SOMETHING

Full Murderhobo Book One

DAKOTA KROUT

MOUNTAINDALE
PRESS

ACKNOWLEDGMENTS

To my Patreons who are supporting me directly, thank you all so much! Especially to Justin Williams, Samuel Landrie, William Merrick, John Grover, Jim Eleven, Mike Hernandez, and Garett Loosen.

A big thank you to everyone who told me that my naming conventions wouldn't work.

Here is Something for you.

PROLOGUE

"Shut th' abyssal door!" a guest at the tavern bellowed at the traveler that had swung the heavy oak slab open to step inside. He grabbed an empty bottle to throw at the newcomer, nearly falling from his seat with the motion. "I *jus'* get dry, and you decide to soak us again? *Shut* it!"

"Kel, I think you've had enough." The bartender deftly pulled away the empty bottle and tucked it under the counter. The Hollow Kingdom had put out a blanket hire of skilled artisans, which meant glass was getting harder to come by these days; no need to be wasteful. "This drink is on me, how about? I think your missus would like you home at some point tonight, so why don't you go *now?*"

The words were a clear order, and the drunk sputtered - and had to be slapped away when he started grabbing at a few drinks - before reluctantly complying. Turning to the soaked man pulling off his body-length rain cloak, the bartender continued in the same calm tone, "I apologize for that; all are welcome to share in my fire... so long as they have the coin."

He glanced meaningfully at the drunk he was sending home. The new arrival moved into the light for the first time since entering, and the bartender sucked in a shocked gasp as he recognized the raiment of a *True Bard* - a man trained not only to play, sing, and pass information, but to weave his magic throughout all of these, creating his art in the senses of those he chose. There was a clear hint of fear in the bartender's eyes. Was... was this Bard *bound*?

Slowly releasing his breath, the bartender ran a keen eye over the man in front of him, appraising the slowly fading glory of his once immaculate clothing. "You... you *do* work for the Hollow Kingdom? You know as well as I, we would both hang if I let an unbound True Bard..."

The Bard touched his own face, and with a slight chiming noise, the Sigil of the Kingdom appeared over his forehead, visible to all. In the back of the tavern, a man scrutinized the newcomer, eyes widening as he looked at the sheer *intricacy* of the Sigil, then narrowing as he realized who the man must be. Though it was a fact only known to a few, Sigils changed shape over time to reflect the power, oaths, and prowess of the *Ascender*. Quietly rising to his feet, the grizzled drinker stealthily exited the main room, going unnoticed by almost everyone as he went up the stairs and out the window.

"My thanks," a musical voice flowed from the Bard as his eyes tracked the 'sneaky' man. "Though, I was hoping to save my coin, if possible. I was thinking we may be able to come to an... understanding."

"An understanding? Indeed! That, I can do!" Motioning one of his serving boys over, the bartender gave instructions to spread the word that a *Bard* would be performing tonight. With a quiet voice, he told the lad that he would get a bonus if there was a full house within the hour. The boy left as fast as he could, eschewing a cloak as he hurried to get as many people packed in as he could find. Bards were rare, especially True Bards, and quickly becoming more so. Bonuses were almost as rare.

"Sit! I'll have you some hot food as soon as it is ready, and you have your pick of drinks. Will you be needing a room?" The bartender shrewdly calculated his incoming profits, hoping that he would stay at least overnight. If the Bard stayed a few *days*, his sales would be enough to more than compensate him for an entire week of free room and board for the performer, let alone a night or two.

"Indeed, I will." The Bard's eyes were dancing at the audacity of the bartender. "My name... is Zed."

"*Ha*! I *bet* it is! Zed is the name of *every* Bard that has been through this city in the last five years!" The bartender roared with laughter as Zed's face twitched. "So I guess that means you are telling stories tonight, not singing?"

"Yes?" Zed was looking rather confused. "I... what?"

Still chuckling, the barkeep announced, "My name is Bob, and I may *look* young, but I wasn't born yesterday. Every Bard - True or not - who feels a bit ill, has a hangover, or just doesn't want to sing for some reason, is 'Zed' these days. No worries; I just hope you can tell a story well. The last 'Zed' in here nearly got my Inn burned to the ground when the crowd turned on him."

"A good story? Well," Zed responded quietly as he examined the spiced cider being handed over to him, "I don't think *that* will be a problem."

He sat down, allowing Bob to administer to his needs. By the time Zed had eaten and warmed himself, the building was nearly full to bursting. Bards were rare in this part of the world, especially since they were so close to the front lines of the last battle of the far-too-recent war with the Dynasty of Dogs. Everyone was clamoring to see him, and a few people who had been waiting at a table were drunkenly shouting for him to hurry up and get on with the entertainment.

Despite being exceedingly boisterous, as the Bard rose from his seat, the crowd quieted in a manner similar to a tsunami moving away from the epicenter of an earthquake. Turning to view the guests, Zed settled into a place where he could be heard, seen, as well as remain comfortable. Quietly, deliberately, he began his tale.

"The war is over for the better part of a decade, and only

now do we learn that we have been living in a golden era! All of this is thanks to a man that you all adore, and those who stood with him. The choices of *The Four* have brought about peace and security for those of us lucky enough to live."

The crowd roared in approval; stories of *The Four* were always well received.

"The Archmage, the Terraformer, the Mindbender... and the Murderhobo. What strange names we have been given over the years." Here Zed paused and took a deep breath, his trained voice shaking with emotion. "But... as you may have heard - and yet simply choose to ignore - there is a fact that will soon become evident. The Ascenders have begun to lose hold of their power and authority."

The crowd was silent for a different reason now: this Bard had just spoken treason and heresy in a single breath. Even the most drunk patron was listening with rapt attention, caught between hearing everything, and fleeing before the guards could arrive. "This world, this entire *civilization*... is ending. Tonight, I will tell all of you *why*."

"It started in what was once a small town named Woodswright, now the largest city after the capital itself." Motioning to the fire, swirling gold-tinged mana spread from his hand. The flames grew in size, until all could see them resolve into images that slowly gained clarity. "We shall begin on the day they realized that their lives were about to change, with the previously unknown origin story of the first among *The Four*: Luke, the Murderhobo."

CHAPTER ONE

- LUKE -

Luke moved through the forest, being careful not to startle anything that might be nearby. It was mating season for boars, and unexpectedly showing up near one of them tended to get a person gored. Intestines rotting away due to a tusk in the gut was a particularly nasty way to die. Actually, there were lots of nasty ways to die that Luke had been watching for recently.

A war had just started on the eastern front of the Hollow Kingdom, and while volunteers were appreciated, conscripts were far more numerous. In a few days, a King's Legion and *Ascender* corps were due to arrive, and anyone of age was to be tested for magical potential. Luke swallowed, remembering that *he* was of age. If he was found to have 'potential', then he would be pulled into the secretive training to which *Ascenders* were subject. After that, it was said that power, wealth, land, and all your desires were within reach.

However, anyone without the power of myth and legends would be joining the Legion as either a volunteer or conscript. To hide meant death for the entire family of the 'coward', but to join was equally dangerous to the individual. As it happened, dying on the front lines wasn't even an assured way out of the war, as Necromancers on both sides were apt to use the fresh corpses in some foul ritual.

Hearing a rustle from the undergrowth nearby, Luke froze, then slowly reached for the bow strapped to his shoulder. With only the rustle as a warning, a singular of boars burst from the brush, squealing as they raced away. Realizing the danger, and having been prepared for the charge, as it *was* that time of year, Luke leapt as high as he could, catching a branch and pulling himself onto it in time to avoid the screaming boars running beneath him.

"I love trees. Didn't even realize how much until now!" Attempting to catch his breath as his heart beat wildly in his chest, Luke started laughing as his adrenaline spike slowly abated. He had been feeling so confident with his bow, but this was the first time he had remembered that he had it with him. He searched the forest floor but swung off his tree after not seeing anything that might have startled the creatures. Patting the wood in thanks for the rescue, Luke continued on his way *much* more hastily. Coming to the last set of snares he had set, he found a plump rabbit, as well as a fox; both struggled in the thick twine of his traps. "Well, *there's* a story they won't believe!"

He chuckled as he finished off the animals, collecting the small bodies into a leather bag after gutting and cleaning them. Resetting the traps, he started his careful journey home, not wanting to run into the same situation of being forced to scramble into hiding. Returning to safety would only take about ten minutes, since he tried to arrange his traps to loop him around the forest. That way, he would be dropped back home at the end of each excursion.

"Today was a nice day," he spoke aloud, causing the birds in the area to go quiet. "I'm bringing dinner, didn't die, and I'm done early. Hmm. Yup. Good day."

Walking through the verdant woods allowed his mind to wander, and he was nearly surprised when he broke through into the clearing around the village. Large *town*, more like. Plenty of people were pouring into the area these days, since the King himself had commissioned a keep to be built on the outskirts; he had claimed the town to be a strategic location for defense. Upon hearing this, carpenters, stonemasons, and artists had all rushed to the town, driving the price of day-to-day living into the non-feasible range for most of the established citizens.

Luckily, the influx of hungry people had also drawn the attention of traders and merchants from all walks of life. As they set up their shops, even more people were needed in order to get their shops built and staffed. Huge amounts of resources were being poured into the town, which only made the demand higher. Food was now far too expensive a luxury to buy at a store for the likes of him, but luckily, business was starting to pick up.

Luke, like the rest of his family, was a leatherworker. He had been trained to create beautiful, as well as functional, armor from nearly any hide that he had. As metal was notoriously expensive in the forested area - the main export from *Woods*wright being *wood* - he had a solid collection of people that would pay top coin for a few more layers of protection between them and possible death.

Arriving home, he slammed the door open, shouting, "The fu~u~un has *arrived*! I'm back, Mom! Dad! Mom? Cindy? Anyone? No? ...Okay, then."

Grumbling about underappreciation, he stalked into the kitchen and started making a stew from the available vegetables, then cut some rabbit meat and added it into what would hope-fully be a nutritious, if not tasty, dinner. If he were lucky, someone else would notice that he was cooking and come to season the meal. The fox wasn't as lucky, most likely the meat would be discarded and the pelt would become a scarf.

"Luke?" He heard his dad shout. "You in here?"

"Yeah!"

"We got an order; the advance unit for the Legion came

today, and they need boots." His father, John, appeared in the kitchen. "The girls are mixing up some tanning fluids. We need to get some deer hide stretched, or we're going to miss a good chance here. They are paying *gold*."

"Gold!"

"Yes; something about the boots they have not holding up too well around here. I guess they were designed more for a city with plenty of cobblestone. I took some measurements, and their feet are *horribly* blistered. Lots of blood." As an afterthought, he added, "Pus, too."

"Bleh."

"Yup. Anyway, hurry up. I'll send Cindy to take care of the food. I need you out there, and we both know your food tastes like sipping a muddy cesspool. Two good reasons to keep you out of here."

"Thanks; so glad that I keep you fed. Maybe I should focus on learning proper cooking instead of catching the wild game that we eat?" Luke's dry monotone made his father roll his eyes. "How many sets did we get an order for?"

"Nearly fifty pair, and all other orders are on hold. The King's Legion takes precedence. *Always*." John muttered darkly as they walked behind the house. He stopped himself before he went on a tirade; there were better ways to die than the consequences for speaking treason. The workshop was closer to the forest than the house, situated at the bottom of a hill in an attempt to minimize complaints about the smell. Luckily, they didn't use urine and feces, as did some other tanners in nearby cities. Instead they used bark liquor, composed of finely ground bark stored in twenty gallon barrels of water, which was left to ferment for several weeks at a time.

Their process still smelled fairly horrible, but it was not nearly as bad as the other available options. There were some necessary precautions that were needed, as bark liquor was highly flammable. The most important rule was that they only worked when there was natural light, and no open flames were allowed within any enclosed area.

As they approached the workshop, a well-ventilated building that was mostly a roof with the sides left open, John called out, "Cindy! Dinner is in the pot; Luke got some rabbit in his snares. Can you go take care of that so we don't need to eat his cooking?"

"Sure! We just sealed the lid on this barrel, so if Mom says it's okay…?" Cindy looked over at her mother.

"Yes," Joanne allowed wearily, "I'm sure we are all hungry, so when it's done, bring it down from the house, please. We don't have time to stop working if we want to complete the order. We have only three days before the Legion arrives in town, and a week from then until they need the boots for marching. Let's get moving, people!"

With renewed vigor, the family worked until night had fallen completely, their efforts focused on softening the leather as much as possible. They then stretched the material as far as they could in preparation for the morning before making their way home.

"We did a good job today," John complimented calmly. "Good work."

Luke and Cindy grinned at each other, knowing how rare it was to hear praise. Joanne smiled at her husband, quietly taking his hand and holding it as they walked home.

CHAPTER TWO

The week passed exceedingly quickly, the days filled with the work needed to complete such a large order as soon as humanly possible. Though he was exhausted, John bowed respectfully and focused on the conversation at hand. "We should be able to have your order ready a day early, Sir."

"Spectacular!" An Officer of the Legion who had come to check in on his investment bellowed happily. Noticing Luke's wince, he grinned wryly. "Sorry; when you need to yell all day, you tend to stop noticing when you aren't commanding troops. I'm Lieutenant Baker, by the way. Mind if I take a look at some of the boots? I know you have a good reputation for quality around here, but this *is* a rather large order, and we are from the capitol…"

"Sir, not at all! Luke, take him down to the workshop? Also remember who you are talking to when you walk." Turning to the Lieutenant, John quickly assured him, "I would take you myself, but we are running low on bark spirits, and I was just on my way to barter for some…"

Waving his hand at John in a shooing motion, Lieutenant Baker started following Luke down the hill. The giant man wiggled his eyebrows and grinned, bellowing, "Whew! Gah. *Wow*! I can see why this is so far away from the town! My eyes are watering already! Smells like your family can really hold their liquor!"

Luke chuckled appropriately at the… attempted humor, and continued the brisk pace to the shop. Reaching the rows of completed boots, he pulled off the set that had Baker's measurements and offered to let him try them on.

"I'd love to, but…" Baker hesitated, flushing slightly from embarrassment, "I need to warn you, there *is* a reason we are getting new boots…"

With that, he started removing his footwear, which fell apart with the first pull, tearing along the poorly-made seam. Emerging into the open air was a foot that seemed nearly rotten, with open sores and a stench strong enough to overpower the strong liquor smell. Looking fully embarrassed, Baker quickly reached for the boots Luke was holding, but missed as Luke set them down and reached for a container.

"Sorry, Sir, I forgot that you had those sores. My dad told me about that the other day, and my sister brought this from the apothecary. Rub this gently on your feet." Luke held the box out to the Lieutenant.

"What is it?" Baker eyed the container suspiciously.

"Oh, right. It's a powder compound we use around here; it contains magnesium, silica, and a chalk powder. The blend helps to keep your feet dry and stop those blisters. They mix in mint and a couple other healing herbs to help the blisters you already have. It also helps with the, um… smell." Luke finished rather indelicately. "Pardon the bluntness…"

"Oh. I'll try it out, I guess. They can't get much worse, and the healers are already overworked." Rubbing some of the powder on, the smell noticeably dissipated and Luke handed him the boots to put on. The powder reduced the friction of putting on the new boot, and with the correct measurements, Baker felt relief for the first time in weeks.

"That feels *so* much better! The other ones are assigned to us; if the things don't fit, they just give us larger ones until we can put our feet in 'em. Felt like I was walking on a bunch of snakes, always trying to squirm off my feet."

Luke shuddered at the image the man put in his head, and let Baker walk around to get a feel for the boots.

"Perfect! Can I wear these back? My other ones…" He looked meaningfully at the ruined boots on the ground.

"I see no reason not to let you," Luke agreed easily. "They are already paid for, and I know that you must be an honorable man to have such a powerful position."

"Thanks! Ha, silver tongue like that; you sure you're not a Noble brat? You've got all the fancy words!" Baker joyfully stomped around. "About that powder? Where can I get it?"

"You can have this box for free. The apothecary wanted us to let your men try it out. Otherwise, just ask around for him. I bet he would cut you a good bulk deal."

"I really appreciate it, son! We march all day, and damaged feet… we've actually already lost people to infection, and we haven't even fought anyone!" Baker confided in the young man. "Oh! Are you going to be at the testing tomorrow? We aren't conscripting for the Legion–yet–but everyone needs to be tested for power. How old are you? You look just about-"

"I'm seventeen, Sir. I thought it was *mandatory* to be there?" Luke glanced at the Lieutenant out of the corner of his eye to watch his reaction.

"It is; I'm just checking. You seem like a good kid. If you don't have 'potential', you should still think about joining up. I could put you in a good position, making and mending our leather supplies, and it would pay an abyss-load more than being conscripted as a lancer."

"I'll… think about it? I am *really* needed here, though. Lots to do, after all." Luke chuckled nervously at the thought of being dragged off to fight someone else's war.

"Right! Well, I'm off. Gotta get back before my men turn into drunken morons and need to be led around like dogs. See you tomorrow. Remember, sign up before you're forced to do it!" On *that* cheerful note, Lieutenant Baker left, enjoying the feel of softened leather swaddling his medicated feet. Luke, now feeling rather nervous about what the next morning could bring, got back to work on detailing the next set of boots.

"*Lukey*! Did you remember to put our crest on his boots? I saw him leave wearing a pair!" Cindy breathlessly shouted as she ran down the hill. "Did he like them?"

"I wouldn't forget that! Free advertising, right?" Luke grinned at her. The family mercantile crest was a set of triangles that joined together to form a single large triangle, which was stamped on everything they made. With boots, it was etched into the heel, so every time a step was taken in soft earth, the symbol appeared. It would be kind of fun to see so many sets leaving trails when the Legion left. It would look like a pack of angular wolves were following along behind them. "And of *course* he likes the boots! We *did* make them."

"Good!" Cindy grabbed an unfinished set and started stitching along the edges. "So what is going on? What is the testing? I know you have to go, but the rest is just rumors."

"Mmm. The testing is where you are, well… tested," he winced, expecting a snarky comment to be forthcoming, "to see if you have the power to become an *Ascender*."

"I obviously know the word, since you've thrown it around so often. Ugh, seriously, you need another hobby. You've been wanting to join them ever since the start of the draft, but what do *Ascenders* actually *do*?"

"They… help the empire?"

"Are you intentionally making me wait for this information? You know what I'm asking. If you don't want to talk, just say so. You just always seem to know what they're doing! Most of my friends can't even read, or I would ask them. You read all the time, thanks to your girlfriend. Can you just give me a good explanation?" Cindy grumped at him.

"Taylor isn't my girlfriend; you know that. She's a Noble. There's no way it could happen. Besides, she and I couldn't ever be more than friends. She's… anyway, sorry, not trying to dodge the question, I'm just nervous. Lieutenant Baker was… abrupt. So anyway, an Ascender is someone who can move between various… how to put this… dimensions?"

"You're useless." Cindy turned to leave, taking the boot with her.

"Let me finish!" Luke demanded, trying to get his thoughts in order, "There are a bunch of different kinds of Ascender, I'm just thinking about the best way to explain this. Right, so, even though there are a bunch of specializations, they all are called '*Ascender*'. Just like a square and a rectangle are both squares, even though a rectangle is different, right? A few of the more well-known are, let me think…"

Luke snapped his fingers. "Mages, who access elemental power from their dimensions. Summoners, who go through their dimensions to fight and capture creatures, then bring them here to fight for them… um… oh yeah, Necromancers, who pull some kind of energy from dead things and bring them back as husks that fight for them. Healers, who heal people, kinda the reverse of Necromancers. There's a *ton* more, I just can't remember them right now. Also, there is a lot of information kept away from people that don't need to know it. I only know this much mostly from rumors, my books have nothing to do with them."

"Fine. You aren't *totally* useless, I guess… but I've never seen any of those people, so they literally don't matter to me. Why 'Ascender'? Just because they can cross back and forth between those dimme-thingies?"

"*Dimensions*. Well, they have other titles, but 'Ascender' works because they get stronger and stronger over time. They're all 'ascending' to something, but no one knows what. Oh! Some of them are strong enough to bring people with them to their hidden worlds, and for some reason they can move across huge distances in a really short amount of time. They are really sought after by the Kingdom, as well as by merchants. There are other types that can only enter or leave their dimension at certain points and are stuck if they can't get to those spots."

"All right… next question, because I can't think of how this helps me. Can I come watch you get tested?" Cindy turned pleading eyes up to meet his.

"Sure? I don't think it'll be a big deal, though. Ask Mom?"

"But I *want* to go. I'll ask Dad."

Luke shook his head and snorted. "Ha! It's *really* not a big deal."

CHAPTER THREE

"*Luke*! Where have you been?" bellowed Andre, Luke's best friend since childhood. The thick giant of a young man appeared behind Luke like a mountain being revealed through fog. Luke was swept into a crushing bear hug that threatened to snap his back. "This is *such* a big deal! Like, the *biggest* deal we have had in this town since *I* was born! Or the keep was announced!"

"Why? It's just like every other town getting tested, isn't it? You know? *Mandatory*?" Luke managed to wheeze out of his collapsing lungs while simultaneously rolling his eyes.

Abruptly dropping his friend, Andre adopted a look of fake horror, "But this is *our* town! Soon, we shall have the glory! Power! Feasts! …Beautiful women."

The last was stated in a sultry tone as a small group of girls looked over at them. Winking at them and leaving them giggling, Andre turned back to Luke. "Come on! We have *power* to quest after!"

Unnecessarily pushing people out of the way, he pulled Luke closer to the front of the lines that had formed. People chuckled as Luke was pulled like a cat on a leash; that is, being dragged most of the time. John called after his son's receding form, "Good luck, son!"

"Traitor! *Help* me! My own *father?*" Luke's words were laughed at, though John caught Cindy's arm and made her wait in line with them. The sun was cheerfully gleaming from the eastern horizon, and dawn hadn't been long ago at all. After hearing that Cindy wanted to go and watch the testing, Joanne had made today a holiday of sorts to keep an eye on both of them.

The event was situated near the center of town, which used to be a bustling open market where people would trade, barter, or sell their excess goods every Loredas, the sixth day of the week. With all the new shops and hungry people, excess goods were quickly becoming a thing of the past. The square was now filled with people lining up to be 'tested'. Anyone from seventeen to thirty was tested, but if they were found to have no power - and were male - they had to give their name to the Legion recruitment agents.

"Why are you in a rush? Stop pushing people. No one cares about this enough to try to slow you down! They'll just let you go ahead of them." Luke attempted to pull his arm away, which was equally as successful as his attempt to reason with Andre. The massive teen was a blacksmith-in-training, and his grip was nearly as unbreakable as the finished steel that came out of his family forge. "*Andre!* That guy wasn't even in line! You went out of your way to chase him down! He's bleeding!"

"Heh."

"We're here! Stop!"

"Let's watch! I wanna see what happens." Andre gushed like a guy with his first crush, finally letting go of Luke's arm. Seeing no issue with waiting after finally being able to free his arm from the soul-and-bone-crushing grip, Luke joined the crowd in watching the day's entertainment. There was a festival mood in the square, and enterprising businessmen were already selling sweets, weapons, and drinks, all at massively overinflated prices. The main attraction was a stage set in the center of the square, where two scarred and heavily-armed soldiers were standing a few paces from what appeared to be an overstimulated twenty-year-old man.

"Next! C'mon, c'mon, let's roll! Hurry up! Things to do, people to test; where's my *water*? Who's next? Move it!" The man was bouncing from foot to foot, and if it were another person, Luke would have thought he needed to pee; but this guy just seemed hyperstimulated. "Good, good, good! Who are you? Where are you from? Any magic in your family?"

As the poor victim of the man's attention stumbled over his answers in an attempt to get the correct order, he was interrupted by a sudden, "Doesn't matter! Come, come, come! Hands on the orb; let's see what we're working with! What are those readouts? Any base class to work with?"

At Andre's questioning glance, Luke explained what he had read about the process. "As far as I know, 'class' simply means where your magical talents lie. Necros hate healers, right? Imagine being sent to the wrong training area. Most of this is general knowledge, but anything in-depth is *really* secret; I just don't have specifics for you."

"That's neat. Yup, very cool. Oh look! Something interesting is happening!" Andre refocused and gestured toward the stage. As the befuddled man laid his hands on the globe offered by the chipper tester... not a single thing happened.

"No worries, my good man! Nothing wrong with not being magical. Look at these fine examples of mundanes standing next to me! One of them will escort you off the stage and over to the recruiting station!" The tester did his best not to sound disappointed, and *almost* succeeded. Leaving the stage among cheers and some friendly ribbing, the failed hopeful stepped down, only to be greeted with an ale provided by his friends.

"Hi Luke, Andre! What did I miss? Anyone get in yet?" Taylor, the Noble girl Luke had known as long as he had known Andre, suddenly appeared behind them and poked Andre in the ribs.

"No!" Andre bellowed as he spasmed from the prod. "What have I told you about doing that?"

"What?" She innocently tossed her short brown hair out of her eyes. "Pay more attention, and you won't freak out when people talk to you."

"That is *not* the issue, and you know it!" Andre grumbled angrily as he rubbed his sore spot. "You always gotta poke the bear. Always the same spot, too! Look at this; I have a bruise there!"

Lifting his shirt, he showed that he did indeed have a bruise the exact same shape as Taylor's fingertip. There were lighter and darker spots, clearly highlighting a bruise that had healed over and over, but kept getting injured.

"Cry about it. You bruise like a peach." Ignoring Andre's reddening face and turning toward Luke, Taylor lifted an eyebrow. "Have you seen Zed today? He's been acting odd all week."

Luke paled and looked around before motioning them closer and whispering, "He's trying to *run*."

"*No!*" Andre gasped dramatically. "He can be executed for that! It's treason!"

"Why?" Taylor demanded, looking at Luke intently.

"You see," Andre started explaining, putting a hand on her shoulder, "The Kingdom needs people who-"

"Not *you*, dumb-dumb," Taylor calmly interrupted the sarcastic giant. "Luke?"

"He wouldn't say. He just had this look like a hunted animal every time it came up."

"That's odd. He's usually so... collected." Taylor tapped her chin in thought.

"I know. I'm worried about him. As much as... I just hope he's okay." Luke finished lamely, returning to stoic silence. Shaking their heads, the group turned back to the spectacle at hand. Seeing a line forming, Andre got excited again and started yanking on Luke so they could be near the middle.

"Hey guys, want some food?" Taylor questioned as she

walked with them, "My dad gave me a bunch of coin, since I probably won't come back from testing. His way of saying 'sorry, I'm too busy to watch where the Kingdom chucks you.'"

Taylor had been having power outbreaks for nearly a year, usually when asleep. They had started small, but recently, maids had been walking in, screaming and nearly messing themselves when they joined the other objects that were floating around the room. Taylor had been *very* anxiously awaiting testing.

"Yes! Um... please, that is," Andre coughed into his hand. "I'll hold your spot. Yes. Food. Need food."

"Sure, thank you," Luke agreed.

"Having the Baron as your father must be nice," Andre murmured after Taylor walked away. Taylor's family had been nearly as poor as their subjects before the keep had gone under construction, but massive upswings in taxes, as well as grants from the king, had suddenly made them more wealthy and powerful than they had been in generations.

"Hey, easy. At least she didn't become all snooty like her brothers," Luke protested on their friend's behalf. Andre had been acting strange around the third member of their group ever since Taylor's family became rich.

"It's just... Luke, let me be frank." Andre turned to his friend with a dark look.

"Hi, Frank," Luke responded flippantly.

"Really, man? Feh. Listen. I really like her."

"So do I. Hence the 'I'm glad she didn't get snooty'."

Andre took a deep breath and tried again. "No, man, I *like* her. And... I think she likes me, too. She touches me a lot."

"Oh. I think the touching may be because you 'bruise like a peach and blush like a sunset'." Luke waxed poetic, making Andre grimace in disgust. "C'mon, I *know* that she pokes hard; you don't actually bruise that easy."

"Luke, *man*. I mean that-" A low sound came from Andre, though he suddenly stopped moping as Taylor returned with fried meat skewers.

Looking past them as she handed over the skewers, Taylor

pointed to the other side of the crowd and gasped. "Is that Zed?"

Both young men turned to get a better view, noticing that it was indeed their missing friend. The townspeople began rumbling as they saw Zed being manhandled, but a group of spearmen stepped forward and blocked anyone from approaching.

"Let me *go*! I've done nothing wrong!" Zed raged and thrashed, half dragged between two overly-muscled members of the Legion.

They did let him go, but not in a polite and friendly manner. Instead, they threw him down at the feet of the tester. "Caught this one trying to run through the forest, Lord Mage."

The one on the right spoke up, his voice reminiscent of a duck gargling sewage. "Thought you may want a crack at 'im."

CHAPTER FOUR

"Right you *were*, gentlemen! Why so *nervous*, young man? You may not even have any power! If you do, it isn't like you become a slave! You get paid well, live in luxury… so many benefits, just for serving the Hollow Kingdom!" Zed just shook his head and took deep, panicked breaths, eyes darting around in an attempt to find a way to escape from the situation. "Well, if you are *that* nervous, might as well get this over with. Then you can get locked away in prison for draft dodging, or sent to the front lines by tomorrow! Come here, young man."

The Mage motioned Zed closer. Expressing a look of utter defeat, Zed trudged forward and slowly reached for the proffered orb. As he lay his fingers on it, touching it as minimally as possible… nothing happened. A look of relief crossed his face nanoseconds before a deep chime emitted from the orb, akin to a bell being hit by a hammer. Swirls of golden color shone within the orb, vibrant bursts of illusionary light that reminded those watching of either fond memories or horrific scenes from their past.

"*Bind him!*" screamed the tester, eyes wide and shocked. His voice spurred the nearby Ascenders to stand forward, releasing energy into the air with a *whoosh*. In moments, Zed was nearly obscured behind several different shimmering fields; his face crumpled into abject terror as the restraints obscured him from view. The tester looked at the guards with wide eyes. "I never thought that those wards on your armor would see use!"

The guards that had dragged Zed in chuckled nervously, shaking their heads in agreement. The audience stood dumbfounded, horrified by this unexpected turn of events, as well as the testers' cavalier attitudes. A few citizens started shouting angrily, ready to rush the stage in spite of the Legion and Mage Corps being in the way, all to save the well-loved child of the village. The tester's face darkened, and he shouted over the crowd, clearly hoping the scene would not dissolve into a mob. "*Please*! I'm sorry that happened! No! Listen, good people of Woodswright, let me explain!"

"You better speak *right* quick!" came a voice from the rumbling crowd.

"Thank you! Please understand, this man is an untrained, unbound... *True Bard*!"

A few people of high standing among the crowd gasped... but the majority stood by, anger rising at the minimalistic explanation. "So?"

"*So*? Do you not understand what this means?" The man stared about the crowd incredulously. Getting mostly blank looks in return, he shook his head and muttered 'stupid backwater' before launching into his explanation.

"A Bard is a *mind* Mage. They are one of the few types of Ascender which can access their power without training. It spills out of them, causing people to trust without reason, allowing the Bard to manipulate others with a mere whim. If he is unbound and powerful enough, the king *himself* would happily hand over his throne, thinking the Bard more suited to the task of ruling. Let me give you an example," the Mage continued, speaking ever faster as the looks of anger started to turn to something more fearful. "Where does this boy live? How long has he been here?"

"He's been here forever," Called a matronly woman.

"The boy showed up last year," A stablehand barked out at nearly the same time. They looked at each other in confusion as similar assertions were called out around them.

"*Exactly!*" The tester announced, "Who actually knows? *Hmm*? I can tell you the answer right now! You have known him exactly as long as it took for you to trust him, and I would bet my last coin that he has asked favors from all of you, promising payment or some such in the future. Favors that you never really... *questioned?*"

As the nods slowly increased, he spoke again, "Hopefully you now understand. You all know that there is a binding oath involved with becoming an Ascender, yes? Normally, this oath is optional. If they say no, we block their magic and send them on their way. A True Bard, by their very nature, cannot be blocked in the same manner. If he refuses the magically binding oath... he will be put to death on the spot, for the protection of the realm."

With this pronouncement, he turned to the shimmering cocoon surrounding Zed. The crowd seemed to be struggling with the news, but the Mage moved faster than they could make up their minds.

"Release his head. Boy," he softly spoke to Zed, "if you say *anything* but 'I hereby swear' as your next words, you will die. I... I *am* sorry. There is no other choice. Nod if you understand."

Zed nodded solemnly, tears streaming down his face as he tried to come to terms with his upcoming life of forced servitude. "Do you swear upon your magic, and your life, to serve the Hollow Kingdom, the King, and your direct superior in all things relating to your training, your service, and your magic, until such a time as you are released from this oath by King Alexander or his heir?"

Shaking with uncontrolled emotion, Zed replied brokenly, "I... hereby swear."

With a *crack* and a deep chime similar to the one that had

announced his magic to the world, the Sigil of the Kingdom appeared upon Zed's sweat-soaked forehead.

"Release him." A Mage in grand robes emerged from a nearby tent and sent the original tester away. "You all have nothing to fear from him now. Given the circumstances, I will take over this ceremony from this point forward. Boy, what is your name?"

"Zed."

"Zed, although this is a poor start to a relationship... I hope you understand why this was needed, and that you will work with us to discover and enhance the mastery of your magic. Please call me by my rank and name, 'Master Mage Donec Arriperent'. You can call me 'Master' or 'Master Don'. I will be the one who determines your path forward from here."

"I do. Thank you, Master Don. This is... a lot to take in," Zed looked up at the many faces in the crowd, many of whom were wearing conflicted expressions, "I apologize to you all. I didn't realize the extent to which I was influencing you. I truly thought everyone here was just really... friendly."

"You owe me money, *freak!*" shouted a stable boy. The crowd started rumbling, some shouting for recompense, some trying to shout the angry voices down.

"*Calm* yourselves," Don growled, his voice layered with power. As the mob was forcefully influenced toward calm, he continued speaking, "Anyone with a legitimate claim against Zed may bring it to the scribes. As a forced Initiate, he is granted immunity from the crimes he may have committed as an untrained individual. As for the rest of you, the testing continues. Line up."

The festival air ruined, most of the people not invested in the testing ceremony started to disperse. Soon only the people to be tested, their families, and disappointed food vendors remained in the area.

"Well, that was intense and horrible." Taylor garnered droll looks from her friends. She started again, glancing around nervously and leaning in toward them. "Look, you guys... if you are found to have power, don't refuse the oath. Promise me."

"Why?" Andre appraised her serious demeanor. "Look what they did to Zed! Why would you want us to be a part of that?"

"I… I can't tell you." At their skeptical looks, she sighed, "I physically *can't*. I'm under oath. But, remember how they say it is up to you to accept or not? Just *think* about that."

"If you refuse, you are stripped of all power, so you can't learn some other way." Luke shrugged and scoffed, "That's common knowledge, Tay. He announced it, even."

"Yes," she desperately ground out, "but have you ever *heard* of…"

She doubled over in pain, suddenly and violently vomiting onto her shoes.

"Celestial *feces!*" Andre instantly moved to help her.

She waved him off, looking around to make sure no one outside of their group had seen her lose her breakfast. "I'm fine. Just being punished."

"You're under a *geas*? Not just an oath?" Luke gasped and recoiled. "Andre, stop asking her questions. She could die if she pushes too hard."

"Who the abyss did this to you?" An infuriated Andre clenched his fists and looked around.

"Easy, big guy," Luke responded, attempting to calm down the highly muscular smith. "A *geas* can only be entered willingly."

Andre whirled on Luke, fists clenched. "Like Zed just entered service 'willingly'?"

"He…" Luke couldn't find a response. "A fair point."

"I was actually willing to enter mine. I wanted information, and this was the only way to get it." Taylor wiped her mouth. "I need something to drink; I should have chewed that meat better. Got chunks of it stuck in my throat."

"Nasty." Luke recoiled from both the smell and the words.

"Well?" Tay threw her hands into the air in exasperation. Giving up their positions in line, they approached a vendor and got some cider. Taylor swished it around in her mouth before drinking deeply. They turned to watch other people getting tested, the majority failing. Though a few were discovered with talents, none made the ball swirl or chime so powerfully as Zed.

"So… what is that ball actually *doing*?" Andre wondered aloud.

"It tests the inborn power of each person. None of us are trained, so they can't exactly 'see what we can do', ya know? The color is what type of Ascender you are; the more intense the swirl, I think, means they have more inborn mana, so they can cast more or longer from the start. That natural ability allows for more rapid mastery of spells. I think the sound indicates how powerful of a spell they can cast. So, loud *and* lots of swirling? Big, powerful spells from the start." Luke looked at Taylor for confirmation, and she nodded reluctantly.

"More to it than that," she contended, see-sawing her hand back and forth.

"So that's it? A *ball* determines my future?" Andre grumpily eyed the orb.

"Well, that's only the natural starting point. Everyone with the ability to Ascend can increase their power with training and practice. I think the current Archmage holds the record for the smallest starting mana pool."

That made Andre pause. "Oh. Why isn't everyone at his level, then?"

"I'm not sure. I think learning spells is harder than it sounds… not many people seem to survive the training." Luke considered the small collection of Mages doubtfully, then glanced over at the huge and still-growing crowd of volunteers for the regular army. "I wonder why?"

"It's because they…" Taylor doubled over again, clutching her stomach.

"Sheesh! Looks like even the training is a secret." Andre pulled Taylor in close for a half-hug until she could move again.

Taylor nodded, looking miserable. "We'd better get in line. Looks like most people are through."

They began walking toward the stage. Their families saw them pulling away from the remaining crowd and began cheering for them, making Luke blush and Andre wave. Taylor kept her eyes forward and ignored the fact that she was alone. Approaching the foot of the stage, she moved to the front of the group and started climbing the stairs.

"Well, *hello*, young lady! Ready to learn about your future?" Master Don asked her, grinning and holding up the orb like a fortune teller.

"Try and stop me!" She was grinning right back, their open friendliness indicating that they were already familiar with each other. Reaching out, she firmly grasped the orb. A riot of purple colors and deep swirls overtook the stage, and a low tone rang out, deep and sorrowful.

"Well, that's even more than I was led to believe by your father!" Master Don cheerfully exclaimed. "This town is full of surprises! Two *wondrously* powerful people! Well, my dear, state your name for the scribe."

"Taylor Woodswright."

"Well, Taylor, if you aren't a Namer, I'll eat my spell book. If you would like... I'll take you as my personal apprentice." As Master Don made the offer, gasps of shock and outrage rose from the staff surrounding him. If Taylor had been undecided, the involuntary astonished responses from his entourage were enough of a push to make her agree.

"That would be most kind... Master?" she half-questioned, taking his hand and shaking it.

"Correct!" he jovially agreed. "All that remains is your oath."

Becoming serious again, as he had with every applicant thus far, he repeated the now-familiar words. "Do you swear upon your magic, and your life, to serve the Hollow Kingdom, the King, and your direct superior in all things relating to your training, your service, and your magic, until such a time as you are released from this oath by King Alexander or his heir?"

"I hereby swear," she solemnly supplied her portion of the

ritual. As with the others, the Sigil of the Kingdom appeared on her forehead with a chime before quickly vanishing from sight.

"A round of applause for the Hollow Kingdom's newest Mage *Namer!*" Master Don shouted as the remaining crowd broke out in cheering, though the other Mages were staring at her in horror. With a grin, Taylor motioned her friends forward to complete their own testing. Andre leapt forward, hoping that he could get in on the applause. Waving at the crowd, he strode boldly over to the Master.

"Humph. Make 'em big here, don't they? All right, mountain man, you ready?" Andre's only response was to push his hand forward, waiting for the orb. The Master acquiesced, dropping the orb into his hand. With an explosion of power, light, and sound, the orb shattered with a flash of green light and a concussive boom that echoed across the instantly-silent crowd.

"Yup. Lots and *lots* of capacity," Master Don wryly stated as a shield vanished from around the duo. Shards of crystal rained to the floor as the captured fragments were released. "Certainly too much for this weak testing orb."

"King Alexander's wrinkly *balls*, Andre, what the *abyss* was that?" Taylor shouted with a shocked look.

"Language, young lady! Words hold *much* power," Don scolded her with a dark look. "This happens every once in a while. Rare, but it *does* happen. A smith?"

At Andre's nod, Don continued speaking loudly so everyone could hear, "I bet your work is somehow too good, and your master has been taking credit for it?"

Another nod and a sheepish cough from the smith, who had attended the ceremony. "Well, the green shows us right where your talents lie, hmm? First things first; do you swear upon your magic and your life to serve the Hollow Kingdom, the King, and your direct superior in all things relating to your training, your service, and your magic, until such a time as you are released from this oath by King Alexander or his heir?"

"I hereby... swear." Andre agreed after a long look at Taylor, still seeming a bit shell-shocked.

Master Don pulled him in for a hug, something he hadn't done even with his own new apprentice. "Excellent! Thank you! *Thank* you, lad! Good people, welcome our Kingdom's very first... *Druid*! The chosen one has been found!"

The crowd froze, then burst into amazed cheering. Don quietly spoke to Andre before pushing him gently toward a tent. "You have a hard road ahead, but we need to get you trained quickly. You will likely have a huge bounty placed on your head by many different factions."

Luke felt uncomfortable under Master Don's scrutinizing gaze as he moved forward. He was confused about what to do now that there was no orb. Although he was happy for his friends, he still felt distinctly apprehensive about his own future.

"A bit of advice," The Master spoke quietly to Luke, "guard your emotions better than you are currently. Don't take this as an insult; you just are quite easy to read, and therefore manipulate. You seem like a good kid, but others will happily pull you into their schemes if you let them. Ah, I get ahead of myself! My apologies. I am a teacher at heart; I cannot stop myself. And, voila!"

Don pulled a new orb seemingly from the empty air and held it forward. Luke, nonplussed by the sudden lecture, tentatively grasped the proffered orb. No change came over the orb, and Don nodded almost in relief. "That was a tough act to follow. Sorry about that, lad. Well, don't be sad. The world certainly needs soldiers-"

He stopped, finally noticing that Luke was entranced by the orb in his hand. It was slowly shifting colors, bleeding from clear to a bright blue; the color spreading from his palm like mercury poured into water. The gradual stain continued until the orb was a solid blue, and then the color simply continued to deepen until it was as dark as midnight. The entire process took nearly five minutes.

"That's... new." Don looked at Luke, a question in his eyes.

"Well, there is no question that you *have* power, even if I am unsure what it *is*. Name?"

"It's… Luke, sir."

"Well, Luke, do you swear upon your magic and your life to serve the Hollow Kingdom, the King, and your direct superior in all things relating to your training, your service, and your magic, until such a time as you are released from this oath by King Alexander or his heir?"

"I so swear."

The Sigil of the Kingdom appeared on his forehead, but unlike the others, it seemed to slowly *flow* onto his brow, then vanish, fading far faster than it had for the others.

"How strange… I look forward to learning about your abilities with you, young Luke."

CHAPTER FIVE

"Are you sure you'll all be okay without me? I know there are a bunch more boots to make," Luke nearly begged his father.

"We'll be fine, son. We're proud of you, by the way."

Luke looked over, startled at the sudden emotion in his father's voice. "Dad?"

His mother leaned forward, giving Luke a hug as his father tried to hand him a leather pack. When he was released, he inspected the pack and gasped. "*Dad*! This is too much! You could sell this for enough money to feed me for a year!"

"Well, it was supposed to be your birthday present next week, but I'm guessing you will be wanting it before you go, hmm?" His father kindly patted Luke's arm, taking a deep breath to stave off the shuddering sob that tried to escape.

The pack was well-worked leather, the family crest embossed into the back. The outside was crafted from hardened leather, which would protect the interior from being crushed, as well as protecting its contents due to being waterproof. The interior, composed of soft, supple doeskin, had been expertly sewn into segmented compartments. It was a large pack, designed for travelers who carried everything they owned. The pack was suspended by straps designed to hang over the shoulders, as well as two straps that could be tightened to secure the pack to the wearer's chest and waist; making the load feel as light as possible.

"Thank you. Thank you all so much." Luke addressed his entire family. It was obvious they had all contributed to this.

"Anything for you, big brother," Cindy tearfully swallowed as she gave him a big hug. "Be *careful*, okay? They said training is two and a half years, right? You're going to miss my sixteenth and seventeenth birthday, so bring me something nice from far away, alright?"

"I put some tools in there for you, keep in practice," His dad ordered sternly. His parents gave him one last hug as the call went out to gather; the Ascender corps was about to move, and the trainees were feeling a compulsion to join the group. Luke itched at his forehead, already a little annoyed by the functions of the Sigil.

"Goodbye! I'll write when I can," Luke promised as his feet forcibly began to move him toward the waiting Ascender Corps. He quickly made his way to his friends, settling into place in the loose formation that began taking them east and away from home. Every new person was nervous, and they were all trying to alleviate the underlying tension by laughing, joking, and generally making a ruckus. The march lasted a surprisingly short amount of time, only reaching a few miles away from town before the Mage halted their progress.

"That'll do. Thank you for the escort." Master Don waved off the soldiers accompanying them. Lieutenant Baker turned his men around and commanded a return to the village, clapping Luke on the shoulder and shooting him a quick smile as he walked past. "Gather around me, please, Initiates. There is *much* information that you need to know; knowledge that is not allowed to the general public. *You* will only be allowed to know because your vow to the Kingdom will force you to keep your mouth closed."

"First of all, I want to know *why* you think we are recruiting right now." Master Don paused, then pointed at a man near the front.

"Well… it's the war, innit?" piped up the reedy voice, a merchant's son that Luke had never really gotten along with.

"Partly." Master Don waved his hand back and forth.

"*Monsters.*" Taylor was just loud enough to be heard.

"Correct!" Master Don confirmed with surprise, giving her a contemplative look. "You and I will have a talk about how you know that."

Raising his voice slightly, he returned his attention to the entire group. "As you will all soon learn, the worlds that we travel to are not safe, by any sense of the word. When we open portals between these worlds, if we are strong enough or the gate is opened forcefully enough, it will *stay* open until it is closed. This is called a 'Scar'. It will remain open until someone trained in opening portals to that world closes it. In some cases, this is easy; in others… well, there are worlds that only one or two people *total* can ever reach. Finally, there are gates that open naturally in the world. That is, in fact, how the first Ascenders came to be."

After a short pause to let this information sink in, Master Don continued, "Recently, some faction has been moving through our Kingdom, and those of our allies. They don't attack, they don't take credit for the destruction they cause. All they do…"

Master Don scanned the small crowd and gazed into the eyes of the anxious young people, "is tear open, and *leave* open, Scars into some of the most dangerous worlds that we could ever envisage. We call them Anarcanists, as they use arcane methods to spread anarchy. People are *dying*. Normally, we don't allow people so young to attempt to use their power. Even with your oaths, and all the training you are about to go through, you will likely kill someone - or many someones – or yourself by accident before you can fully control yourselves."

"What we need are powerful people that can slay man and beast alike. If you aren't at the warfront, you will be hunting monsters that have become mankillers and finding ways to close Scars. Prepare yourselves now, because this is a task that never seems to end." The Initiates were starting to pale as they came to know what they had actually gotten involved in. "Now, we are going to begin. I am going to use your mana to open a portal to whichever dimension calls to your power."

"In each of these worlds, the person most qualified to protect you and teach you how best to use your powers should soon arrive and explain everything else. Obviously, this is a long process. Does anyone know *how* we are able to train everyone we find?" A sea of blank expressions met Master Don's question. "Then does anyone care to guess my age?"

Silence continued to reign over the group, and he grinned, almost to himself. "I love this part. While we do require much from you, the rewards are worth everything else. First... the process of *Ascending* slows the aging process. I am over six *hundred* years old."

The silence shattered as people exclaimed in awe or disbelief. "Calm down, calm down. It's true, and this is also what allows us to train you in time to be useful. Across the portals, time moves... disproportionately. The average speed is four times faster than this world. While you are in another world, your body doesn't seem to age at *all*. There are some theories against this, because your body will still grow hair, nails, heal, and scar as usual; but the fact remains that you will go in and come out looking the same age as you do right now."

"It is *highly* likely that you will not return to this world - this plane - until you are trained. By the timing of this plane, you will be gone roughly two and a half years. For the vast majority of you, it will be nearly ten years. For those with the most difficult paths... it could be *much* more." Shock and outrage raced across the faces of the Initiates, warring heavily with greed and excitement.

"Why do *you* decide who the best person to train us is ? Shouldn't we get to choose who we are bound to?" Andre demanded as his shock dissipated.

"A very good point, young Andre. The simple answer is: *I* am by far the most qualified person to determine your path. Beyond me, there is no higher authority in the Hollow Kingdom except the King himself."

"But that means…" Taylor interjected with shining eyes.

"Correct! I am Archmage Donec Arriperent, High Authority on all things magical, considered the most powerful in the land, and yes, Taylor, you are still my apprentice."

"King Alexander's wr… *cough*… I guess that explains why your people were so shocked." Taylor composed herself and only let a small smile shine through.

"Unflappable. I *knew* there was something I liked about you," Master Don complimented her. "Time to go, everyone. Line up and prepare yourself. Portaling can be a bit… disorienting."

The emotionally and mentally confused Initiates shuffled together into a rough line. They watched in awe as a gate to another world was opened. Don reached into the air, light emanating from his fingertips… and *pulled*. Unnatural light started to pour out of a small space, growing into a door shape as he continued to strain against something invisible. The entire process took about two minutes, and the Archmage blew a sigh of relief as he finished. "*Goodness*, that takes a lot out of me. The framework is set, all we need is a mana input. Right, who's first? Make sure to say your goodbyes, as it may be a *long* time before you see anyone here again."

Andre stepped forward, showing his willingness to go first. He waved sadly at his friends; they had already said their good-byes. Master Don nodded approvingly. "Good man. Now, just so you all know, you will be *compelled* to return here after two and a half years have passed on this plane. Make sure you are strong enough to make your Kingdom proud."

With a wave of Master Don's hand, light passed through Andre. It entered his body as a light purple, and exited as a deep green. The light was swallowed by the portal, which solidified into a single color. The land beyond was beautiful, but all the creatures visible within moved across it at insane speeds. "That's just the time dilation effect; don't worry. Step through, and your trainer will arrive shortly. *Don't* keep him waiting."

Indeed, a man was sprinting toward them at a godlike speed. He stopped at the edge of the gate, beckoning to Andre with a hand that fluttered faster than a hummingbird's wings. Master Don prodded him impatiently, "Sound doesn't cross over very well. Get going."

Andre stepped across the shimmering boundary and into the strange land. The last sight the group saw was the pair walking away faster than a horse could gallop.

"Amazing," Luke whispered, awe evident in his voice. "So that's what it looks like with time passing faster on that side?"

Others converged on the portal, and for each one, the process repeated. The portal opened, someone sprinted up, then the selected person zipped away. Taylor drew nearer, but Master Don stopped her. "No, you will be coming with me. Luke, you are up. I think we will try you with the... healers, perhaps, just like this last youngster? As soon as we use your mana, we will know for sure, but since the way is open, I'll just have them wait a moment longer; just in case."

Master Don sent the light through Luke, then more, and more. The Archmage's eyes narrowed, and a *storm* of mana rushed out of him and into Luke. A bare trickle of it took on a blue tint and filtered into the portal without changing the landscape beyond. "Ah, I *love* being right! A healer! Such a noble occupation. Let's go, lad."

Luke stepped forward and waited until someone ran up to the door from the other side. He moved to cross the gate, but as his foot passed over the threshold, the blue power that stained the gate flashed into a *deep* blue for a bare instant. He was *sucked* though, vanishing from sight. When the blue tint cleared in the blink of an eye, the healer on the other side shrugged and waved his arms in an 'X' to show that Luke hadn't arrived.

"Well, *that's* new." Don's brow furrowed quizzically, and he cast a few spells at the portal in an attempt to see what had gone wrong. "I've never seen someone vaporized just trying to *use* a portal. Ah, well; we were expecting *some* losses. This one was simply a little early. Probably his mana channels; those were damaged beyond belief! Likely for the best, though. It seemed like his power had something to do with resisting oaths. That'd be a death sentence anyway, though he likely only had another few years left with mana channels like that… send someone to notify his family, Reginald. Ready to go, Taylor? Lots to do!"

Taylor simply stared at the shifting portal with moist eyes, a hand pressed to her mouth.

CHAPTER SIX

Luke flew out the other side of the portal, landing heavily on his back. Luckily, his pack took the brunt of the fall, saving him from shredding his skin on the rough stone floor. Gasping in an attempt to regain his breath, he searched around wildly, trying to understand what had gone wrong. There was very little light, but he was able to see that he was in a cave of some sort. He could hear water running nearby, leaving him with the hope that he would be able to survive long enough to find help.

Something had clearly gone wrong; this wasn't the world that he had intended to step into. Luke forced himself to his feet, standing unsteadily and trying to find a way out of the hole he was in. There were many paths, but even from where he stood, he could see that most of them were dead ends. He started down a likely tunnel, one where light was filtering in. Luke walked further and further, the sound of rushing water increasing as he advanced along the fissure. Finally reaching the mouth of the tunnel, he found daylight shimmering through what had to be the bluest waterfall he had ever seen.

"Of course." Luke put his hand out, trying to see how deep the water flowed, but the pressure forced his hand down before he could reach past it. His hand also tingled unpleasantly as he shook off the water, but he chalked it up to the sudden, intense pressure. He looked away, never realizing that the remaining water simply... evaporated, leaving not a single droplet of wetness behind. "It's never easy, is it?"

He snorted, annoyed that he had been forced into such a situation by the 'Archmage'. Determined to find another way out, Luke backtracked and spent several hours searching for another point of egress. Sadly, he could find nothing else, and the light in the cave was beginning to fade. He raced back to the only exit and decided to camp next to the roaring waterfall for the night.

Luke pulled a carefully folded bedroll out of his pack, and as he laid it out... a folded note fluttered to the ground. In the fading light, he could just barely make out the words 'We love and miss you already, son. Never doubt how proud we are of you'. Luke teared up, but only allowed a few drops to squeeze out.

"I'll make it back to you," Luke whispered his promise to his family, who were now equally only a step - and also impossibly far - away. A restless night passed, and morning came quickly. He awoke feeling *filthy*. While eating a breakfast of dried meat and some of the limited stores of water from his pack, he mulled over his options.

Luke believed that he had searched the connecting tunnels in their entirety. If he was correct, then there was only one way out without tunneling through the stone, and at best, he only had another few days' worth of food. Certainly not enough to sustain him while creating a tunnel through solid rock with no tools. Packing everything as carefully as he could, he cinched the strap on his leather pack to make it as watertight as possible, and braced himself for the pain of being crushed by the intense flow of water.

"Survival is what matters. Get as far as possible from where the water lands, because there are likely rocks at the bottom. Try to cannonball; cross your arms and protect your head," he coached aloud, psyching himself up for the jump. "Now, stop thinking so much and *do* it!"

Gritting his teeth, he ran at the wall of water and jumped out as far as possible, pressed down by the torrential downpour as he passed through. Upon his escape from the falls, he dropped at *most* two feet before hitting a large pool of water, belly-flopping painfully.

"King Alexander's saggy wand!" he gurgled beneath the waves, clawing his way to the surface. Luckily, his bag acted as a floatation device, dragging him upward faster than he had any right to emerge. Sputtering, Luke made his way to a sandy beach located only a few feet away and finally looked up to observe his surroundings. The view took his breath away more effectively than the water had; the enormous vista boggled and confused his mind.

The visible land was only about a half mile wide, and there were distinct *edges* to the terrain. Luke found himself standing near a field that stretched for miles to the east, sloping downward to a point on the horizon. He could see some kind of animal playing in groups, but the distance and long grass was too great to see them clearly. To the north and south, the land vanished. He couldn't understand *how*, but he would go see for himself. The strange cut-off was only about a half mile away.

However, the most stunning aspect of the landscape was the *color*. Everything was stained in the most *violent* shades of blue. Luke looked behind himself and gasped again, this time in panic. Behind the waterfall was *nothing*. The land ended at a cliff, another drop off. In other words, the cave he had come out of didn't exist. Luke was trapped on this new world, and as far as he could see...

He was the only human.

CHAPTER SEVEN

- TAYLOR -

"What just *happened*?" Taylor was panicking. Her lifelong friend had suddenly vanished, and no one appeared to know *why*. In fact, Master Don said he was *dead*?

"I'm honestly not certain," The Archmage admitted, but he simply moved on. "This has never happened before, Taylor. To be frank, I do think that he was killed instantly. I am sorry to be blunt, but sadly, the facts do not care for your feelings like I do."

He motioned to his retinue and gave specific orders for them to attempt all magical means of pulling Luke back if - no matter how unlikely - he was in another world. Still, he didn't countermand his order to tell Luke's family that he had died. "Taylor, I'm sorry. We can't wait here, though. There is simply too much for you to learn. I have chosen you as my apprentice, therefore it is my duty to personally train you, which means that I need to relinquish some of my more pressing duties to the King."

"You may not understand how *much* this will affect the

realm, but please know that we need to begin your training immediately. Grieve during downtime. Come along." He shifted the portal, opening it to a strange-looking place none of the others had entered. Master Don stepped through, impatiently awaiting her on the other side. Much more hesitantly, Taylor edged across the threshold and looked at what her future would hold.

"What is this place?" Her eyes were already roving the world around her, and she was breathing heavily in relief that the portal hadn't fried her.

"Taylor, it is my great pleasure to be the first to welcome you to '*mundi sunt nominibus singulorum*' or, roughly translated: 'The World of Names'. *Literally* translated, it is: 'the names of each of the world'." Don chuckled at a fond memory, taking a deep breath. "It is *good* to be home."

They were standing in what appeared to be a living library. A short distance away, an extremely tall bookshelf held thousands of books neatly stacked in rows. Orderly calligraphy swirled and shifted across the ground, flowing like a river to the south. Animals, made of all sorts of different materials for writing, roamed the moors of the Library's orderly stacks, which seemed to stretch forever in every direction.

"Oh... *wow*." Taylor's fear for her friend had been completely overwhelmed by the vastness of the new world around her. "This is... this is *amazing*. This is home?"

"Isn't it, though? I'll never forget my first time here; I imagine my face looked just like *that*. Well, no time like the present. We need to get you a spell book and teach you how to tame spells!" Don started toward a distant stack of books.

"Okay, let's - wait, what? *Tame* spells?"

"Yes."

"I don't understand."

"Good! I'm being purposefully unhelpful. Let's begin." With that frustrating conversation as the starting point, Master Don guided her toward a bookshelf. He pointedly ignored all of

Taylor's questions, until she took the hint and stopped asking. Approaching the shelf, he gestured to the neatly organized volumes.

"To entice your first spellbook, you need to *slowly* release your mana into the air around you. It will be much easier in this world, and as such, you need to be *very* careful when you do so. Here, mana is to creatures what blood is to sharks. When you release it, you need to know *exactly* what you are trying to entice, or everything in the area will try to feast upon you."

"If they succeed in overpowering you, they will only stop when every bit of your body has been consumed. First, you make this hand symbol, which means 'release mana'." Don motioned with his hands, and had her repeat it until he was satisfied that the motion was correct. "Then you focus on what you are trying to lure, and relax the control you have in your brain. Literally try to relax your 'brain muscle'."

"*Why* am I doing this, if everything is going to try to eat me?" Taylor shook herself, already regretting asking the dumb question. She grinned wryly. "Sorry, I'll just do it. Also, I bet Andre would be *great* at relaxing his brain."

At her botched attempt not to laugh, Master Don snorted with only a touch of mirth, "Laugh it up, but if you find a *better* way to describe it, please let me be the first to know. I get laughed at every single time I say that line, though I admit you hid it better than most. Now, Taylor, I want you to focus on those books and try to convince one of them to be your friend. The *strongest* one you can convince."

She glanced at her instructor, trying to determine if he was messing with her. Noting his serious demeanor, Taylor shrugged and got into position, made the symbol with her hands - pinkies together like she was holding a book - and tried to release her mana. Feeling foolish, she peeked at her Master, but quickly refocused after he gave her a dark look.

"Convince them to be my friend," she whispered, trying to relax. "Never been good at that. Only had three friends my whole life, and one of them was a Bard that made me *think* he was my friend. Come on, mana. Come *on!*"

Taylor aggressively attempted to breach the barrier in her mind. With that push, she felt punctured, like a water skin with a dagger stuck into it. Feeling as though her hands were gushing blood, she opened her eyes in a panic... only to find mana dripping from her hands like purple-tinged water. Upon contact with the air, it evaporated and rose like a cloud.

"Too much already... try and stop," her master calmly ordered. She tried to close the breach in her mental space but was immediately distracted and lost focus as a horrendous *shriek* filled the air. The cloud had reached the first row of books.

The books erupted into motion, exploding into the air like a murder of crows. The covers flapped like wings, and the volumes *literally* flew above her, crashing into one another and fighting in an attempt to be the *only* one to feed on the free mana source. Taylor panicked, and the mana redoubled its explosion from her body, getting caught by an updraft and reaching almost all of the higher shelves. The air was suddenly teeming with flying books, some of them larger than she was by a significant margin.

"*Help!*" she cried to her Master.

"I cannot." Master Don's bearing was still calm, but his words made Taylor realize a terrifying fact: he wasn't going to step in. No matter what. "You're *fine*. If you can't overcome *this* fear, you will never make it as a higher level Namer. Hurry up; one of them will win soon. You want to be ready for it."

Breathing deeply, Taylor tried to regain control, building a dam to slow the rushing ocean of mana. The flow cut off as suddenly as it had begun, making her stumble as though she had taken a blow to the head. She scrutinized the swooping books and still-spreading cloud of mana, and tried to focus all her thoughts on gaining a new friend and partner. Her intent reached out to her mana and released a concussive wave that knocked several books from the air even as it nearly flattened her.

"Good, you gave your mana a purpose." Master Don was still calmly observing the hurricane of books overhead.

Taylor ignored him and kept her thoughts on her need, focusing on the chaos above her. Books returned to their places on the shelves, quivering in apparent fear. Some flew away as fast as they could, and Taylor felt an echoing concussion rebound onto her. It knocked her to her knees, and a long moment passed before she was able to determine what had caused the shockwave. Then she saw *it*. Her mana had reached the highest shelf, and the only book upon it had just peeked over the ledge.

"Oh, dear." Master Don maintained an infuriatingly calm tone. "*This* should be interesting."

Several of the books were still bickering when the top-shelfer started to tumble down. About halfway between its starting point and the ground, it opened its covers, gaining speed like a raptor and attacking the still-flying books *viciously*. The few tomes that hadn't returned to the shelves or escaped were quickly reduced to confetti, which was somehow feasted upon by the victorious book. When the sky had been cleared, the book circled Taylor once, then descended to float a few feet in front of her face. Words scrawled across the open pages, adjusting themselves until she was able to read them.

<Delicious mana. More.> it read.

"Make a deal with it. Agree to feed it mana and spells, so long as it allows you to cast from its pages." She repeated his offer to the spellbook, and the volume halted in midair, as though considering. Eventually, it bobbed, agreeing with the deal.

<Fill my pages with the *tastiest*. No disease or disease-like, or I leave. Allow me to read you?>

"Yes, sounds good!" she confirmed, even as Master Don shouted in a voice suddenly *far* from calm.

"*No!*"

Too late. The pages swirled with color as she re-lived every moment in her life, the book recording it all and reducing the story down to a single page.

When Taylor was finally able to look away, it was well past dark and they were in a different location entirely.

"*What?*" she croaked as she attempted to stand, swayed, and fell to the ground.

CHAPTER EIGHT

Master Don seemed to be alternating between annoyance and... something else. "You let it *read* you! It now knows absolutely *everything* about you, and will record everything that happens from here on! Think of this as the most intrusive diary ever. Should this book ever leave you and partner with another, that person will be able to read your entire life. All your strengths, all your weaknesses. All emotional high or low points. *Everything.*"

"*What?*" she spat in horror. She looked at the book, now cradled in her arms. Was it... sleeping? "What *is* this?"

"This is your spell book, your Grimoire," her Master replied with a sigh, letting his anger go. There was no help for it now. "Here is where you keep all of your spells, and how you will cast magic. If it helps you feel better, you have started with a Grimoire of *exceptional* quality. If a book from a low shelf had read you, I would have simply destroyed it and made you start again, but then you would have lost your starter bonus."

"What do you mean?" Taylor pulled in the book protectively, even before she realized what she was doing.

"Well, the quality of these books has an effect on your

48

ability to progress. Basically, the number of spells you can learn is based, in part, on how many spells the book can hold, in addition to the quality of those spells. Here in the Library, books are like birds, and they follow a hierarchy. The overpopulated first few rows are pigeons, plentiful but stupid. They eat and eat, but only give you scat in return. You can learn tier one spells at *best*. As you climb the shelves, the books become smarter, eating less, but requiring a certain," he waved his hands, "*something*. They want a specific diet."

She nodded, easily following along. Master Don continued his impromptu lecture, pointing out a few still-fluttering covers. "Also, they are made from better material. The low levels are made from papyrus, a weak material, a weak Grimoire. As they go higher, the durability increases. Paper, vellum, hard leather, and finally, whatever the top predator is for the shelf. In your case, it appears that yours is made from the hide of a cockatrice, which should make it nearly invulnerable to physical harm. Again, an excellent start for you. Less chance of losing all of your hard work to a simple swing of a sword."

She looked at the book in wonder, surprised by how *interesting* it was. The book was surprisingly light, and had no markings of any kind on it. This was to become her book of spells? It seemed too... *alive*. Taylor voiced her concern while continuing to cradle the precious tome.

"Of course! To be magic is to be alive, and to be alive is to be magic. Even humans, whether or not they become Ascenders, have some mana in them. That is what allows healers to cure injuries, and Necromancers to animate corpses. Earth Mages don't actually move the earth; they move the mana that flows *through* the earth like rivers, the ley lines. *Everything* is interconnected, and mana even has physical properties if enough of it is released, as you just observed for yourself. In the right conditions, it acts like water before evaporating."

"Oh!" Taylor exclaimed as she remembered something. "What did my book mean by 'no disease, or I leave'? That has to be part of its 'diet', right?"

"Correct. There are spells that you can cast that cause disease or specific illnesses, perhaps self-propagation as well, and to some books they 'taste' foul. Every book seems to have particular palates, as I mentioned." Master Don shook himself and started looking around the shelves.

Taylor waited, but he didn't continue speaking. "What did you mean about the starting bonus?"

"Oh, that." Master Don pursed his lips, hesitated, then decided to answer the question. There was no point in hiding the information. "The maximum tier of the first spell you can learn is determined by an aspect of your Mind characteristic called 'talent'. The very first spell you learn, or in our case, the first *Grimoire* you bind to yourself, is not beholden to your natural talent. It can be practically any tier, so we as trainers watch *very* closely at the start. That's why I brought you directly to one of the most dangerous areas you could survive in right away. That Grimoire is tier five, and I know that means nothing to you right now. Just know that it does mean to cast a spell above tier five, you will need a new Grimoire. You can have as many as you can control, but they are *very* territorial."

"Can you explain more, so I *do* understand?" Taylor pressed him. "Can I increase my 'talent'?"

"Yes; very easily, in fact. But… all in due time. Too much information all at once is like filling a glass with water. If it over-flows, you lose whatever is on the ground." Master Don turned to his pack and pulled out some rations for them to munch on. They sat quietly for a while as Taylor looked at the wonderous world around her, ate her food, and stroked her practically purring Grimoire.

"This is all so *amazing*." Taylor took a deep breath. "Master, can I try casting a spell now?"

"You don't have any, do you? How could you cast one?" Don smirked at her stricken face, and coyly offered, "Would you like to go get one?"

"*Abyss*, yeah."

"We'd better get moving, then. Nowhere around here to

sleep, anyway." They began walking, and Taylor made it nearly a half mile before she fell flat on her face.

"Ow."

"I *did* tell you not to let out so much mana, didn't I? Even if you can regenerate it, unless your mana channels are well-practiced at handling large mana flows, you can utterly exhaust yourself." Taylor's suddenly-hated mentor chuckled. "I suppose a break is in order… can you sit up? Good. Eat this."

"I obviously didn't give you enough to eat." Handing her some dried meat, he started going through his pack as she voraciously gnawed upon the salty beef. "Drink some water, and eat some of this honey. You used *far* too much energy in one go. With the amount of mana you pumped into the air, I could have burned a small village to the ground. I have, in fact. While we are here, why not read what your book has to say about you?"

CHAPTER NINE

Taylor looked at the book in her lap, contemplating it for a moment before running a finger down its spine. It shuddered and fell open, revealing details of her life that even she had forgotten. "Oh neat, it details the date that Zed showed up in town! I've only known him for six months? *Sheesh*... that was a messed-up situation. What's this section?"

She covered most of the text, leaving only the page filled with numbers. Master Don looked over and nodded. "That's an easy one, and an explanation of something I referenced earlier. It is *you*, boiled down to numbers. They are 'characteristics,' or 'stats' if you are lazy. Your body, mind, senses, and presence. Those can be grown from study, training, and... ugh, *leveling*."

"Leveling?" Taylor poked at the obvious sore spot.

"Yes, some *morons*... no... let me do this properly," her mentor growled and turned to face her directly. "When you start defeating monsters, either here or back in our world, you will gain a portion of its *potential*. Specifically, you will gain 'Etheric Xenograft Potentia', commonly known as 'exp' or 'Potentia'. As a better explanation, it is the 'total potential energy field of an outside source'. When you kill something, you add a portion of their Potentia to your *own* potential, and slowly start to become more than you were. This will change you. Power, strength, speed, willpower. Eventually - if you live long enough - you will stop being a mere human, and become an *Ascender*."

"I don't know what you mean. Aren't we already Ascenders?""

Don shook his head slightly. "I mean that our world will no longer be enough for you. It means that to get stronger, you will need to search for bigger, deadlier, more powerful planes of existence. But once you ascend... you can never return. If I were to ascend, I could meet someone on *this* world, The World of Names, but never back on our own world, known as the 'base world'. I can't really tell you much more. Not many Ascenders have ever bothered to offer details."

"I see... if there is nothing else, can you tell me about my stats?" Taylor politely asked him.

"*Characteristics*. Don't fall into the trap of those... reductionists. Yes, just hold on one moment. 'Leveling' is the term some bureaucrat came up with to generalize mutating and altering yourself. It means that you have gained enough Etheric Xenograft Potentia to *radically* improve a single aspect of yourself. You can save it and store it up, gaining many levels at once if you want. There are certain incentives to doing it like this... but there are drastic downsides as well." Master Don took a deep breath and looked into her eyes so that he had Taylor's full attention.

"Once the process of leveling begins, it *must* be completed." He swallowed in an attempt to soothe a suddenly dry throat. "If you try to level yourself too much at once, there is a likelihood that you will not be able to endure it, or you will mutate into something *else*. I have seen people die from trying to gain too much at once. I have seen others turn into literal monsters as well. On the other hand, you can devote some of your 'exp' to your spells to increase their potency as you level."

"This is why people will often delay leveling themselves.

They can pour exp into their spells, and still train their body to its natural maximum potential before ever using their gained Potentia to do so. The trade-off is that you stay weaker for longer, but your spells become more powerful. Some do the reverse, and work to train their current characteristics to the maximum before using the leveling bonuses. Still, there is a *limit*. The Sigil we placed on all of you Initiates contains a few safety features to help you survive. Now, say 'status'."

"Status?" Taylor yelped as a chiming sound played in her head.

Contribution Activity Log is online! Scanning...

Unbeknownst to Taylor, the Sigil on her forehead was glowing, now fully visible to anyone looking. Mana left the Sigil, spiraled around her body, and returned to her head.

CAL Scan complete!
Level: 0
Current Etheric Xenograft Potentia: 15/100 to level 1!
Body: 1.1
Mind: 3.75
Presence: 1.9
Senses: 2.25
Health: 59
Mana: 92
Mana regen: 1.83 per second

"Now, you see that data in front of your face?" Master Don wryly shook his head as he told her, "It should match up with your book *exactly*, and the *Sigil* is how we see that data without the potential of losing it to someone else."

"I get it; don't let books read me." Taylor checked her book, and it did indeed match up, at least what had been revealed so far. "Okay... but what does each one *mean*? Also, there are more in the book than on this screen!"

"Take it easy; I'll explain. I'm just going slow." Master Don handed her another strip of meat. "'Body' controls your overall health, fitness, and strength. It impacts the amount of damage you can take, also shown as 'health', determines how much you can lift, and how hard you can push yourself without collapsing from fatigue."

"It is important to improve your body, because spellcasting is *stressful* and frequently damages your body. Also, remember that health is a resource that does not replenish quickly on its own. You can use mana to heal your body, but without associated abilities to target that healing, there are often side effects. Health is *not* a resource to be spent lightly."

"Got it. Healthy body, healthy mind, just like Momma used to say." Taylor nodded to show her understanding.

"Nice way to push the conversation along. We'll work on your subtlety. '*Mind*' is your overall intelligence, knowledge retained, and talent toward learning and using spells. You need all of these to successfully cast spells. A very clean system, if I do say so," Master Don grimaced distastefully, "even though certain *aspects* of it are taken lightly. Abyssal Enchanters, always taking the artistry out of things and inserting numbers."

"What about Presence and Senses?"

"Presence is... hmm." Master Don hesitated. "These two stats are less *quantifiable*, but equally as important. You will need to decide whether or not you want to increase them, and by how much. Presence, also sometimes called 'aura' determines how much force you exert on the world around you simply by *being* there. With your basic score in Senses... I bet you can easily sneak up on people, correct?"

"That's what high Senses does?" Taylor thought about how often she had jabbed Andre in the ribs, and felt a wash of homesickness. It had only been half a day! "I could easily sneak, yes."

"Good. Now, this is what it is like when you have a *huge* Presence." Master Don nodded sagely, and suddenly... he was *massive*. No... he was *there*. Taylor couldn't look away from him, and she started gasping for breath, the sheer *magnitude* of the man in front of her causing her lungs to seize. Then her tutor was normal again, and she started gulping in air. "Obviously, you need to learn to control it. Also, to clear any lingering concerns, it is *very* hard to kill things with Presence alone. You may have passed out, but you would have been fine. Probably."

"Senses are essentially the opposite, as they allow you to *feel* things even when they have very little Presence. It also controls your actual senses, and increasing them will allow you to see, hear, smell, taste, and *feel* more powerfully. Observe." Master Don *looked* at her, and Taylor could *swear* that a predator was watching her and finding all the weaknesses that she had to offer. "As you can see, there is a feeling of danger associated with someone turning their Senses on you, also called 'blood-lust' or 'killing intent', so keep that in mind."

"Just…" Taylor wasn't even sure what she had been planning to say. "How do *I* get to that point?"

"Every time you… *level*," Master Don's nostrils flared as he ground out the hated words, "you choose one of the sub-characteristics of those main characteristics to increase. Each increase is a flat five points. Now… think on this for a moment. What happens if your mind is a hundred times more powerful than your body? Can your body keep up?"

"…No?"

"Correct. There is a limit to how much you *should* devote to a single characteristic." Master Don looked at her numbers again. "Now, say 'Sub-status'."

"Sub-status." Taylor's view revealed more information, but still not as much as her book contained.

Level: 0
Current Etheric Xenograft Potentia: 15/100 to level 1!
Body: 1.1

- *Fitness: 1.3*
- *Resistance: 0.9*

Mind: 3.75

- *Talent: 5.5*
- *Capacity: 2*

Presence: 1.9

- *Willpower: 1.7*
- *Charisma: 2.1*

Senses: 2.25

- *Physical reaction: 2.7*
- *Mental energy: 1.8*

Health: 59
Mana: 92
Mana regen: 1.83 per second

"As you can see, these are the sub-characteristics. When added together and divided in half, you can see that the subs equal the main characteristic." Master Don regarded her book and cheerfully smiled. "As expected, your natural talent is crazily high for a newly Initiated Ascender."

"Also, consider this: if you were to level right now and increase your Fitness by five points, you would increase your *entire* body by fifty percent. Later on, five points will seem a small thing… but right now, you would feel like you were going to die from all the changes that would be done to you. When you level, make *sure* I am watching over you, and you are in a safe place. You might literally die from starvation otherwise, or just from something taking advantage of that moment of weakness."

"Yes, Master Don." They lapsed into silence as Taylor contemplated her options, but she couldn't hold back her questions for long. "Why would anyone *increase* their Presence? Wouldn't it be better to be able to sneak around?"

"For certain people, yes. Mainly assassins and rogues,"

Master Don answered calmly, obviously having given this talk many times before. "Do you recall how you could barely breathe a moment ago when I released my Presence?"

"Clearly."

"That was actually merely my Charisma sub-characteristic. To fend off Charisma, you need to use your own characteristics to fend it off. Your Willpower is the most direct way; it is a direct contest between mine and yours." Master Don explained as if this were a simple concept. "There are other ways, of course; either a Mind that could withstand it, a Body that can power through, or manipulating the Senses to find a way to turn yourself inward and fend off the effects."

"There are many things that refuse to acknowledge beings with a lesser Charisma, which makes the stat important for people who are intending to tame things. That means *us*. There are *many* spells that will never allow themselves to be cast by someone they see as weak."

"I'll think about this," Taylor told him as she took another bite of food.

"See that you do. We will discuss what each of the sub-characteristics control at a later time."

"There's *more?*" Don rolled his eyes at her question, not deigning to reply. A few minutes after Taylor finished her impromptu meal, they got back up and continued walking. "Thanks, I needed that. So, not to be pushy, but what spells are we going to get?"

Her book perked up, peeking out of her backpack like a pet hearing that a treat would soon be offered. Master Don flushed a deep red. "It's a... surprise."

"Don't want to say it?"

He cleared his throat. "Not really. We will just... *show* you, if that's okay."

"All right? *We?*" Taylor's question went unanswered.

They continued in silence for a bit, Master Don sweating lightly until he suddenly felt the urge to continue teaching her. He launched into a lecture without preamble, "About this spell that we are going to get… you have to understand, mana either comes from somewhere either deep in the earth or from the sun. It is required for all things to live, and all living things contain mana. In fact, *everything* about you contains magic, including your sweat, because it comes from you."

"When you use all of your mana quickly, it depletes your very essence. You can replenish yourself best with liquids and dense foods. Liquids, even water, can help you regain mana quickly, but you can't drink enough to make it useful over time. Dense foods, like honey, are the best sources, because they contain mana from so *many* different sources. It is jam-*packed* with power. Now that I mention it, jam is pretty good too."

"Oh. That sounds good. I mean, it makes sense. Um, sorry to bring this up, but I really need to use the bathroom…?"

"Hold it." When Taylor gave him a scathing look, Don swallowed and stated, "I have a good reason for it. We are almost there."

Taylor looked around, but saw only empty shelves. "Where are we?"

"We are about to get your first spells!" Don informed her brightly. "They are considered tier one, the weakest of all spells. Still, every Mage worth their salt has these particular spells; they are *that* useful."

Taylor looked around *much* more eagerly, trying to spot whatever she was about to tame. "I don't… see anything. Is my Sense characteristic too low? Are you sure we're in the right place?"

"Positive. Now, let me explain something. Sometimes when collecting spells, you use force, and you'll need to fight *desperately* to survive the encounter. Sometimes, you bend them to your will through sheer *Presence*. Other times, you can… make deals or bribe them. This is one of those bribe spells, but unlike your book… the spells here aren't after 'pure' mana."

"So, what do I need to do?" Taylor pulled her book out of her bag, and it rustled menacingly and floated up to perch on her arm like a hunting falcon. "I'm ready to do whatever I need to do, Master Don!"

"Ahem. Um. Well, that's good. The two spells in this area are known as 'Cleanse' and 'Purify', and both are *immensely* useful! Though *nearly* every Mage has them, you never hear how they are captured because… it is not very… *dignified.*"

"What do you mean?" Taylor was becoming concerned at Master Don's non-forthcoming manner.

"You have to bribe them with their… ahem… *function.*"

"I don't…"

Turning beet red once more, Master Don looked away and spoke in a rush, "You have to mess your pants!"

"No!" Taylor flushed scarlet at the words. "*What? No!*"

"Trust me… you absolutely *need* these spells. Listen, being a powerful Mage means huge compromises with dignity, and some people are just too *proud* to do what needs to be done. Are you one of those people?" Her Master turned to face her, and it seemed like his face was carved from stone. "Are you *actually* willing to do whatever you need to do to become powerful? Or will you falter at the first step because it is *embarrassing?*"

"I… what do I have to do?" Taylor spoke flatly, her face burning red.

"Good. Go over there, and… do it. When they swarm you, only let two versions of *different* types come near, and make them a deal. One will look like a fly, one will look like a firefly. Here is the deal you offer. They get everything your body collects and produces normally, like dust, sweat… *poo*, all forms of excreta… and you are able to use them on other people and things."

Swallowing hard, Taylor nodded once and trudged like a condemned person around the bend. No words were passed between them. A few minutes later, she came back, *perfectly* clean. Sweat and dirt that had clung to her were gone, as though she just had taken a bath; her clothes were clean and apparently ironed.

Master Don chuckled and started to speak. "Good! I see you succeeded! Now that you have your first two spells-"

"We *never* speak about this again."

"Taylor, those spells don't even require mana! They pull it directly from what they take, and are therefore essentially *free* passive spells. We should really discuss the benefits-"

Taylor whipped around, looking Master Don in the eye, "*Never speak about them again*, Don!"

CHAPTER TEN

- ANDRE -

"This *sucks*," Andre stated petulantly as they plodded along the seemingly endless plains.

"Yup," his teacher agreed sullenly. He had his own reasons.

"Are we just gonna walk forever, or are you gonna actually *teach* me?"

"If you were paying *attention* to the land around you, you would *possibly* notice that you didn't exactly come through to the safest area in this world," his new Master spat at him. "And you either call me 'Master' or 'Xan'. Here, first lesson for free: respect in *all* things, *Initiate*."

"Fine, *Xan*. Are we just gonna walk forever or are you gonna teach me eventually, *Xan*?" Andre grumpily demanded.

"You know *what*? I just realized! We can master your powers right *now*! Surely *you* can do it really fast, even though no one *else* ever has without a solid *decade* of study! Abyss, *six* times time dilation? Making it one of the most *dramatically* large time dilation effects so that you can learn properly? Who needs *that*? Tell you what; there's a bugbear tribe over that hill. Go tame them, and learn what they offer the earth. Any *questions* before you become all-powerful?"

"Yes!" Andre angrily exclaimed. "*What…* is a bugbear?"

"Hopeless." Xan sighed and stared up at the green-tinted sky.

"*Excuse* me?"

The trainer took a deep breath, "Can you not just *wait* until we get to a safer place?"

"C'mon, man. *Something*! I'm so ready… I wanna do something cool!" Andre's eyes were shining.

Xan eyed his pupil with disgust. "Do you ever wonder why they didn't take people so young into training before? You. *You* are the reason, and are also everything that is wrong with this whole debacle."

Andre waved the admonishment away and flashed a brilliant smile. "I'm adorable. C'mon, you know you wanna show me how to blast people."

"*Blast* people…? You're not a *Mage*! Do you know what being a Druid even means?" Xan was working hard to keep his jaw from dropping as he caught the obliviousness on Andre's face. "They sent you here with *no* knowledge? Nothing?"

"Nope. Are you gonna… *teach me?*" Andre wiggled his eyebrows at the man that appeared to be just barely older than himself.

"*Fine*! *Abyss*, but you are annoying! Sit down."

Andre plopped onto his butt with a feces-eating grin spread across his face. Xan snarled at him, "You put the 'suffer' in 'insufferable'. What do you know about Druids? What we do, where we go, how our power works?"

"Nada," Andre smiled cheekily.

"Great. Just great. Our Archmagis make a deal to solidify the alliance and save tens of *thousands* of lives, and yet *I'm* the one stuck teaching you basic information that every *child* in my country knows. You're lucky I can't die of old age or I'd be *really* furious."

"Burning daylight, *Xan*."

"Shut it, mouthbreather. First and most important: a Druid is a person inextricably linked to the land, with *everything* that entails."

"Such as?"

Xan took a deep breath to collect himself, then spoke with gritted teeth. "Mouth. *Shut.* A Druid can interact with everything natural in the world: dirt, water, metal, plants, natural forces, and animals. With the proper *instruction*, you can be *useful* by interacting with these forces for the good of everyone."

"Neat."

"If *you* say another word, *I* won't." Xan looked at Andre until it was obvious that he was staying silent. Xan calmed himself with another deep breath. "Look... I'm not from your Kingdom, but your *survival* has been entrusted to *me*. Not only that, but as a Druid, you are *very* needed on our home plane. Do you want to know *why* there will be people trying to kill you?"

Andre nodded his head with a look of confused horror on his face; the warning about talking seeming to be taken to heart. "You were sent here by your Hollow Kingdom's Archmage, right? Where was your Arch*druid*? The leader of your Druidic groves? You can answer this *one* question."

"There... isn't one? The Mage guy said I was the Kingdom's *first* Druid." Andre proudly announced.

"So, what does that mean for *you* when you are trained?" Xan made a 'come on' gesture.

Andre opened and closed his mouth a few times. "What do you mean?"

"If your Kingdom has *no* Archdruid, and you are your Kingdom's *first Druid*..." Xan leadingly taunted the lad.

"*Me?* You're saying *I'll* be the Archdruid?" Andre gasped as a look of glee appeared on his face. He had just realized that he was even *more* important than he'd *thought* he was!

"*Correct!*" Xan agreed patronizingly. "Do you now understand why I'm trying to get you out of an area that *I'm* unsure I can survive in?"

"Got it. Let's make some tracks." Andre hopped to his feet and walked in the direction they were traveling.

Xan gasped and put his hands over his mouth. "Look at *that*, Andre! You *are* learning!"

"Is your full title 'Xan the *grumpy Druid*', or...?" Andre quipped.

Several hours later, trees started appearing on the horizon. Xan and Andre slowed down when they reached them, and Xan's face started to relax. He pointed out a house built between a few trees which supported it. "Up you go."

Xan pulled out a rope ladder dangling from the small building and handed it over. Andre looked at the rope in his hand, then up at the Druid. "A tree fort? What, are we stopping for the day?"

"Yes and no. This is where you'll be living for roughly the next... oh, ten *years* or so." Xan grinned at his student's horrified expression. "This is a neutral Grove."

"*That*? It looks like it'll fall at the first sign of wind!" Andre was seething at the unfairness of the situation.

"Would you rather sleep on the ground? I'm *sure* you'll survive the nocturnal predators," Xan offered hopefully.

"You have a *sick* sense of humor, don't you?"

"Just move, ya abyssal brat."

"Fine!" Andre climbed the twisting ladder, squeezing himself into the opening at the top and becoming instantly and *thoroughly* unimpressed by the accommodations.

"Home sweet home." Xan fondly stated, climbing up behind him.

"This is... 'home'?" Andre irreverently scoffed.

"You'll come to love it." Xan clapped Andre on the shoulder. He seemed *far* more relaxed, now that they were off the ground. "Took me a while too, a couple hundred years ago."

"Hundred...! I thought Druids were supposed to *love* nature?" Andre looked at the man askance. "Why are you adamant about getting away from it?"

"Look, yes, I love nature; but nature *really* loves to kill and eat you. *So*," his words were steel, "Let's stop getting *snarky* with the guy keepin' us *alive*, hmm?"

"I mean... sure, fine, fair enough." Andre sighed but then perked up and looked over hopefully. "Ready to start teaching me to Druid?"

"Wow. 'Teaching me to Druid'. That's... that's a new one. Yeah, may as well. The faster you learn, the faster I'm free of you. Lesson one: get some food. This is an apple tree; convince it to grow some apples," Xan ordered his Initiate offhandedly. "Good night."

"Ok!" Andre stared at the tree for a long moment, then looked back at Xan, who was starting to climb out of the window. "How?"

"Establish a connection to the tree, open your mana to the tree, and *politely* ask it to give you apples. You will be giving it everything it needs to grow them, so it won't matter that it is out of season. If the tree accepts, it will give you apples. Depending on how much power you give, it will produce more apples. Contingent upon how much it *respects* you, the tree will give you better-*tasting* apples." Xan explained verbosely.

"Whoa. That's a *lot* of words for you." Andre earned a glare with his attempt at a joke. "What do you mean by 'ask it'?"

"If you have mana going into it, the tree will be able to understand your intentions." Xan replied frostily. "I *hope* you succeed, as I just decided that you will be getting *all* your own food from now on. Hope you brought something in your pack."

"Well, that's just plain rude." Andre put his hand on the tree. "How do I open my mana channels?"

"*Carefully.*"

"You know, the sooner you are done teaching me, the faster you can go back to being a lonely curmudgeon..."

"Insufferable little... you had *better* knock that off. Respect in *all* things. This is your last warning. Listen, *Initiate*, mana has certain qualities, and can act like water or gas. Theoretically, it *could* be a solid, but that has never been seen before. When mana is passed *directly*, it goes where it is needed in that organism to increase its natural functions."

"Is this *going* somewhere, or…?" Andre was getting grumpy from lack of information, and he was *hungry*.

Xan was visibly restraining himself, but also slowly climbed back through the window and stood at his full height. "You need to learn *patience*. That is the *art* of the Druid. Seriously, you don't understand anything. The backlash of the things you're asking for could crush you like an insect-"

"Any time now, old man."

"That's *it*! You're an infant playing with blasting rods! Time for you to be *taught* respect, since you won't *give* it!" Xan glared at the wood Andre was standing on. In an instant, two spikes shot up and impaled Andre's feet. Andre screamed and toppled backward, but never touched the floor. More wood rushed up, wrapping around him like vines. One went around his mouth, *tightly*, cutting off his screaming. Andre stared at Xan in horror, appalled and shocked at the sudden brutality.

"I *did* warn you. Nature is violent." Xan stood up, walked over to the ladder, and started climbing down. "Tomorrow, I'll see if you have a new outlook on being a Druid. Until then, think about something for me: you have always been *large*, yes? Muscular? The girls fawn over you, people laugh at your mindless 'witty' banter? Even at your choosing ceremony, you were the 'extra-special Druid'?"

He scoffed and moved downward. "You have no *respect* for the power you have the potential to wield, and apparently none for *me*. You won't die overnight, but you had *better* decide what kind of person you'll be. If you choose wrong… I'll kill you myself, and deal with the consequences of that action. The world has no need of another rogue Druid, and this place does not suffer fools. I *refuse* to lose *my* life trying to teach you. Sleep well, *Initiate*."

With that, Xan climbed down the ladder fully, leaving

Andre with tears streaming down his face, blood dripping out of his feet, and eyes begging not to be left alone for one of the first times in his life.

CHAPTER ELEVEN

- LUKE -

Luke skirted around the pool of water that he had fallen into, inspecting the waterfall that was seemingly pouring from the sky. There was no evidence that the cave he had jumped from had ever existed. The world just *ended* behind the falls. He crawled to the edge of the land and peered over, gasping at the scene.

This place was full of surprises, it seemed. The entire *world* was shaped like a massive corkscrew, seemingly held aloft by nothing. Far, *far* to the north, he could see the earth turn and slope downward, which was apparently the only way down without wings. There was a strange fog that roiled everywhere, making seeing any real distance a trial in itself. Near the platform he was on, it wasn't so bad, but it was already thick in the area just below the edge.

"Amazing," Luke whispered aloud. He pushed himself up, dusting off his clothes. Deciding he had better start looking for shelter, he filled his empty water skin from the falls and started

walking down the gently sloping land. Just then, he realized that his clothes were already dry. How had that happened?

"Everything is downhill." Luke realized that he was speaking out loud a lot, not due to insanity, but mainly to stave off the crushing loneliness. "Well. Downhill, unless I want to come back here…"

He began searching for anything that could be used for shelter or a fire, but across the vast plain, there was only longish blue-hued grass. Not wanting to start an out-of-control fire, and due to the environment not being cold, he simply kept walking until he heard an odd sound.

Thud.

Thud.

The sound kept repeating, sometimes punctuated with a high-pitched squeal. He pushed aside the long blue grass blocking his vision, and tried his best to understand what he was seeing. Two long lines of what appeared to be tiny goats stood facing each other, and every few seconds, one goat would charge an opposing one and bash heads. He moved a little closer, scrutinizing their heads. They had four eyes - two on each side of their head - and recognized extensive horns protruding from the tufted hair of their small heads.

"What the *abyss*?" He was still talking out loud, not yet realizing what a mistake that was. The massive herd of tiny goats turned toward him, many letting out bugling screams. Differences apparently forgotten, the two lines ran and jumped at him, gaining speed quickly. *Far* too fast for him to block them. They bounced forward, the leading one reaching him and ramming his leg. It felt like Andre had just punched him as hard as he could, which made no logical sense when considering the size of the shin-high goat.

"*Ow!*" Luke screamed at the onslaught of the worst beating of his life. Well, worst beating *so far*. After only a few hits, his legs gave out and he dropped to his knees on the loamy ground. The goats then were able to reach *much* more of him, smacking into his body repeatedly. His back, luckily, was protected by his pack, and he started swinging his fists at the goats as they jumped at him. This was not a great success, as he started getting hit on his arms as well. Luke rolled forward and stumbled to his feet as the abuse continued, managing to start running back the way he had come.

The goats pursued, raining blows on him from all sides as he sprinted up the gentle slope. His legs were heavily bruised, likely fractured, and nearly gave out as he *forced* them to work. Luke dodged a few bounding goats and took a wild swing at one as it passed him, managing to hit the goat just behind the head where the skull connected to the spine.

The goat had locked its neck and spine into position to brace itself for impact; specifically, an impact from the front, which it could easily absorb. When it was hit from the *top*, it flopped to the ground with a broken neck. Just like that, Luke realized how to fight back. Shockingly powerful blows were still rocking his legs, but Luke set about punching as accurately as he could, felling a dozen of the oddly fragile goats in only a few minutes. A loud shriek sounded from where the goats had originated, and the remaining attackers abandoned their prey and sprinted off.

Luke collapsed, breathing heavily. The pain was becoming *intolerable* as his adrenaline wore off, and he rolled up his pant legs to assess the worst of the damage. Huge bruises were forming, and he could tell from the discoloration that his bones were splintered in several areas. Pulling the pants back down, he slowly and painfully started to collect the bodies of his fallen foes. Retrieving his hunting knife from his pack, he quickly cleaned and skinned them as tears rolled down his face. It was an odd, yet satisfying revenge.

Deciding that he would risk a grass fire, he gathered as much of the long blue grass as he could easily crawl at. Shuddering every once in a while when he jostled his legs, Luke made an impromptu camp and fireplace. He pulled out his bedroll and sat on it, trying to keep his weight off his swelling legs. Luke had absolutely *zero* idea what to do to help himself, but since he wasn't bleeding… he didn't know if binding them would help? Perhaps to keep the swelling down?

Trying to focus on what he *could* do, he pulled out some flint, and struck sparks into the grass. If there was a wildfire, at least it would kill all the goats as well! With a *whoosh*, the fire caught on the first strike, blazing very high; *far* too fast.

"Wahhh!" he yelled as he fell backward in an extra-manly way. Looking closer at the burning grass, he realized that it was giving off almost no smoke. While the fire was *high*, the grass was disappearing slower than he expected. Putting his hands out, he could feel that the flames were *exceedingly* hot already. Overall, both fire and water seemed to act oddly on this world, but he wasn't complaining.

While he was pulling the meat off the goat, he found something strange. Long years of proper care for hides had taught him how to collect them efficiently, and that meant taking the head off. Since he would need some tools to oil the hides later, he also removed the horns to eventually make some. That was when he saw the lightly glowing pearl. It was no larger than the toenail of his smallest toe, and he almost missed it. The fact that it was shining was the only reason he found it. Luke pulled the item out from the goat's skull and held it up in the fading light. He gently set it down and checked the other carcasses. *All* of them had a glowing pearl, so he made sure to collect them. If he ever got out of here, he could sell them to a jewelry maker.

"Or Cindy would like it, I bet. I'll owe her birthday presents…" He wiped away the tears that formed at the thought. His legs were broken; he likely wouldn't survive a full week. Fighting the despair, Luke forced himself into motion. He placed the small cast iron pan his mother had packed onto the fire, cut off some fat from a small carcass, and used it to grease up the pan. When that started sizzling, he put on some of the meat, crudely frying it into something he *hoped* was edible. A few minutes later, he was staring at the cooked meat; praying that it wasn't poisonous.

He ate all the meat that had been on the goat, and not noticing any ill effects, fried another entire creature. It took *three* of the creatures to fully satiate his gnawing hunger. After he was done, Luke reached for his water skin and took a few long pulls. It took him a moment to notice, but the water was *burning* in his throat and stomach, like the strongest alcohol he had ever tasted. He gasped, gulping in air in an attempt to alleviate the unexplained throbbing.

Allowing the discomfort to pass, he sipped a bit more water and swished it around in his mouth, spitting it out after a long moment. A cloud of blue vapor appeared, a cloud which quickly dissipated. It took a moment to realize that no liquid had reached the ground.

"What *is* this?" he looked at the water skin, more than a little concerned that he had just drunk whatever that was. Still feeling his stomach burning, he tried to discern if it was hurting him. As he waited, the burn resolved into a warm glow that seemed to fill his body. A sense of well-being settled over him, easing his pain and tempting him with lethargy. Knowing that he had to try to increase his supplies if he wanted to survive, he ignored the lethargy as much as possible, and began experimenting with the water.

"What *are* you?" he asked the 'water' as he poured some onto the dirt. Nothing happened, and it acted just like he expected water should. It slowly seeped into the ground, leaving a small wet spot. Next, he poured a bit onto the ground and *spat* on it. It evaporated instantly wherever the spittle hit it, releasing a small puff of vapor into the air that quickly vanished.

"Huh." Pouring a bit more, Luke spat out a mouthful of saliva and the reaction was even more impressive. The vapor formed a translucent fog, which drifted away slowly; brushing against his arm. He winced as it stung him slightly. Looking at where it had touched him, he saw that a patch on his arm was now completely hairless.

"*Should* I be drinking this?" he nervously muttered. Then an idea hit him, and his eyes started to sparkle. Grabbing the pelt of one of the creatures, he worked up as much saliva as he could, made a hole in the dirt, and combined spit and water. The vapor streamed out of the hole and he held the pelt over it, making sure he coated the entire skin with the stuff. As the vapor started to dissipate, he watched the hair on the pelt begin to fall off, leaving it bare and soft. He poured the water on the bloody side, and the same reaction occurred without him needing to spit. Now both sides were clean and hairless.

"*Perfect!*" he celebrated. That would allow him to skip several steps in tanning, particularly the nasty ones that - without proper tools and chemicals - could only be done by soaking the pelt in urine and feces or letting it rot. He was now holding what should be rawhide when it dried. He pulled on it, testing how much effort it would take to stretch, and was impressed by how elastic the skin was.

"This is some high-quality hide…" Using some large rocks, he pulled the hide, stretching it as far as he could. After the first was set, he got up to get the other skins. "Wait."

Luke stopped, realizing that something was… different. He took a step, and felt very little pain. Pulling up his pant leg, the bruises remained, but the horrid discoloration that indicated broken bits seemed to be less inflamed. "Is this *healing* water? Or is my mind failing me already? Was the bone *not* broken?"

He couldn't say for certain that his leg had been broken, but it had certainly *felt* like it was. Luke returned to the pelts, repeating the process he had tried on the first, and soon had a pile of skins stretching under several rocks. "Another dozen of these, and I'll be able to replace the pants they ruined with even better ones. Poetic justice, really."

Digging a channel with his hands under the hairless skins, Luke formed a pit on one end. Collecting grass, much easier now that he could walk properly, he started a fire in the pit. Warm air moved through the ditch under the skins, and he hoped that they would properly dry. By the time he finished, the sun was just beginning to set.

Luke hunkered down and drank deeply from his water, grimacing at the burn and hoping the fire would keep away any goats that were looking for revenge.

CHAPTER TWELVE

Two weeks passed quickly, and Luke had given up on hope of rescue. With all the other Initiates to manage, and a new personal apprentice, it was unlikely that the Archmage was going to devote too much time to rescuing him. Luke had long decided that he needed to find his own way out. He took a deep breath and held up the patchwork goat hide pants that he had made. "Not even close to perfect, but good enough."

He pulled on the stiff pants and stood up, looking around at his growing campsite. The grass had been working really well in lieu of firewood, and a handful of it burned as hot and long as an entire log of oak. He cracked his neck and looked in the direction of the goats. Luke had been forced to attack them a few times, basically whenever he was running low on meat. After half a month of getting battered and broken, he was finally getting the hang of fighting them, as well as gaining an understanding of how they attacked.

The trick was to hold still until the goat jumped, then side-step and punch down. Also, whenever at least a dozen died, the rest would run away. He had still been overwhelmed a few times, but he was getting better. The water did seem to have healing properties, and when he was... *damaged*, Luke was always back on his feet in record time. "Time to make a spare shirt, and then get started on making hardened leather leg guards. I need to be able to take a few hits from these things."

Luke was doing his best to distract himself, and throwing himself into work was the most logical thing to do. Had he been whisked away from everything he knew, and abandoned in an instant? Sure! But he had his tools, and his dad *had* told him to practice. This counted, right? Plus, there had to have been a 'first' human that had gone to another world. There *had* to be a way to learn how to escape, but it was likely not going to be near the entrance. No... Luke had to travel to find a way home, and the only possible direction was *down*.

He started whistling as he walked toward the goats. He was going to gorge himself on goat meat tonight to celebrate his first fortnight in... "Never named this place, did I? Let's see... how about 'Murder World', since I don't know what it actually is, and apparently everything here wants to kill everything else?"

Chime.

Ignoring that sound, which was very faintly emitting from his forehead and had happened a few other times with no explanation, Luke focused on his upcoming hunt. He was getting close to the goats, so he quieted down and started creeping through the grass. Just as every time before, the goats were locked in combat with each other. Luke had watched them long enough to realize that it wasn't just a mating competition. Every time one of the goats was knocked out, the winner would slowly eat them. Yup. The goats were omnivores, at the *minimum*. Their teeth screamed 'carnivore' though, which might explain the grass remaining long.

Now, from his study, Luke had realized that the different markings on the goats seemed to indicate herd affiliation. They didn't attack their own herd, only those with different markings. For some reason, whenever he was seen, all of that went out the window and they attacked him together. Over the past couple of weeks, Luke had started testing something.

When he killed off the goats now, he tried to target one herd exclusively. *All* of them ran whenever twelve died, but the practice was starting to impact the population in a very minor way. Each day, the left herd - as he called them - gained a quarter-inch or so of territory. The right herd was getting beaten down more often, since they were outnumbered. With the sheer *number* of goats, it was hard to tell if you weren't looking for it, but still... Luke needed a hobby, so he made this his goal.

Crack.

Luke joined one of the fights, killing the goat and grabbing it in one fell swoop before legging it. As always, the goats screeched and started to follow him. A tide of tiny goats galloped through the long grass, mimicking a wind blowing through the area. He knew better; in the entire two weeks Luke had been here, there had been no wind, or rain, or any sign of weather patterns at all. Simply light... or dark. There also didn't seem to be a sun, so the light was strange and flat.

He finally reached the rock that he used as a fighting point and got into position. Luke tossed his first goat to the side and started punching small creatures gleefully. He tried to focus on the right herd, but one or two of the left herd was always in the way. They were *really* fragile, if hit correctly. Just a few minutes later, a squeal rang out and the remainder of the herds galloped off.

Luke sighed and stepped off his rock. "That'll feed me for a day or two. Good... on to the next part!"

After cleaning the goats, he added the horns and pearls to his growing collection. The pouch he was storing the pearls in was starting to get pretty full, so... Luke frowned as he realized that it *wasn't* as full as it should have been. He opened the pouch and looked inside, finding that a full *fifty* pearls were missing. With today's haul, he should have had an even eighty-four, but instead he now had... thirty-five? So, he wasn't missing fifty *exactly*... wait.

One of the pearls was... *different*. It wasn't much, but the pearl was slightly brighter, more... pearlescent. Luke winced as he had that thought. Puns were not his strong suit. "All right, little guy… where did you come from? I have thirty-four regular pearls, then *you*. I know you weren't here before…"

It took two more days, but Luke finally gained his answer after his next hunt. Since he had lost forty-nine pearls and one had seemed to become brighter, Luke assumed they had done something magical. Instead of taking his normal twelve goats and retreating, he attacked again. This had apparently *infuriated* the goats, and he had to kill off another twenty-four before the shrill cry came again and made them retreat.

Luke had honestly thought that they were going to keep going until either he or *all* of them had died, so he nearly kissed his fighting rock when he stepped off of it. "I *know*, Rocky! That was dumb, I get it. But at least I know that I'll need to kill a full thirty-six if I attack twice in one day. Twelve plus twelve times two? Does that mean if I go further, I'll need to kill eighty-four, or seventy-two? Does it double, or is it only an *addition* of twelve?"

Trying to understand without testing to see for sure was a fool's game, so he made his way to the campsite and poured all of his pearls into his pouch. Having nothing to do beyond watch it and clean goats, he got to see when the reaction began. The cluster of pearls started to shine, and what he assumed to be forty-nine of them melted and flowed into the fiftieth. That one became brighter and *fractionally* larger than it had been.

"So now we know for sure that these aren't *just* pearls." Luke muttered to himself as he inspected the new version with slightly still-bloody hands. "But what *are* they? Should I… what should I do with them?"

Not having an answer, and not too desperate to figure out the mystery, he simply decided to hoard them as originally planned. Now that he had a goal, it only took another week of his routine for him to consolidate his pearls into four of the better versions. That night was also the first where he had trouble during darkness since arriving.

He awoke to a soft bleating, and was careful not to move as

he opened his eyes. A small herd of goats had invaded his camp, and he realized that his fire had gone out. Luke cursed himself for his complacency, and jumped to his feet as he heard something tear. A goat had chewed through the side of his pack and currently had its head inside. Luke shouted and started goat punting, and the creature in his pack scrambled back.

One of Luke's pearls was in its mouth, and it panicked as Luke killed more of the goats. He started toward it, and it bleated a challenge at him. Then it stumbled and fell over. "I'm going to skin and *eat* you-"

Pow!

The goat exploded into meaty chunks, and Luke fell flat on his back as gore rained down on him. What was left of the goat was a smoking ruin, and when Luke went to check... there was no sign of the pearl. "There's *one* question answered... don't eat the pearls. Go full hoarder mode. Keep in storage device *far* away from mouth."

By his third month in the world, Luke was getting sick of goat meat; but no matter how he tried, he couldn't get through goat territory. He had attempted it a few times, but once he was *inevitably* seen, the goats didn't stop swarming until he was out of their area. Since all he could see for a *huge* distance was swaying grass... he had to turn back, time after time. He *was* getting better at killing them, and he knew that progressing was only a matter of persistence.

Luke had stopped hunting for meat alone out of sheer boredom, and was now starting to attack the goats either just to train his reactions, or to kill time and goats. Luke remembered how that had been taboo back home, as slaying creatures for no real purpose was a way to send creatures into extinction, and also removed a food source. Here, though, on Murder World, there was no other way forward. There was also a seemingly *endless* number of goats, and if he made them go extinct... "*Good.*"

Three months and twenty-five *hundred* goats. That was lowballing the actual amount he had slain, as he had gone on a rampage a few times deep in their territory, trying to break through. Luke's legs were armored with layers and *layers* of goat skin, which he had hardened and stitched together, to the point that he took off the top layers and used them for pillows at night. By now, he had killed at least that many goats for a very simple reason: after the last fifty pearls had melted together, the *upgraded* pearls had all melted together and created an even larger, shinier, *more* beautiful version. He rolled it in his fingers, "You're a *beauty*."

It was useful in a few ways. It now gave off enough light that he was able to use it instead of a torch of grass, and he had found that the goats really, *really* wanted to eat it and blow themselves up for some reason. Luke had been forced to relocate his camp all the way back to the sky-waterfall pool area. The goats were now seeking him out whenever he was near, and no amount of stealth allowed him to sneak up on them. They could apparently *feel* the third-tier pearl, as he had started calling it.

In fact, Luke could feel it, too. It was a presence similar to having his back to an open flame. It felt *hot*, and he could always point at it perfectly, no matter where it was. Not that he often let it out of his range: the goats might get it. "Then I'll have to kill enough of them to replace *my* pearl! The goats can't have *my* pearl!"

Luke's hand was shaking so much from rage at the thought... that the pearl slipped out of his hand. Normally, it wouldn't have been much of an issue, but he was at the edge of the pool. The pearl fell into the edge of the water and *vanished*. Both from sight and feel.

"No! *No!*" He screamed and dived after it, coming to his senses as his face hit the water. What was he doing? He could still see it; the light that it was giving off let him know that it still existed. Why had he thought it vanished? It took him a moment, but he realized that it was because the constant warmth and direction that it had *always emitted* had vanished. He pulled it out of the water, and the feeling returned. He dunked it back in, and the feeling vanished, except where his hand was clenched around it.

"Well, that solves the *stealth* issue," Luke muttered, already planning on making a new waterskin out of goat hide. "Ha! It will be my goat *hide*! I'll hide the pearls in it! Ha, ha!"

He broke down into laughter, and after a while, felt that his cheeks were wet. Luke touched his face, still laughing. That was odd... water didn't stay *wet*... wasn't it just supposed to vanish after a few moments?

CHAPTER THIRTEEN

- ANDRE -

Andre munched on an apple as he listened to Xan's lecture. The last month and a half since he had entered this world - unimaginatively named 'The Grove' - had been... informative. He had been doing nothing but twice-daily multi-hour exercises and reading the massive volumes of information that Xan provided him. Andre wasn't allowed further than the shadow of the tallest tree in the grove, and the forced limit was grating on him. Not that he would complain about that out loud. Though it had taken a while, he had learned better.

After spending his first night pinned tightly to a tree, Andre had been completely silent for *days*, one hundred percent terrified by the man that seemed ready to kill him for literally no reason. He had followed all instructions as well as he could, and on his third day in 'The Grove', he had managed to connect to the apple tree and feed it mana. That was good, as he was literally beginning to starve by that point. Xan had kept his word and hadn't fed him even a single time.

The apple tree seemed to like him, pleased by his gifts of

blood and mana. He hadn't yet managed to *bind* to the tree, but his teacher's lectures had shown him that was likely going to take a long time. Still, he could make good, nutrient-packed apples. But as a human, he needed a variety of food, and after a long month of constant exertion, he could feel his shrinking muscles *begging* for meat.

So, when Xan had told him that it was time to learn to hunt, Andre had nearly cried with happiness. Then Xan had clarified that he had meant it was time to learn how to make a *weapon* that he could hunt *with*. Not that there would be meat on the table. Andre's mind had nearly shut down at that point, but it drove him to use every single second of his free time practicing binding to a single chunk of dead wood. It would be his staff, and once he had bound to it, the staff could be whatever weapon he needed. Well… so long as he had enough mana control.

Say what you will about the brutality of Xan's methods: they were *effective*. It only took a week for the staff to suddenly come to life in Andre's hands. The dead wood gained strength and elasticity, and a few leaves even sprouted on it. The young Druid was shaking as he felt his connection to the wood; it was a piece of *him* now. The living chunk of wood could be his *arm*, such was the strength of the bond he had just made.

Xan appeared by Andre's side in an instant. "Ah… you succeeded. Without an ability, even. Congratulations. You now understand the depth of what we do, and I can start treating you like an actual person, instead of what you came in here as. Come up and have dinner."

Andre looked up from his staff, the mention of food breaking through his fugue. "You… what? Dinner?"

"C'mon, kid. Now that you've made a bond with a thing that was dead and brought it back, you've created what will likely be the most *difficult* bond you will ever make." Xan helped the lad to his feet and marched him along. "Record time, too. I *told* the Circles that they were too soft with Initiates. You've helped me prove my point; now this is going to be standard training. Took me this long just to make my first apple."

Andre's mouth fell open. Despite wanting to scream and rant, he nearly collapsed when Xan tried to make him climb the rope. Then the rope composed of vines wrapped around him and lifted him in, where somehow Xan was already waiting; though he had been behind Andre on the ground. "I'm sure you have questions. First, drink this, and eat this."

A bowl of honey and what appeared to be meat that had been pulverized were handed over. Andre wasted no time, pouring them together and licking the bowl clean. Spoons and manners were never even considered. Xan nodded approvingly. "Good. You are finally starting to get it. Efficiency is your best friend. Listen. This was a trial training method, and if you had gone much longer without success, I would have reverted to the standard practice."

Xan kept talking as more food was carried over by vines. "Also, that was a compound that will make your body and metabolism function at ten times the normal rate. Eat everything you can get your hands on; we have almost two months of starvation to fend off. We can fix it all right *now*."

That was all the encouragement that Andre needed, and he dove into the food. Xan lectured as he ate. "All right, listen. The breakthrough to your Druidic powers can only be done in an incredibly meditative state. The normal practice is to teach you to reach this state, running through forms and positions that would help you clear your mind. I theorized that sudden trauma, followed by starvation, while forcing intense physical activity, would let you reach that state ten times as fast."

"I was right." Xan was deadly serious, and Andre was too busy shoving food in his face to attack the man like he wanted to do. "You did in *two months* what normally takes three to five years to achieve. Now, you still need to learn all of the other things, but we can start with the *practical* applications of your power *years* before it is normally possible. Even though it seems terrible, it was all done to benefit you."

Xan stopped talking, because Andre had fallen asleep. "Ah… the medicine is as effective as advertised. Right on schedule. See you in the morning. Sleep well."

Hours later, at the exact moment when the sun touched Andre's new staff, his eyes popped open. He stretched and felt *good* for the first time since before he had arrived on this cursed world. "Master Xan?"

"Ah, you are awake!" Xan leaned over and looked at his charge. "Tell me… how much of your time here do you recall clearly?"

"All…" Andre's brow furrowed. Most of his time seemed like a damaged dream. Well… more a sleep-deprived nightmare. "Not… much, actually?"

"That's fine. I didn't expect that you would. Your mind needed to find a way to make you stay sane, after all. The Sigil even helps with that when you get proper food and rest. It balances you forcibly. It's a touchy subject, that. But, it keeps people from going off the deep end." Xan took a bite of an apple and tossed Andre his new staff. "Don't leave that lying around. It's an object of power now, and can be used to *badly* hurt you. Now, about the properties of the staff."

"This is your connection to plants." Xan explained seriously. "*All* plants. Though you don't *need* it when you are binding to plants, the fact that you turned a dead stick into a Livingwood Staff means that all plants will resonate with you through it. It will make your life a *lot* easier. We are going to start the practical applications of what we can do soon, but just know that the bond you have with that staff will be the same with *everything* you bind. It will *all* feel like your body."

"That's why you were so mad at me when we got started, then?" Andre nervously questioned.

"You wanted to 'blast people'." Xan scoffed and clapped his charge on the arm to put him at ease. "A Druid is the ultimate *defense*. We don't go on the offence except *in person*. We bind the land and everything in it to ourselves, which means our

Kingdom literally becomes our body. We'll talk on that more later. Now, I want you to say 'status'."

"Status?" Andre repeated in surprise. "Why-"

Contribution Activity Log is online! Scanning...
CAL Scan complete!
Level: 0
Current Etheric Xenograft Potentia: 130/100 to level 1!
Body: 2.45
Mind: 3.65
Presence: 2.25
Senses: 1.35
Health: 71
Mana: 127.8
Mana regen: 1.4 per second
You are able to increase in level! Do so now? Yes / No.

Xan asked for the numbers, and nodded along. This was roughly what he had been expecting. "Good... creating and connecting to a Livingwood Staff gives a full one hundred exp. The rest must be from the apples, you lucky dog. There's no more Potentia in those for you now, I bet, but it was nice while it lasted. You came here with a crazy high Capacity for a newbie, but that's expected as a Druid. Choose 'yes' to leveling, and put the point into 'Mind', sub-characteristic 'Talent'. I'll explain after you're done, but you *need* to do this. If you put the point anywhere else, I'm going to kick you out as a failed Initiate. That means death."

"*Sheesh*, Xan!" Andre selected 'yes'. "I thought we were past this."

Xan only bothered to reply with a flat glare and, "Just make sure to speak out loud."

Level up Initiated! Integrating Etheric Xenograft Potentia into host! You have one level to use, where would you like to add the bonus? Body / Mind / Presence / Senses.

"Mind."

'Good, that's the first one you need." Xan snarked at Andre, getting only a glare in return.

Mind selected! Select sub-characteristic. Talent / Capacity.

"Talent?" Andre's voice was questioning, thrown off by Xan's attitude.

Increasing sub-characteristic now!

Andre's world went black, and when he came around... everything was different. Xan's words floated into his ears, and he understood *exactly* what the man meant when he stated, "Congratulations. You now process thoughts nearly six *hundred* percent faster. That won't translate into 'thickheaded' like you might think; quite the opposite. You will likely be *much* more on board with my training, and I'll need to know if you would recommend this harsh training for others. Also, say 'sub-status'."

"All of *that*..." Andre sputtered as his status appeared in front of him.

Level: 1
Current Etheric Xenograft Potentia: 30/200 to level 2!
Body: 2.45

- *Fitness: 2.8*
- *Resistance: 2.1*

Mind: 6.15

- *Talent: 6.2*
- *Capacity: 6.1*

Presence: 2.25

- *Willpower: 2.7*
- *Charisma: 1.8*

Senses: 1.35

- *Physical reaction: 1.7*
- *Mental energy: 1*

Health: 71
Mana: 135.8
Mana regen: 2.06 per second

"It was…" Andre locked eyes with Xan. "It was worth *every* second of the abyss that you put me through."

CHAPTER FOURTEEN

"Oh… *god*. I can't believe I would ever do something that dumb." Andre was rehashing old conversations with Xan, who was laughing at the embarrassment that the Initiate was feeling.

"You were given the mind of someone almost a decade older than you, essentially overnight." Xan finally started helping the young man calm himself, his fun now had. "Of *course*, you are going to regret things that 'younger you' did. If you look back on what you used to do and cringe, it means that you have grown as a person. The important part is that you will be able to keep up with my lessons from now on; I'm sick of explaining things more than once."

"I… what's the next step, then?" Andre took the offered gift of a topic change.

"We are going to go ponder nature." Xan told him. With that confusing reply, they dropped out of the treetop and started walking. They quickly passed the marker that had denoted Andre's free roaming space, and continued for a little over an hour. Xan spoke nearly the entire time, mostly pointing out types of bugs, trees, and animals. "Now, we are going to walk through what will become your daily routine until you are... strongish."

They sat on the side of a hill, and Xan waved at the world in front of them. "Everything the light touches is... no, wait. That's a different speech. This is more than that. So much *more* than we can see is our domain. You have created a Livingwood Staff and can now start connecting to plants. Your task every morning will be to sprint here - yes, the entire way - and bind with all the plants on this hill."

Andre looked around, but had no idea what the man was talking about. "Three trees and a flower? Okay...?"

"Forgetting anything?" Xan smirked at the youngster. He waited contentedly until he saw realization dawn on the lad. "Ahh, there it is. Yup, *all* the grass."

"But that's-"

"Going to take a long time, I know. Remember how I told you that you needed to cultivate patience?" Xan watched his charge's face fall, and decided that an example was in order. "Andre, why do you think it is important to bind *all* the plants? *Especially* grass?"

"I don't know; the stuff is *everywhere?*" Andre spat in frustration.

"*Exactly* correct." With that, Xan started flowing across the grass faster than a horse could gallop... still in his reclined seated position. He made a circle and came back, "A simple Druidic ability, Forestwalk. Still, it is effective for movement and... other things. Come here."

Andre stood and started walking over to his teacher. He frowned, realizing that the man wasn't getting any closer. Andre started running, sprinting, then he *dove* at the man. In all that time, he hadn't managed to move from his starting point on the grass until he jumped. By the time he stood again, he had been returned to his first position. "All right... when do I learn to do that? I want that."

"You need to bind enough plants." Xan informed him with a shrug. "The more you bind with, the more likely that you'll get an actual ability. It seems random when you get them, because you cannot *seek* abilities. All abilities are gifts from the earth, and they differ slightly for each Druid. Variation will often get you interesting abilities, and by that, I mean binding to *numerous* varieties of plant. Honestly, I have no idea how long it will take, or even what abilities you will gain with your starting bonus. All I know is that you gain mainly plant-based abilities from plants."

"What's a starting bonus? Wait... where is your staff?" Andre had just realized that he had never seen his master carrying one. "I thought they were really important for-"

A staff shot out of the ground into Xan's waiting hand. "Right here. I'm a Druid of the Third Circle. I have bound with plants, animals, and the earth. That means I have a Living-wood Staff and a Livingstone Focus, as well as a familiar. Creating a Livingwood Staff means that you are a First Circle Druid, and you gain a promotion to a 'Novice'. Congratulations."

"But where was the staff...?" Andre couldn't stop himself from asking the question; he knew it was dumb.

"It was in the earth. It is *Living*wood, which means it needs nutrients and such. Start here, and work out in a circle. No cheating by going out to other types of plants, not until you've *earned* it." Xan placed the staff upright on the ground, and roots grew out of it and into the ground. "I'm gonna go take a n... that is, ponder nature over there. Don't bother me until you run out of mana at least five times."

"How do I-"

"You know how to do this now, Andre." Xan waved and walked off.

Andre looked at the grass around him and sighed. This was going to take a *long* time. He reluctantly started, poking the grass and coaxing mana into each blade. The grass *loved* the attention. It stretched toward him as if he was the sun, and accepted the bond he offered without the slightest hesitation or haughtiness. As he connected to the grass, he *learned* about it.

He suddenly knew what the soil was like, if the grass had proper access to light, if its roots were fighting for a tasty, nutrient-rich patch. Before he was even fully aware that there was an issue, Andre collapsed to the ground with a nose bleed.

Current mana: 0/135.8.

Your attempt to use mana has forcibly drawn mana from secondary source.

Current health: 69/71

"Watch your mana!" Xan called over as soon as the first drop of blood touched the ground. "It's a bad idea to use your body like that; it can lead to all sorts of nasty side effects. Don't use your health as a source. It only heals naturally! There is no health regeneration characteristic."

"Didn't know hurting myself was *possible*, Xan!" Andre called back, his irritation flowing across the distance. There was no reply, so Andre scoffed and turned back to his work. "I'm gonna ponder nature, all right, old man. The nature of *violence*."

His mana regenerated at two-point-oh-six mana per second, which meant that it was going to take about seventy seconds to get back to full. Not a terrible trade-off. He sat and meditated as he had been taught over the last month, peeking at his status every once in a while. When his mana was back, he looked at the amount of grass that he had been able to convert and sighed. His hand would cover the entire area with room to spare. This was going to take a *long* time.

Two weeks later, Xan seemed to think that Andre had suffered enough. Andre had increased the borders of his bound area to roughly fifteen square meters, which encompassed over ten thousand stalks of grass. He was getting close to the flower on the hilltop, and was almost *drooling* at the thought of gaining a connection to a new type of plant. Grass was great, but… it was grass.

"Andre, now that you've shown your dedication by doing each blade individually, I am going to show you how to bind to a swath of plants all at once." Xan's remark made Andre slowly look up, and he was clearly trying to hold back *unkind* sentiments.

"You mean to tell me that I don't have to destroy my back leaning over like this? That I could be *done* already?" Andre opened his mouth to continue, but Xan held up a hand to stop him.

"No, doing this was actually very important." Xan promised him calmly. "You needed to get an instinctual feel for the amount of grass you could bind using the entirety of your mana pool. You'll understand why in a few moments. Come close and follow my instructions."

"Do you remember when I called you a 'First Circle' Druid? That has more meaning than just a title." Xan sketched out a swift circle on the ground, the earth moving the grass away so that there was a perfect circle of bare earth. "This should be about the correct size... now, use your mana to form a circle around these plants."

Andre concentrated and attempted to follow instructions, but struggled mightily. The mana wouldn't stay in any shape, instead billowing away as a gaseous cloud whenever he attempted the process. Xan watched his lack of progress, confused, but his expression cleared as he realized the issue. "Ah... right... you don't have several years of practice manipulating your mana internally. That may be an issue, but I suppose I'll just need to *incentivize* you."

"Please no."

"It'll be *fun!*" Xan rubbed his hands together. "I'll teach you the forms, cycling, and mana control exercises over the next month. After that, every week that you are unable to complete this task, I'll reduce my protection on the area by a set amount. Each week, the beasts and creatures will get just *that* much closer. I'll *probably* be able to keep them off you, even if we get really close... but hey, I need to test my limits as well, right?"

"Learning is *just* the best," Andre stated flatly, specks of blood leaving his lips as he added too much mana to another failed circle.

CHAPTER FIFTEEN

- TAYLOR -

"You're pretty messed up, Master Don." Taylor was scrutinizing the landscape, the stacks of books that went on forever, and the flames that were reflected in Master Don's eyes. His peaceful smile as he had sent the undulating ball of plasma into the sheaf of happy spellforms would appear in her dreams tonight for certain.

"Ahh... apprentice." Master Don took a deep breath, relishing in the scent of burning paper and boiling ink. "Ask yourself, how did a man with the *lowest* starting mana pool in history become arguably the most *powerful* Archmage on our planet?"

"Before I got to know you, I'd say that it was likely a combination of working harder than everyone else combined, plus a lot of luck." Taylor took in the crisping landscape as oily smoke rose into the air. "Now... I'm going to have to guess... specializing in area-of-effect spells?"

"All of that, and just a *smidge* more." He started striding toward the exterminated spellforms, motioning for her to hurry up. "One, I had an *excellent* teacher that truly cared about what happened to me, and he helped me learn the very important lesson that I have been guiding you toward for the last half year. What is that lesson, Taylor?"

"There are no compromises on the path to power, unless the compromise is worth more than you give up," she recited clearly, knowing from experience that if she mumbled he would make her repeat herself. "Everything here is a step on that path, and if it doesn't join you, make sure to take its Potentia."

"No, that's the lesson that I have been *teaching* you." Master Don tapped his chin as a spike erupted from his book and skewered a charging *Knockback*. The bull-shaped spellform unraveled, falling apart into ink, paper, and a cloud of light that drifted over and sank into Master Don or the Grimoire that he never let Taylor see.. "The lesson that I have been trying to guide you toward is that there is no such thing as *honor*. Dignity is a fool's word, and I needed to grab power, no matter what the cost."

"Frankly, you're better than I was." He nodded at her respectfully. "That's why I changed the lesson that you were *going* to be taught. I think that you have what it takes to be the next Archmage. The Kingdom needs someone that can take my place, and be *respected*… not just feared, like I am."

"There you go again!" Taylor threw her hands into the air. "There's no *chance* that I become the next Archmage! Plus, people respect you. They have no choice!"

"Wrong. I have the power and authority to make them *regret* acting out." Don sternly stopped her. "I know that they despise my methods, and most think that I am nothing more than the Kingdom's trump card. They are correct, but for the wrong reasons. I was simply taught that my success was the most important thing, and the lesson stuck. You, though-"

Taylor interrupted, quoting the words she had heard dozens of times: "'I can train you properly, and you'll be a shining light in the darkness of the Hollow Kingdom'. I know it, Don, but I just can't believe it."

"Which is why we are going to my *personal* hunting grounds.

We are going to fill your spellbook with the most powerful spells we can find, and then make you practice using them until you can ruthlessly destroy anything they put in your path," he explained patiently. "Ooh. I like that word. *Ruthless*. Perhaps I'll make it the title of my autobiography one day."

"So much for not being feared, and who is this ephemeral 'they'?" Taylor tiredly inquired. While they were speaking, she stole a glance at her status, pleased with her progress, though she didn't want to tell Don that. He was being irritable today. She had gained a level every other month, and that was even while she was devoting Potentia to her spells to upgrade them.

CAL Scan
Level: 3
Current Etheric Xenograft Potentia: 445/500 to level 4!
Body: 1.4

- *Fitness: 1.7*
- *Resistance: 1.1*

Mind: 8.9

- *Talent: 10.5*
- *Capacity: 7.3*

Presence: 1.9

- *Willpower: 1.7*
- *Charisma: 2.1*

Senses: 5.1

- *Physical reaction: 8.1*
- *Mental energy: 2.1*

Health: 61

Mana: 165
Mana regen: 3.5 per second

Spells
T1: 2
See full listing?

Although she didn't yet know what exactly they did, any increase was a good one. Taylor was pleased that she had managed to increase *everything* a little without using her leveling points. Since she was in a 'party' with her master, she got a fraction of the Potentia that he earned, and just the small amount had been enough to push her most of the way to level four. The direct increases had gone into Mind sub-characteristics twice, and she had been forced by her Master to increase her Senses to stay alive without any defensive spells.

Taylor froze and dismissed her status when she realized that Don had gone silent. She glanced over at him guiltily and was confronted by an arched brow before he continued speaking. "All *done* preening over your stats? That is considered *rude*, you know."

She flushed at the reminder. "I know, sorry."

"Hmm. *Courtly mannerisms.*" Master Don shook his head in disgust. "Lord of Flame's fiery beard, I need to teach you *etiquette* as well, don't I? Good thing we have a few more years... which is also the answer to your question. The 'they' I had been referencing includes Nobles, Merchants, the Royal family, and the various guilds that represent the commoners. When I say that 'they' dislike how utterly *needed* I am, just feel free to believe me."

"Ignore that for now; it is *finally* time to get you a defense spell. With your Talent already above ten, there are so *many* spells you *could* learn. If you manage to do so..." he shook his hands at the sky and shouted, "I can finally go take a *nap*! Hah! In all seriousness, I will be letting you go off and discover things on your own - most of the time - after you are more well-protected."

Taylor perked up at that, looking forward to the upcoming trip just a *little* bit more. They walked through the herd of decimated spellforms and paused near the stacks of books. Master Don gave her a level stare. "I need an oath from you. You will never show anyone how to do this, except the person you plan to have replace you as Archmage. Your *personal apprentice*, not just another Namer that you train. Understood?"

She nodded, but was required to give a verbal answer. She rolled her eyes, but did it. "Yes, I swear."

Don stepped toward her as her sigil lit up and a thin line raced across it, signifying that she had been bound to her word. He pulled her close, then reached out and grasped a book. Instead of flapping and attempting to escape like any *normal* book would... this one let out a *click*. All Taylor could manage to get out was, "*What?*"

Then they fell through the ground.

Before she could even scream, they landed, and Taylor was able to see the illusion they had just passed through. Master Don started walking forward right away, grimmer and more serious than she had ever seen him. "Taylor, do you know why I call you a 'Namer', and not a 'Mage'?"

"I honestly have no idea." She took a deep breath, gathering her courage. "Can we talk about how I thought we were falling to our deaths just now?"

"It's because you have something just a little bit *extra*." Master Don considered his words carefully, swallowing deeply before continuing. "Now, I took you here because I have determined that you are to be my successor, and that means I plan to give you *everything* I know. I'm not just *training* you like I would another. A Mage and a Namer are the same in all things... except *one*."

Taylor had to try *really* hard not to smack the information out of him, remaining cool and aloof while he pondered how to teach her. He mumbled after a few moments, "Now I know why my Master had such a hard time doing this... can never practice *explaining* it to anyone."

"A Namer is a Mage that can control a spell through *another* means. Specifically, there is a chance that they can 'read' a spellform while it is gorging on their mana. Similar to what happened with your Grimoire and you, actually." Master Don paused and pressed an elbow against the wall, which swung open to reveal daylight. A small smile appeared on his face as he took in the familiar surroundings. "You will be attempting to tame the spell in the usual ways, and all of a sudden, you will be able to see everything about it in a manner similar to reading your status. When you speak that name..."

"You gain *total* control of that spellform." He locked eyes with her, all traces of happiness missing; only a mad hunger for power filtering through. "You still need to empower it as usual, but it becomes what is called an 'inherent' spell. It is a spell that you will never need to re-tame after casting. It will always meekly return to your spell book as soon as it can. Even if you lose a Grimoire or need to upgrade, it comes back when it can. If at all possible... train this ability and use it on *every* spell you ever tame. It must be yours, if you never want to fear losing it like your other spells, which are only bound to you via bribery and emotions."

"That seems a little dark...?"

"*Everything* here is a step on the path to power, and if it doesn't join you, take its Potentia." Master Don shook his head and grumbled, "If you can't make this moral leap, how would you ever cleanse an infected civilian town? You would never sleep again! Get used to making the tough choice *now*, Taylor. It only gets harder when you are the Archmage."

"I-"

"Hush. You will be the Archmage, because I am *ordering* you to become qualified for the position." Don waved her forward, and pointed at gorgeous fluttering insectoid spells. "These are one of the best possible passive defensive spells, and they are *very* rare."

"Butterflies?"

"*Evil* butterflies." Don's eyes shifted back and forth as she stared him down. "Fine, not really evil, I'm just trying to get you in the right headspace for this. They are *Nulli-flies*, and with them, you can create the spell 'Nullify'. This spell activates when a hostile spell is cast on you, and it nullifies all incoming magic for five seconds while... basically screaming. An alert and protection all in one. Also... single use."

Taylor winced. 'Single use' spells were spells that you needed to fully re-enter The Library and find again in order to retame. They tended to be powerful, but were *rarely* used, as they would be gone after doing so. Don waved at her. "Go, tame one by Naming it. If it doesn't work, move on to the next one. Don't worry about getting all of them; a Nulli-fly will never stay in a Grimoire with another of its kind."

"I obviously want them, but I need to ask... why the secrecy? I'm *sure* other people know about 'Namers', right?" Taylor remembered something just then. "You even talked about Namers in front of people back when we were tested!"

"Yes, other people know about Namers, but not often what that really *means*. Nor to what spells we gain access. Look," Her teacher waved around at the area that was enclosed by shelves on all sides, "when I said don't tell anyone about this, I meant this *area*. This place is secret, and there is an abundance of Nulli-flies here for only one reason. This is the *spawn* point for this spell. This is the only place in the world where they come into being. They spread out from here, but they are so small and rare that it is nearly impossible to find *exactly* where they spawn."

"You're a *spawn camper*?" Taylor blinked in surprise. "You called spawn campers the scum of all the worlds...?"

"*Other* people doing the camping should be put down. *Us* doing it is simply being prudent." Don announced proudly, like the hypocrite he was. Taylor rolled her eyes, but she wasn't about to complain. She was about to reap the benefits, after all. "Oh, as for why this is so important; there are a finite amount of spellforms in the world. I am pretty sure that there are only ten total Nulli-flies at any given point in time. Ever."

"Really? There are three right here!" Taylor looked at the pretty spells.

"Three of *ten* that exist *at any time* in the Multiverse." Don informed her sharply. "Ultra-Rare spells are that way for a *reason*. Either someone snapped up so many that the spell *became* rare, or there just aren't many in the first place. This means that the rarer something is, the more it is worth. Yes, you can sell or trade spells, so long as they weren't *Named*. That is what scrolls are for."

Taylor nodded and moved. Her mana reached out to only one of the creatures, and soon, it fluttered over to land on her finger. It was the size of a small eagle up close, and was draining *far* more mana than any spell she had attempted to capture previously. She stared at it, waiting for the moment when information would be revealed to her… and waited. Her mana was reaching the limits… it was gone. Her nose started to bleed, and Master Don called out, a flame appearing on his palm.

She ignored it all. It was right there… she could *feel* it. There! "*Destrueret totum industria. Comedent illud usque ut nihil supersit!*"

"Celestial cowbells chiming in the wind, you actually did it." Master Don gasped as the Nulli-fly unraveled into a swirl of ink and a single page, all of which melted into her Grimoire. "Now, what have I told you about your *health*?"

"Wait… you're *surprised* that I succeeded?" Taylor wiped the blood from under her nose, and it vanished as her Cleanse passive spell ate it away.

"I mean… we hadn't ever tried doing this before, had we?" Master Don showed her a half smile. "It was the last test before you could be my apprentice for *real*, and you got it on the first try!"

"Test? Wait… that…" Taylor opened her Grimoire, flipped to the spell, and almost collapsed again.

Spell Named: Nullify. (T4): 0/100 to level 1!

Effect 1: Release a klaxon call when a hostile mana source would hit you. Spells, abilities, and all other effects included.

Bonus, at range: Effect 1 activates when hostile mana source is about to impact the user.

Effect 2: Block the first incoming hostile mana source aimed at you.

Bonus, Multitarget: block all incoming magic for 5+.5n seconds, where n = spell level. This bonus maximizes at tier threshold (when tier five is reached.).

~~Single use~~ (Overridden, Named.)

Spell prerequisites: ~~Body: 25. Mind: 25. Presence: 30.~~ (Overridden, Named.)

"Are you *kidding* me, Don?" Taylor rounded on her Master. "I have *none* of the prerequisites! That would have *killed* me if I didn't Name it!"

"I would have stopped the process on the first two; they *are* very fragile as a spellform." Master Don told her calmly.

"But there are *three* of... oh. You would have let the last one kill me." The last of her words were stated weakly. "Ah... that's the real reason I didn't get to have offensive or defensive spells, huh? In case I decided to fight back at this stage? How many people have you taken as 'apprentices' and told them that they were 'definitely' Namers?"

"Too many, Taylor." Master Don intoned heavily. "Too. Many. Hundreds of years as Archmage... I knew that I'd have to be correct *eventually*."

"So that was why all those people gasped when you took me as a 'Personal Apprentice'." Taylor spat the words as if they disgusted her. "Not because they were shocked that you would do so... it was because no one ever survived before. Are you evil?"

He ignored the accusation, glancing at the other two Nulli-flies that were fluttering in the spawn point. Lightning flashed, and they withered and faded; crumbling to the ground as waste paper. "There's a reason there were three of those here, in their spawn point. They have a respawn rate of ten our-world years. That means I've either attempted to train a new apprentice each time; or I couldn't bear to do so, and simply made the journey to destroy them every ten years."

"This will become your responsibility when you succeed me." Master Don started toward the exit. "There are now seven Nulli-flies that have been captured or escaped this spawn point long ago. If you ever see someone else with a Nulli-fly, destroy them or make sure that they lose the spell. Otherwise, the person *you* train… will only get *two* tries to become a Namer."

CHAPTER SIXTEEN

"Fireball, heed my call, burn the world, burn it all!" Taylor sent a fireball spinning toward the fleeing *Fear*, the spider-shaped spell-form screeching as it dropped to the ground and tried to put out the flames. Taylor grumbled as she stalked toward it. "Oh, *sure*, imagine that. You're a spider almost tall enough to reach my shin, and you're afraid of *fire*."

Mana: 143/165

The *Fear* crumbled, leaving behind a puddle of ink and a few pages of high-quality vellum. She grabbed the vellum before her book could and promised it as a treat later. "That should be just enough…"

A month had passed since her close brush with death at the hands of the Nulli-fly, and she had been unleashed upon the unsuspecting denizens of this world to release some steam. "Current Potentia."

Current Etheric Xenograft Potentia: 310/500 to level 4!

"Excellent; that was worth even more than I thought it would be." With a gesture, her Grimoire released her Nullify spell, and it swirled up and out until it was a large butterfly shape once more. "Increase Nulli-fly to level three."

Etheric Xenograft Potentia: 10/500 to level 4!

Spell: Nullify has reached level three! 0/500 Potentia needed for the spell to reach level four!

Level increase effect: Nullify now lasts for 6.5 seconds after activation! Cooldown period: 24 hours. Effective cooldown: 23.1 hours.

"Ugh… just… why couldn't he explain why the cooldown is reduced? 'The sub-characteristics each control one and a *half* aspects of your growth, figure out what they are'!" Taylor mocked Master Don and dismissed the spell information, and it sank back into her book. "I can see what they are in my paper, but they don't *mean* anything to me! Know what? Forget him for now. It's time to get stronger. Fireball is at level two, and Shatter is at level three, so it is time to focus on *me!*"

Rhyming and wordplay helped with the fact that there was no one else around for miles in any direction. That was fine; at this point, her Master had driven into her that *all* other people had serious and dangerous ulterior motives. She wasn't to trust *anyone*, including him. He had proven time and again that she needed to hide things from him. If she found something impressive and showed it off, he would kill it or use it to make *himself* stronger.

Fireball (T2): 13/300 to level 3! Mana cost: 12

Effect 1: Create a ball of fire that detonates for 10 fire damage within a ten-foot sphere; centered on impact. To cast, the full chant of 'Fireball, heed my call, burn the world, burn it all' must be used.

Bonus 1, at range: the ball of fire can now be used at range, up to thirty feet. Damage becomes $10+5n$ fire damage, where n = spell level. (Starts at T2, no level cap.)

Shatter (T2): 0/500 to level 4! Mana cost: 10

Effect 1: Create a spike of ice that chills the target, dealing 5 ice damage and 5 force damage. To cast, the full chant of 'Destruction, neither frost nor force, the best of both. Shatter' must be used.

Bonus 1, at range: the spike can now be used at range, up to twenty feet. Damage becomes $10+(2.5i+2.5f)n$ damage, where i = ice damage, f = force damage, and n = spell level. (Starts at T2)

A quick glance at her Grimoire helped her remember her

limits. Fireball was a special type of tier two area-of-effect spell, which did five points of fire damage per level within ten feet of the impact point, when it was cast properly. Since it was level two, that meant ten damage total; apparently, multiplying by skill level zero still meant that there was 'zero' bonus damage. Shatter was a single-target spell that dealt two-and-a-half points of both frost and force damage per level. At level three, that meant the spell did twenty-five points of total damage.

She turned back to look at the hole in the ground that Fear had crawled out of; there were almost *certainly* more in there. It was time to hunt. She ran along, carefully measuring her pace so that she was always going at roughly eighty percent of her maximum speed. If Taylor wanted to increase her stats naturally, she needed to take every opportunity to do so. If she had to go somewhere, she ran. If Taylor needed to *kill* something, she killed it with *maximum* efficiency. No mana was wasted if at *all* possible.

"Destruction, neither frost nor force, the best of both. Shatter!" A small elemental left her Grimoire with the speed of a flying arrow, impacting the oversized Fear spellform that she was aiming at. The spider froze in place, literally, and then the elemental *pulled*. Single target, yet even more *beautiful* than a giant fireball. The Fear shattered - just as her attack spell implied it would - and fell to the ground. A near-invisible light of Potentia drifted into her, swirling around before being filtered into her Sigil.

Mana: 133/165

Taylor ran and flipped into the dark cavern, launching a fireball ahead of her. The Will O' The Wisp that flew from her Grimoire detonated and flash-fried everything within ten feet of itself. A tortured screeching impacted Taylor almost like a physical blow, as dozens of Fear-spiders started pouring out of the cave mouth. She wanted to freeze, but knew that showing her fear would empower the spellforms. Instead, she landed on one, squishing it into an oozing ink-sac.

"Two... one... Fireball, heed my call, burn the world, burn

it all!" The Will O' The Wisp appeared from Taylor's fluttering book once more, happily launching itself into the spells that were still pouring out. The fireball roasted the Fear spells with *exactly* as much damage as they could take. "Lord Frankfurt's crusty *nostrils*, there are so many of them! Did I find a spawn point for Fear?"

Mana: 122/165

Her two offensive spells were being cast as soon as they returned to her Grimoire, after what Master Don called the 'cooldown' period. Even so, she was having to get into closer range than she wanted. As the spiders started leaping at her, Taylor had a crazy idea. "I've been leveling the spell… now is as good as any time to test it!"

Having decided, Taylor sprinted *into* the cave mouth as fast as she could go. "*Whoa*! Fireball, heed my call, burn the world, burn it *all*!"

As she leveled the spell, Taylor assumed that she would be able to say less of the chant and have the same effect, or say the full chant and *really* power it up. Master Don refused to confirm or deny her hypothesis, telling her to figure it out. As it was, the fireball hit everything within ten feet and burned *hot*. The fire at the center of the blast had turned blue, and Taylor let a cocky grin emerge when she saw that her path forward had been cleared.

As the last of the fire burned down, her smile vanished. A new spellform had stepped into the open area, though she only caught a glimpse of its bulbous, grotesque shape as the fire puttered out.

Scree!

"What was *that*?" Taylor abandoned her previous plan and turned to run. That creature *kind* of looked like a Fear, but it was as tall as she was and had a monstrous body. It seemed like a combination of a spider and a wood tick, and she was *not* going after it alone.

Too bad for her that the thing didn't share the same sentiment.

A weight took her to the ground, but the spellform didn't actually *touch* her. Just before the thing would have landed on her, a klaxon call sounded and Taylor was surrounded by a swarm of tiny Nulli-flies. It seemed her plan had worked after all. "Six and a half seconds to destroy this thing!" She popped to her feet and turned on the beast. It was heavily damaged, as any part that had touched her had been *nullified*. Fear spells started throwing themselves at her, falling to pieces as they got into range.

"Get over here; time to gain some *Potentia*! Destruction, neither frost nor force, the best of both. Shatter!" Taylor wasn't certain why some of these spell chants seemed nonsensical, but she suspected that her Grimoire translated them into her language so that she could use them correctly.

Mana: 101/165

Her elemental raced from just above her head, slamming into the large beast and seeming to do very little damage. Yikes... shatter was tier two, level three; it should have *wrecked* anything in this area. There was only one thing that she could think of to try. She *dived* into the creature and allowed her nullify spell to eat away at it. It was sliced in half just as her protection wore off. Breathing heavily, she waited for the rush of Potentia, but felt nothing.

"It's not *dead*!" She scrambled away, looking at the creature fearfully. Its head was separate from the body, but the jaw was still opening and closing. "Wait... it isn't *dead*!"

Taylor released a small stream of directed mana, allowing it to waft into the face of the creature. She was down to nearly half mana, but that was fine with her; it was regenerating quickly. The spellform shifted in her sight and the new information started to make sense to her. "You're... Mass Hysteria? I name you as-"

Splat!

The connection cut off, and Taylor screamed as she saw her Grimoire lifting from the crushed head of the now *fully* dead spellform. "Grimmy, why would you *do* that?"

<Mass Hysteria, spell usage. Upon cast, create a node of hysteria that casts fear spells into other creatures within range.>

Taylor read the words on the page of the book, not losing her glare. "*So?* That seems *really* useful!"

<Mind Disease,> the Grimoire explained by writing out a string of text, *<Disease is disease. I refuse disease. You want I leave?>*

"No... stay." She was still fuming, but Taylor reluctantly allowed that the book had a point. "*Fine.* But what if I get a self-casting spell that does something like cast lightning? I *want* that sort of power!"

<Fear. Affliction/debuff.> The text scrawled across an otherwise blank page. *<Disease. Affliction/debuff. Bad. Not tasty. Chain lightning. Destruction/direct damage. Good. Nummy.>*

"Well, I'm glad to know where you draw the line." Taylor snarled as she plopped down into a small puddle of ink. Her Cleanse spell was really getting a workout *today.*

<Line is drawn between words Affliction and debuff. Is known in general language as a forward-slash.> the Grimoire informed her helpfully.

"*Thanks*, Grimmy." Taylor wanted to drop her head into her hands, but there were likely Fears in the area still. Getting eaten and broken down into base mana because she was mad about the inability of a book to understand sarcasm would have been beyond embarrassing.

Her Grimoire, liking the affectionate name 'Grimmy', flapped to her head and rested on it like a hat. "Hey, that's bad for your spine! You should close fully."

It ignored her, and Taylor didn't bother to force the issue. She had other things to look at anyway. "Current exp."

Etheric Xenograft Potentia: 670/500 to level 4!
You are able to increase in level! Do so now? Yes / No.

"What in the...! How did I gain so much Potentia?" Taylor meant it rhetorically, but was given an answer anyway.

Accessing combat logs...
23 Fear (T1) defeated: 460 exp.
1 Mass Hysteria (T4) defeated: 100 exp.

Spawn point cleared and captured! This was an unknown spawn point. Bonus Potentia gained from absorbing all ambient Potentia accumulated within unknown place of power: 100 exp.

Add spawn point to Kingdom map records? Bonus exp will be granted. Yes / No.

"No, add only to *personal* map records." She ignored the last question. Why would she give up the information to an *awesome* training spot? That'd just be stupid. Instead, Taylor started thinking about what she should do with the unexpected windfall. Clearly, she was going to level up, but where to put the points? "Mind is the best bet, of course... but... Naming...? I *almost* had that spell; I could *feel* it. I couldn't get all the fine details, though. I need better *Senses*."

Taylor knew that her instructor had a plan for her development, but she really, *really* wanted to test her theory. She was certain that her ability as a Namer would allow her to bypass the requirements that higher spells demanded. So what if she didn't have enough Presence to make a Volcano spell whimper? If she could get its true name, it would be hers either way.

Plus... it would be nice to have at least a small way to rebel against Master Don. Decision made, she agreed to level. The point went into the Mental Energy sub-category, bringing her Senses total up to six-point-six, and for a long moment, the world was dark. Her eyes popped open and locked on a hairy leg that was *slowly* extending around the corner, it was a Fear inching toward her through the darkness. She smiled widely; the low light wasn't *nearly* as much of an issue as it had been only a few minutes ago.

She had made the right decision. Maybe not for Master Don, but for *her*. "Fireball, *heed* my call...!"

CHAPTER SEVENTEEN

- LUKE -

Luke scraped at his combat perch stone and grunted happily. The last two and a half years had been intense, and was basically a blur of killing goats and increasing his battle prowess. A diet of only protein hadn't been *great* for his system, but he wasn't malnourished in the slightest. In fact, between the constant combat and the huge number of protective hides he wore to prevent getting beaten to death by goats, he had gained an impressive amount of muscle mass.

He was scraping at what he had thought was stone for a simple reason. Earlier today, it had cracked and flaked when it was hit by a leaping goat. When the top layer of grime had dropped off, Luke had been able to tell that it wasn't rock at all. It was *bone*.

Goat-bone tools had been the norm for well over a year after his dagger became too dull to handle the tasks he needed it for. So when he found so *much* bone as a single piece, he got both excited and a little nervous. First, he already had a use in mind. Second, what had been so large in this world that its bone could be mistaken for a rock for over... what, two years?

Luke had started digging, and found that the mindless task was a nice change of pace. When the bone was fully unearthed, he was still confused. It didn't look like any bones that he was familiar with, such as a femur or fibula. No, this was a crooked teardrop that was flat on one part of the wide side. About halfway down its length, there was a spar of bone that jutted out perpendicular to the rest of it.

"Hello, new weapon." Luke spoke flatly, not having the mental energy to get excited about something like this. "Well... now I get to learn how to use a two-handed club. That should give me something to do for the next few years. A new hobby might be nice, *heehee*... though digging was interesting as well! Diggy, dig, dig!"

Luke took the bone back to his base by the water and started using some goat bone and rocks to smooth and carve into the large teardrop. It was *dense*, so the task took some serious doing. That made him happy, as it meant that it would survive heavy usage and give him a short-term hobby. Days later, when he had a place to wrap leather for a grip on both the tapering end as well as the spar, Luke decided to wash off all the excess dirt in the pool. He stood, dragging the oversized weapon behind him. When he was ankle-deep in the water, he dipped the club in and started washing.

When he was done, the bone *gleamed* like the pearls he had been saving up. It was a beautiful blue-white, and it almost looked like the water had left a film on the bone. No. Wait. Yes. The bone... a few of the scratches, nicks, and blemishes had vanished from the surface. That meant... this bone absorbed water to repair itself! "So cool! The water impacts even *dead* things!"

Intent on testing this phenomenon, Luke fit the leather grip onto the bone and held the entire thing underwater. As he suspected, after about ten minutes, the bone was entirely fixed up. Bone had grown around the edges of the leather, holding it in place better than sinew ever would. Luke hefted his new weapon and gave it a few test swings. "Good enough."

Still, he had to frown at the item. It *really* was familiar, but he had no idea *why*. "Let's go looking at bones, then. Ha! *There's* a phrase I would have never been able to say around... hmm... what's his... it was... *Andre*! Wonder how that guy's doing?"

Luke walked to where the day's meat was waiting to be processed and carefully dismantled the first goat. While he was butchering it, he found nothing that looked even *remotely* like the bone that was now sitting next to him. Luke pulled out the pearl and added it to his bag with a **plop**. He had given up one of his waterskins specifically so that he could fill it with water and hide the pearls. It was effective, and at full capacity, the skin could hold a few hundred of the tiny pearls. Not that it ever *needed* to do so.

He had gotten to a point where there were *almost* a few hundred pearls in his waterskin, but one day, the water had started churning when he dropped a few in. He had waited a few minutes, then dumped out the water and found that he had a bunch of the third-rank pearls and only two of the first rank ones. At least he would know when they upgraded; the process was somewhat violent as they got stronger. Luke sighed and shook his head.

A third-tier pearl made him *sad*, because that meant that he had killed yet another twenty-five hundred goats and added their pearls to his collection. Currently he had forty-eight of the tier threes, and twenty-six tier ones. Relatively soon he would be able to witness a tier-*four* pearl, and he wasn't sure if he should be sad at all the killing he had done, or excited to have a goal. To make a *single* tier four pearl... fifty of the first, second, third... that would be exactly one hundred and fifty *thousand* goats that he had managed to pull a pearl out of.

If the goats hadn't been carnivorous, he would have been drowning in blue goat meat. Also, instead of the population dropping like he had expected, there had been a population *boom*. At least, for the left herd. Since their competition had been killed off to the tune of over a *hundred thousand* deaths, and most of the meat was left for them to eat...

"*There* it is! Oh... *Celestial Feces.*" Luke had finally found the bone that matched the large club. He held it in his hand, which was shaking slightly, mainly due to his sudden realization. The bone in his palm was almost the exact same shape as his new oversized club. He had pulled it out of the goat's skull, specifically the ear. "You are a malleus... also known as the 'hammer' portion of an ear bone. Also known as the *smallest* bone in the body."

Luke looked at his weapon again and gulped. It was at least four feet long and about two feet wide at the thickest point. "Good thing whatever this came from is already dead..."

Over the next three months, Luke worked to familiarize himself with his 'hammer'. It was as though he was learning to fight all over again, and only the fact that he had been conditioning his body every day for over two years allowed him to survive until he had gained some proficiency with the club. Every time the bone started to get cracks or flaws, he would put it in the pool until it regained its luster and smoothness.

As time went on, he found that the outside of the weapon was getting damaged less frequently and was becoming more and more *blue*. Luke was using his hammer weapon regularly, and had even named it! 'Crustulum Capra', nicknamed 'Crust'. That translated as 'Goat Paste', which was what the goats turned into when he got a good hit in on them.

It could *also* translate as 'Goat Cookie', which still made him laugh a month after he had realized that fact. He had immediately thrown all other names out and started calling his weapon 'Cookie'.

Then, disaster struck. During one particular excursion, Luke was swarmed and Cookie got caught between the ground and several charging goats. Their odd magically-enhanced horns made them hit harder than they had any right to be able to do, and the portion that he used as his normal handhold snapped off. Not the spar, but the actual *end* of the teardrop.

Luke managed to finish off the remainder of the goats by falling back on punching them to death, but he was *furious* at himself for his carelessness.

He collected all the new pearls and the broken chunks of his weapon, then made his way back to camp. He carefully inspected the break and quickly found the issue. "Ah... I see... the outside has been getting harder to damage, but the interior is still soft bone. How can I..."

Luke scraped at the bone and discovered that the inner area formed by marrow, was far softer than the exterior had ever been. "Now *this* gives me an idea..."

Cookie was out of commission for the next few months, which *infuriated* Luke. Luckily, he had a ready and never-diminishing population of small animals to take his frustrations out on. During the day, he destroyed goats from the right herd. In the evenings and nights, he slowly hollowed out the enormous bone. When he needed to do something less tedious, he shaped the bone that had broken off.

Eventually, Luke had most of the teardrop hollowed out. He had even used bone shards from the goat horns he collected to drill through the spar and made a twisty 'U' bend in the marrow on the interior. He lifted the broken teardrop tail and started to turn it. The shaped screw fit into the main body and held! "Yes! Now to fill you up with water..."

He hurried to test it, first washing out the bone scrapings that had accumulated, then filling the entire thing. He simply left the bone underwater overnight, making sure that it was totally filled with water. In the morning, he saw that blue gas was leaking from the hole in the spar that he had drilled, and nodded in appreciation. It was working *exactly* as he had hoped it would. Time for the next test.

He twisted the screw, *really* putting effort into it. The end eventually popped out, and he grinned as the remainder of the water trickled out. It wasn't as blue as the exterior yet, but that had a few months of extra time where it had been hardening.

Still... Luke refilled the hollow portion and replaced the bone screw, then turned his attention to the shifting grass.

"Cookie is back on the table."

Luke charged downhill and into battle, crushing twelve goats and laughing the entire time. No longer did he need to slowly dig the pearls out; a simple *smash*, and the pearl practically *rolled* out of the broken skull on its own! "Time to make some goat paste."

He spent the next few weeks making minor adjustments to his weapon and fighting style, and was finally ready to make his next big push. "Three years and... four months? Better make sure I keep that tally up to date..."

Luke was covered in six inches of padded leather across his whole body. His neck and head were wrapped with hardened goatskin, and Luke felt that he was as prepared as he was going to get. "No stopping, no slowing. It's time to get past these creatures. You ready for this, Cookie?"

There was no reply as Luke scooped up the pearls and added them to his goat *hide*. "Hey. *Cookie*! Come on, don't give me the silent treatment like that. I just wanted to grab these pearls; no stopping after this. We're still gonna go break that-"

Heat.

Luke yelped at the foreign sensation and jumped away. It didn't help. His leather was on fire! *Actual* fire! He dropped and rolled, smothering the flame. Luke searched around to determine what had happened, and his eyes locked onto a nearly see-through pearl that was generating enough light that only the fact that the sky was brightening allowed Luke to look directly at it. Beyond the sight, he could *feel* it. His skin under all of the armor tightened and twinged as though he was standing next to a burning building. "Where did...?"

"You have *goat* to be *kid*ding me." His eyes widened as the area around him started to fill with noise; he grabbed the pearl and sprinted toward the pool. As he did so, a cry went up from all around him. Luke had just created a tier four pearl, and the goats *wanted* it. Luke tried to think over what had just happened;

nodding as everything fell into place. The water had boiled and churned even when the smaller versions of the pearl had been created. With this one, the reaction had apparently flash-boiled the water and caused him to catch on fire.

Fire was over-effective here, on all things, and he had no idea why. Luke was just glad that he hadn't started a wildfire. If this blue grass path had caught… it was unlikely that he could survive very long. The goats, as much as he *hated* them and *wanted* them to burn, were his food source. Also, who could tell how long the area might burn for? He could be trapped in the pool for weeks, and he wouldn't survive that either.

Still, what mattered right *now* was surviving the next few *minutes*! He could hear hooves stampeding, so much so that it felt like the entire population must be heading his way simultaneously. The pearl in his hand was *hot*, not in a way that was physically burning him, but in a way that made him aware of *exactly* where it was. It practically *screamed* at him, and he was sure that everything for miles around was coming for him.

"If I can get this home… make it into a necklace…" Luke puffed as he ran uphill, "Sell it to some random lady. Make sure no one can eat it and explode. She becomes Queen, no one can take their eyes off of her. She gives me a Noble title as thanks, I hide from the world forever. No goats allowed on the property. Yeah. There we go."

Luke reached the edge of the pool and dived in without hesitation. Instantly, the *hot* feeling vanished. The loss hit him so hard that he almost sucked in a breath, just *barely* managing to refrain. That would have been bad, being underwater and all. He came up and could hear confused calls coming from *everywhere*.

"*Baaa!*"

"Yeah, like I care that you're unsure of yourselves. Stupid carnivorous goats." Luke idled in the water for a while, relaxing and floating until his skin started to pickle and the noise level had reduced to normal. "Good thing that happened this early in the day. If every one of them was awake and worked up… I can't imagine that I'd have gotten away."

Luke looked down and saw that the entire pool was *filled* with light, thanks to the pearl in his hand. He could see all the way to the sandy bottom a dozen feet below him, and was a little disgruntled to notice that the bottom was positively *filled* with bones. He dove down, and as he got closer; he saw that most - but not *all* - of the bones were from goats.

He knew what goat skeletons looked like; he was likely the foremost expert on goat skeletal structure right now, on Murder World or his home world. Luke surfaced and took a long breath of fresh air, then explained what he was doing to Cookie. "There were some human bones in there. I'm not the first to arrive here? Am I the first to *survive*, for some reason?"

"Come to think of it, I can't remember the goats *ever* drinking the water." He knew for certain that there was nothing else in the pool. In fact, it was the cleanest, clearest water he had ever been in. "I wonder why? Also, why are these ones in here? They died of old age, maybe?"

"Now, what to do with you?" Luke looked at the innocently shining pearl and smiled. His waterskin had burst and was now a set of tattered hide; but there was an easy solution to this problem. He already had a tool ready-made for this! "Looks like you're going in the Cookie jar."

Luke unscrewed the end of Cookie and rolled the pearl inside. There was plenty of room for it to move around, and he wasn't at all worried about it getting stuck in there. Since Cookie was already filled with water, the pearl stayed 'cool'. He heaved himself out of the water and started walking. There were goats to get past, and today was the day.

CHAPTER EIGHTEEN

Luke broke into a downhill sprint, moving as fast as he could while wielding his massive bone and being covered in several inches of leather. The water on him was vaporizing, turning to gas as he charged along. Some goats got in his way, but he simply plowed over them, breaking bones as his huge weight crushed them into the ground.

He was starting to have a following, a few hundred of the bleating beasts were charging along behind him. "Short... legs... *suck*, don't they! Ha!"

"I can keep this pace up for *days*!" Luke called back about five minutes of running later, when his following had turned into a few *thousand*. The galloping beasts behind him bleated in reply, and Luke decided that it was almost time to put his plan into action. Two minutes passed, and he took a sharp right. He cut in front of the leading edge of the herd, and they followed him, deep into the heart of 'right herd' territory.

Once he was pretty deep into the right side of the downhill path, he turned so that he was running directly down again. A long few minutes passed, where he was uncertain if his plan was going to work... then he heard the herd. A deep, bellowing, "*Baaa!*"

The right herd hadn't really acknowledged his presence, but it was hard to miss the *thousands* of rivals in their territory. A full-on territory war began, and the left herd was blindsided by the attack. Their focus was solely on him, so the right-siders were picking them off with impunity. Luke had killed one and a half *hundred thousand* of them over the last few years, and the population decrease was met with a subsequent boom for the left-siders.

This meant that Luke could run with less conflict on this side, but if he had *started* on this side... he would still have been overrun. A veritable *wall* of goats was charging uphill toward him to meet the invading goats, and Luke could have *sworn* he saw surprise on their goateed faces when they saw him. "Get 'em, Cookie! Paste those stupid *bleaters!*"

He half-turned to fully swing Cookie, and any goat hit was either sent flying or was turned to bloody paste. To be fair, the creatures only came up to his knees, and were about as light as a Noble's prize-winning poodle. Luke ran faster, holding Cookie to his side and leaning to the right to compensate for the weight. He attacked again and again, killing indiscriminately as the goats came after him. "There's something *different* over there! Oh, celestials above, there's a change in scenery! Get out of the *way*! I see *shrubberies!*"

On the horizon, small green plants dotted the ever-downward slope. The thick knee-high blue grass was replaced by *ankle*-high grass, and there were even *other* types of plants! He would have cried for joy if he hadn't been running for his life. Several minutes later, he leaped into the new area and spun around, swinging his weapon as hard as he could to catch the goats that were hot on his heels.

His strike met only empty air even as a weak chime came from his forehead. Luke looked into the grass, and saw that the goats had stopped and were watching him. Ever so slowly, they melted back into the sea of grass. Luke glanced around him and found... nothing. There were no visible monsters here. The reaction of the goats though... that was concerning.

First order of business: the shrubberies! Luke raced over, excited beyond belief about this simple change. A new plant for the first time in over three *years*! He got closer, closer... then jumped in the air and swung Cookie down in a devastating overhead blow. The plant, berries and all, was pulverized and rendered into splinters and splattered juices. Luke circled around the newly-made crater and searched to see if it had been hiding a creature, or if it by itself was deadly. As far as he could tell... there was nothing.

Luke started walking, hoping to find a safe haven or place he could use as a base while he figured out why this area was dangerous. It *had* to be dangerous, right? "Hmm... the width of this area is larger. I'd say... three-quarters of a mile, instead of half of one? If there aren't any monsters here, I'd best move on and get through before this place changes its mind."

His run across the lush grasslands had only taken about thirty minutes, so Luke had the entire day to work. He scoffed as he thought of how long he had been trapped with the goats, only to escape by running without stopping for a mere ten miles. Then his mind stuttered, and Luke realized that he had just run *ten* miles in *thirty* minutes, while fighting. "What... I'm not even winded...? How did *that* happen? Was it really ten miles, or did it just *feel* that way?"

"How fast are goats? How fast was I *moving*? That's not possible. What... what am I?" He needed to understand what had changed. Luke did something that he hadn't done in almost two years.

He started removing the *entirety* of his armor.

Layer after layer landed on the ground, and the extra-beefy form slimmed down further and further, until he was looking at pale skin that reflected the ambient light in the area. Though it still grew, he had no hair on his body; the water had taken it off him every time he dunked himself in and the liquid started to evaporate. Luke inspected his arm, musing that it would look more at home on the arm of the old blacksmith in his home-town. Still, his skin was unblemished and smooth.

His hands, which had held weapons, wielded tools, and beaten down goats for years without pause... had no calluses. They were as smooth as a scholar's, but the skin was as tough as hardened leather. "Well, can't say that this place has been bad for my physical health."

There was no excess fat on him, and with his armor off... Luke started to circle the area, swinging Cookie around and moving through the primal martial art he had created. It was focused on direct, brutal attacks. There was no subterfuge; every motion held the intent to kill if it landed. Beyond being a veiny chonk of hairless muscle, Luke found that he was *fast* without his armor on. He started sprinting and used his momentum to tumble while running at full speed; Cookie stayed nearly stationary in the air as Luke used it as a counter-balance.

He had long since gotten used to this sort of motion, and it was second-nature to him now. Still, when he sat and thought through what he was doing... he had no explanation for the rapid improvements. Three years shouldn't have been *nearly* enough time to transform him like this. Not with his poor diet and lack of a proper training plan. Luke wanted a mirror, or a reflecting pool.

"Oh... I hope I can find some water in this area." Finally done admiring himself, he turned back to the task at hand. "Cookie? I need to get as far as I can today... but imma crush every bush I come across, just to be on the safe side. That work for you?"

Cookie bobbed in Luke's hands, more than enough of an answer. He started putting his armor back on, and soon was back in full gear. Luke took off running, and true to his word, demolished every single bush he came close to in passing. He found that the downhill slope had a slight leftward curve, which would make sense in this odd corkscrew world. Since the whole thing appeared to be a flat spring shape, the only way it would have a *right* curve would be if he were going *uphill*! Who would want to go *uphill*?

"Pfff. Uphill; am I right, Cookie?" Chuckling at the inane thought, he gauged the distance he had traveled. It was almost halfway through the light cycle of the planet, and he was pretty sure that he was going to be nearing the next area soon. "Looks like this zone was… fifteen miles? Does every zone increase by half? Half again as wide, half again as long? This place was *specifically* created, then? It's artificial?"

Luke looked back, and saw nothing beyond grass, shrubberies, and *pulped* shrubberies. "What a strange area… onto the next!"

Slowing as he reached the clearly-defined edge of the next territory, there was a sharp line where the grass ended and stone began. Luke looked upon the next challenge that awaited him. He could see a creature, and it appeared to be waiting for him. It didn't step onto the grass, but its eyes followed him exactly; and it moved to intercept if he veered off toward another direction. The creature waited for him just past the point the grass faded into rocky earth, and it wasn't going to let him pass for free.

It appeared to be a gorilla, but its front limbs ended in an oversized metallic plate that could separate into three distinct bladed claws. The creature, like everything else in Murder World, was blue. In fact, because of that, Luke almost didn't notice that it had no fur. Instead, it appeared to be coated in a fine gravel grit. "Great. A stone monkey with metal claws. Oh, and it's *following* me. Perfect."

"Are you my trainer, finally here to teach me the way?" He didn't hesitate, charging forward with a scream of glee and swinging Cookie with all his might. "I bet you have a pearl, too! Time to go into the Cookie jar, ape!"

The bone hit, and a cloud of dust exploded from the beast as it tumbled away. "*Yea-*"

Luke went flying, and Cookie twirled in the air beside him. He landed with a sick feeling, and found that gasping in air was *difficult.* He sat up, coughing blood and phlegm to the side. "What..."

The ape was back at the edge of the territory, staring at him impassively. There was no indication that it had been hit, and nothing that made him think that it was angry... but he had the feeling that if he had landed on its side of the distinct line in the dirt, he wouldn't be getting up right now.

He felt at his armor, and found a row of three gashes that went through two full *inches* of his goat-hide wrappings. "Is this some kind of... *wheeze*... sick joke? I fought murder *goats* for three years, and the next trial is an abyssal metal-and-stone murder ape?"

Chime.

As per usual, there was no reply to his shouting into the air. He sat down and opened his pack. Repairing his armor and healing were both going to take time. Luke took a long drink of water, then poured the remainder over himself; wincing as it burned in - and on - his body. It always seemed to hurt a *lot* more when he was injured.

Over the next week, he tried everything he could think of to get around the ape. It was always waiting for him, however, and eventually Luke started to run out of food. He made the trip back to the goats and tried to enter, but it seemed a full-scale war was raging. They were also on the lookout for him, and whenever he got close, a *'bahhh'* would ring out, and a wall of flesh stood prepared to attack him if he entered the grassland.

He also found out why they didn't cross the edge of their designated area. Luke decided to force them to come to him, and pulled out the tier-four pearl. The draw had been too much for the goats that were right at the edge, and they swarmed toward him. As soon as they crossed into bushland, their bodies exploded, starting with their heads.

Luke was shocked, but honestly didn't mind all that much. The only real downside was that only an inedible paste remained of the goats. To counteract his ability to draw them in, the goats moved back further into their own territory. It was a game that he didn't have the time to play; Luke was *hungry*. He managed to pull a few goats over after crushing their heads, but it took at least a dozen a day to keep him from starving, and he just wasn't getting that.

Finally breaking down, Luke went to a shrubbery and ate one of the berries. Honestly… it felt like eating a *steak*! Cow meat! And *so* juicy! He waited a few minutes, and found that his body wasn't having a bad reaction to it. Luke ate a few more and moved on, collecting and eating as many as he could find. "So simple; such sensually succulent steak."

It was only later that he found the issue with the berries; Luke lay on the ground, staring up with overly-large pupils. "*Why* do the pink fluffy unicorns dance on the rainbows? They could be doing anything… they can *fly*! Instead, they dance there for *hours*!"

The Sigil on his forehead was sparking madly, and with a tortured *chime*, it popped and went fully dark. Luke nodded as the singing unicorns suddenly got louder and more numerous. "It makes so much *sense*! Do what makes you happy, fluffy critters! Except *you*. I don't know what you are trying to pull, but I *know* you're a goat!"

The fluffy unicorns in the sky swarmed the imposter, goring it until it fell to the earth far in the distance and exploded into glitter and rainbows that the unicorns could dance on. Luke nodded as his eyes started to flutter shut. "Good call, 'Corns. Goats are pure evil… and they got weird little square eyes. Taste good, though."

CHAPTER NINETEEN

- ANDRE -

"You know what?" Xan told a sweating and bleeding Andre. "A year isn't all that bad for figuring out how to make your first real circle. "Beyond that, you are *really* embracing the theory more than any other generation of Druid."

"Perhaps it has something to do with the fact that you let those bear-hunting bees at me when I didn't fully internalize the lesson?" Andre replied in a dead-tired voice around still-swollen lips.

"*I* didn't let them through. *You* did, because you thought that you could skip steps." Xan shook his head with mock sadness. "That doesn't matter right now! You made your first circle!"

Andre let his head fall to the side, taking in his surroundings. There were wolves, chittering bugs, horrible yet natural amalgamations… if he hadn't succeeded this week, he would have been in range of the creatures that seemed to be afflicted with an unnatural hunger for his flesh. "*Ya~a~ay.*"

"So… how do you feel?" Xan expectantly prodded.

"I've been stung by insects that can kill bears, slashed by insectoid talons and... and..." Andre blinked, sitting up and feeling at his previously swollen skin. "What's happening?"

"Oh, did I not mention that when you are in an area fully bound to your magic, the bound objects happily donate their essence to empower you? No?" Xan tapped his chin. "Strange, that seems like something I would tell you. Didn't we have that lesson?"

"Xan! Empower me? What just happened?"

"Ugh, *simple* terms are still needed?" Xan *tsk'ed* at his charge, but his smile was getting harder to hide. "The things bound to you will boost your recovery when you are in range. Healing, mana regeneration, stamina. Everything. With enough bound to you, you will eventually be as difficult to destroy as a natural mountain. Druids are lucky in that, normally people need to just wait to heal, or get a personal healer. But, well, ultimate defense means *ultimate* defense."

"Now we're *talking*!" Andre sat up with a wild grin on his face, but was slapped back down by Xan.

"Let's not forget that you are only bound to *grass*. You have empowerment and boosts from a weed, Andre. Also, *only* when you are on the ground bound to you." Xan laughed as his charge spat out a mouthful of blood and looked around fearfully. He was now surrounded by beasts on all sides. "Oh, don't worry about them. Those are my bound creatures."

A bugbear walked past and gently high-fived the Druid before skittering off. The others also dispersed, and Andre could only stare around in exasperation. "A year of threats, and none of it was real?"

"It was *all* real, Andre." Xan waved at the area around them. "How do you think I bound them? I needed to get them all in circles, and you didn't seem to mind being the wriggling bait for me."

"As respectfully as possible, I really kinda hate you, Xan." Andre closed his eyes and swallowed.

"I'm glad that you are putting respect in all things, Andre." The Initiate ignored the snickered response and looked at his status.

CAL Scan
Level: 1
Current Etheric Xenograft Potentia: 57/200 to level 2!
Body: 3.2
Mind: 8.2
Presence: 3.75
Senses: 3.45
Health: 76
Mana: 170
Mana regen: 2.43 per second

The constant running, meditation, and control exercises had allowed Andre to increase every aspect of himself. Not terrible increases for the last eight-ish months, certainly not something that could be done back on his mana-poor home planet. Even so, a few measly points was all he had to show for an entire year of throwing himself into his studies as if his life depended on it. Not even level two, and his abilities were at the very minimum necessary to do the work Xan required of him. It was enough to drive a man into doing very dumb things. "Xan, how far can I increase my stats through non-leveling?"

"He wants a lecture after tuning me out to preen over his stats?" The instructor shook his staff at the younger man, then shrugged and sat beside him. "Sure, why not. Call it a reward for your first circle. Through training, you can get any sub-characteristic up to ten. That is considered the 'mortal limit'. For Ascenders, that's easy to move past; only two level-ups away at any time. After you break through the mortal limit by leveling, you could continue increasing your characteristics indefinitely. There are simply diminishing returns with any training you can do, so that would take a *long* time in a mana-rich environment to see significant gains. Tell you what; say 'extended status sheet'. Time for you to learn what all your characteristics do for you."

"*Thank* you." Andre had never seen this portion of his characteristics before, and new meant exciting! "Extended status sheet!"

CAL Scan
Level: 1
Current Etheric Xenograft Potentia: 57/200 to level 2!
Body: 2.45

- *Fitness: 3.8*
- *Resistance: 2.6*

> Total Health points: 76
> Total Physical Output: 190 kilos
> Poison/disease resist: 3.2%

Mind: 8.3

- *Talent: 7.3*
- *Capacity: 9.1*

> Mana regeneration: 2.43 per sec
> Total mana: 170.2
> Spell Cooldown reduction: 5%

Presence: 3.75

- *Willpower: 4.7*
- *Charisma: 2.8*

> Dominate resist: 14.10%
> Dominate chance: 8.40%
> Stealth break: 18.75%

Senses: 3.45

- *Physical reaction: 2.9*
- *Mental energy: 4*

Dodge chance: 2.90%
Magic resist: 4.00%
Stealth engage: 17.25%

Health: 71
Mana: 170.2
Mana regen: 2.43 per second

"As you can see, there are three sub-sub-categories. Each sub-category impacts one and a half of the doubles-subs." Xan wrote out all of Andre's characteristics in the sand. "Fitness determines Physical Output, fifty kilos of lifting power per point, and determines half of Poison or Disease resistance. Resistance is the other half, as well as determining your total estimated health; fifty points plus ten health per point."

"Okay…" Andre looked at that information and sighed. "I *feel* strong and healthy, though. That number seems so… low?"

"Prove it wrong, then. No one *else* ever has, but you go ahead." Xan snorted at his Initiate's sour expression. "Mana regenerates at a third of your talent, and talent is worth four total mana per point. Capacity is worth ten mana per point, and everyone has a base of fifty mana. Also, Capacity allows you to use abilities faster. You already have a five percent cooldown reduction; that's *outstanding* for being natural."

"Thanks…?"

"I hope you're seeing the pattern here, though." The Druid pointed at the next point of data, "Dominate resist, a third of willpower divided by ten. Two-point-five times Willpower and Charisma, divided by one hundred, boom, Stealth Break. Charisma uses the same formula of Dominate Resist to generate Dominate *Chance*."

"Last one, Dodge Chance and Magic Resist are just their main characteristics divided by one hundred. Use the incomplete data to extrapolate which is which. The two, multiplied by two point five and added together, divided by a hundred, give you your stealth option. Questions?"

"Ah… one. Here." Andre pointed at 'total mana'. "This one is in the center of the sub-sub-characteristics, and is the combination of it's two parent sub-characteristics. All the other combos are the bottom line, why is this one different?"

Xan slapped him to the ground, erasing the numbers and letters that had been scraped into the dust. "You think I understand what was going through some moron Enchanter's head when they decided to *brand* us like cattle? Who cares which line is which!"

"I just like consistency!" Andre cried out in shock and anger. "Abyss, Xan, you're so slap-happy today. So, now what? How long is training supposed to last? We get to level ten, and make it back in time for the time limit?"

"Notsomuch." Xan leaned back and looked upward. "It sometimes takes *centuries* to reach level ten. Think like this: you need two hundred Potentia to get to level two, yeah? *All* of that is used up to get you that level, it is now gone. You start back at *zero* exp, and need *three* hundred to get to the next level. But! What's *this*? Fighting the same monsters over and over gives diminishing returns on Potentia? You need to fight a *variety*, or find some *tens of thousands* of the same creatures and slay them to gain fractions of Potentia points?"

Andre nodded in understanding. "The patience, and the length of time needed to gather that many of the same creatures, would be better used simply seeking new challenges."

"Correct again." Xan looked at Andre suspiciously. "Did you level up and increase your mind again?"

"Nice, Xan. I'm *smart*, drat it!" Andre huffed at his bearded fellow. "So… total experience to get to level ten? That's… all the individual levels added up… are…"

He sketched out the sums on the dirt in front of him, "Twenty-three thousand, one hundred."

"That's right." Xan spat out a pile of mush, yanked up a blade of grass that Andre had bound recently - making the young Druid flinch - and started chewing on it. "It's very doable. Lots of High Humans in the employ of the various Kingdoms. By the way, 'High Human' is the race humans are named after reaching level ten. Want to figure out why there are... like... *two* Paragons that interact with our plane? That's people at level twenty or above, though at level twenty-one, the base world forces them to stay off of it. Do the math for one reason, and I'll tell you the other."

Andre started drawing on the ground, and it took him a few minutes to struggle through the large numbers. When he gathered the result, he was slightly pale. "Two million, eight hundred sixty-five thousand, five hundred total Potentia? That's *possible?*"

"More than possible." Xan bobbed his chin, now fully stretched out on the grass. "That's also if you use all your Potentia *only* on upgrading yourself, but that would mean you only *ever* have level zero or level one abilities, whatever tier they might be. You think that your Archmage is gonna have only level *one* spells? He might *have* a maximum tier-ten, level nine spell. Imagine that: a spell that gained enough power that it is on the cusp of tier eleven. That's enough exp to level it to level nine, then double the requirement of level nine to reach the next tier, repeated ten times if you start with a tier one spell. Insane, right?"

"Yeah... I suppose that's one of the reasons people want to start with higher-tiered spells, or in our case, abilities? What's the real difference between tiers, beyond ease of leveling up to maximum?" Andre prepared to do more math, but Xan waved him off.

"We'll talk about that another time. You don't have any abilities, anyway; why worry about 'what ifs'?"

"Huh." Andre tried to think of the sheer amount of death that one person must have dealt out to gain *millions* of Potentia while Xan nodded at him. "You said that there was another reason there aren't many Paragons on our world?"

"Yup." Xan stood up suddenly and dusted himself off. "You think that Sigil on our heads can force a Paragon to do *anything*? At level twenty... a Paragon can just leave. Also, the reason we are treated so well in our respective Kingdoms? Paragons *can* leave... but imagine what happens if you had been treating your powerhouses *poorly*, and they reach the highest level of power possible for this planet. Your control over them is suddenly gone... what next?"

They both shuddered. Andre ventured a question, "Has that *happened*?"

"Of course it has." Xan quietly responded. "Ever heard of the Scarocco desert?"

"Yeah?"

"Used to be the Rocco *grasslands*."

"Ah." Andre swallowed deeply. "That's a part of *my* Kingdom, isn't it?"

"Sure is." Xan patted him on the back. "Why do you think it's so important that your Kingdom gets a well-trained Druid that they treat well? What class of Ascender do you think was treated so poorly the first time around that they went mad and killed everything they were bound with? Now, I think break time is over. Now that you can make your circles, you can *finally* start improving your craft."

"Eight months of being stagnant in Potentia has really been getting to me." Andre agreed with his mentor. He hefted his staff and started walking alongside Xan, having plenty to think about. "What's next?"

"What are you talking about?" Xan stopped and looked at the young man quizzically. "All you did was learn how to make your first binding circle, Andre. You haven't completed the task I set out for you. You still need to bind everything on this hill. Get to it."

"You *suck!*"

"Respect your Master!" Xan's response was to slap Andre in the face and walk away laughing as the youngster spat blood onto the ground once more. "You know, you're right! I *am* feeling slap-happy!"

CHAPTER TWENTY

"Circle is complete… now let the mana flow away, but only toward the interior of the circle…" Andre was breathing heavily as he forced his mana to work as he needed it. "*Done!*"

His concentration broke, and the excess mana flooded away into the air. It had taken him a *month* to gather the entire hilltop under his control, and three entire days of that had been spent making the flower like him enough to bind to him. "Now to reap the fruits of my labor!"

Andre walked into the circle of his plants, and instantly felt his mana regeneration speed tick up. Internally it felt like drinking ice water during a heat wave, and having it all reach the stomach at the same time. He stared at the tree that was now at the edge of his circle, and decided to tackle that project next. Trees were difficult, stubborn things. They didn't *want* to be bound, often not changing in hundreds of years, if left alone.

Although they could be coaxed into doing things for a Druid, the act of *binding* them was at a higher magnitude of difficulty. Since his circle was now large enough to boost his mana regen by about thirty percent, Andre could stand in it and work on the tree at the same time. As his mana reached capacity, he controlled it and encircled the tree trunk.

"Here you go, tree. Nice, tasty mana... *bind with me!*" There was no reaction, though the tree was starting to push out some fresh leaf buds. "Come on, tree... I need this by the end of the day. Xan was looking for honey yesterday, and he thinks those bear-killer bees are hiding something tasty. I need a good reason not to go with him..."

Mana: 0/170.2

His mana bottomed out. Andre tried again and again, speaking with the tree the entire time. As dark approached, he pushed too hard and he tapped into his health pool. "Son of a... *tree!* Bind with me already!"

Health: 66/71

Mana: 0/170.2

Flecks of his blood were spat into his circle and absorbed by the tree. With a dark flash of green, he *felt* the tree in his mind. Andre dropped to the ground as the tree joined his circle. Information on this Juniperus Virginiana, that is... the red cedar in front of him, entered his mind. "You need a healthy dose of nitrogen, huh...? Good to know... I bet that's a common problem here, and the other trees would be willing to bind with me if I fixed that issue..."

Chime!

You have generated an ability!

"I did?" Andre blinked and started to smile. "I did! I did it! What... what is it? My first ability! What did the starter bonus get me-"

Ability generated: Bind by Blood (T6).

Bind by Blood (T6): 0/100 to level 1!

Effect 1: By using your blood when creating a Druidic binding circle, you can gain additional benefits from the bond.

Bonus 1, at range: Circle can be created within line of sight.

Effect 2: Bond is 30+n% more likely to succeed in any circle your blood is added into, where 'n' = cumulative levels after tier 2! (T3 level 0 and beyond counts toward the percentage.)

Bonus 2, Multitarget: Increases resource gain among bound presence from $r*5^-6$ to $r*5^-5$ of offered resources, where r = offered resources!

Effect 3: Offered resources now include any Etheric Xenograft Potentia generated by bound beings within touch distance.

Bonus 3, AoE: 'touch' distance is now considered anywhere within the circular binding. Any future abilities generated that require 'touch' can be activated by any plants you are connected and in communion with.

"Celestial *Feces*." Andre sat up and stared at the display that was generated by his forehead Sigil. "This changes *everything*... I got a tier *six* ability? What... what does that mean? Three effects, three bonuses? Is that it?"

Before he had gained this ability, his path forward was going to be a mix of Body, Mind, and Senses. Now... he planned to *only* improve his Mind. Perhaps a few points in Senses, but his Mind was going to be his heavy focus. "If I can make larger circles, I can add blood and still be fairly certain that they'll succeed in binding. By binding things, they can generate Potentia for me. That means I can generate Potentia without killing!"

The only downside was that the ability could be *mistaken* as... somewhat sinister. He didn't need people thinking that he was like the Necromancers and Blood Mages that devastated and terrorized the front lines of warzones. Andre decided to keep all information about his ability - especially the tier - to himself for now.

He decided to start over with the area he had bound, this time using his blood. To Andre's delight, he found that everything was synergizing well. The damage he dealt to himself to make the bind was healed quickly by the health being donated to him by the plants. The mana he spent was given the same treatment.

It took him a *week* to bind the remainder of the entire hill, where just the top had previously required a full month. When he had captured the designated area, he used the remainder of the day to bind the path home. That was easier, as his circles only needed to be the size of his running body, and he could stand in a circle and create a new one anywhere within line-of-sight. Dark was approaching when the grove came into view, and Xan was suddenly next to him.

"What are you doing?" Xan glared at the Novice Druid. He looked back the way Andre had come. "You realize that *only* the area I left you in is protected, yes?"

"I do remember that... now." Andre scratched his chin, sheepish about his forgetfulness. It could have gotten him killed, and he hadn't remembered that in his excitement. "I wanted to surprise you with my progress. I finished the hill and bound the grass between here and there as a path!"

"Yes, I can see that." Xan snapped his eyes back to Andre. "You must have generated your first ability, then. All right, tell me what you got?"

Something was off in Xan's eyes. For the first time he could remember, Andre directly lied to his mentor. "Enhanced Bond. It increases the likelihood that any circle I try to make will be accepted!"

"Ah... I know that one. Not bad at all for a tier one ability. Too bad that's what your starting bonus came up with." Xan's nonchalance rang the warning bell in Andre's head.

"I hate to contradict you, Xan, but it's a tier t... *three*."

There was a moment of silence, and Xan narrowed his eyes. He lifted his hand... and then clapped it on Andre's shoulder. "*Congratulations!* Not only did you get a *great* first ability, you resisted the urge to lie about it! All known abilities are recorded and chronicled, so we know most of the general abilities tier and their chance of appearing. Okay, now that I've tested your trustworthiness... a word of advice."

"Our Kingdoms are allies, and *we* should trust each other. But never forget that there is a chance in the next *hundreds* of years that we are going to live... there is the possibility that we will be at war." Xan paused and let the information percolate through his mentee's mind. "Never tell anyone else the abilities you gain, their rarity, or the exact effect, unless you trust them implicitly. From the results of your initial testing, we knew that you were going to get powerful abilities, but starting at tier three is still *right* at the edge that outside parties could handle without getting... overexcited."

"I assume there are people out there that will kill to stay as the 'most powerful'?" Andre questioned halfheartedly.

His mentor leaned forward and spoke softly, looking off into the distance. "There are people *here* that would do that as well. Remember that nature is *always* listening, and Druids are one with nature. There are a few that are on the cusp of becoming Paragons, and they can hear nearly anything you say or do. *Especially* in the grove, which is why I've never interrupted you during your frequent nighttime... *indulgences* with yourself."

"Message received, find more privacy." Andre was sweating, both literally and figuratively. What would have happened if he hadn't seen the trap? If his lie had been detected? Worst of all... what if he had told the *truth*? "Should I look into finding a way to hide future ability gains?"

"Hmm. Not the direction I thought you were gonna go with that, but sure." Xan pulled the two of them to the top of the treehouse and waited a few moments as food started arriving in front of them. "Steak today, as a celebration of completing your Initiate training."

"*Steak*! Wait, you said that I was a *Novice* before? I got demoted?" Andre didn't think too hard on it; there was *steak* to be eaten!

"Right, but you passed your Initiate *training*." Xan smirked as he saw the juice running from Andre's mouth as he tore into the meat. "You've learned all the things you were supposed to learn in the first few years here. Next we are going to spend half of the day with combat training, and you are going to keep binding territory for the other half."

"Now, back to hiding abilities... it is neither possible nor needed." Xan's words made Andre look up in confusion. "Do you remember how your Archmage used your mana to open and create a portal for you? An invasive scan is the only thing that can list your abilities, and now that you can internally manipulate your mana, that is nearly impossible to do without your permission."

"You mean that if I had never told you my ability, you wouldn't have even known what it was?" Andre narrowed his eyes in thought and took a slow bite of his steak.

"Correct, but I would have been able to see the difference in what you do." Xan smiled as he saw his charge enjoying his cooking. Not that *he* had cooked it, but his abilities were very versatile at this point. "I might not be able to know *all* the effects of every ability, as each one is often *slightly* different, but I'd still have a good idea. Starting with a binding ability is very common, as nature wants to give you what you *need*."

"I see." Andre stated, wiping his mouth with the back of his sleeve. "Combat and more binding, then? How long will this continue?"

"Unless you show a surprising gift for it, you'll stay here till you are out of my care... in about a decade. Remember, I have you for two and a half base-world years, with a time difference of six. I have to spend fifteen years making sure you don't die when you leave this world," Xan told him bluntly. "You may progress to a Druid of the Second or even Third Circle by then, maybe have more abilities, but unless something changes; this is your life until you leave."

"I see..." Andre took a look at his current Potentia.

Level: 1

Current Etheric Xenograft Potentia: 58/200 to level 2!

In the short time since he had started with his new ability, he had already passively gained one point of Potentia. He had a whole *world* that he could eventually pull from... but he would need to hide his power from the old monsters hiding amongst any kindly-seeming Druids, that much was certain. Andre grinned cockily at his Master, "Sounds like a party, old-timer. Let's go learn how to combat."

"Oh, look. The joker is wild again." Xan stood up while shaking his head sadly. "Welp, time to smack some more sense into him."

CHAPTER TWENTY-ONE

- LUKE -

Luke's hands shook as he swallowed fistfuls of berries. He waited and waited, but there was no effect. He screamed into the void, "I want my *hallucinations*! Give them back!"

He had been trapped in the second zone for the last two years, and it seemed that he had finally adapted to the toxins created by the berries. Luke was finally immune to their effects... and he hated it. He had spent every day training with and without Cookie, and he felt that he had finally reached his peak physicality. There was something blocking him from reaching further, but he *still* couldn't get past the Stone Ape. Not for lack of trying. "I'll kill you!"

At least once a week he threw everything he had against the beast, and every. *Single. Time*. Luke was sent to the ground with serious injuries. Once he had landed on the ground in the third zone, and he had been torn *up*. Luke still wasn't sure how he had managed to get away, back into the second zone, but he thanked his lucky stars that he had. He had a sneaking suspicion that Cookie had rescued him, but she was playing coy and refusing to answer.

But now... now he was *really* trapped. There was no way to progress; he could *feel* it. That meant that there was no way forward, no way back... "And now my *berries* are useless!"

He threw the remaining berries at the Stone Ape, but they popped and sizzled away into nothing as they crossed the zone dividing line. Luke couldn't even use them as a distraction; the stone ape just didn't *care* if he threw things at him. "I need... this all needs to *end*. I just want it all to be over! I've been trapped here forever!"

Luke trudged to the edge of the world and looked over. Just like every other time he had been here, his broken Sigil mustered the power to chime, and he was unable to take any further steps. "I can't even throw myself into oblivion because of that *abyssal* Kingdom that sent me to *rot*! If I *ever* get the chance for revenge...!"

He stood at the edge and screamed for a while, then cradled Cookie and wept blue tears. Night fell, and he simply lay on his back and stared at the empty sky. No stars, no sun. No dancing unicorns. Only time of light, and time of darkness. No wind. No rain. No change of any kind, except the swirling blue fog that made it hard to see any real distance on this plane. "Thanks, Cookie. That helped. I love hugs. Still, I *need* to find a way to make this all *stop*."

Cookie fell against his leg, and he stared at the corkscrew at the end of her teardrop. "Cookie... I understand. Thank you for mentioning that, I know it must be hard for you to suggest that, since you'll be all alone when I'm gone. Oh! I know! You can hang out with my skeleton; it's named 'Douglas'. He's not very talkative, and I know you aren't acquainted, but don't worry. I give you permission to have a friend other than me."

Luke unscrewed the cap and started pouring the water onto the ground. He drank some of it to lubricate his throat, no reason to be uncomfortable when he died. Finally, the only other thing inside Cookie fell into his waiting hand. The shining tier four pearl. All the smaller ones were still in his goat hide canteen. "No danger here, Kingdom Sigil. Just a shiny rock, nothing for you to worry ab-"

Without waiting another second, he slammed the pearl into his mouth and swallowed. Then he chugged as much water as he could manage… and waited. "Ha! Sucker Sigil, I found a way around you! So long, Murder World! I did it; I *did* it! *Hahaha!*"

Already his stomach was burning, a heat that his body simply couldn't contain. "I'll count down… I bet I'll pop by the time I get to one. What? What do you *mean* you'll take that bet, Cookie? Just because *you* could stomach it doesn't mean that I can! Don't you put that evil on me!"

Chime!

"That… that was louder than usual." Luke shook his head at his silly weapon and lay flat. No need to make a mess on her. Looking up, he gasped for a moment in delight as his *hallucinations* returned! No unicorns this time… for some reason, it was *words*? Unbeknownst to him, the Sigil in his forehead had fully come to life for the first time in years, and the lights it released were spinning madly.

Contribution Activity Log is online! Scanning…
CAL Scan complete!
Level: 0
Current Etheric Xenograft Potentia: 37,777/100 to level 1!
Body: 10 (Mortal Limit)
Mind: 0/0 (Damaged: repairs needed)
Presence: 10 (Mortal Limit)
Senses: 10 (Mortal Limit)
Health: 150
Mana: 0/0 (Mana channels damaged to non-usability.)
Mana regen: 0/0 (see above!)

Massive damage to mana channels has been found. Carving new mana channels... processing. Large amount of mana is required. Find a mana-rich area! The more abundant, the better the resulting channels will become!

Extreme mana surplus detected within flesh, stomach, and ambient environment; all needs met by a factor of 1.1k. Caution: due to surplus of mana, survival depends on channels that can properly direct mana. Requirement determined: Prismatic Channels required for life. Carving new mana channels... beginning.

Luke screamed as his body was lit up from within by undulating blue lightning. Whips of raw mana started flaying his flesh from the inside out. He wanted to black out, but he was too used to the berries - which he had eaten for the last few years - impacting his mind and altering his senses. Powerful sensations had been something he had been *seeking* on a constant basis... but not like this.

Lethal hallucinogenic poison levels detected... processing... process-proc-proc-

Pop.

The Sigil on Luke's head started to steam and shifted into a new configuration; even as the skin around it blistered and burned.

Sigil damaged due to extremely low internal mana and extreme concentrations of ambient mana! Mortal tier safety protocols overridden. High Human safeties activated. Scanning the local environment.

"*This one is* Mine."

The words resonated throughout the entirety of the corkscrew world, and the Sigil reformed once again; this time into an entirely different and *much* more intricate configuration. Then it shifted slightly, a camouflage that made it appear to be only a standard and basic Sigil.

Luke's eyes were rolled into the back of his head, and he stared up with only the whites showing as he choked on his own saliva. The voice came again, sending every intelligent being into hiding as pure power converged on Luke's changed Sigil from the foundation of the world.

"*Data...* granted!"

High Human safeties overridden by UnKnOWn. Data packet added to framework. ? Source-cerer protocols granted by same entity?

Skill *acquired!*

You have enough Etheric Xenograft Potentia to level up! Do so now? Yes / Yes.

Source-cerer protocols are auto-assigning Potentia, as host is not in a fit state to do so. Scanning… overabundance of Potentia will destroy the host body if used to improve characteristics across the board. Prismatic Mana Channels found. Mana uncontained within system. Body will burst unless characteristic is increased. Leveling up host. Leveling gained skill with death-inducing excess. Activating in 3… 2…

As the process started, Luke began to stretch grotesquely as his body gained mass and muscles. His arm swelled up like a stretched waterskin, then shrank down to become proportional to the remainder of his body. This happened over and over, with different limbs. His skin shifted back and forth, and his bones groaned as they broke and repaired themselves again and again.

Leveling complete.

Current Etheric Xenograft Potentia: 3,000/3,400 to level 8!

Your skill from a pearl has reached tier 7! 477/8,900 to level 10!

You have created a skill? Impossibility found. Checking… data accurate. Deleting Power On Self Test from logs.

Say 'Status' to open or close this screen. Say 'Access' to access the data packet granted by unknown!

The sky brightened. The Stone Ape looked on impassively as Luke lay unmoving on the ground. Darkness descended. This pattern repeated twice, and finally, Luke blinked and reached out. "C… Cookie?"

Abnormal mental state detected. Balancing… error. Baseline measurements corrupted. Averaging aggregate data… balancing based on pathways carved in last several years. Current mental state set as the new normal.

The Sigil chimed, and Luke blinked. He sat up, and the screen followed his movements. "Ugh… what in the… what happened to me? What is this?"

He read over the screen, and his eyes widened again and

again, then narrowed. "The Sigil had a function other than forcibly controlling self-destructive urges? Why didn't they tell us *before* we left?"

Luke shook his head and read through all the text that had been generated. He stood, wiped dried and crusted blood out of his eyes, ears, mouth, and nose, and walked to the edge of the world, bowing, and shouting. "Hey, unknown entity! Thanks!"

No response, but that at least was something that he was used to getting. Luke plopped down and looked at the information. "All right, stats - oh, come on. *Status.* I feel like this should be more *intent*-based. 'Characteristics' were auto-assigned? What does that mean?"

CAL Scan

Level: 7

Current Etheric Xenograft Potentia: 3,000/3,400 to level 8!

Note: the arrow next to characteristics denotes a change granted by leveling up.

Body: 20

- *Fitness: 10 -> 30*
- *Resistance: 10*

Mind: 10 (Prismatic mana channels)

- *Talent: 10*
- *Capacity: 10*

Presence: 10

- *Willpower: 10*
- *Charisma: 10*

Senses: 12.5

- *Physical reaction: 10 -> 15*

- *Mental energy: 10*

Health: 150
Mana: 190
Mana regen: ~~3.33~~ 100 per second (Overridden by local ambient levels.)

Skills
T7: 1
T3: 1

To access historical data, say 'Access'.

"I'll get around to it. Calm yourself." Luke told the final - flashing - word. He glanced to the side, and nodded at Cookie. "I told it, don't worry, Cookie. I was listening. What's the skill I got?"

Skill page requested. Skills: 2
Fully geared. (T7) Level 9. 477/11,000 to level 10!
Effect 1: You are able to absorb natural weapons and armor (Claws, fangs, scales) by touching them. By absorbing a certain amount of the same type of weapon or armor, you are able to 'equip' it on your body. Only one type of weapon can be created at a time, and only one type of armor per slot. Choosing a new type of weapon or armor will replace the previous type once it is complete. Weapons and armor cannot exceed current tier and level.
Bonus 1, at range: You are able to absorb a weapon or armor type within five feet of your body. No longer requires active attempts after the item is selected.
Effect 2: You are now able to absorb weapons or armor created via natural metals. Natural metal weapons and armor cannot exceed current tier and level. Natural weapons can exceed tier, so long as they are within three effective levels.
Bonus 2, Multitarget: You can now select to absorb all weapons or armor of the same type within the range of bonus 1.
Effect 3: You are now able to absorb weapons or armor created via unnatural metals (magical weapons/armor). Weapons and armor cannot exceed current tier and level of this skill. Natural metal weapons can exceed

tier, so long as they are within three effective levels. Natural weapons can exceed tier, so long as they are within six effective levels.

Bonus 3, AoE: You can store the weapons and armor you create. You are able to select between all different versions you have previously created!

Effect 4: Each active weapon or armor slot now costs a flat percentage of your mana pool to maintain! To achieve the exact damage or protection potential, ten percent of your mana must be applied. Each percentage added or subtracted will change the potential armor/damage by one percent.

I Have Concerns. (T3) Level 0. You have gorged yourself on potent hallucinogens and high-ambient mana for years, and they have finally given up. They have thrown in the towel. You win.

Effect 1: Never again will poison or pure mana be able to damage you. Your flesh contains potent power and mind-shifting effects. Anything taking a bite out of you should be prepared to feel like unicorns are goring them to death!

Bonus 1, at range: Poisons in the air, such as toxic fumes, will restore your health and mana over time. Amount regained is based on potency and time spent in the poison.

Effect 2: You are able to consume concentrated mana to restore health and mana, or hallucinogenic materials to further increase restored health and mana.

This skill cannot be increased via additive Potentia.

"Helpful, but not really. I don't know what any of this means. What are Prismatic Mana Channels?" Luke sighed and decided to get on with the next portion. "Alright, ya blinking screen. Calm down. *Access.*"

Data packet from unknown accessed... updating log with provided data... cross-referencing with Source-cerer *protocols... complete! Messages will be displayed in order of creation.*

You have entered Unknown World!

You have been exposed to concentrated mana! Damage reduced from 100/second to 0.003/sec. Scanning body... mana channels damaged and blocked to the point of extreme host mana deprivation. Sigil enters low-power mode until mana can be absorbed from host to sustain systems.

You have entered Tutorial zone, Zone one! While in this Zone, you may notice a few small creatures! Don't underestimate them, but do your best to move to the next area quickly to earn a bonus! The longer this Zone goes without crossing into the next Zone, the more creatures will be generated to ensure that you are being properly tested! This Zone will help you to understand your own body and some of the challenges you will face on the lower stretches of Unknown World!

You have slain Battering Ram (level 1). Bonus Etheric Xenograft Potentia granted for slaying a creature of a higher level than yourself! (Battle log condensed, display entire log?)

Concentrated mana ingested! Preparing for death of host. Death not achieved. Impossibility found. Deleting data. New effect noted. Health… regenerated? Error. Divide by zero. Impossible situation. Data unavailable. Deleting data.

You have gained a skill pearl (T1) from a Battering Ram! You can either use the pearl right away by swallowing it, or combine fifty pearls to upgrade the skill rarity you can attain! Please note, each type of creature will only allow you to use a single pearl per tier. Example: 1 T1 skill. 1 T2 Skill. T3 or above is possible, but very unlikely due to the massive amounts of pearls that would be required!

World name changed from 'Unknown' to 'Murder World' by host.

You have combined fifty T1 skill pearls! Congratulations! Upgrading starting bonus due to extreme patience!

You have slain Battering Ram (level 1). Etheric Xenograft Potentia has been reduced for slaying too many of the same creatures! Error. Bonus Etheric Xenograft Potentia granted for slaying a creature of a higher level than yourself! (Battle log condensed. Total of 150,000+ messages over three years aggregated. Display all?)

You have combined fifty T2 skill pearls! Congratulations! Upgrading starting bonus due to extreme patience!

You have combined fifty T3 skill pearls! Congratulations! Upgrading starting bonus due to extreme patience! Please… eat the skill pearl.

Zone one cleared! Congratulations for setting a new record clear time! New record: 26,729.4383 hours! Now people following in your footsteps have something to strive for!

Battering Ram respawn rate has been reset from 886 goats per hour, to 1 goat per twelve hours! Bonus Potentia gained for clearing a Zone: 100. Optional: Finish off all enemies to earn another bonus! Feel free to return at any point, but be warned: the creatures will be extra-hostile since you escaped them once! Fear the fluffy death!

You have entered Tutorial Zone, Zone Two! This Zone is designed to test your Mind! You may find a bush or two in what is otherwise a safe zone. You can either ignore them, or sample the berries to very slightly train your mind through the use of hallucinations! Caution: the berries are slightly toxic and you may suffer some damage!

Zone two cleared! Congratulations for setting a new record clear time! New record: .489 hours! Now people following in your footsteps have something to strive for! Bonus for clearing the Zone: 200 Potentia. Hidden achievement: Eat no berries! 100 Potentia gained!

You have entered Tutorial Zone, Zone Three. This Zone is guarded by various defenders depending on the section of the Zone you enter! No matter which route you take in personal progression, you must find a way to clear this Zone! Do your best to defeat the guardian and move to the next area quickly, as each defender you destroy will spawn two defenders that are out for revenge!

You have eaten a toxic berry! (total of 200,000+ messages over two years aggregated. Display all?)

You have eaten a Tier four (T4) skill pearl! Starter bonus applied! Skill being generated! Error. Mana channels damaged. Skill use is impossible with this body. Body shutting down due to overload. Death is imminent.

Intervention by Unknown entity. New mana channels carved. Optimized mana channels carved by Unknown. Starter bonus increased by ambient mana levels. Increased by improved channels. Increased by entity! Applied. T4 skill increased to T7.

Characteristics assigned: +7 to Fitness, +1 to Physical Reaction.

Prismatic Mana Channels: Mana usage will not tire the host. Losing all mana may be annoying, but cannot impact the user's mental or physical state. Channeling of any amount of mana is theoretically possible.

There was nothing else, but still there were tears flowing down Luke's face as he laughed in pure joy. "It… there was supposed to be a *reason* for this area? I wasn't abandoned here? This place wasn't a mistake? Then why… why did it all go wrong?"

He remembered the human bones in the pool of the tutorial, and things started to fall into place. "Think... the goats had been spawning at a *crazy* high amount, which would have started the first time someone arrived here. I drank 'concentrated mana', except... I never drank anything but spicy water."

Luke put his head in his hands. "In other words... that wasn't water? I knew it was different. That was all 'mana' somehow, and only the fact that my body was damaged to the point of almost dying whenever mana tried to go through my 'channels' somehow allowed me to survive *touching* it? I've been *drinking* that for years, *bathing* in it. I used it to *craft* - ahh! I forgot about *Cookie*!"

Luke grabbed Cookie, who was *shining*. He picked up the bone, and it *flashed*. The surface turned a deeper shade of blue, and he felt something inside him connect to it.

The basic two-handed bone weapon 'Cookie' has finished reacting to your skill 'Fully Geared'. Would you like to start absorbing 'Cookie' into a weapon slot? Caution: weapon will be destroyed in the process.

"How *dare* you threaten Cookie!" Luke's fist lashed out as he screamed, impacting only air with a **wub**. He jumped to his feet. "What was *that*... right! I got stronger! I'll figure this all out later. Let's go try to get that goat Zone-clearing bonus, Cookie!"

CHAPTER TWENTY-TWO

Goats ran away bleating in terror as the personification of goaty death loomed large behind them. A blue-white streak whirled through the air and left behind nothing but pulverized grass. At first the goats had made a proud and noble stand, but now the unified herd that controlled the entire grassland of the first Zone was in full retreat.

"Ha, *ha*! Thirty points in Fitness!" Luke bellowed after the fleeing creatures at the top of his lungs. He flashed forward, catching up to his target as if it had been standing still. Cookie came down, and Luke caught the escaping pearl on the first bounce. Collecting all the pearls was easy, as that was the largest object left after each Cookie-cutter smash. The pearls didn't seem to mind the force, but skulls didn't particularly care for it.

"How hard must I be hitting in order to totally demolish the entire goat like that, Cookie? How do I transfer points in 'Body' to a usable metric?" Luke pondered this thought while working to destroy every other living thing in the Zone. That included the grass; it was working with the goats to hide them! When it was as short as the grass in Zone two, he left it alone after careful consideration and a long conversation with Cookie.

"I could have burned this place down, and the goats would have just respawned anyway, huh?" Luke mused calmly. "Ah, no point in worrying about it now."

He spent the next few weeks utterly annihilating the entire Zone. At the start, he was killing dozens of goats every minute, but now that he needed to chase them; he was only getting that many every *other* minute. Luke was also attempting to find his limits, and found that after four days straight of wakefulness, his mind couldn't handle the stress anymore.

Every time that happened, he would retreat to Zone two and rest, then get back to work as soon as he woke. A month into his new pet project, he had cleared about half the Zone and was finding fewer and fewer Battering Rams. He almost slipped as he returned to killin', as there was so much blue blood on the slope that it couldn't dry up in a reasonable amount of time. On a positive note, it made getting to the second Zone both fast *and* easy! He jumped and slid on the proper-length grass; treating the gentle slope like the largest slide in existence and traveling to Zone two in style. "*Whee!*"

Another month, and the excitement had worn off. There was one major positive: Luke finally finished off his grim task. Over the last few weeks, he had explored all the changes to his body and now had a good grasp on his limits. The feeling that he was stagnating was gone. Now he was disgruntled that fighting such weak things had kept him trapped for so long. Even worse, with his new level, they gave him such a small amount of... *exp*... that he hadn't gained even a single point.

Challenge completed: clear all Battering Rams from Zone one! Reward: 200 Potentia!

"Hooray." Luke growled at the words that he still held a slight grudge against. "It was so *worth* the effort."

He sat down in his old camp next to a pile of discarded bones, horns, and hides that was piled higher than he stood. Leaning against the hides, he took a short nap, awakening feeling refreshed and relaxed. He had finally gotten revenge on the goats for the years of torment, and avenged the 'right herd'.

Yes, their extinction *had* been his fault, but when he thought about that, *something* always-

Battering Ram Horn (x500) have finished being absorbed by skill 'Fully Geared'. You are now able to slot the Ram Horn as a fist weapon for either right or left hand slot.

"I'm some sort of enchanter class, right?" Luke massaged his head and tried to remember the stories he used to read, but he couldn't think of anything else that was similar to what he was doing. "Horns, huh? That's *bone*... come on, Cookie, let's see what happens. Bind horns to the right fist?"

There was no clear change, though when he looked at his status, the weapon had apparently bound to his fist.

Gear

Head: None.

Shoulders: None.

Gauntlet: None.

Torso: None.

Legs: None.

Feet: None.

Right Hand: Battering Ram Knuckles. Effect: +5% physical damage (Blunt). Right hand treated as a weapon when attacking.

Left Hand: None.

"I see nothing. This place is messing with me again." Luke grabbed the horns on the ground that had the deepest blue coloration and headed toward what he now knew was a waterfall and pool of concentrated mana. He dipped a finger in, cautious now that he knew what he was dealing with. There was no pain, no sudden death. That was a plus. It still seemed like simple water to him, so he stepped in and got to work.

He used his pure strength to forcibly smooth the damage that had been done to Cookie by the guardian of the third Zone. He soothed her the whole time, knowing that the process must be painful. Still, since she was so egotistical about her looks, Luke knew that he should try to fix up all the scars. Shaved goat horn, mixed with the water, acted as a kind of glue. When he was finished filling in everything that the water couldn't do by itself, Luke gently placed Cookie into the pool. He waited by the poolside for a few days, letting the mana thoroughly soak in, and fretting for her the whole time.

During that time, he found that the mana pool had carved a channel down through the exact center of the Zone and into the next one. He took a half hour and explored the new stream, finding a new pool in the center of Zone two that had *definitely* not been there before. "Yet *another* mystery to explore!"

After a week, he pulled Cookie out of the water and tried to shave down any new protrusions, even going so far as to smash Cookie against the ground as hard as he could over and over. Luke wasn't worried; during the week, she had started to shine a deeper blue that let him know she would be harder to break. The extra bone material stayed on, and seemed almost as strong as the original. "Good… good… time to flatten a monkey."

He followed the stream downhill and charged straight at the Stone Ape. It watched him come, and prepared itself to counterattack as it always had. Cookie swung around into its face… and the Stone Ape shattered just like that. Luke was shocked, but dove forward and caught the pearl that fell from the creature.

Damage dealt: Unknown. You are using a weapon that has not been quantified by your skills.

"Stop trying to make me eat *Cookie!*" Luke screamed at the screen, his eyes wild and his chest heaving.

You have slain Stone Ape Guardian (Tier 2, level 3). Potentia gained: 1. Slaying a creature two levels lower than you reduces Potentia gained! Caution! Defeating a guardian will spawn two more at the same level! All new spawns will remain for twelve hours after the most recent guardian was defeated, then fade away until only a single guardian remains!

You have gained a skill pearl (T2) from a Stone Ape Guardian! You can either use the pearl right away by swallowing it, or combine fifty pearls at a time to upgrade the skill rarity!

Luke scanned the notifications and looked into the distance. Two slabs of stone lifted from the ground over ten seconds and resolved into Stone Apes. "Well, now I know what I'm gonna be doing for the next year or two!"

He dove into the fray, shattering the two guardians with a swing each. Four more appeared, and soon there were so many spawning and attacking all at once that he had a seemingly never-ending stream to fight against. "Level five, huh? Wait, no. It said three. Why did I think it was five? I wonder how hard it's *supposed* to be to kill you?"

Hundreds of guardians were popping out of the ground every second, and Luke was starting to get torn up by their claws. Even though he could kill them with one hit using Cookie, he couldn't react fast enough to dodge what was now a swarm. His armor was rags at this point, the metal claws easily able to tear through the goat hide. Only the fact that he had started with half a foot of leather made it difficult for the guardians to get at him. A deep slash opened up his side along his left ribs, and Luke roared furiously. Changing his grip, he started swinging Cookie in a huge arc; becoming a whirlwind traveling toward the edge of the Zone.

He made it, barely, and fell into a heap once he had found safety. With trembling fingers, he unscrewed Cookie and drank the water stored inside. Soothing warmth emanated from his stomach, and the raw mana traveled along his new mana channels like the world's best medicine. It actually *was* this world's best medicine, as far as he knew. Luke's wounds didn't close instantly, but when he pulled up his status, he could see the number ticking upward.

Health: 87/150. Caution! You are bleeding heavily!

You have slain Stone Ape Guardian (level 5) x439. Potentia gained: 439.

Current Etheric Xenograft Potentia: 3,439/3,400 to level 8!

You are able to increase in level! Do so now? Yes / No.

"What? I thought I was something like fourteen thousand away? Let's see... oh. That was the skill, not my level. Got it. Hmm. No." Luke stared at the Potentia hungrily. "What are you… is there anything else you're used for? My skill wants you too, yes?"

Checking access levels… no trainer present within [error] miles. Early access granted.

Etheric Xenograft Potentia is used to increase the potential of your being, or applicable skills to bring them to the next tier or level.

"How much do I need to bring Fully Geared to the next level?" Luke had finally found *something* to be excited about.

Current exp in skill: 477/11,000 to skill level 10! Level ten is an important threshold, the barrier between tiers! To break through the tier, you need double the experience of level 9 (5,500) to break through to the next tier.

"I have nowhere near what I need…" Luke took a long breath and continued to wait until his health had returned. "I have two options, Cookie. Level myself so that I have a higher reaction speed, or save up the exp. But if I level myself, I might not get any exp from the guardians anymore…"

A third option appeared in Luke's mind, and his eyes lit up. "It said that I can get a skill per pearl tier from each monster!"

Luke had pearls for days. He pulled out a T1, T2, and T3 from his goat hide canteen, swallowing them down in order.

Skill gained: Bum Rush. T1, level 0. Mana cost: 10

Effect 1: At the cost of 10 mana, once per minute you can empower your forward charge, allowing you to cross the distance in one second that you can normally sprint in five seconds. Extra effective for knocking over defensive lines!

"What's a Bum?" There was no answer to Luke's question, so the next pearl went down.

Skill gained: Goat Call. T2, level 0. Mana cost: 10.

Effect 1: Lure goats to your location, forcibly. Near impossible for any goat to resist.

Bonus 1, at range: Lure goats from up to a mile away.

"All right, so not every skill is a winner; good to know." Luke grimaced at the new skill. Why would anyone *want* more goats near them… wait. He could lure them closer and then *kill* them! This skill was *amazing*! The next pearl went down.

Skill gained: Innate Balance. T3, level 1. Mana cost: none.

Effect 1: You gain an innate balance when walking on narrow ledges or anything that you are attempting to walk on that requires good balance. This skill is modified by the sub-characteristic Physical Reaction. Current balance increase: 5%. (passive ability)

Bonus 1, at range: When jumping or leaping, balance bonus doubles.

Effect 2: The bonus is active at all times, not only when on narrow walkways.

Just to see what would happen, Luke then ate another T1 pearl from a goat. No new skill appeared, so he put the others away carefully. No need to waste them, who knew if he would someday come back and get these pearls all the way up to tier five? In fact... now the pool of water that had formed in the Zone took on a new meaning. Should he hide his pearls in the water? He decided that would be better than lugging them around.

"Then I'll lure in my dinner!" Luke considered his new skill with glee. The goats had been trying to hide recently. Now... now he could *force* them out into the open.

"Goats! I. Am. *Hungry!*"

CHAPTER TWENTY-THREE

"Goat Call! *Baa!*" Luke ordered his skill to activate, and a strange bleating tore out of his mouth and resounded through the air. It didn't take long before a couple of goats started running toward him, clear confusion in their annoying square eyes. Right now, Luke was after food, so he decided not to use Cookie to turn them into inedible paste. He set her down and took a step forward, driving a fist down as the goat passed.

Splat.

For an instant, there was a shimmer over Luke's hands that formed two curled goat horns. The horns started in front of his knuckles and curled back and over his wrist. As soon as his attack ended, so did the shimmering blue horns. Luke looked down at the demolished goat and frowned.

Damage dealt: 110 blunt damage. No Exp gained.

"How much health does a goat have?" Luke asked the air, getting only silence in reply. When the next goat jumped at him, he swatted it with his left hand much more gently. No horns this time, and Luke's actual fist hit the goat.

Damage dealt: 88 blunt damage. No Exp gained.

"Huh." He hit the next goat as hard as he possibly could,

his fist meeting the charge directly. The goat detonated into gore and bone fragments.

Damage dealt: 315 blunt damage. Critical hit! (current maximum damage achieved!) No Exp gained.

That last hit had contained everything Luke could muster, and he was panting after putting that much force into it. He thought over it for a while as he went to the top of the Zone and sat amongst the bones that he had collected. "Absorb goat horns."

Fully Geared activated. Target: horns of Battering Ram. Absorbing... 1/500 in progress. 500 total needed. Time until completion: 4:59:59.

"I hate that I need to reabsorb them if I want them on my other hand." Luke sat amongst the disintegrating horns and thought about the changes in his body. He had always thought that it was using Cookie that killed everything in a single hit, and she was definitely deadly... but part of it was definitely his own power. Using only about a third of his strength with Cookie, he could reduce goats to a splatter. He wasn't sure how to feel about the fact that he could achieve the same effect by putting everything he had into a punch, but he was happy to know that using Cookie was the superior option.

While he sat there contemplating, he used Goat Call every once in a while. The goats tried to run away when they got close to him, but the compulsion drew them in. To get food, he took them and gently snapped their necks, building up a pile of meat. Five hours passed as he sat there in silent thought.

Battering Ram Horn (x500) have finished being absorbed by skill 'Fully Geared'. You are now able to slot the Ram Horn as a fist weapon for either right or left hand slot.

"Left." The skill bound onto his left hand, and he punched twice. As his hands shot out, blue energy horns appeared over each hand for a bare instant. "Neat. Good to have a backup for when Cookie needs a rest."

Luke got to his feet and jogged down to the guardian area. Dozens and dozens of guardians stood at the edge of the Zone, and he remembered that twelve hours hadn't yet passed since his last fight here. "Isn't there supposed to be different types of you based on the location? Monkeys as far as the eye can see… or does it change further into the Zone? Is that what it means?"

Mana: 142/190. (38 mana (20% total) reserved by right and left fist weapon)

He activated Bum Rush. Luke's legs tensed, mana flowed into them, and he shot forward. He crossed the final one hundred feet in that single flash of motion, and joined combat with a roar, slamming Cookie through three stone heads before she started to lose momentum and he came to a halt. Their bodies crumbled, and he laughed at the rush he felt from traveling so fast. "Once per minute? That's fine by me!"

Luke lashed out with Cookie one-handed, backhanding an ape that tried to jump on him as the weapon passed.

Damage dealt: 91 blunt damage. (Physical damage reduction detected.)

The ape was reduced to powder, only leaving behind its metal claws and a pearl. That seemed to happen about ten percent of the time; usually, the claws also vanished into the ground. Luke was looking forward to absorbing these items and seeing how he could use them going forward, but that was a thought for later.

Now that Luke had realized that he could use his hands to attack without damaging himself, he was having an easier time fending off the onslaught of these huge creatures. In a real way, he had been intimidated by them at first. Going from fighting shin-high goats to fighting eight-foot-tall stone apes was quite the shift. It was only as he battled them that he realized their size was actually a disadvantage for them.

There was a large surface area that he could land a hit on, and they could only attack with a small amount of that: claws, teeth, and so on. Similar to a human, Luke supposed. While he *was* enjoying himself, injuries were starting to appear again as the sheer numbers began to overwhelm him. His armor was tattered, and he hadn't taken the time to fix it up before leaping into the fray.

With a wild swing of Cookie, Luke cleared the area around

him and activated Bum Rush to bring himself out of the Zone. He slowed down gracefully, likely on account of his Innate Balance, and glanced back at the throngs of apes standing patiently at the edge of the Zone. "So creepy."

Luke drank some 'water' and healed up, watching the huge horde that wanted to tear him apart but couldn't come any closer. He took off his armor and looked it over, grunting at the deep slashes that had torn through the first few inches. "Can't fix that…"

Although his 'Fully Geared' bonus said it could absorb armor, it didn't seem to count the hides that he wrapped around himself as armor. To be fair, it *was* simply extra inches that kept blades from his actual skin, but wasn't hide a type of natural armor? Not according to his skill. Too bad. Perhaps if he took the time to create actual, *working* armor by using his rusty leatherworking skills, the skill would count it? Luke glanced at the guardians again and shrugged.

"Welp. I guess I need something to do while I wait the twelve hours it takes them to go away." He worked for the next few hours, moving all the gear from the top of Zone One down to his new area. Then he focused his efforts on the small mountain of cured hides, finding the production to be rather calming. He drove a small rock through the hide easily; there was no need for some of the usual proper tools when his strength was enough to shatter six inches of solid stone.

"Gonna need some stretched sinew." Luke worked single-mindedly deep into the night, only looking up from what he was doing when a strange sound reached his ears. The sound turned out to be gravel falling to the ground as all the Stone Apes - except one - were reduced to rubble. Luke was pleased to see that the metal claws and pearls from the ones he had defeated remained on the ground, shimmering or reflecting light.

He stood and stretched, then went to collect all the drops. A casual swipe sent the only guardian to join all the fallen ones, and Luke had a minute before the others would come after him.

He managed to get everything back to camp, and activated his skill to absorb the metal.

Fully Geared activated. Target: Metal Gauntlets of Stone Apes. Absorbing 1/10. 1000 total needed. Time until completion: 37:58.

"A *thousand* are needed?" Luke snorted as he looked at the *ten* measly items he had grabbed. There were more a little further into the next Zone, but certainly not a *thousand*. He ran over to collect the rest of the metal claws, and dragged them back over the cooling remains of the two guardians that had tried to stop him. "Now I have eighty, but... this'll take a while."

He got to work on his goat-leather cuirass, finishing a rough version after only another half a day. Now that he had made a test model, Luke knew that he could do it faster. There would be fewer mistakes next time; working off a prototype would help. The metal gauntlets had all vanished into... his skill or something, so now he decided to see if he could start absorbing the chestpiece. "Fully Geared, activate!"

Fully Geared activated. Target: trash-quality mana-dense cuirass. Absorbing... 1/1. 100,000 total needed. Time until completion: 00:59.

"Yeah, no." Luke cancelled the counter and started over, making a new chestpiece. "I just needed to see if that would work."

Over the next few weeks, Luke continued to grab gauntlets and improve the quality of items he was making. Every time he made a new design, he would throw it away unless it reduced the number of items required.

Fully Geared activated. Target: flawed-quality mana-dense cuirass. Absorbing... 1/1. 10,000 total needed. Time until completion: 00:59.

Fully Geared activated. Target: common-quality mana-dense cuirass. Absorbing... 1/1. 5,000 total needed. Time until completion: 00:59.

Fully Geared activated. Target: excellent-quality, intricate mana-dense cuirass. Absorbing... 1/1. 500 total needed. Time until completion: 00:59.

"All I needed to do was make it the highest quality I could, make patterns on it, and use the best material I had on hand!" Luke pretended to be cheerful, but the words were bitter. He had spent a *week* detailing this piece. "It won't take as long next time, just gotta keep telling myself that…"

A month passed, then two. By that point, he had absorbed enough metal gauntlets to be able to use the claws himself! Luke got ready to start tearing large chunks out of the Stone Apes, but found himself disappointed at the result.

Metal Gauntlet (x1,000) have finished being absorbed by skill 'Fully Geared'. You are now able to slot the Metal Gauntlet as a gauntlet (Armor) for both right and left hand armor slot.

"Armor? But… they're claws!" Luke really disliked the seemingly nonsensical nature of this skill. "Ugh… right hand."

Gear

Head: None.

Shoulders: None.

Gauntlet: Metal Gauntlet (Stone Ape). Effect: +10% overall health. Hands are considered armored when attacked. Strength: slashing/piercing attack reduction (80%). Weakness: Blunt force, magical, elemental damage reduction (2%).

Torso: None.

Legs: None.

Feet: None.

Right Hand: Battering Ram Knuckles. Effect: +5% physical damage (Blunt). Right hand treated as a weapon when attacking.

Left Hand: Battering Ram Knuckles. Effect: +5% physical damage (Blunt). Left hand treated as a weapon when attacking.

"Oh! It goes over *both* hands? I am confused by the strange, and at times, nonsensical, way things work. Okay, ten percent health? Not bad; I can see how that's helpful. I like life." Luke stepped toward the edge of the Zone, steeled himself, and blocked a metal claw with his left hand.

Clang. The attack stopped just above Luke's skin, and a translucent three-fingered gauntlet appeared over his hand and halfway down to his elbow. Luke gripped the monkey, then punched with his other hand to demolish it. "Interesting. That still hurt a little… it reduced eighty percent of the damage, but the force of the strike still hurt. Just like wearing armor naturally. Now I'm not bleeding, though, so that's extra-handy."

Health: 162/165.

The real danger from the Stone Apes was the damage over time that he took. Bleeding, infection if the wound would ever be left unattended, and so forth. His layers of hide were usually enough to stop his guts from getting exposed to the open air, but it was still concerning when he was surrounded. Luke had come close to death *far* too often to take these creatures lightly, no matter how easy it was to kill them.

"Let's see... the skill says I can devote more mana to it for increased power, right? Let's add all of my mana, except what I need for my Leap... that's... twenty percent to my weapons, and seventy-four percent to my gauntlets, leaving eleven mana. Perfect." He accepted the changes, and his hands lit up. The armor that had only appeared during a block was now clearly visible as a shifting layer of blue energy over his hands.

Health: 259/261

Mana: 11/190 (179 reserved)

"Enough of this; there's work to do." Luke ran out and began testing the capabilities of his weapon and armor, trying to see how far he could get through the area. He even considered trying to get through and clear the Zone, but as soon as he passed what he estimated to be the one-third mark, all the creatures sank into the earth behind him and an equal number of a *new* type appeared in front of him. These were Stone Leopards, and they were *fast*. Beyond that, they had the same metal claws as the apes, but on all four paws.

Slash.

Health: 220/261

"Hold on a min-"

Slash.

Health: 172/261

"What in the actual *abyss!*"

Unless he caught the attacks with his hands or forearm, the attacks seemed to take huge chunks out of his health; *way* more than those of the apes. No... it appeared that *only* his armor had the health boost? Luke had no choice but to retreat, and as soon as he passed the previous one-third mark, the leopards vanished and the apes appeared again. He needed to test the capabilities of this armor, and see what it was doing to him.

CHAPTER TWENTY-FOUR

On the eighth month after he'd started working on his cuirass project, Luke finished the final chest piece he needed. He absorbed it right away, and thought over what had happened in the last six months.

Luke recognized that his carelessness in charging through guardian territory had nearly cost him his life, and he had done extensive testing with his armor since then to see what *exactly* it did. As it turned out, the 'extra health' was another way to say 'armor durability', but his Sigil hadn't known how else to quantify the skill. As soon as he had made that realization, the skill had shifted to showing health and armor. Luke scoffed when he thought about that mistake, which had nearly killed him.

The armor effect only came into play when an armored area was hit, which was why it seemed like he was losing such massive chunks against the leopards. Now - today - he would finally gain proper chest armor.

Excellent-quality, intricate mana-dense cuirass (x500) have finished being absorbed by skill 'Fully Geared'. You are now able to slot Goat-hide Cuirass for the torso armor slot.

Gear

Head: None.

Shoulders: None.

Gauntlet: Metal Gauntlet (Stone Ape). Effect: +10% of overall health is added as armor. Hands are considered armored when attacked. Strength: slashing/piercing attack reduction (80%). Weakness: Blunt force, magical, elemental damage reduction (2%).

Torso: Goathide Cuirass (Crafted). Effect: +4% of overall health is added as armor. Torso is considered armored when attacked. Strength: slashing/blunt attack reduction (60%). Weakness: piercing, magical damage reduction (1%).

Legs: None.

Feet: None.

Right Hand: Battering Ram Knuckles. Effect: +5% physical damage (Blunt). Right hand treated as a weapon when attacking.

Left Hand: Battering Ram Knuckles. Effect: +5% physical damage (Blunt). Left hand treated as a weapon when attacking.

Luke grunted in dissatisfaction at how much *less* protection the leather offered compared to the metal gauntlets. Still, the 'torso' was where so many of his important bits were located. He reallocated his mana, sending fully half to his torso, twenty-four percent to his gauntlets, and leaving his weapons alone. He still did enough damage to kill the creatures with a single hit, so long as the horns appeared, and he didn't end up punching stone with his bare knuckles.

Total Armor: 109

Torso: 71

Gauntlets: 38

A glance at his status showed new information, and Luke was pleased. Having his torso protected with about a third of the total damage he could otherwise take was *great*. It was time to challenge the third Zone and finally clear it. Standing up, he prepared himself. Today was the day. He had a plan. He had a goal. "*Go!*"

Holding Cookie in his left hand, Luke started sprinting toward the Zone boundary. The guardian was ready, and it reared back to strike at him. "Bum Rush!"

Luke zipped past the glistening claws, *almost* too close, only slowing eighty feet behind the ape. He didn't look back to confirm, he just *ran*. His goatskin-wrapped feet were pounding against the rocky ground, and he laughed at the fact that the ape was *far* too slow to catch up.

CAL Scan
Level: 7
Current Etheric Xenograft Potentia: 7,304/3,400 to level 8!
Body: 21.65

- *Fitness: 32.2*
- *Resistance: 11.1*

Mind: 13.35

- *Talent: 13.7*
- *Capacity: 13*

Presence: 11.1

- *Willpower: 12.2*
- *Charisma: 10*

Senses: 14.75

- *Physical reaction: 19.5*
- *Mental energy: 10*

Health: 161
Mana: 235
Mana regen: ~~3.33~~ 100 per second (Overridden by local ambient levels.)

Over the last year or so, only his Mental Energy and Charisma had failed to increase. The Mental Energy made sense; how would he train it? The other, Charisma, only made sense after he realized that he had already maximized his relationship with Cookie. There was no more 'up' to go, they were the best of best friends!

Luke crossed the boundary, and a single cat appeared in the distance. Success! The number of creatures here *was* determined by the number of apes! "Here, kitty, kitty...!"

The leopard came after him, and as it jumped, Luke *rushed*. They passed each other, and this time Luke took a slash in passing that would have opened up his stomach even an hour previously. The reaction times on these things were *way* too high! Something in this world had to be broken; there was no way an actual novice was ever intended to come through here. "Tutorial, my *tush*. Without armor, that would have taken at *least* forty of my health, and more over time from bleeding."

Health: 153/161

Torso Armor: 47/71

Ghostly cracks spread all over his cuirass, and Luke landed and started sprinting in a panic. He had a head start, but the cat would be faster; it had proven that already. Putting everything he had into it, Luke dashed forward, leaning over so far that he needed to use Cookie as a counterweight to keep him off the ground. Just before he passed the next third of the Zone, a slash opened up the muscle on his right leg, and he tumbled into the open space.

Health: 138/161. Caution: leg crippled. Move speed -30%! Seek medical attention to regain full use of leg!

"Now I need *leg* armor? Filthy mongrel!" The cat had vanished by the time Luke looked around - since he had reached the third section - so he hurriedly opened his canteen and sucked down some water, then poured the remainder over the grievous wound. It started to close, and after a minute he was able to put weight on it. Soon after that, his health and armor had recovered, and the debuff blinked before vanishing. Now mobile again, Luke began cautiously treading through the remainder of the area. It took a short stretch of cautious movement, but he finally found the next guardian… as well as why it hadn't appeared earlier.

There was a massive stone walkway ahead, a flat bridge that connected this guardian Zone and the next. Not for the first time, Luke wondered what the *abyss* was going on with this world; the land ahead seemingly floated on nothing. On the bridge itself stood a single stone creature, which appeared to be a cross between a snake and a human.

"Lamia…?" Luke remembered reading about these so long ago in his storybooks, where monsters were *supposed* to stay! He felt a deep pain in his heart as he looked at the most human thing he had seen in almost a decade. More than a decade? In… Luke had lost count. He… what was he doing? He had been *abandoned* here-

Chime.

Luke blinked and cocked his head to the side as he tried to think of the best way to destroy the monster that was waiting for him. Even if it were larger and stronger than the others, faster, whatever, Luke was sure he could still kill it if he got close enough. "No time like the present!"

He activated Bum Rush and appeared right in front of the creature, killing it easily and walking proudly forward to claim his reward-

"What?" Luke had certainly gotten *closer* to the beast, but he hadn't attacked it yet… what was happening? "Are you magical, you sneaky snake? Are you a sorcerous slitherer? Can you make unicorns with your hallucinations? Can you give me hallucinations?"

"Wait… it was…" he had a dark thought, and the small grin on his face twisted into dark rage. "You… it was *you* who took away my hallucinations, wasn't it! *Wasn't it?* Give them *back*!"

Now he really *was* running at the guardian. He felt something brush his thoughts, but he shoved aside the attempt to control him and lashed out with a fist. The snake dodged, using its impressive mobility to sway under his attack.

Humanoid hands tipped in metal claws created sparks as they skittered over his torso, opening up the goat-hide wrapping but failing to penetrate the magical armor that his skill generated for him.

Health: 160/161

Torso: 62/71

The distraction apparently opened his mind to an attack, and for another moment, he was triumphantly stepping over a pile of rubble on the long bridge... then he snapped out of it and landed a swift strike on the lamia's left arm, reducing the stone limb to dust. "Nice one! That's the way Cookie crumbles! *Haha!*"

Another hit, and the lamia was a full snake, no extra limbs. "That's better! Now we... a unicorn!"

A pink fluffy unicorn had captured Luke's attention and held it only until he glared. He was in the middle of a battle; he didn't have time for-

The slight whistling that had captured his attention turned into a stone tail that struck him on the side; not damaging him, but sending Luke sprawling *far* too close to the edge. He rolled himself closer to the center, managing to miss the swipe that was going to send him over and to his death. But... *but*! Cookie took the hit that was meant for him, and flew into the air. For one long, chaotic second, Luke thought he could catch her. Then... then she went over the edge.

"No! *No!*" Luke was on his feet in an instant. Without a conscious choice, his armor fizzled out and one hundred percent of his mana was diverted to his right fist weapon. His punch hit the lamia so hard that only an outline of dust remained, the rest having turned into shrapnel that spun out into the void. A pearl dropped to the ground, rolling to the edge and pausing as if waiting to be picked up.

Luke didn't notice. He was half-hanging over the edge of the bridge, screaming after Cookie. He could see her twirling, and knew that she must be terrified right now. Cookie was afraid of heights, and he had actually made *fun* of her in the

past for that by showing off how great his balance was on the edge of the world, time and again!

The blue air only allowed for a certain distance to be visible, acting like a light fog that increased in density the further away you looked, but today, just for an instant, Luke was able to see Cookie stop on something. She had passed a bridge, two... then she had stopped, and was swallowed by the fog once more. "You made it to a lower Zone! You're *safe*, Cookie!"

Luke stood and bellowed over the edge, "I'll come for you! No matter how long it takes, I'll find you! Don't be too scared... I know being alone is terrifying, Cookie. I'll come for you. If something gets in my way... I'll *kill* that *something*."

Standing up, he found that there were two lamias slithering toward him with the grinding sound of stone on stone. His eyes flashed darkly, his armor came back into being, he charged at them. Luke needed to vent some of his fury, and they seemed to be happy enough to be his targets.

"Greetings, *something*."

CHAPTER TWENTY-FIVE

- ANDRE -

Andre stood on top of a cliff, gazing down at the dry valley below him. He had been preparing for this moment for years and was looking forward to seeing how his regrowth project panned out.

This was going to be his first proof-of-concept attempt. If he could use his power to grow plants in the harsh terrain below him, Andre would feel much more comfortable with his long-term mission of returning the Scarocco desert to a grassland, and potentially even to farmland or forest. "First step… adding mulch and dead matter!"

Mana poured out of him, a huge amount from the environment bound to him, which his studies proved no Mage or other person could even really handle. The truth of the matter was that the mana wasn't *really* coming from Andre. He had bound the *entire* forest behind him, and he was drawing on that accumulated mana to fuel the process. The valley below started to change in texture and coloration as a thick moss grew over the sand and rocks, absorbing nutrients, but especially living and dying much faster than was natural. Sand vanished and rocks shattered as they were eaten, absorbed, or had root systems plunge through them.

Moss gave way to fungus, which sprang up, blossomed, and withered, leaving behind fertile mulch. Andre threw a pouch into the air, where it unfurled and rained seeds into the valley. All sorts of seeds and spores had been stored within: ferns, weeds, flowers, and other nutrient-fixing growths. By the time all the seeds landed, they had already begun to sprout. Andre dropped to a knee and spat out a mouthful of blood; a backlash from channeling too much power. He was rapidly healing, thanks to his binding ability, yet it still took a lot out of him.

He looked over the valley. While it couldn't yet be described as lush or verdant, it was on its way. Andre stood and wiped his mouth, feeling the weight of the last few years on his mind. He had tested out on all the required learning of plants and mana manipulation formulations, and had graduated *years* earlier than expected from his official training as a Druid of the First Circle. Andre knew there were other reasons that he had been left to his own devices, but he liked to think that it was all due to his adept handling of his abilities. To be on the safe side, he met up with Xan once a month and discussed how things were going, but in general, he was on his own. "Heh. Old man thought I'd be forced to stay with him the whole time."

In fact, he had been hoping to see Xan soon and had rushed this project so that he could show off his progress. There were only two years remaining before his Kingdom-mandated training was over, and he wanted some achievements under his belt. Xan was getting praised up and down for his newly developed training method, and all future Druid Initiates were going to be subjected to it. Andre winced at that; he didn't want any part of the credit. *Someone* would eventually want revenge for the brutal training regimen.

Andre took a deep breath and opened his status, hoping against hope that *this* success would finally generate a new ability for him.

Level: 8
Current Etheric Xenograft Potentia: 7,421/5,500 to level 9!
Body: 8.7

- *Fitness: 8.3*
- *Resistance: 9.1*

Mind: 28.05

- *Talent: 20*
- *Capacity: 36.1*

Presence: 8.65

- *Willpower: 12.2*
- *Charisma: 5.1*

Senses: 7.55

- *Physical reaction: 8.9*
- *Mental energy: 6.2*

Health: 141
Mana: 491
Mana regen: 6.67 per second

Abilities: 1

Andre sighed at the sight of the very lonely 'one' that showed in his abilities section. Years ago, when he had first gained Bind by Blood, he had thought that it was the start of an *amazing* journey to make him a super-Druid. But… since then, there had been *nothing*. No new abilities, though at least he had gained huge surges of Potentia. All of his leveling bonuses, seven levels' worth, had gone into increasing his Capacity so that he could channel vast amounts of mana.

While his current ability was great - more than great, really - he had no combat utility. Without an ability to cause harm, he would remain trapped at the First Circle. There was simply no way to make the living creatures submit to bindings, not unless they either *had* to, or a Druid could *convince* them. His Charisma made that second option useless, and Andre wasn't going to give up improving his Capacity just so that he could skip steps.

Just as he turned to head over to his current campsite, Andre froze and dropped to his knees as weakness and *loneliness* washed over him. "What…? My connection to the forest?"

"We got him, friends." A *human* voice? Three people that were very much *not* Xan walked into view. Andre didn't know who they were, but in order to not only sneak up on him, but also cut off his connection to the woods, they needed to be powerful Druids themselves. At least, more powerful than he was. Going by the large beasts accompanying them, they had to be at the Second Circle.

If they were at the Third Circle or higher, Andre would already be dead. Unless you were at a similar level of power, the ability to command the *earth itself* tended to generate instant death against your opponent. Target acquired? Earth opens up and swallows them, slams shut. Death, unless you could counter it somehow. Andre got to his feet and lifted his Livingwood Staff in a defensive position. It wouldn't help against their abilities, but it made him feel better. "Who are you, and why are you attacking me?"

"Attacking you? No… we're just here for a friendly little… chat." The lead Druid stated with a nasty smile as his scarred hyena companion chuckled. The other humans smirked and fanned out. Just like that, Andre found himself trapped against the edge of the cliff.

"Not attacking me?" Andre pushed mana into his lungs and shouted the next words as loudly as he could, making the leaves in the trees rustle softly in reply. "Pursuant to Druidic accords of conduct, chapter four, section seven-point-one, these three have initiated hostile actions toward me, a First Circle Druid still within the Kingdom-mandated training period!"

The three Druids paled, and their animal companions snarled and took a sharp step toward Andre. There was *always* someone listening in this world, and unless they could guarantee that it was only *their* people... the situation was going to change rapidly. "Abyss it, just kill him, Quin!"

"Trevor, you idiot! Don't use *names!*" The leader lashed out and slapped Trevor across the face. "His mentor is at the Third Circle! *Quiet!*"

The third was silent, taking the opportunity to simply dash forward along with a medium-sized Direwolf. Andre met the two with his staff, and the sharp retort of clacking wood sounded over the valley behind them. There was a yelp as the Direwolf took a smack to the head, and Andre kicked it to the edge. It scrabbled against the rock, whining deeply as it began to slip backward, pulled by its own weight.

Andre had no damaging abilities. Knowing this, he had thrown everything into his staff and hand-to-hand fighting when training with Xan, rapidly becoming as proficient as his mentor in technical skill. Xan had spent decades of time in which he had hardened his body and trained his fitness; in a real match, Andre stood no chance of winning. But, right now, he didn't need to win. He needed to *delay*. The man he was fighting lunged and grabbed the wolf's paws, saving it from falling but having to devote himself to that task fully. The struggling animal almost pulled both itself and the Druid over, but vines wrapped around the Druid's feet and helped yank them up.

Thick thorns sprouted around Andre's feet, penetrating his soles and giving him a vivid flashback to his first night in this world. Andre yanked himself away from that spot and rolled, avoiding being rooted. He tried to get into the woods, but the branches of the trees blocked his escape. Teeth closed around his arm, and he simultaneously was pulled back and lost a chunk of his underarm. He *knew* what that portion of his anatomy was called, but the pain didn't allow him to focus enough to think about it.

"You abyssal little *brat!*" There were three staves cracking down on Andre, and the hyena tore into his thigh. "You tried to kill Spot? *Suffer* for your insolence!"

A handful of spores were poured on Andre's face, and he screamed as they sprouted and created blisters and welts in an instant. The pain was incredible, but Andre maintained his will to live and focused on surviving. His bones had cracked wherever the staves came down, so he protected his head and spine. Teeth were tearing into him, so he only showed meaty, non-essential areas.

Then it all stopped in an instant. Not the pain, but the attacks. A soft grinding of stone was all Andre heard before his connection to the land came roaring back; bringing regenerating health with it. His flesh started to knit, and his bones started to realign.

Health: 36/141. Bleeding. Concussion (Major). Internal organs damaged.

"I was almost too late. They *warned* me, and I was still almost too late." Xan's voice reached Andre's ears. It was oddly muffled, and Andre idly noticed that was because his ears had blood pooling in them. "I knew this was a possibility, but I never would have guessed that it would be so soon. Sending Second Circles out like this? Tch… too bad they can't tell me who sent them…"

"Where…?" Andre managed to get out.

"They're just nutrients for your pet project now." Xan informed him darkly, looking over the edge of the chasm before focusing entirely on Andre. "You won't have to worry about them."

"Who?" Andre coughed out a ball of blood as his innards expelled some damaged bits.

"Mercenaries. Druids whose Kingdoms or tribes have fallen, people that refuse to put down roots and call one place home." Xan came into view finally, and Andre blinked away the red tint that was coating his eyes. "The worst kind of Druid; one who doesn't care about the land anymore. It gives them freedom, and certain amounts of power, but they can never really progress further. How's the healing going?"

"It's coming along." Andre used his mana and created a circle around the ball of blood that he had just spat. Since his blood was so liberally sprinkled through the area, he gave away none of his secrets by doing so.

"I like what you've done with the valley. Very nice. Fertile. That'll be a good place to look for magic herbs in a few decades." Xan had walked to the edge of the cliff, and was pretending to admire the view while actually double-checking that the dead Druids were actually dead-dead. There were lots of tricks that they could pull if they had the right kind of abilities for it.

"Thanks, Xan. I figured I needed to get some practice if I'm going to fix hundreds of miles of desert." Andre stood up on shaky legs. His wounds had closed, but the scars were still healing, and he was weak from blood loss and pain. Xan supported him when he faltered, and they looked over the now-green valley one more time before turning and moving deeper into the woods.

"I can't let myself be weak anymore, Xan. I'm gonna have to become deadly."

"I know it, Andre." Xan sighed as he half-carried his charge along. Even with the incredible healing rate he had, the young Druid's wounds had been *fatal*. They were going to take time to fully recover. "But you're a good kid. I hope you never lose that."

"Me too, Xan." Andre's hard eyes didn't match his words in the slightest. They were slightly distant as he read words that only he could see.

Ability generated: Bloodthistle (T4). Passive, Active.

Bloodthistle (T4): 0/300 to level 2!

Effect 1: Marinating a seed in blood will allow you to use mana to grow and control it while it is in your hand. Costs 20-n mana to begin the growth process, and 1-n% mana per second to control it, where n=skill level. Minimum of .01 mana per second.

Bonus 1, at range: Can control the grown plant within line of sight.

Effect 2: If a plant has access to blood, it uses the blood instead of mana. Removes mana cost of controlling plants until all blood is all absorbed.

Bonus 2, Multitarget: You can now control multiple plants and seeds at the same time. This is modified by your 'Talent' sub-characteristic.

"I really do hope that you always consider me a good person." Andre just barely managed to slip the congealed ball of blood and pain-inducing spores that he had bound into his pocket, and forced one more sentence before passing out.

"It matters to me."

CHAPTER TWENTY-SIX

"No, I *know* these don't naturally pollinate each other... I just don't care!" Andre laughed at the silly samples that had been sliding out of his sterile stash for a sesquihoral. He was in hiding and had spent the last few months working with his new ability to create something he could use as a weapon. Currently, he was arguing with a plant that he had created, a combination of fungal spores and dandelions. His goal was to make spores that not only got into the air, but could drift over a huge area like dandelions did.

Since they were sterile, he didn't need to worry about them self-propagating or losing control of them to another Druid. Someone losing their plants to *him* was how he had acquired the weaponized spores in the first place, after all. The fluff that had been created would get into the air, scatter around, then activate only when and where he told it. "Good... just like that... a single pound is enough to cover half a mile if needed. Perfect. *Ooh*! How about you?"

Andre had discovered a deep love of altering plants and combining their species. Currently, he had an ivy plant wrapped around himself that he could use as a whip. Thanks to Blood-thistle, he didn't need to use his hands to control it, leaving staff combat as a viable option. Both the whip and his staff now had thorns filled with paralytic poison that would unfurl upon command, or could be released to give his weapons a ranged option. Andre had vowed that he would never be caught out without protection again.

Beyond his growing weapons, he had made another firm choice. After his connection to his bound plants had been interrupted, the young Druid had decided that he needed to start pouring his Potentia into his binding ability. It was finally time to start doing that; he had been hesitating for far too long. He had high hopes that if he got the tier and level high enough, it would become impossible to tear away his connection to his plants.

Andre had never run into that situation before his life was almost lost, as the Druidic training area was intentionally unbound from any Druid after they were done with the area. This was the only place in The Grove that was kept safe and was *also* not bound. Usually, you had to choose one: be safe, and stay within someone's territory, or be out of controlled lands and fend for yourself.

Perhaps someone with a more powerful binding ability could still take away his bound plants, but he had to hope that he would be able to keep ahead, since he had such a strong head start. Though he wasn't sure that was *exactly* how it worked, Andre could only test his hypothesis by putting in the effort; it wasn't like he could go ask Xan if getting his *tier six* binding ability to tier *seven* would let him fend off the bindings that others attempted to create or destroy in his territory. Asking that out loud was like signing a death warrant.

"I can never tell anyone my actual level, especially not until I can fight off people that will want to hurt me for it," he muttered softly. Here, in the interior of the tree trunk, he could talk to himself without fear of being overheard. The tree, and all the flora in and around it, were bound to him. They wouldn't give up his secrets easily. "Still, I need to tone down how quickly I grow. All the Potentia I'm gaining will be diverted to skills until further notice... that way I will still be able to surprise my enemies."

The nice thing about passive Potentia income was that he gained it all the time, even if it was only gradual. Andre's eyes practically glowed as he glanced over the Potentia he had saved up. Beyond what he had used on himself already... he had eight thousand three hundred and ninety-one Potentia that he had gained without killing *anything*. The people that he knew were watching him would *never* expect that he was this far into his levels and ability increases.

"Devote Potentia to Bind by Blood until a new level cannot be reached." Andre watched as his Potentia drained. His ability level increased to one, two, five, and stopped at tier six, level seven. He nodded appreciatively; there was still three thousand ninety-one remaining, but the next level would cost him thirty-four hundred. A quick calculation later, Andre was smiling brightly. "This means I now have a sixty-eight percent chance of any bond succeeding!"

It was time to set out and start creating a safe haven for himself. This world was vast, as was the base world, and there were less than a hundred living Druids *total*, including the rogue ones that had just died. Some of the remaining Druids had even Ascended, and no longer cared about what they saw as the petty squabbles of a weak world anymore. On the base world, their systems would remain in place... for a while. In The Grove, it meant that if he traveled far enough, he could eventually get out of the influence of others and create a space that was entirely his own.

"Surprise, surprise. I need to make a *circle* if I want to go home." Andre rolled his eyes, and sighed. Thanks to his training, he knew how to draw a portal to leave this plane, but his Sigil would not allow him to leave until he was *supposed* to do so.

Even so, he could seek out his own safety on this world. He needed to do so. Far too many people were watching him at all times, and he needed to vanish so that he could return and have a good reason behind his power. He started writing a note to Xan, thanking him for everything.

While he composed his farewell, his vines began whisking around the area. The interior of his current home was easy to empty. A wash of mana, and suddenly all the experimental plants he had been working with were seeds. Anything that didn't produce seeds was wrapped around his body, and carefully controlled so that it would assist in all his motions. The tree filled in with wood as he left, healing in moments what would have taken decades otherwise.

With an intense mental trial, he dissolved his bonds to every plant, undid every circle, and opened the area for whoever else would need to go through training in this area. It hurt, and it made Andre feel *terribly* alone, but it needed to be done. After finishing up and pinning the note to the tree, Andre picked a spot on the horizon and started sprinting.

"Sure would love an ability for movement…! Anything? No? Ugh. Manual manipulation of plants, it is." The vines that were around his legs acted like coiled springs, making each step faster and allowing him to cross vast distances easily. The plants on his torso stayed slightly tensed, supporting his body and letting him mostly relax. Soon, too soon for any *proper* Druid trying to appear haughty and mysterious, Andre had left the training territory he had bound and was shooting across a fertile valley that he recognized from his work a few months back. "Mm. Looks good. Test was successful! That desert is going *down*! Up? I'll heal it."

He landed on the other side of the split in the land, pressing onward. Andre continued running for four days straight, pausing only when he absolutely *needed* to bind something and heal his overexerted body; or when he found something extra interesting. Easily half of all the travel time was used by going around areas where dangerous creatures or plants roamed, but this close to the Druidic training grove, there wasn't much of interest. Still, there were a few seeds from fruits or vegetables that he could coax into providing him sustenance wherever his new home would end up being.

"Just keep running, just keep running!" Andre sang as he continued running for a week, then two, then a month. It was clear that he hadn't brushed up against any areas controlled by Druids for at least a week; the area he found himself in plainly showed that lack. When a Druid had an area under their control, nature harmonized with itself; everything grew to be beautiful and lush. Here, the ground was rocky and vegetation was sparse. There was a higher likelihood of finding rare or magical ingredients, minerals, or creatures, but he also knew that the danger was on a different scale entirely.

He took a day to recover from all the mental and physical strain, bringing his body and mind into a centered state, thanks to the Druidic teachings and practices that Xan had trained him in for almost a decade. When he finally reached balance, Andre moved out, searching for the place that would eventually become the grove for his Kingdom. There were many requirements, but chief amongst them would be safety and an abundance of resources. He would be the guiding light for any Druids that came after him, and he would also need to be able to train them in a safe and secure environment.

The path of the Druid seemed simple and straightforward, but there was a dire and necessary responsibility hidden in what they did. The truth of the matter was that a Kingdom with an active Druid had healthier residents, a higher probability of Ascenders, and more *power*. The more land in a Kingdom that was bound by a Druid, the more those three things appeared. This meant that the world was in a constant state of war, as the only way to gain more Ascenders - or more *powerful* ones - was to snatch up territory.

Andre's Kingdom had been on the decline for well over a century, ever since their last Druid had become a Paragon and lashed out against them. Right now, the only reason their

Kingdom hadn't been overrun was because the last Druid had accidentally put a 'protection' in place: the Scarroco desert. In fact, the desert was the reason his home country was named the 'Hollow Kingdom', as the loss of so many lifeforms had drastically hollowed out the power of the Kingdom. No Druid *wanted* to clean up that magical mess, and most places were fine with watching the Kingdom decline for a few more decades. Only one *wasn't* – the Dynasty of Dogs - and that was why a war had started just before Andre had come to train.

The Archmage had been very serious and sincere regarding how badly Andre was needed, and he had let this information slip to him before opening the portal. He *hadn't* explained that keeping the *kingdom* weak was the motivation for people to kill him while *he* was still weak – straight up politics - but Xan had picked up the slack in that regard. Andre stopped suddenly, feeling a shift in the basic harmony of the biosphere. Something was pulling at the ambient mana in the air, and the minor fluctuations pointed toward a magical plant of some kind.

Andre followed the pull to the source of the fluctuations, feeling them increase in power the farther he walked. He was getting ever more excited; if this plant was generating such powerful fluctuations, it was likely about to break through a tier. If he could claim it for himself... the rewards would be immense.

The terrain had gone from 'rocky' to 'severely damaged' as he continued following the mana fluctuations. He would have sworn that he was being *pulled* toward it, and wondered why. Examining the ground, Andre wouldn't have been surprised if a glacier had come through here at some point; the ground was dug down to the bedrock in places, creating a naturally breathtaking stony vista. He felt somewhat uneasy, as there were very few plants in the area. It was understandable, as there wasn't much soil. However, that meant he needed to rely on his own natural regeneration if combat broke out. Andre traveled across the steep slopes, encountering minimal vegetation, a lack of a substantial regolith, and high drainage density. "This would be a *terrible* place to stay for any length of time."

The ambient fluctuations were coming from just ahead, so he made sure to move carefully. Other things would have been drawn here as well. He knew that if he could feel everything, creatures or other people also could. Even so... careful wasn't enough. As he peered around the edge of the towering rock formation, Andre discovered a cave formed of beautiful rock striations. The fluctuations were clearly coming from inside, but the issue arose from locking eyes with a massive Cave Bear that was blocking almost the entire entrance.

It didn't seem happy that Andre was here. To be fair, Andre wasn't happy that the bear was here. As the beast lumbered out of the cave and stood to its full height, Andre started regretting arriving. There was a certain hierarchy that could be followed when sizing up beasts. Typically, a Tier one creature was pretty normal. A bear back on Andre's home plane was usually just a non-magical–also known as Tier zero - bear. However, a bear that was exceptionally strong but still non-magical *could* poten-tially qualify as Tier one.

A Tier two bear would be called a 'Dire' bear. A Tier three would be called a 'Cave' or 'Ancient' bear. After that, they became something like 'Demon' bears. But, as there was a Cave Bear currently staring at him, nomenclature wasn't Andre's concern at the moment. As a Tier three creature, his studies reminded him that the bear had some kind of empowered melee attack; as well as one that could be used at range.

The Cave Bear was standing at its full height, its head a massive fifteen feet in the air. It bellowed at him, blowing Andre's long golden hair back even from that distance. Then it appeared to be dropping down to charge at him... but Andre spotted the mana gathering at the tips of its claws. He threw himself back behind the rock formation as the front paws released claw slashes that tore deep gouges through the stone where he had been standing.

Andre didn't hesitate; as soon as he was stable, he legged it.

He had run at least a quarter mile before he realized that the bear wasn't following him. Andre looked back and considered his options. "Why would a Cave Bear bother to live in a place like this? There... hmm, there can really only be one explanation. You're trying to hoard that plant for yourself, aren't you? I can work with that."

CHAPTER TWENTY-SEVEN

Andre had left the badland area and gone searching for plants that he could use to subdue that bear. It certainly wouldn't be an easy task, but there was only profit in this plan. If he took down the bear non-lethally, he could attempt to bind it and reach the Second Circle. If he couldn't... he would eat well and wear a fashionable bear pelt cloak. Though reaching the Second Circle only meant a huge push forward in prestige, it would also give him a companion that could help in fights. Another reason that he had waited this long to bind a creature was that it *had* to be done on his own, and the strength of a Druid's first creature determined what they could bind at a later date.

Binding a tier three would allow him to bind a tier one and a tier two as well, if he found ones that he liked. Once he got one of his creatures to tier four—also known as the Multitarget Tier— Andre could have as many ones, twos, and threes as he wanted. That was also why it was so terrible for bound creatures to die. If his bound tier three died, he would need to raise a tier two all the way to tier four in order to gain the multitarget ability. Breaking through one tier was already hard; going through two of them would take *decades* longer.

All in all, getting a tier three to start would give Andre a solid advantage, but actually making that happen was *definitely* at the edge of his capabilities. All of the risks were absolutely worth it in his mind, especially since he would never get close enough to be in danger of an attack. At the end of the day, he would also gain the Potentia from whatever that plant was; the one gathering mana to push through into the next tier. Andre looked at the plant cuttings and seeds that he had and prepared to start investing mana. "Skunkweed, rotting corpse bloom, sapstick, numbing nettles…"

Mana poured out of him and into the plants, and his selections grew, bloomed, and faded in minutes. Andre collected all the pollen and seeds, then started again. On the second run, he integrated the collected pollen. The process repeated over and over as he selectively bred the plants that he needed. In the natural world, these combinations would never happen. They were different plants, and different plant *systems*. It was only through forcing his mana to react with the plants that he eventually achieved what he wanted.

He stared at the abomination… no, *plant*, that had been created; a fleshy bulb that looked like a cross between a pine cone and a succulent. It was small now, but when he wanted it to grow, it would reach maturity in moments. Once it did, it would release a stench that could only be surpassed by smashing the 'fruit'; which was filled with a paralytic sap and thousands of seeds. Additionally, once the sap reacted to the open air, it became incredibly sticky. When the bear attacked it, the sap would get into its fur. That meant the seeds would as well.

Andre had made sure that he could control everything about the plant using Bloodthistle. After a few solid trial runs, he took a deep breath and nodded firmly. It was time to begin.

Circling around the area, Andre found the rock formation that housed the cave and bear, and climbed the back with the help of his powerful body, as well as his bound vines that lashed out and pulled him up the steep rocks seemingly of their own accord. At the top of the stone, he was still only about thirty feet off the ground. The perch was too close for him to feel *comfortable*, but it would have to do. He had originally planned to lower the newly-named Stink-sac plant with a vine, but at this height, a new, *better* idea had popped into his head. Andre sent a pulse of mana into his Livingwood Staff, and a vine began to grow from the top to the bottom.

Both his staff and the vine followed his mental commands perfectly, and soon the staff began to bend. Unlike other woody shafts, his staff would never break from something as simple as *leaning* a little. A few moments later, Andre held a large bow in his hands. He had used a bow fairly regularly when hunting, but he was a terrible hunter. Andre was planning to mitigate that fact by controlling the bow, the string, *and* the ammo with his mana. With an influx of power, his staff grew a branch that fell off the main trunk of his bow: a perfect blunted arrow. The Stink-sac plant wrapped its roots around the top of the arrow - becoming the most bulbous arrowhead he had ever had the misfortune of seeing - and Andre wasted no time in firing it at the bear.

He missed.

On the positive side, the plant landed right next to the bear, which roused from the noise of the impact. Then the creature twitched and sneezed. It hadn't taken long for the bear to notice the stench, and as the plant grew… the smell only got worse. Much worse. Andre had wrapped multiple layers of lavender-infused filter flowers around his face, and the smell *still* got into his nostrils. The Cave Bear screeched like a bobcat and glared at the wriggling Stink-sac, then tried slapping it away. Andre grinned. The pod burst, and the sap splattered the ground and the paw of the bear.

The creature was annoyed at first, then became increasingly desperate as it tried to remove the sap. It was a beast at the third tier, and the Potentia that had mutated it meant that the bear had reached a point where it could be considered *extraordi-*

narily intelligent for an animal. There was no way that it was going to stick that mess into its mouth and bite or lick it off. Instead, it was rubbing its paw against the ground and walls, tearing off tufts of fur and wreaking havoc on the cave's entrance.

Andre knew that he needed to act fast. Mana whirled out of his hands and forced the seeds covering the paws to grow. The bear stiffened and reacted to the mana influx by coming fully out of the cave and glaring up at Andre. The youngster grinned weakly. "Oh… hi there, big fella."

The bear bellowed and jumped at him, scoring deep lines into the stone. When that didn't achieve the intended effect, it reared back and gathered mana on its claws. Andre's pupils dilated as he focused: this was what he had been waiting for! Mana roared out of the Druid, and the small pods stuck on the bear swelled to the size of watermelons. The creature swiped, releasing claw-mana slashes, but the first casualty was the pods.

Andre rolled out of the way of the remainder of the attack and looked down at the miserable bear. It was now coated head-to-toe in sap and was struggling to breathe as the paralytic effect came into play. "Yeah… I'm really sorry about this. I *really* need you out of the way, though."

The bear was starting to blink rapidly, and Andre knew that the thick coating of numbing nettle sap that had settled on the bear was having an effect. If this creature was any smaller, it might have actually died from the sheer amount of poison. He'd known that a small amount of the toxins wouldn't do much, and it was great to see his plan to *marinate* this beast come to fruition. Mana lurched out of him, and in moments, the bear was covered in so many 'fruit' that it looked like a plump rasp-berry. "A rasp-*bear*-y! I love it! The fruit is even pink! Mr. Bear, I'll at least warn you. If you move at all, things are only going to get worse."

Mana: 89/491

Andre quickly checked his mana, swallowing at the low numbers he was seeing. Without a large circle of plants, he could only rely on his personal stores to see him through this trial. If the Cave Bear could get through this…

Wham.

The bear dropped to all fours, and there was a huge splash from all the sap that washed over its legs. It leaped forward and up, digging its paws and claws into the rock face. As a fringe benefit for the young Druid, all the plant matter - and now dirt and rocks - were stuck to the front of the beast, slightly slowing it down. However, this was a powerful magic creature! It wasn't going to be brought down by something *stinky*!

Vines lashed out from Andre, adding an additional and more *potent* paralytic to what was already coating the bear. With a thought, all the pods on the bear burst at strategic locations, ensuring that the vast majority of the sap was soaking into its fur. "Listen, furball. I can do this all day—*abyss*!"

Andre dove off the rock formation as the bear surged upward suddenly; nearly three times as fast as it had been a moment before. It *climbed* the rock wall, and was almost on him in an instant. Madness shone in its eyes, and there was a faint red outline around the beast's entire body. "It has an enrage ability! Bad!"

He was rapidly approaching the ground, but a swinging vine grabbed at an outcropping and swung him around the rock and up to another. This motion just *barely* kept him ahead of the bear, which had dived off the rock and charged after him. Attacks were coming through the air thick and fast; Andre's vine was slashed by a ranged claw swipe as he pulled himself along, but the Druid fired off a vine from his bow that took the place of the first easily. As he swung up, his back and the long green Druid robe he wore were both slashed deeply by the very edge of a claw-shaped mana strike.

Health: 121/141. Bleeding heavily! -4 health per second!

"*Ahh!*" Andre screamed in pain, directing several of his plants to wrap around the wounds and bind them tightly. Before he had dropped a dozen feet, thorns had pierced his skin and sewn the gashes closed. It still hurt to move as recklessly as he was doing, but the other option was death; so he continued swinging along. Each time his wound reopened, a thorny vine pulled it closed. Excruciating, yet effective.

Bleeding effect removed!

Andre landed on top of one of the rocks, panting heavily and finally out of the bear's line-of-sight. He fell to the ground and held still. "Pods... break!"

Mana: 10/491

This was his last-ditch effort. If he didn't have enough time to regenerate his mana, there was no way to escape. He waited with heaving breaths as his mana pool slowly trickled upward, and there was no sign of the Cave Bear. A few minutes later, Andre carefully crawled to the edge of the rock and peered over. His nose nearly touched the bear's, and he leapt back like a fish trying to swim upstream; screaming at the top of his lungs. "*Ahh!* Ahh...?"

The bear didn't move, except for its eyes, which were locked on Andre and filled with hate. Andre drew closer and found that there was a thick coating of debris and plants holding down a thoroughly paralyzed Cave Bear. The red aura was gone, and he realized that the effect must only have a short duration, then weaken the creature for a while. "Well... my mana is back, so no time like the present to become more powerful."

CHAPTER TWENTY-EIGHT

His blood was still running down his back, and there was a shallow pool of it on the top of the stone. Because of this surplus, the circle he created in an attempt to bind the bear was more like an oval, but even so, Andre had high hopes for taking the next step. The Cave Bear was weakened, it couldn't struggle out of the circle, and its personal mana pool had run dry. The conditions were perfect. "Hope this works... I've got the theory down, but never had a chance to test it before. I'm sure you understand."

"*Bind by Blood!*" The Druid roared in agony as the wound on his back popped open and a surge of fresh blood joined what had been added previously. His freshly regenerated mana pool plunged; blood and power circled the bear in two distinct circles before joining together into a purple stream. Symbols and runes formed as Andre's hands rapidly formed seals, the apparent ease actually the product of a decade of study and practice. The circle shrank, moving from surrounding the entire bear to wrapping around its head like a crown.

Then it sank into the bear's flesh, and the bear fell unconscious.

Binding successful! Cave Bear (T3, level 8, Male) has been bound!
Would you like to name this creature?

"Name him Arthur." Andre sighed in relief as the binding took hold. Elation started to flow through him: he was officially a Druid of the Second Circle! Since he had started with one at this rank, he could get two more. Should he get a bird so he could have a scout? Maybe a pet, too, he could use some companionship. He stiffened as a new question appeared, one that his mentor had never hinted about.

Erase the mind of the creature to impose your own will, or imprint the creature?

"I don't understand the difference?"

Erasing the mind will allow you to have perfect control of your bound creature. However, the creature will not take actions on its own. It will need to relearn all instincts over time.

By imprinting the creature, you will make it impossible for the bound being to attack you, but it will be up to you to convince it to follow your orders.

"Imprint." Andre ordered firmly, the mana shifting into a new configuration on Arthur's head as soon as he spoke. "I only wanted to get past this thing in the first place."

Imprinting. Congratulations! You have imprinted a living creature! You have gained the qualifications of a Druid of the Second Circle!

You have gained Potentia: 2,200. (1,200 exp pulled from 'Arthur', 1,000 exp from your Kingdom by achieving the Second Circle while still in training! Make them look good, and the profit will continue!)

"Xan never explained how the Sigil can give us exp…" Andre squinted suspiciously at the text hovering in the air. "I bet they hold back on what they allow us to use after we gain it, or siphon it off somewhere."

There was nothing he could do about that, so he simply decided to tend to his new bear companion. With a thought, all the plants fell off the bear's body, taking most of the debris with it. Andre poured some fungus on the thickest sap and stimulated its growth, and in moments, the bear was covered in rapidly-growing, sap-eating mushrooms. He left it there to recover and climbed carefully to the ground. "Time to go look at the rewards!"

It was highly unlikely that there was going to be anything deeper in the cave. If there had been something stronger than the bear, well... Arthur would have been eaten. Anything weaker than Arthur would have also been eaten, but by the bear. "Ah, nature at work."

Andre shook off his thoughts and reminded himself that this all came together to indicate a safe trip deeper into the cave. He entered the rocky enclosure, finding that the cave was as beautiful as he had expected it to be. After he had side-stepped all the bones and offal that the bear had left at the entrance, he started looking for the plant that was practically calling out to him. The fluctuations were reaching a peak, which meant that the breakthrough was about to happen. He picked up the pace, finding that there was a huge network of tunnels hidden by the cave entrance. Without the energy guiding him, Andre would have become lost very quickly.

He dropped glowmoss as he jogged along so that he could find his way back, and soon he came upon a huge, almost entirely empty, underground cavern. There was a soft sound of running water, and a single crack in the cavern high above allowed a stream of natural light in. This light fell upon a single flower, which was glowing both from the sun as well as the energy building up within it.

Andre slowed down as he stared at the beautiful golden flower. He could tell that its petals were normally white, but at the moment, *all* of it was gold. "What *are* you?"

There was clearly not going to be an answer, and Andre needed to make a choice. If he bound this flower right now, he would be able to pull out all the accumulated Potentia it had stored up. Breaking the tier limit meant that it was just reaching level ten in whatever tier it was in. Thanks to Bind by Blood, *all* of that pure Potentia could be his, right now. Or, he could see what the transformation would accomplish, and bind the flower after it had gone up in power.

It was a tough call, but he decided that he would let the process finish. He surrounded the flower with a binding circle and waited. Hours later, just before the last of the natural light vanished, all the fluctuations coming from the flower stopped suddenly. The golden light faded away, leaving a milk-white bloom. Then, red started to color the white of the petals, stopping halfway up each of the delicate corolla. As soon as the process ended, Andre bound the flower. He had been expecting resistance, a denial, a full-on magical fight. Instead, he swam through a feeling of gratitude as the flower bound to him. The plant was quasi-intelligent!

"Why do I get the feeling that this is thanks for not taking the Potentia?" he muttered uneasily. Plants, even magical-ish ones, had never sent along a concept like *gratitude*. It was far too alien for their instinctual lives. Intelligence in a plant indicated *power*. Dangerous, deadly, focused power. "Let's see what you are…"

"I…! That's not possible! I don't understand… how… *what?*"

Sanctuary Lily (T10). This is the final form of a Peace Lily that has lived through a massive outpouring of death. After absorbing enough blood, the Peace Lily becomes a War Lily, a Lily of the Valley, a Plains Lily, a Death Lily, then finally, a Sanctuary Lily.

Would you like to see the ability of the Sanctuary Lily?

"Yes!" Andre shouted instantly, his eyes scanning across every word that crossed his vision.

This flower has seen peace, war, the rising and falling of the world around it, and become death for thousands by draining the life, mana, and Potentia from all living things around it for decades.

Sanctuary Lily (T10, level 0), Full Domain: Harmonious existence. This Lily will only bind, or remain bound, with something that has not directly killed any sentient being. Any living being which enters the area of its domain will have their bodies and mana held in a harmonious state, unable to stimulate either in a way that would intentionally harm or kill another, as well as being unable to deteriorate.

This does not impact the bound Druid. As the flower's master, you are able to use your abilities to their fullest.

Domain size: 1 kilometer per level.

"I have a *domain?*" Andre fell to the floor, his mind weirdly whirling. When an ability, or apparently a plant, reached tier ten; all the other abilities that it had evolved over time became fused into a single 'domain' that perfectly controlled the area around it. There were higher evolutions, but those were things that only Paragons would likely ever see. Something at tier eleven could only be controlled by a Paragon, and even then, it was… unlikely. Most of the time, natural treasures that reached that point of development were *incomparably* violent. "Hah…! A Druid of the Second Circle has a *domain.*"

Seeing that the Sanctuary Lily had just changed from a *Death Lily* that drained the life out of everything in a large space around it, the desolate badlands surrounding this area - a place where nothing could grow - made much more sense. It was likely that if Andre had come here sooner in the life cycle of this treasure, or drained away the accumulated Potentia to get stronger, it would have reverted to eating him in return to empower itself. "All right. I can't kill anything sentient. That's the first rule. Good thing that I have the ability to gain Potentia in other ways…"

"I can use my mana to damage others, and I can use it to grow things, but no one else can do anything harmful in the domain?" Andre threw a handful of glowmoss up, controlling it as it landed on the ceiling. Mana poured out of him, and the patch of moss rapidly grew until it covered the entire ceiling and provided a soft twilight. "That's a 'yes', then. I wonder what it means by 'unable to deteriorate'? Can people not die in the area of effect?"

A few attempts later, the young Druid found that he couldn't give any Potentia to the Lily. That was settled, at least. The Domain would need to grow naturally over the years, decades, or centuries. On the positive side, if there was one thing an Ascender had, it was time.

"I'm going to need to get on good terms with Arthur, and then start bringing life back to this area." Andre briefly pondered how he kept getting projects that made him start from nothing and shrugged. He might as well get good at doing it: the Scarroco desert stretched for hundreds of miles. Anything he could do now to refine that upcoming process could potentially save him decades. "Interesting... I need to reform the life above this area, but I could start by making this entire subterranean network into a hidden grove."

"That means I would need to find or breed plants that can handle the dark. Then I need plants that can live in sparse soil for a long time before I transition to larger and more stable plants. Night plants, regular plants. Animals, too; gonna need to build an entire ecosystem. Eventually gonna have to do the land as well, if I want a true foothold for myself and my Kingdom." He scratched his beard and looked up at the rocky, moss-covered 'sky'.

"I have no idea why this sort of thing is appealing to me. All I'm doing is making my life harder than it needs to be. I shouldn't take on so many decade-spanning projects." Even though he said those words, Andre was beaming at the rocky ground that had *nothing* in it beyond a single flower. "All right, I've decided. It's a fixer-upper, but it looks like I've found my new Grove."

CHAPTER TWENTY-NINE

- TAYLOR -

"Taylor, you are six years into your training, and I still have to look over your shoulder to make sure that you are doing what I tell you to do." Master Don's voice was calm and collected, but it still made Taylor shiver to hear his admonishing words.

She had seen all too much of what Master Don was like. Over the years, the veneer of being a good person had faded, and faded... until one day he had just given up all pretenses. The Archmage wanted out of his deal with the Kingdom, and the only way that he was going to be able to focus on Ascending was to stay in the World of Names at all times... and place *her* in charge of *his* responsibilities. "Master, the issue isn't that I don't *want* to listen. The problem is that you are looking over my shoulder. Look at this wreck of a man."

Taylor waved her hand at the etiquette trainer that Don had brought in to train her. He was shaking like a leaf, and had soiled himself *again*. "He's terrified of you, and every time you appear, we lose an hour's worth of our time. Cleanse, Purify? Fix him up *again*."

The stench roiling from the rumpled, sweating man vanished even as his clothes smoothed themselves. Taylor nodded as her spells came back to swirl around her, acting like small dogs that needed attention. Master Don looked at the trainer and softly asked, "Is that true? Am *I* the issue, or is Taylor not paying attention as she should be?"

"M-m-master D-don, there is no way that *you-*" No more words got out of his mouth before Master Don had grabbed his neck with his left hand and had a sparkling icicle pointed at the man's eye with the other.

"There is *no* call for lying to me, *Rupert,*" Master Don practically whispered. "I have trained Taylor *personally*, and if you think I don't know *exactly* what she is capable of… hmm. Tell you what? I haven't ever hurt you. But if you fail to train her properly, I will. I will *hurt* you. You won't even remember *why* you are in pain for the rest of your life. Do the job you are supposed to do, and this will only be a dream. You'll have a week of your time vanish from your memory, and a fat sack of gold to retire with. How does that sound?"

"S-s-so *generous!*" Rupert managed not to faint, his own personal training the only thing allowing him to remain conscious. Master Don nodded and walked out of the room that they were staying in, and the man started shaking.

Taylor rolled her eyes. "Cleanse, go on out *again.*"

After Rupert was cleaned up, he started teaching Taylor with a vengeance. Classes had been on-again-off-again over the last few days, but now he was motivated to focus. Taylor appreciated this. When Master Don was watching her as carefully as he had been the last few days, she couldn't make progress.

She had thrown the Archmage's training program away long ago, but she had still been exceeding expectations. Still, she wanted her methods and secrets to *stay* secret. As Rupert babbled, Taylor pulled up her status to see what had changed in the six years she had been training.

CAL Scan

Level: 7
Current Etheric Xenograft Potentia: 2/3,400 to level 8!
Body: 4.15

- *Fitness: 5.2*
- *Resistance: 3.1*

Mind: 12.15

- *Talent: 13.1*
- *Capacity: 11.2*

Presence: 3.4

- *Willpower: 4.7*
- *Charisma: 2.1*

Senses: 20.05

- *Physical reaction: 20.8*
- *Mental energy: 19.3*

Health: 81
Mana: 214
Mana regen: 3.5 per second

Spells
T1: 2
T3: 2
T4: 1
See full listing?

Flame Lance, Shatter Shot, Purify, Cleanse, and Nullify. Against the orders of Master Don, she hadn't taken on any other spells than these. Taylor chose only to look at what had once been Shatter and Fireball, the only two offensive spells to which she currently had access. Thanks to dedicating herself to these two spells, she had brought both of them up a tier and evolved their next spell traits.

Flame Lance (T3): 0/500 to level 4! Mana cost: 12

Effect 1: Create a ball of fire that detonates for 10 fire damage within a ten-foot sphere centered on impact. To cast, the full chant of 'Fireball, heed my call, burn the world, burn it all,' must be used.

Bonus 1, at range: The ball of fire can now be used at range, up to thirty feet. Damage becomes $10+5n$ fire damage, where n = spell level. (Starts at T2)

Effect 2: This spell can be used as a single-target spell. If it is, the damage is doubled, as is the mana cost. A chant is no longer needed to cast this spell.

Shatter Shot (T3): 0/500 to level 4! Mana cost: 10

Effect 1: Create a spike of ice that chills the target, dealing 5 ice damage and 5 force damage. To cast, the full chant of 'Destruction, neither frost nor force, the best of both. Shatter,' must be used.

Bonus 1, at range: The spike can now be used at range, up to twenty feet. Damage becomes $10+(2.5i+2.5f)n$ damage, where i = ice damage, f = force damage, and n = spell level. (Starts at T2)

Effect 2: This spell can be preemptively shattered to create shrapnel that flies out in a cone for ten feet. If it is shattered before landing, only the ice damage is applied. A chant is no longer needed to cast this spell.

Raising these spells to their current rank and level had cost her almost the entirety of the Potentia that she had gained, but she unraveled spells - how they described forcing the spells to respawn - so often and casually now that she had been able to bring her personal level to seven. It still made her grit her teeth in anger that she wasn't able to improve herself faster. Master Don kept bringing her to more dangerous areas to force her to find 'creative' ways to survive, and if her spells were too weak to unravel her opponent, she *would* get killed.

"...which brings us to the newest addition to the... the lineage of the Royal family, Crown Prince Vir! He stands to gain the throne of his father, and oh, Celestials above, *please* be paying attention. I don't want to get an icicle through the eye!"

Rupert muttered these last words when he saw the far-away look in Taylor's eyes.

"Rupert, I can repeat verbatim every word that you've said in my presence since you arrived." Taylor grumped at him, forced to look away from her status. "Relax. I am the best student you will ever have."

"And *so* humble." Rupert scathingly retorted, turning to the board he was writing the royal genealogy on. But when he faced it, Taylor was already in front of him, inches from his face. He screeched and jumped back, "Ah! How did you-"

"*Rupert*. Whether I like it or not, I am the next Archmage. Don has already told you that your time here will basically have been a dream. But, when I leave here, I *will* remember everything about my time. Everything. Keep that in mind." Her words were perfectly inflected, respectful, and in accordance with the etiquette she was learning.

Even still, Rupert's eyes were rolling around, and he seemed faint again. The elderly instructor frantically nodded and bowed several times. "Is there any training method you prefer; anything that I can do to help with your absorption of this information?"

Taylor appreciated his shift in his attitude, and decided to be as direct as possible. "Yes. I need all of the information that you have. I can remember it all, I just need it in front of me. After that, we will work on anything else that is required. Utensils for salad, how low to bow or curtsy, any dances that I will need to know, proper forms of addressing each member of the Noble class. Give me the *information*. Expect that I will understand it and be able to put it into practice immediately. Save your snark and your casual dismissal for the Noble brats that you usually have to train."

What followed this short conversation was sixteen hours a day of information spewing from Rupert's lips... for a week straight. There was so much data stored away in the man's head, specifically so much information that Taylor considered ninety-nine percent useless, that he physically injured himself by trying to verbalize it all in a single week. When he declared with his now-raspy voice that he had told her everything he knew, and had walked her through all of the proper motions that were necessary for courtly etiquette, Master Don suddenly appeared in the room with them.

"Excellent. Test her."

Rupert was incredibly startled, yet so drained from the week of work that he could not muster up a reaction. He simply started calling out what the situation was, and the person she was addressing. "Viscount Frankfurt Turtle, in the palace, at a social gathering of nobility including the Royals. You are not yet the Archmage."

"It is lovely to see you, Lord Turtle." Taylor swept into an elegant curtsy, only lowering herself until her knees were just barely bent. Her eyes remained level with Rupert, then she stood quietly.

"Perfect," Rupert sighed at the response, starting to relax. She had been as good as her word. She *remembered*! "You *are* the Archmage, same situation."

"Evening, Frank." Taylor barely nodded in his direction, making Rupert sputter with indignation.

"You can't just-!"

"Rupert, if I am the Archmage, I can do whatever I abyss-well please," Taylor snapped at him. She let that sink in, noting the faint grin playing on Master Don's lips. Then she gave Rupert what he wanted to see. "However, what *propriety* would call for, is this:"

"Lord Turtle. A pleasure." Taylor bobbed her head respectfully.

"...Correct." Rupert was fully disheartened over the fact that Taylor was going to follow in Don's footsteps so exactly. They went over dozens more situations, and each and every time, she was able to give the perfect response. They held a mock dinner, breakfast, brunch, high tea, and multiple other scenarios. They danced, they held conversations, they dueled.

At the end of it all, there was nothing further that Rupert

could recall to test her on. "She is… perfect. If I had five students like her, I could hire them all to do my job and retire. I have nothing left to teach her."

Rupert's words, though hesitant, showed exactly how impressed he was by her learning capabilities. "Still, to get her used to the treacherous life in the courts, I think you should-"

"Don't tell me what to do." Master Don grabbed Rupert, slapped a sack of gold into his hands, and shoved a spell into his head. Rupert's gaze became blurry and far away. The Archmage shoved the instructor through a portal that came into existence for a brief moment, then turned to Taylor. "Excellent! Now that you are a proper inheritor of my position *socially*, it is time to see if your *self-made* training program will grant you the power that my training program was supposed to do… *if* it had been followed."

Taylor couldn't help but swallow nervously as Master Don grabbed her arm and they teleported away.

CHAPTER THIRTY

"Oh, Taylor... I waited for fifty years. Fifty *years* of trying to find someone to take this Archmage position without killing me off for it. To think I once desired this position, and held it for *centuries* while slapping down competition." Don had an iron grip on Taylor's shoulder and was frog marching her along through a thick morning fog. "Now I am seeing the light at the end of the tunnel, and you... you just decide to do your own thing."

He chuckled, but there was no happiness in the sound; only frustration tinged with fury. "One of the only things that I can't order you to do is spend your Potentia as I see fit... a failing of that Sigil on your brow. *Power*, Taylor. Only power, and being able to *showcase* that power, will convince the Royal court that you are fit for the position. Brutality is the only way to fend off everyone who wants the position. Recall how I have told you that there are only two ways that this title gets passed on? An apprentice takes it, or someone kills the Archmage in a direct, sanctioned duel. Let's be realistic, no one is taking *my* life."

"But by ignoring my orders, you are threatening my freedom, Taylor. My *freedom*. Since you seem to be fine with this, since you seem to want to do things your own way, we will compromise. You get to do things your way, but where I tell you to do it. You have roughly three years remaining before you can leave and return to the Kingdom. Three years before I need to introduce you as my Apprentice... if you are still alive. A question for you, Taylor: will you follow my training from now on, and become what I want you to become? *Speak Truth*."

Taylor opened her mouth and tried to say that she would do what he wanted. However, the words wouldn't come. In her heart, she knew that she didn't want to be anything like this calculating, corrupted Archmage. "I'll become the Archmage."

"Heh, ha! Not good enough. Not even close. Well, let's make a bet. Prove to me that I made the right choice, and you did as well. If you win, we'll do things your way, and I'll never raise a hand against your past or future disrespect. If not... well. Let's just see if you survive. *Resist Gravity, medium*."

"What?" Taylor recognized that a spell had just been cast, but she had no chance to think on it further before Master Don threw her off a cliff. She hadn't even realized that they were *on* a cliff thanks to the fog surrounding them. Taylor hurtled through the air as if she had been the ammo for a trebuchet. She was screaming, but was falling much slower than she had initially expected. This also meant that her travel was a large, gentle parabolic arc. Thanks to that, she was still falling half an hour later.

Eventually, she was far angrier than afraid. "Celestial Feces, just let me get back on the ground already!"

Between the wind, the power behind the throw, the fog, and the much lower gravity that she was being subjected to, there was no way to tell how far she had traveled. By the time Taylor actually got to the wooden flooring that covered this portion of the World of Names, she was ready to fight something out of sheer frustration.

That was the right mentality to have, because as soon as

Taylor touched the ground, she was under attack. She landed on the wooden surface and found that it had odd protrusions. Though the fog was still present, it was starting to clear, which allowed Taylor to see that the bumps on the floor were now staring at her. "He threw me right into a spawn point? That son of-"

Taylor jumped and rolled as a half-dozen stone spikes drilled through the wooden floor and into the spot where she had just been standing. Her gaze traveled over the bumps that were looking at her, and noticed that they resembled stone-clad hedgehogs. "Spikers. Great. At least you're Stone Spikers, and not something annoying like Wind Spikers."

With a wave, fire condensed into an orb on her hand and almost lazily flew toward the largest cluster of Spikers. The fiery explosion created a strange reverse concussive blast from the sheer amount of air it ignited at once; it gave her hope that when she ranked this spell up a few times, it would transform into a type of implosion magic. That sort of thing happened very infrequently, and it was hard to tell if you had gained one, but variant spells did exist and usually had strange effects like this when they were low-ranked.

Damage: 115 x12 (Fire damage). Exp gained: 82 (T2 Stone Spikers x12 destroyed.)

"Why is it that the same monster has different amounts of Potentia? I understand that they are growing at different rates, but it just seems so... messy." Taylor cracked her neck, her hair flowing back into a perfect position. She had to admit that Cleanse had been worth getting so many years before, but she forced her mind away from that memory. "Shatter Shot."

She stated the words casually, but the icicle that went flying didn't lose any power because she was being flippant. When it was most of the way to the next group, she squeezed her fist closed and let the shrapnel shred the Spikers.

Damage: 67.5 x8 (Ice damage). Exp gained: 79 (T2 Stone Spikers x8 destroyed.)

The creatures bled ink as they dissolved into illegible words and stone quills. Taylor scooped a few of the quills up. Even if she didn't have anything to write on, they would work well for marking her surroundings if needed. At that moment, Taylor was more annoyed by the inconvenience of needing to find her way back than she was concerned for her safety and the future. That changed as lightning flashed through the air and she heard two spells clashing.

The ground around her started to shift, and when she looked into the distance, she could see that the wooden ground was shifting, shattering, then lifting into the air and flying toward the commotion. Her face went pale and she started sprinting away from the battle. "Tier eight! Multitarget Area of Effect! That's just *death!*"

Creatures like spells, monsters, and constructs were all rated with the same tier system for an easily explainable reason. Just as when humans were able to control or use them, the results were easily quantifiable. At tier eight, the spell would have four effects, and four bonuses. The bonuses always grew in the same way: the spell became ranged with bonus number one, multi-target with bonus number two, then gained an area-of-effect with the third. Finally, when something became tier eight, the fourth bonus made a *separate,* multitarget area-of-effect. This was the most powerful bonus until tier ten, when the spell shifted into a domain that was created by combining all the other effects and bonuses.

Theoretically, every Ascender wanted to go out and gain spells, abilities, summons, and other enhancements that were already at the highest tier possible; if only so that they didn't need to invest all their Potentia in raising them higher. In *practice*, there was a limit to what any one person could handle. If Taylor ran to a fight where two tier eight spells were fighting, there was an *extremely* high chance that she would just flat-out die. Even if she could nullify magical damage for a few seconds, those wooden spikes that had been fired at her were physical objects. They would pulverize her even if the magic controlling them faded.

After about a mile of running, the echoes of the battle had faded to nothing. She kept going until she could no longer see the direct effects of the battle, but it was impossible to miss the swirling thunderstorm that was moving toward the battle. Taylor watched it move, and very, *very* quietly started to slink away. "Celestials above, a Domain spell..."

Controlling the weather, by definition, was a tier ten spell. A lightning bolt, tornados, and so forth could all be lower... but no one under the domain level could control the *actual weather*. "Don, you terrible, *terrible* person... just where did you send me?"

There was a threatening *cracking* that was coming closer at a high speed, so Taylor rushed toward a book stack and focused on retracting her Presence. In an instant, she was merely a part of the scenery. Her eyes flashed to her characteristics, and she took a deep breath to steady herself.

Senses: 20.05

- *Physical reaction: 20.8*
- *Mental energy: 19.3*

Stealth engage: 100.25%

In order for the mysterious entity to break her stealth, it would require the ability to *do* so. That meant either Senses at the same height as hers, a Presence stat that could directly break her stealth, or some equivalent spell of the Mind or Body designed for that purpose. With a bonus of over a hundred percent chance to her stealth, Taylor felt more comfortable than she should have.

The cracking advanced and soon revealed itself as the ground breaking apart. The shattering earth slowed, then stopped. A small round creature emerged from the ground, and she almost laughed at herself. It was a simple Digrett, a tier one spell creature that made tunnels or pitfall traps. As she was about to stand and kill it, the ground surrounding it crumbled. The 'Digrett' rose higher and higher into the air. It was actually only the *nose* of the huge beast that clawed its way into the open air. Taylor almost spoke out loud in shock, but somehow kept the words from falling out of her wide-open mouth.

"Tier *five* Fissure. Don, you despicable son of a-"

CHAPTER THIRTY-ONE

Taylor had been trapped in the same spot for the last few hours as the Fissure crawled along and snuffled. It was clearly searching for her, as it kept returning to the spot where she had entered stealth. It looked like an abstract cross between a giant lizard and a mole, and she wanted nothing to do with it. The words that made up its body were sharp and full of scribbles, like a twelve-year-old's drawing of something 'scary'. Every once in a while, it would screech and charge in a random direction; clearly attempting to make her break stealth and run away.

"Why is it after me?" There was no reason that a spell at this level should be continually hunting for her. If she had come into its territory, it should have searched for her but eventually determined that she had left. Hunting her like this… that was something that only blood, tracking, or curse spells usually did.

The Fissure chuffed, a sound she hadn't heard before. Then it grunted a few times, and Stone Spikers started pouring out of the tunnel that it had made. Realization hit Taylor hard enough to make her wince. The Fissure must be an evolved form of the spikers, and she had unraveled as many as she could before making her escape. She realized her mistake clearly. "I should have unraveled *all* of them so that there were no witnesses."

If she had just run, and not unraveled the spikers just because she was frustrated, they would have stayed in their area and left her alone when she got far enough away. However, the instant that she turned one of them into a goopy mess of ink and stone, she should have made sure they couldn't seek revenge. How many times had Don told her to do *exactly* that? He was righ-

"*No.*" Taylor stopped that traitorous thought before she could finish it and narrowed her eyes. She had chosen her own path, and she was determined to walk it.

There was a reason that she had chosen to do the things she had done. She had abilities that were apparently incredibly rare. She wasn't just a Mage, she was a *Namer*. So why would she take the same path as the regular Mages? Taylor stood up and walked away from the area. Anyone looking in her direction would only see a vague shimmer in the air, only hear the paper streamers that replaced grass rustling in the wind. Scent? Removed at all times by Purify. Taylor believed that only by touching her would anything be able to find her location.

However, the Fissure stiffened as she carefully walked away. Its sensitive hairs trembled in time with her footfalls as she stepped on the bare earth and sent the most minute of tremors through the ground. It screeched and charged after her, this time not bluffing. Taylor realized that she was caught, so she sprinted away. The ground around her started to break, walls of rock shot out of the ground, and yawning chasms opened up in an attempt to ensnare her.

"Focus *harder!*" Taylor hissed at herself. "If I want to survive, I need to be *perfect!* Not just here, but in *everything* I do!"

Her footfalls lightened, and she ran faster. Taylor was working so hard to control her body perfectly that she missed the moment when her Physical Reaction characteristic went up by point-two.

Physical Reaction has reached 21!

All Taylor really knew was that she was faster and more capable of avoiding the stone shards that were peeling off the walls and flying at her. She started to pull away, and within ten minutes, she could hear the Fissure bellow in fury at having lost her. There was no slowing down. All she wanted to do was put as much distance between them as possible, and maybe start looking for a defensive spell that could be used more than roughly once per day.

"Where do I even start?" At that moment, the Sigil on her forehead flashed and released a loud:

Chime.

There was clearly *one* thing that she could do, and that was to retaliate against the Fissure. It was still hunting her; she knew that much. Perhaps it was time to let it 'find' her? Taylor *needed* to make sure that it was never a threat again. "No. Wait. I just got away... why am I thinking like this?"

However much she tried to avoid the thought, the knowledge that the spell would be after her spurred her into doing something that she really hoped she wouldn't regret. Taylor looked for a book stack and tossed a fireball onto it. There was a huge *fwump* as the air ignited, and Taylor felt the ground shake from the aftershock.

Beyond that, the books on the shelf flew into the air with a mad flapping of pages, creating a plume of smoke and flying books that could be seen for miles around. If this didn't draw in the spell that was after her, she'd take a bite out of her Grimoire. The next step of her plan was to get into position and prepare her ambush.

This part was deceptively simple. All she needed to do was wait, and not get caught. Then, she'd kill the Fissure and everything it brought with it. Not even realizing that she was doing it, she whispered the words that Master Don had told her every day since they had first arrived in The Library. "Everything here is a step on the path to power. If it doesn't join you, take its Potentia."

Her body started trembling, not in fear, not from any realization of moral failing, but because the Fissure was moving so fast under the ground that the whole earth felt like it was falling down. She started preparing an attack, holding the spell and wrapping mana around it until it appeared to be cocooned in shimmering purple power. "Here we go."

The beastly Fissure exploded out of the ground in a shower of stone and dirt, screeching as it saw that the commotion was a basic fire. Taylor finished her spellcasting, and Shatter Shot zipped away from her hand, trailing dense mana like a spider-web. The icy spell penetrated the Fissure, and Taylor started dumping power into the connection, screaming as weakness gradually overtook her. "Let me *read you!*"

A screech was her only answer, and the Fissure attempted to turn. To her benefit, the spell was fast only in straight lines, giving her a few extra seconds to make her attempt at Naming the creature. "Come on. Come *on!*"

The childish scribbles that made up a large portion of the spell started to twist. It stomped the ground in a fury, and Taylor was forced to dive to the side as a field of stone spikes shot up from the ground in an attempt to impale her. She maintained the mana connection, even though it was empowering the spell attacking her. Taylor returned her full attention to the Fissure as it charged at her... at the same moment as the scribbles formed into words.

"*Crus clypeos et hastas saxa!*" Taylor's eyes slammed shut as the creature rammed her.

Health: 32/81.

"I'm gonna die!" was the only thing she could think as she hit the ground and blood welled up through her teeth. Her body went flying, but the follow-up attack she was expecting didn't land. She watched as the Fissure *unfolded*, its ink splattering all over papers that seemed to come out of nowhere. The papers reached her Grimoire and were absorbed by the suddenly cheerful-and-active book.

<Yum. Thank.> Grimmy flapped up and landed on her head, sleepy after such a large meal.

Spell Named: Fissure. (T5): 0/100 to level 1! Mana cost: 30/second.

Effect 1: Perfect stability. No matter how much the ground moves or grooves, your balance is perfect.

Bonus, at range: So long as you are walking on dirt or stone, you will be able to walk normally, no matter the condition, movement, or angle.

Effect 2: Send a spike of stone at a target, dealing 10n damage, where n = spell level. This is maximized at the start of the next tier.

Bonus, Multitarget: Create a field of stone spikes that can be left on the ground as a hazard, or fired as projectiles. These deal 10n damage each, where n = spell level. This is maximized at the start of the next tier. 5 Second cooldown.

Effect 3: Earth shaping. Take direct control of the ground within ten feet of yourself. You can use mana to shake the ground, raise or lower slabs of dirt and stone, hollow out areas, or create stone spikes. Damage is limited to prior tier maximums. No cooldown.

Spell prerequisites: ~~Body: 20. Mind: 30. Presence: 51.~~ (Overridden, Named.)

"All right, this 'being a Namer' thing is pretty awesome. Fine... I will admit that not *everything* Master Don told me is absolute garbage. I will take the advice that works for me, and use it as I need to use it. I will be the best, I will be powerful, I will be *perfect*." She sat up and looked at the Stone Spikers that were starting to emerge from the hole that the Fissure had left behind. Her eyes flashed dangerously, and a Flame Lance appeared in her hand.

"As for not finishing them all off the first time around..." The fire left her hand at high speed, slamming into the nearest rank of stone spikers and detonating. Another spell was already prepared and in the air before the first shrieks of pain were able to reach her.

"I will *never* make the same mistake twice."

CHAPTER THIRTY-TWO

- LUKE -

"Years." Luke sighed as he gazed at all of the scars that criss-crossed his body. They were faint and silvery, but he had only ever healed perfectly when he had been able to fully submerge himself in a pool of water. "Cookie is waiting for me, but it's taken years... five? Eight? Ten? Just to get through another two. I'll find people to help me rescue her."

Alert: system clock registers time since Sigil application as Years: 29 Months: 11 Days: 12 Hours-

"Just stop already!" he shouted at the Sigil, trying again without success to tear the branded enchantment out of his flesh. However, just like every other time, he was only able to tear furrows into the area around the Sigil; if nothing else, the control aspects were still active. "It keeps track of time for me? At least I found a new function..."

One of the most annoying aspects of the magical *thing* was that he never knew when something he had done a thousand times before would make it speak up. Luke snarled and did one of the harder things he had to do nowadays: he tried to think back and make a plan instead of just being reactionary.

There were times where he wondered if the choices that he was making were the right ones, but he was always distracted by an enemy whenever he started planning. They always seemed to know when he wasn't fully focused, and used that time to launch a sneak attack on him.

In fact, the reason that Luke had been trapped in this spot for so long was exactly the creatures launching sneak attacks. This Zone had apparently been designed to prevent him from running straight through it, because there was some kind of energy barrier set up at the end of it. He still remembered the day that he had first arrived within this Zone, and had gained a quest from his Sigil.

You have entered Tutorial Zone, Zone five! This Zone is designed to test your reaction speed! There are a few enemies here that will hit you with a stick if you can't take them down fast enough! Caution: the longer you go without defeating your enemies, the more devious and dangerous they will become. They might even get better weapons! Finally, more enemies may spawn, depending on how many you have left alive at the end of each day!

Quest received: Open the way. Defeat all the enemies in Zone Five! Reward: barrier vanishes, tutorial is completed, skill granted based on total accumulated unused skill pearls. Enemies remaining: 18,000/1,000

Since that moment, Luke had been doing everything he could to kill the enemies as fast as possible. At the start, he had been able to kill hundreds every day. They would swarm him with their katanas, spears, and rapiers, attempting to bring him down through sheer numbers. Luke would have been fine with this type of battle, except for the small fact that his opponents were intangible until they attacked. Luke had exactly one full second to take them down before they couldn't be hurt again.

Now... *years* into fighting against them, the 'Physical Phantoms' had been reduced to under a hundred from their swollen population of *eighteen thousand*. With how fast more of them appeared, he had likely killed over twenty to twenty-five thousand. There was no way to tell for certain, since *none* of them dropped skill pearls. Luckily, their respawn rate seemed to be tied into how many existed in the area, meaning that as he killed more of them over time, fewer and fewer returned.

"Maybe that's where they all go at night? To 'repopulate'?" Luke chuckled even as he whipped around and slammed his fist into a semi-ghostly skull. The humanoid popped like a soap bubble, and a rush of Potentia filtered into Luke's Sigil.

Damage: 210 (blunt damage). Exp gained: 1 (T3 Physical Phantom destroyed.)

"One Potentia?" Luke punched the ground where the being had stood and snarled. "This place is *useless!*"

To gain increased Potentia, please fight new types of monsters, or more powerful ones!

"Sigil!" Luke bellowed, spinning and backhanding another beast.

Damage: 280 (blunt damage). Exp gained: 1 (T3 Physical Phantom destroyed.)

Enemies remaining: 56/1,000

Alarm: you have requested to be alerted when you have gained enough Potentia to increase your skill 'Fully Geared'. Would you like to do so now?

"I… what? When did I do that?" Luke narrowed his eyes at another popup that told him it had been roughly ten years since then. "Yes, increase the skill."

Skill deactivated while increasing tier! Please use caution.

"Pure hate right now." Luke turned and sprinted away from Zone five. By doing so, he only took light damage to his back instead of having his kidneys skewered. "Why would I get a warning ahead of time that my skill would turn *off?* That would be too well thought-out."

Health: 214/234

His forehead started to burn slightly, and the air around him shivered as double the amount of Potentia needed to reach the ninth level of a skill - a total of eleven thousand - gradually drained away and was funneled into the skill. Every hostile entity that could sense the fluctuations of something attempting to break through to a new tier took that opportunity to rush at Luke. He swatted a phantom, getting both an outgoing and incoming damage indicator upon impact.

Damage: 70 (physical damage).

Health: 212/234

"I took damage from *hitting* it? Wait, it didn't *die?*" Luke's brow furrowed, but he remembered a time in the past where punching things with his bare hand hurt, and rarely did enough damage to kill something outright. It had been… twelve? Eighteen years? Since he'd first gained 'Fully Geared'. He had needed to use some of his Potentia in other ways to survive, but almost everything else had been saved to get this skill to the next tier. Luke spun in place and finished off the staggered Phantom. "My growth woulda been faster if *anything* else gave Potentia!"

Enemies remaining: 55/1,000

To gain increased Potentia, please fight new types-

"*Quiet!*" He crossed the Zone boundary and looked back. Zone five was eight miles wide at its widest point, and there were… he checked his quest, "only fifty-five monsters left in that whole area? Ugh… finding them is going to take forever."

Luke decided that it might be time for a quick hunt. The goat meat that he had acquired a few weeks ago was starting to become rather… sparse. However, there were plenty of vegetables and herbs in the 'safe Zone' that was Zone four. Anything he found that could be considered food here was toxic to the extreme, which had been beneficial in increasing his Resistance sub-characteristic. "Makes things spicy, too. Now I'm hungry."

Since he was in a 'safe' area, he decided to take a look at how he had developed in the last… "Thirty *years*. I'll kill them all, if I ever get out of here."

CAL Scan

Level: 8

Current Etheric Xenograft Potentia: 0/5,500 to level 9!

Body: 26.8

- *Fitness: 35.2*
- *Resistance: 18.4*

Mind: 17.75

- *Talent: 15.5*
- *Capacity: 20*

Presence: 14.6

- *Willpower: 22.2*
- *Charisma: 7*

Senses: 18.4

- *Physical reaction: 23.5*
- *Mental energy: 13.3*

Maximum Health: 234
Maximum Mana: 312
Mana regen: ~~5.16~~ 100 per second (Overridden by local ambient levels.)

"Isolation and constant combat have been good for me." Luke looked himself over, noting the powerful and bulging muscle hidden under layers of filth and blood. His pants were simple wraps of raw goat hide that were tied up with raw ligaments. No shirt. Luke's head and face was now coated in a dense bush of hair. Since he hadn't been in a pool recently to take a bath, his hair hadn't all fallen off in… a few years.

"You know, I never noticed, but my Charisma dropped by three points? I didn't even know that was possible… oh! It's because I don't have Cookie with me anymore! That makes sense; I haven't tried to make myself presentable nor hold a decent conversation in… I don't even know how long."

"I guess it doesn't really matter. I'll clean up my act when I have Cookie back and safe with me." Luke lapsed into silence as the area around him continued to thrum with power. Potentia continued filtering through his forehead and into an unknown location. Was it perhaps his... brain? Is that where skills were stored? Or was it going into some kind of different layer of reality that allowed him to-

Chime.

"I should go kill something!" Luke smiled as he turned around and started walking back toward Zone five. He blinked, remembering what he was doing thanks to the thrumming and shifting air surrounding him. "Right; I need to wait until my skill reaches the new tier."

He sat down right at the edge of the Zone, eating a poisonous potato and snacking on the last of his rotting goat jerky. It was worth doing for Resistance training. Yes. An hour passed, then two, and night began to fall. Still, his skill was deactivated and upgrading. Out of sheer boredom, he decided to look at what had changed over the years. Pulling open his skill list, Luke started to mutter. "Bum Rush got up to level seven, Innate Balance up to level six, and obviously Fully Geared is getting to tier eight."

A deep, shuddering inhalation while he closed his eyes was the only way that he was able to stop himself from devolving into cursing at the people that had put him here. Luke distracted himself by using his finger on the ground to start doing some basic math. No matter what else he had forgotten over the years, for some reason basic mathematics had stuck with him. Seven levels, six levels, I got to level eight... combine that with the final level in Fully Geared... nineteen thousand, two hundred Potentia? Okay... perhaps I should not be too upset with the outcome."

"Wait, didn't I already kill almost eighteen *thousand* Phantoms? Doesn't that mean that I nearly exterminated an entire Zone just to get to this point?" Luke's expression brightened immediately. "So, when I get past this, all I need to do is make sure to kill absolutely *everything* in *every* Zone! That will let me get strong enough to find Cookie the fastest!"

In that moment, he felt a sense of incredible satisfaction. Somehow, he knew that this was the best way forward. A manic smile grew on his face as he planned out the next few years.

CHAPTER THIRTY-THREE

Skill increase complete!

Luke waited for more, but it appeared that the system was done speaking to him for the moment. He sighed, and requested more information. "Skill page, changes only."

Tier seven 'Fully Geared' has become Tier eight 'Walking Arsenal'.

Walking Arsenal. (T8) Level 0. 0/100 to level 1!

Effect 1: You are able to absorb natural weapons and armor (Claws, fangs, scales) by touching them. By absorbing a certain amount of the same type of weapon or armor, you are able to 'equip' it on your body. Only one type of weapon can be created at a time, and only one type of armor per slot. Choosing a new type of weapon or armor will replace the previous type once it is complete. Weapons and armor cannot exceed current tier and level.

Bonus 1, at range: You are able to absorb a weapon or armor type within five feet of your body. No longer requires active attempts after the item is selected.

Effect 2: You are now able to absorb weapons or armor created via natural metals. Natural metal weapons and armor cannot exceed current tier and level. Natural weapons can exceed tier, so long as they are within three effective levels.

Bonus 2, Multitarget: You can now select to absorb all weapons or armor of the same type within the range of bonus 1.

Effect 3: You are now able to absorb weapons or armor created via unnatural metals (magical weapons/armor). Weapons and armor cannot exceed current tier and level. Natural metal weapons can exceed tier, so long as they are within three effective levels. Natural weapons can exceed tier, so long as they are within six effective levels.

Bonus 3, AoE: You can store the weapons and armor you create. You are able to select between all different versions you have previously created!

Effect 4: Each active weapon or armor slot now costs a flat percentage of your mana pool to maintain! To achieve the exact damage or protection potential, ten percent of your mana must be applied. Each percentage added or subtracted will change the potential by one percent.

[New!] Bonus 4, Multitarget AOE: All weapons and armor in your possession and within five feet of you grant you $1n\%$ of their maximum damage or armor. This bonus is maximized at the tier limit.

Luke read over the information, excited about the idea of gaining more power. However, his face fell when he realized that he had no extra armor, no extra weapons, and no way to get or make them. "Maybe I should try remaking some tools? I'm sure that my leatherworking skills have degraded... I bet my father would be disappointed. Didn't I know someone who was a blacksmith once? Maybe I can convince them to give me every weapon that they made since I was *locked up here!*"

Now that his glowing blue armor - and he assumed his weapons as well - were back to full power, he sprinted into Zone five and started hunting for phantoms. There was a good chance that they had been lured into the area from the power fluctuations coming off of his Sigil. Luke was going to take advantage of that, and he knew the best way to do it.

He got to the area he had been aiming for, and laid down. Closing his eyes, he pretended to be asleep. Luke waited, waited... waited. He was far too excited to actually fall asleep, but there was no way that his prey would know this. There was a light hissing sound as a spear was thrust in his direction, and Luke reactively rolled to his feet and activated Bum Rush.

Exactly as he had hoped, he was surrounded by easily a score of Phantoms. These creatures seemed intelligent; very rarely did they come after him one-on-one. Not after the massacre of the last few years. However, he had rarely seen so many of them all together and in one spot for months on end. Luke was going to use this opportunity to the fullest!

Devoting a full fifty percent of his mana to his Battering Ram Knuckles and essentially disregarding defense, Luke began attacking the surprised Zone training devices. They seemed surprised, but he knew better than to pretend that they had feelings or thoughts other than finding more sophisticated ways to ambush him. "Other things aren't real! Only *I* am real! All of you only *exist* to make me stronger!"

Damage: 391 (Blunt damage).

Damage: 286 (Blunt damage).

Damage: 322 (Blunt damage).

The battle was short. The only reason it lasted as long as it did was that Luke needed his opponents to attack first before he could damage them. He took some light damage, but a single sip of water was enough to heal the light scrapes and contusions.

Enemies remaining: 22/1,000

Exp gained: 33 (T3 Physical Phantom destroyed x33.)

"Twenty-two to go!" Luke's eyes were gleaming as he thought of finally, *finally* getting out of the Zone and the tutorial in general. He shouted into the night, "I'm coming for you! I'm coming for *all* of you!"

It took three weeks, but he did it. Just shy of his thirtieth anniversary in Murder World, Luke tricked the last Phantom into attacking him while he was 'weak and defenseless'. When it popped like a bubble, Luke received the message he had been waiting for. He had waited years, *decades*, and it was finally here.

Zone Five cleared! Congratulations for setting a new record clear time for Zone five! New record: 17 years, 4 months, 18 days! Now people following in your footsteps have something to strive for! Hidden achievement:

Defeat more than 1,100 total Phantoms (10% more than needed)! 1,000 Potentia gained!

Tutorial complete! New record for tutorial: 29 years, 11 months, 30 days! no bonus is allotted, as the estimated time to completion for the tutorial was five years, three months. Every aspect of yourself should have been challenged during this tutorial, if you feel that you have not been sufficiently challenged, please contact -ERROR-.

Scanning... no class trainer found. Your reward has increased! As you managed to complete the tutorial without assistance, you have become the default class trainer! As the class trainer, you are allowed to change the name of various sections of this dimension, such as the Zones and Zone defenders. As an example, you have titled this plane as 'Murder World', and that is now the official title of this entire dimension!

"Hold on... I am the only person to ever get through this, and the big reward that I get for it is that I get to provide *naming conventions?*" Luke tried again, unsuccessfully, to tear the Sigil out of his forehead. The only thing that stopped him from trying harder was the next message that appeared.

Quest complete! Go to the boundary of the sixth Zone to collect your reward.

Luke started walking, hoping against hope that this would be his ticket out of this terrible blue abyss. Then again, even if he left for a short while, he would be back to search for Cookie. Until he had her safe in his hands, there was no way that he would ever be able to rest properly.

Soon enough, the boundary of the sixth Zone came into sight. Unlike every time he had ever seen it before, there was no shimmering barrier blocking him from crossing. As he drew closer, a small rumble caught his attention. In the distance, a line had appeared in the ground, and water was flowing down it. He followed the stream, and found a stone plinth; which began to rise out of the ground in front of him as water flowed into it. "Another bonus? Is this what I get for totally clearing each Zone? Well, that's handy."

There was a single hole on the plinth, and as Luke walked over to it, his Sigil projected words above it.

Add as many skill pearls as you would like. Final reward is based on total and quality of pearls added, clear time, and achievements gained within the tutorial.

Luke looked at the solitary small hole, and sighed deeply. He opened his goat hide canteen and started putting pearls into the hole one by one. One, a dozen, fifty, one hundred, and finally a total of two hundred ninety-seven skill pearls between the ranks of one and four were pushed into the hole. "No funnel. Seriously? I had to line all of these up individually?"

Would you like to add any more?

"No."

Processing… please allow up to three to five business days for new Skill Pearl to be created based on the criteria!

"Are you messing with me?" Luke dropped all of his defense, pouring fifty percent of his mana into each of his Battering Ram knuckles. His hands began to glow a brilliant blue, with a depth of power that began shaking the air around it. Just before he lashed out, a single skill pearl was pushed to the surface of the plinth.

As there are no other requirements on the system, the skill pearl was generated in record time! This is a custom skill pearl, and it is very unlikely that you will ever find one like this again! It has been configured specifically to your person; don't let your friends have it!

"Other requirements on the system, my gluteus maximus. It didn't take you any *time*, you were just afraid of work!" Luke snarled as he snatched the pearl and threw it down his gullet. "How can an entire *plane of existence* be lazy?"

Skill gained: Open Up. (T6) Level 9. 0/11,500 to tier 7!

Effect 1: You have gained the abilities to open a small crack between dimensions. By punching into a weak point in the world, you are able to tear through enough to pass between the worlds. Total mana needed to open a small crack: $1,000-10n$, where $n =$ skill level.

Bonus 1, at range: You are able to clearly and easily see weak points in the world.

Effect 2: You are now able to reuse weak points in the world at a much-

reduced rate. Each time you use the same weak point, the mana cost will be reduced by 50%, to a minimum of 25% mana cost.

Bonus 2, Multitarget: No longer are you making a momentary flicker in the weave, you are able to invest extra Mana into the opening to create a stable portal that other people will be able to travel through. Time that the portal will remain open: 60 seconds per 100-n mana.

Effect 3: You are now able to break down the barrier to other worlds in order to enter them. In order to do so, a portal must have been made to that world and closed within at a maximum of 24+n hours.

Bonus 3, AoE: by injecting your Mana into a portal, you can either subvert it to your control, redirect it to [Murder World], or directly close it. Cost: 100-10n mana. Caution: If the person who has created the portal is maintaining control of it, your willpower will clash against their charisma.

"It is my way home!" Luke's eyes welled up with tears, but only for a bare moment before the Sigil on his forehead re-centered him. "I can see my father... his name is... my mother! Sister? I can't... remember them? How long has it been since I thought of them? Are they even still alive? It has been thirty years! Will they even remember me?"

Luke looked around, and found that right at the edge of the Zone there was a vertical shimmering field. "So, you are a weak spot between the worlds? Imma punch you."

It has been exactly 30 years since you entered Murder World!

"Yeah, cool, thank you for the information." Luke snorted as he poured Mana into his newfound skill. He lashed out and punched the weak space, and a small crack appeared for just a brief instant.

Chime!

Connection to main enchantment block re-established! System clock updated! Skill forcefully deactivated!

"What in the actual abyss just happened?" He tried once more to invoke his new skill, however, every time he attempted to do so, it was forcefully deactivated. "Sigil, you had better explain yourself!"

System clock shows that the order of the Archmage is still in effect! Two and a half years of training time has been allotted for new Initiates;

they are not allowed to leave their designated worlds until the required time has passed!

"Not enough time? Not enough *time?*" Luke was flabbergasted by this information; he simply could not understand what the Sigil was telling him. "How much more time do I have to be here? How much time has passed out there?"

System clock has shown that two base-world years have passed! Assessing current differences between system clock and personal clock... Calculating... Congratulations! You have entered a world with the highest time dilation on record! With a 15x time dilation, you have six months of base-world time, or seven-and-a-half years subjective time remaining, until your training is considered complete!

After reading the information, Luke felt something inside of him break, something that the desperately chiming Sigil on his forehead was unable to prevent or fix.

He closed his mouth. He turned. He walked into Zone six.

CHAPTER THIRTY-FOUR

Just outside the small town of Woodswright, where a defensive Fortress had just been completed, a portal appeared and a man walked out of seemingly nowhere. He scanned the overgrown path, specifically at the trees that seemed to stretch endlessly in all directions; then lightly crouched, jumping into the air and searching around. Satisfied that he was in the correct location and there were no actual threats within at least fifty kilometers, he reached into the air and plucked a string of mana.

"I, Archmage Don, hereby declare training complete. All surviving members of the Initiate group are to return here within twenty-four hours of this world." He paused and grimaced at the next words that were required to be said. "I authorize the Sigils of the Kingdom to use deadly force upon refusal of this order."

Master Don waved his hand, and the trees in the area were ripped to shreds. the wood chips flew into the air, congregating into a series of small buildings. A book appeared behind him; a Grimoire as tall as he was that exuded a deathly aura. If any base human had been in the area to see the book, their mind might have been permanently warped from the mere *sight* of it.

He reached out a hand, lightly backhanding the air. The book vanished, and the space that he had touched blossomed into a portal. People began flooding out of the opening; mostly support staff that was present to tend to the needs of the returning Initiates.

Healers, Warriors, Quartermasters with huge amounts of food and gear, and finally some people exuding a Presence that could nearly rival Master Don's. He nodded at them as they stepped forward, "Generals."

"Archmage, it is good to see you back among the living." One of the Generals stepped forward, bowing lightly before taking a step back. "That you are back so late... have you succeeded? Have you found... an inheritor?"

There was no change of expression on Master Don's face, nothing to betray the fury that still boiled behind his facade of calm and control. "Perhaps. Perhaps. We will find out soon."

Over the course of the day, the portal changed colors. Each time it did so, multiple people streamed out of the distortion. More often than not, there were deep wounds, malnutrition, or other small issues that needed to be tended, which the support staff efficiently cared for. Twelve hours passed, and the portal shifted colors once more, this time to a coloration that had been seen several times already. Only one person sauntered out, the Apprentice of the Archmage.

Master Don merely nodded, and his words were cold. "Taylor, it is good to see that you survived. I hope that you found that the path you followed was the correct one. The terms of our deal will be honored."

Unlike the other people that had stepped out of the portal, there was not a hair out of place on Taylor. She wore a bright white robe with purple and black etching, and the robe itself had a beautifully crafted hood that she lowered to show her face. Taylor slipped into a full courtly bow, "Archmage, a pleasure as always! It seems I have won the bet, and we will be doing things my way from here on. Indeed, I believe that you will find only positive changes since our last meeting. Of course, if I ever find a way to reduce you to ashes without damaging the Kingdom or myself, I will not hesitate."

"But of course! I would have it no other way. Keep in mind that I will kill you in a heartbeat should you fail," Master Don replied, turning his eyes back to the portal dismissively. The people around them recoiled sharply; this was not a normal interaction, *especially* not for a master-apprentice relationship. Several of them had seen the Archmage destroy small towns over a threat that was *half* as credible as this one. "An Archmage must be prepared, at all times, forever. If I slip, I deserve what is coming to me. I look forward to the next stage in your training... Archmage-in-Waiting Taylor."

"Pardon me, My Lady. If you could step over here with me, we will update your Sigil and your credentials." A man bowed to Taylor and swept a hand toward a wooden building. "Pardon the repetition if you already know this information, but all Initiates who have passed to the full rank are granted a military position of Captain, and the Noble equivalent title of Baron."

Taylor's eyes traced over the man, and she nodded before following him. "Thank you, Lieutenant. Your assistance is greatly appreciated."

They walked to the small building where another Mage was waiting for them, this one a specialized Enchanter. He gestured toward a seat, and Taylor gracefully took it. "Might I have your name, surname if you were a noble before your initiation, and class name."

"Taylor Woodswright. Specialized Mage, Namer." Taylor's answer was concise, clear, cold. There was nothing wrong with what she was saying, no insult that could be garnered, but still the man across the table became *furious*.

"*Namer*? How dare you claim to have power on par with the Archmage?" Balls of light began appearing in the air around the Enchanter, and he barely stopped himself from attacking. A long beat passed, he looked at Taylor consideringly... when a leer appeared on his face. "I will forgive this insult, and even 'forget' to report it; on the small condition that-"

The shocked lieutenant was barely able to think the words, 'this man is an idiot', before Taylor reacted and the Enchanter's words were choked off. The air around his throat constricted; he blinked and found that a spike of Earth, Fire, and Ice were rotating around his head. Very, very close. So close in fact, that the tips of each spike drew blood as they circled around; leaving red-weeping trails as they passed.

Taylor leaned forward, clearly not having had to move in order to get the spells to enact her will. "Let me try this one more time. I am Taylor Woodswright. Specialized Mage, Namer. Only Apprentice of Master Mage Donec Arriperent, and presumptive Archmage. Would you now like to finish your job, or should I get someone to come in here, clean up whatever mess is *left* of you, and have *them* do the job?"

She left the small building moments later, the Sigil on her forehead shining and in a new configuration: a single book with a border of mystical runes in a circle around it. Taylor was now proudly wearing the symbol of the Namers; though over the next few minutes it faded until only silvery lines remained on her forehead, instead of the shining symbol of her Order.

As Taylor exited, there was another shift in the portal: it began growing a deep green, with flecks of golden light. A strange sense of joy filled everyone in the area, and the few remaining trees started shaking as if a strong wind were blowing through them. Seeds and small plants burst into flowering; all as a thin man stepped out of the bright green portal.

The lightly-tanned man had long black hair that curled into beautiful waves. His shining hazel eyes swept over the area, and everyone caught in the glance felt their hearts beat faster. He took a step onto the ground, and flowers erupted upward to curl around his deer-hide boots and brush against his wolf fur-lined robes. The gnarled staff in his hand bore leaves and flowers on it as well, but a closer look revealed thorns with glistening fluids at their tips.

Everyone that had been gathered near the area ran over and began cheering as Andre returned to the Kingdom. The

Archmage approached and personally shook his hand, pumping it up and down with great enthusiasm. However, the portal did not immediately close. A massive Cave Bear began forcing its way out of the space, which prompted the security team to raise their weapons and shout a warning.

Andre simply looked behind him and patted the bear on the head, stupefying everyone watching and turning the fear into laughter. "Fear not, my friends! Arthur is a comrade of mine, the creature that allowed me to reach the Second Circle several years ago! While he is not tame, so long as you do not approach him or myself aggressively, he will leave you alone."

After looking around the area and ensuring that Andre was safe, the bear gave him a fierce lick and shimmied backward into the portal; which closed behind it, leaving no trace of the animalistic presence.

Very few people understood exactly what Andre had meant, but they all seemed to appreciate his open and caring attitude. Something deep inside them exulted that their Druid was worried about *them*? He made sure to allay *their* fears? What a shining example! As for those who had understood exactly what he meant, they were taken aback, but very pleased by his progress. There would be no one attempting to stifle his progress; in fact, only by increasing his power would the Kingdom become more powerful as a whole.

It was an interesting situation for Taylor as she watched her childhood friend walk into the small building for processing, then emerge with his Sigil showcasing the symbol of the Archdruid. In an instant, he had transformed from an Initiate into someone with technically as much or more political power as the Archmage. However, the current Archmage was clearly more directly powerful, and Andre knew better than to overstep himself.

The two of them vanished for a talk, and it seemed during that time Andre was able to convince Master Don to levitate him a few hundred feet into the air. A few moments later, a halo of energy was released by Andre, a ring of red-flecked green

Mana that expanded... expanded... *expanded*. Andre finally descended to the ground, and as his feet touched down, the overgrown path was suddenly repaired and covered with tight-knit vines that somehow *improved* the quality of the path and made it into an actual road.

The trees around them seemed healthier, and the blooming flower effect spread as far as the eye could see. Taylor took advantage of the moment and decided to reintroduce herself to her old friend. Quietly walking over, she jabbed her finger into the ribs on his back.

"*No!*" Andre bellowed as he spasmed from the prod, "What have I *told* you about doing-? Wait! *Taylor!*"

The young Archdruid whipped around and yanked her into a bear hug that his companion Arthur would have been impressed by. "Taylor! I've missed you so much! How are you? Tell me everything! Where is Zed? Did he get here before us? Oh! Where is Luke? I bet he became something really cool! Did you see what world he was sent to before you left?"

"You still bruise like a peach, huh?" Not really wanting to answer his questions, Taylor deflected and simply smiled at him. "How in the world did you *lose* muscle by leveling up?"

"How dare you." Master Don called over, casually offended by her cavalier attitude toward 'leveling'. "It is *Ascending*, blast it!"

"Ignore him," Taylor dismissed the Archmage's correction easily, causing the people within hearing distance to blanch with fear. "He gets cranky. Probably hasn't eaten, or maybe he only killed *one* member of a family, instead of getting all nine generations or something. Really hard to get a read on what sets him off."

Silence reigned in the area for a few moments, until both Andre and Don began laughing at her. However, Taylor's facial expression did not change a single bit. A new - highly musical - voice called out, "I did *indeed* get here before you, great Archdruid! My oh my, do I have a story for you!"

A golden-haired man strode forward with a lopsided grin.

He was wearing a stiff new formal outfit, the purple-and-gold Raiment of a Kingdom-bound True Bard, and had several instruments strapped to him in the places where others would carry a bow or other weapons. He looked to be roughly twenty, and his eyes showed a hint of amusement… and something else. There was a hunted cast to his face that his friends could not remember ever seeing before.

"Zed!" Andre bellowed, rushing over to embrace his long-lost friend. "How are you? You've *aged*?"

"Yes, well, not all of us got to move to a new universe that allowed us to stay immortally and eternally young. My powers are granted by *this* world, remember?" Zed huffed at Andre, pretending to be upset. "Kids these days! But really, the biggest draw for a Bard is Ascending to level twenty. If I can't do it fast enough, I will become too old to really hold my own in a new world."

"Well, what are friends for?" Andre slapped the Bard on the back, "My Potentia is your Potentia; let's get you some levels! Can we group up or something? Share Potentia?"

"Lord Archdruid, you will be assigned a security team that fits with your power, prestige, and scope of duties." One of the Generals that had been waiting in the area piped up, snorting at the thought of the *Archdruid* teaming up with a barely-trained Bard. "Besides, Bards cannot earn Potentia through combat, only through interactions with other people. It is highly unlikely that you will be grouped together with… ahem… *him*."

"Right, well…" Andre searched around in a vain attempt to find a way to alleviate the awkward situation. "Seriously, where *is* Luke? He should be here by now!"

"Andre, I really did not want to be the one to have to tell you this." Taylor locked gazes with Zed, who also knew the truth of the matter. He wasn't offering to explain, so she sighed and closed her eyes. "When we were first going through portals, all those years ago-"

Crack.

Somehow, impossibly, the portal that was in place shattered

like a mirror that had been hit by a hammer. It shifted into a deep blue coloration, and the world started to *thump*. A sound like a heartbeat filled the area, growing deeper, faster, louder. Just as it seemed as though the Mages in the area would launch an attack at the portal, *something* came through.

It was a hand. A human hand, one which displayed a pair of glowing goats horns hovering in front of it. As the hand pulled back, another joined it and seemed to be pulling the portal in different directions. A light blue mist poured out of the small hole that was being opened, and almost everything that it touched died. *Almost* everything.

"Everyone get *back*!" Master Don roared, sweeping the area with telekinetic force. People were tossed away from the blue mist, some of them sustaining injuries as they went through the walls of the fibrous new buildings.

Andre felt sick and prepared himself to go all out in defense of the world around him. Taylor felt refreshed, powerful, and somehow knew that the energy coming out of the portal was raw, unfiltered mana. Zed leaned forward, interested in the show. "Oh, *this* will make a good story…!"

The portal cracked again, and a humanoid figure forced itself into the world, dropping to the ground for a long moment as it heaved deep breaths. The excess mana slowly absorbed into the area, and only Andre knew that everything that had survived its touch had been incredibly empowered.

Zed, who had decided to get closer to the heaving figure than anyone else, suddenly wheeled backwards, clutching at his face. "Celestials above! What is that *smell*?"

CHAPTER THIRTY-FIVE

"Whatever it is, I believe that it is coming from... him? It appears to be a man." Master Don raised a brow at the strange person covered in half-rotten hides. There was so much muck on the body in front of him that Master Don couldn't tell if the blue-brown hair was naturally that color, or if it was just full of dirt. The smell of blood filled the air on the heels of the scent of rotting flesh, and people once more grew wary.

Luke slowly opened his eyes when he heard the voice that had plagued his nightmares for just shy of forty years. It had been *so* long, in fact, that he was momentarily convinced that he had once upon a time *imagined* the voice of the Archmage; simply ascribing his hatred to a figment of his imagination. However, here was the man himself, and Luke was too weak from running uphill and fighting his way all the way back to the edge of Zone six, then punching open the dimension, to kill the man where he stood.

When his Sigil warned him of impending death, Luke had been stepping into the ninth Zone. He had planned to ignore the Sigil, and had managed to do so for ten entire days. Then there had been *red* text that informed him that he only had four days to escape Murder World and return to the base world before it popped his head like skill pearls popped goats. Though he was loath to give up the search for Cookie, he would escape and resume the hunt as soon as he could manage it.

"Throw a bucket of water on it and see what comes out the other side." Master Don ordered.

"Water! *No!*" Luke's voice was barely intelligible. He had spent so much time making sure that his hair and beard were extra fluffy! He had never felt so weak, the air here was so thin! Still, he struggled to his feet and prepared to fight these new Zone constructs. The people around him took a step back; apparently his weak struggle to his feet was still faster than they typically saw *anything* reacting. He yanked out a goat hide water-skin and took a sip from it, feeling his mana skyrocket back to its maximum. Opening a portal had been trying, and that was when the world around him was feeding concentrated mana to his system at a high rate.

Don! There he was! Luke's hands glowed bright blue, and the ground shattered under his feet as he launched himself at the man that had trapped him in another world. There was surprise in the face of the other man; Luke remembered just enough about human interactions - and he had seen the expression often enough on the things that he killed - to understand that much. His Battering Ram weapons slammed against a barrier of some kind, again and again. Eight attacks in one second, and the energy field around the Mage collapsed.

"What in the-" the Archmage did not stand idly; a spell detonated in Luke's face the next instant.

Health: 180/250.

Luke felt the skin of his face start to drip off; that detonation had some form of corrosion behind it. A sense of danger flooded through him, and he instantly deposited all of his mana into his 'metal gauntlets'. Once more, the sheer amount of power devoted to a single aspect made the air around it warp and shudder. His hands came into position, and only his experience fighting allowed him to catch the bright green Fireball that was coming after him.

'Catch' was a bit of a misnomer, as what he was doing in reality was absorbing as much of the damage as possible, then doing everything he could to deflect the remaining power into the air above him.

Boom.

Luke was knocked to a prone position, his face bouncing off the dirt and stone below him. "What? Brown? Dirt is *brown* here? How strange!"

Health: 132/250. (Concussion, massive.)
Armor: 2/250

He looked upward to see bright green flames spiraling down toward him. There was nothing that he could do, Luke was fully spent. His brain felt scrambled, he was out of Mana, his armor had been destroyed. He watched his death approach... then was slapped out of the way by the branch of a tree that he had landed near. His new resting location had him staring up at a man wearing fur-trimmed robes. Solid and practical choice. Luke approved.

A voice that he somewhat recognized from his childhood shouted out in a heroic tone, "Archmage, he is clearly an Initiate! Perhaps he has simply gone through something traumatic, and needs a few moments to collect himself. Why not put him through processing, and question him after?"

"Andre, he was able to attack me, though the Sigil is *clearly* on his muck-coated forehead." The Archmage retorted coldly as he readied his next spell. "He needs to be put down for the safety of the Kingdom."

"Doesn't processing adjust the Sigil and fine-tune it?" A cold, feminine voice reached Luke's ears.

There was silence for a long moment, then the Archmage appeared next to Luke and slapped him toward a building. "Fine; let's see if that fixes things."

Feeling his body spinning through the air was an uncomfortable sensation for Luke. He hadn't found anything in the last seven years that had been able to challenge him with physical might, and he had *tried*. Perhaps he shouldn't have taken the time to kill absolutely everything in every Zone, but that was the only way to ensure that nothing would come along and stab him in the back. Things *had* tried to do so, had succeeded even, but still he was alive.

The Zones after the tutorial were… different. They were full ecosystems. Full of creatures, bugs, plants, and a myriad of things that he had no phylum for. There were creatures made of the elements, creatures made of pure thought that had to be 'experienced' in order to be defeated… overall, it was a nice change from the single enemy type of each of the previous tutorial Zones.

However, it seemed that some kind of restriction had been lifted. No longer were things respawning or growing at incredible speeds, but the caveat was that each Zone seemed to have some form of 'boss'. Like him, everything there was trying to survive and become the most powerful. Oftentimes, they did not appreciate his attempts to move forward; in one instance, he even had to kill a boss in order to pass through to the next Zone.

Still, it had taken seven years to get through three more Zones. He had *known* that the only reason he had been trapped in Zone five of the tutorial was because the phantoms were hiding from him! "Ha, ha, *haaa!*"

Luke was interrupted from his reverie by a strange man that he found himself sitting across from. But… he didn't remember sitting down? Before he could say anything, the strange man spoke first. "What is going on here?"

Not having had a human interaction in almost forty years, Luke simply sat and stared at the strange, chubby little man covered in odd, shifting writing. There was a small staring contest for a few long seconds, then the man spoke once more. "I can only assume that you are here for processing? Give me your name, surname if you were a noble before becoming an Initiate, and class."

Luke said nothing, so the man rolled his eyes and tried it again. "On my authority in the Kingdom, I order you to answer my questions. What is your name?"

"Luke." Luke blinked as his mouth answered without him intending to speak.

"Surname if you were a noble?" No answer came to this one, so the Mage crossed something off and went to the next question, "What is your class?"

Still, there was no answer. There was a space for a class in Luke's Sigil status, but it had always stayed blank. As the silence stretched on and no answer was forthcoming, the Mage started to become peeved. "Are you intentionally resisting my orders?"

"No." The answer was instant and again unintentional.

"Where are you from?"

"Here." Luke responded honestly.

"What are you?" the Mage responded in an irritated voice.

"Powerful."

The Enchanter slapped his hand on the table, "What is your power?"

"Skill."

"All right, enough of this. You want to do things the hard way? Fine!" The Enchanter pulled out a massive book and slapped it on the table. "What plane of existence did you go to?"

"Murder."

"You went... to *murder*? What does that even mean?" The Mage didn't even bother to look through the book. "Was that an action, or a place?"

"It was the world."

"You went to 'Murderworld'?" the Mage stared at Luke with narrowed eyes, "Was that the official name of the plane of existence you were sent to?"

"There is a space between the two words," Luke calmly replied. "Murder. World. That is where I have been."

"Forget this. I hope you can deal with pain." The Mage pulled out a crystal and it instantly resonated with the Sigil on

Luke's forehead. To the Enchanter, the most concerning part of this process was that Luke did not utter a sound as he underwent what was known to be a *horrifyingly* painful experience. His anger slowly started to transform into fear as the data on the crystal was updated.

CAL Scan
Level: 9
Current Etheric Xenograft Potentia: 3,333/8,900 to level 10!
Body: 30.1

- *Fitness: 40.2*
- *Resistance: 20*

Mind: 18.6

- *Talent: 16.3*
- *Capacity: 20.9*

Presence: 14.5

- *Willpower: 23*
- *Charisma: 6*

Senses: 22.4

- *Physical reaction: 27.5*
- *Mental energy: 17.3*

Maximum Health: 250
Maximum Mana: 324.2
Mana regen: 5.43 per second

"But...! You are an Initiate! You are under level ten! These numbers are *literally* not possible!" The Enchanter quickly scanned the other information that had been pulled from the

Sigil directly. "Murder World. Celestials, you weren't joking. *Unknown* plane of existence? That hasn't been seen in a thousand years! No class, both in the literal and…"

The man paused and looked at Luke's disgusting body with a sneer. "… figurative."

He couldn't help but feel threatened by the enormously muscled man across the table from him. Luke was an anomaly, something that shouldn't exist. Beyond that, he was *far* stronger than the Enchanter himself. "You are coated with rotting animal skins. I literally cannot tell how far under that dirt and dried blood your skin is. It looks like your blue eyes are peeking out through a blue mask!"

Silence was his only response. The taunting had no effect. Luke had not been asked a question; he did not have to answer. The Enchanter snorted. "Typically, when a new class is created, the creator gets to name it. However, in this case I am going to just assign you a combination of your plane of existence, as well as your demeanor as a person. Your class name is officially 'Murderhobo'. Oh, and there *isn't* a space between those words. I don't suppose you would like to offer a diagram design for your Sigil? Of course not-"

He was interrupted by a scrap of leather slamming onto the table in front of him. There was a symbol etched into it, but the leather itself was so filthy and soaked in blood that it was hard to make it out. Luke stabbed his finger onto it, "This is what I remember of my family. This was our family crest. This can represent me."

"I thought you said your family was *not* Noble?" The Mage examined the triangular symbol; it was a combination of four shapes. From left to right: a diagonal line that spanned from the bottom left to the top, an arrow pointing to the left above a line that wrapped around to the center, finally ending with a line looking like a mountain peak on the right. "What is this supposed to be? A mountain range?"

"Four people in my family. Four mountains. Based on some kind of mythos about the best place in the multiverse, a place called Mountaindale." Luke chose not to elaborate further, and the Enchanter simply rolled his eyes.

"All right, your class symbol is set, your class is set, updating your Sigil now." The Enchanter-specialized Mage rolled his eyes and let his Mana flow into the crystal. Unbeknownst to him, the changes in the Sigil consisted both of a cosmetic one, and the *entire reimplementation* of the previously destroyed anti-kingdom-attacking system… which promptly fractured within the Sigil and began leaking mana. "As you become more powerful, and make more contributions to the Kingdom, your Sigil will gain intricacy. We hope that you have enjoyed your time here. Get out. For the love of the celestials, take a shower."

Luke stood up, then calmly turned around and kicked the table. It shattered, sending the Enchanter flying through the back of the building with wooden shrapnel all around him. Only the fact that he was wearing Enchanted garb with passive protections on it kept him alive. "If you *ever* try to control me again, I'll crush your throat before you can get out a single syllable."

Chime!

"Quiet, you! I don't care if you're mad at me." Luke stepped out of the building, finding himself completely surrounded by Mages and warriors with weapons and spells prepped and aimed at him. He heard the Archmage speak to a suspiciously familiar woman.

"Well, that clearly didn't work. Any *other* bright ideas?"

CHAPTER THIRTY-SIX

"Well, first of all, why don't we just *talk* with him, instead of ordering him around or slapping him with spells?" Taylor's tone was caustic, and she stepped forward carefully after answering the Archmage, holding out a soothing hand as if Luke was a wild animal. "Sir? I assume you are a man, thanks to that… rather, um, *impressive* beard. I'm going to cast a spell to clean you up and take care of any surface-level health issues that you are having. This is not an attack. Cleanse, Purify? Take care of him?"

Two insect-like spell forms flew out of a fluttering book that appeared behind her, zipping around Luke in a supersonic orbit. His hand lashed out, catching one of them, inspecting it, and letting it go. He snorted in a gravelly voice, "No protein."

It took a few minutes, longer than Taylor had ever seen her spells require to complete their instructions, but eventually the grime and filth vanished. However, his wrapped leathers and animal hides deteriorated to a point that they vanished into nothingness as well. What the spells left behind was a fully nude man that Taylor had given up for dead long ago. "*Luke…?*"

His brown hair was perfectly styled, his beard plaited, and

thousands of body-covering scars were on full display. Luke felt no shame for his nudity; he had been alone for far too long to give a single abyss about personal boundaries or societal norms. However, hearing his only half-remembered name made his eyes lock onto the person who has spoken it. "How do you know that name? Who are you?"

"Who am I? I'm *Taylor*! I was one of your best friends your whole life!" Taylor moved forward, her nostalgia and slowly-kindling happiness burning down to fury in an instant. "What happened to you? Where did you go? You *died*! We *saw* you die! How could you let us believe that you had been dead all of these years?"

"Let *you*...?" Luke's blue eyes shifted into a deep, electric fury, and foggy mana began rolling out of them. "I was locked away for almost *forty years*! Who are you to lecture me? I don't even know who you are! Why should I care that you were *sad*?"

"I'm Taylor! Your best friend! This is Andre, and Zed!"

Taylor's next words were interrupted as Zed chimed in with, "We are also your best friends; just saying."

Both Taylor and Luke glared at him before looking at each other one more time. The Archmage chose that moment to speak up. "I don't care how well you all know each other; he clearly cannot be controlled. He has to be put down like the rabid animal that he is."

Before the most powerful man in the Kingdom could act upon his words, Zed stood forward between everyone else and Luke. "Hello! I don't know if you all know me, or in your case remember me, Luke. I am Zed; nice to meet you and all that. I'm a Bard, so I know exactly how difficult this sort of situation can be. Why not, instead of threatening each other, we agree to either work with each other or go off and do our own things? I am directly volunteering to go with Luke; it seems like I will get the best stories with him!"

The General, who had disparaged Bards earlier, spoke again with a clear sneer on his face, "*Once* more, you don't get to choose the team you are on. You will likely be in the back lines, in some tavern somewhere. Accept your lot in life, *Bard*."

"No, wait." The Archmage took a step forward; a light smile appearing on his face. "Tell you what I will do... I am going to assign *quests* to all of you! At that point, you can decide whether you want to tackle them yourself, or go with a group."

Master Don looked over at Andre. "Druid Xan has informed me that you have known about your quest practically since your initiation. Now that you are the Archdruid of the Kingdom, you can choose on your own whether or not to accept this quest. For the rest of you, this is mandatory. Andre, your quest is to return life to the Scarroco desert. Bard, your quest is to keep this abomination from killing any servants of the Kingdom. Taylor, your quest is to keep their group from creating any political incidents."

The Archmage's gaze went hazy as he accessed data. "You; *Murderhobo*, is it? I'm sending you to the front lines. You're too dangerous to let roam within the Kingdom itself."

Luke had a message appear in front of his eyes instantly.

Quest gained: Assist the warfront! You have been assigned to the front lines of combat, you will be paid an Ascender's stipend for each week that you are able to follow the orders of your new Commander. Reward: variable. Failure: variable.

"No." Luke instantly refused the command. "I'm going back into my world."

"Sigil, deactivate his ability to return to... Murder World? Until his handlers grant him permission. Upon permission being granted, he gains at maximum thirty days of subjective time before he *must* return to this base world." Master Don easily ordered, offering no compromise and leaving no loopholes.

Luke stepped forward with death in his eyes as his Sigil happily chimed in agreement.

"Right, well, see, what you did there... you only gave *one* of us a quest that doesn't require being all together." Zed tried to explain to the Archmage, stepping in front of Luke once more. "I mean, sure, this is what I was after, but it just seems a little-"

"You got what you wanted. The others can choose whether they want to work with you... or not." The Archmage turned his glare on Zed. "Whether *he* is with you or not, if he kills someone that serves the Kingdom, your quest fails. Quest failure equals jail time or death, based on your level of negligence. Whether there is a political incident determines Taylor's Quest."

"I am certain that she would be able to control that happenstance, either in the capital or with the Murderhobo. Only *Andre's* quest is actually one that is of great importance to the Kingdom; he wouldn't fail even if I did *not* assign it to him. This way, he just gets more rewards. Rewards that he can keep for himself, or share with you." The Archmage finished, and Zed looked over at Andre, his eyes wide and pleading. The General that had been glaring daggers at Zed seemed satisfied by this outcome, and turned to walk away before he was called upon to do anything.

Andre was clearly hesitating; as the Archmage had stated, he would succeed in this on his own. If he included other people in his project, his rewards would obviously be lessened. However, he nodded at Zed, "Yes, let's all group up together! It'll be just like old times."

"I will, of course, go with you," Taylor stated to the others with a slight smile on her face, "It will be much easier to prevent an international incident if we don't... feces, where did the Murderhobo go? I mean... where did Luke go?"

They looked to Master Don to see if he had anything to say, but the Archmage simply shrugged. "I gave you your quests. You wanted him alive, he's alive. Luke is your problem now. He went that way. Good luck."

The newly-formed party looked in the direction that the Archmage had casually indicated with great concern; that was the fortification. That was a town. There were *people* in there that had no defense against an Ascender. If Luke could attack the Archmage, there would be nothing protecting those other standard citizens. They ran after him, each of them speeding forward in their own method.

"I guess I'll just catch up, then?" Zed yelled as Andre and Taylor blasted across the terrain faster than most spells would travel. They spared him a glance, noting that he was running only slightly faster than most normal humans could. However, no matter how fast they were, Luke had quite a head start and they were uncertain of where to begin looking for him.

Andre's eyes widened as he was struck by a realization, "His *family*! He's been gone for so long, there is no way he does not want to see his family! Quickly, we have to get there first!"

Both of them were already traveling at their maximum speed; Andre zipping across the ground, the plants in the area practically launching him forward, while Taylor floated over the ground on a current of invisible mana. They reached Luke's old house in moments, and could see his parents and sister working in their workshop… but there was no sign of Luke.

They looked at each other in confusion, and Taylor spoke what they were both thinking. "Where could he *possibly* have gone, if not to see his family?"

A sound like a tree being shattered with a single punch reached their ears, quickly followed by screams. Without hesitation, the two of them reacted by moving as quickly as they could toward the source of the disturbance. What they saw confounded them to the point that they weren't certain how to react.

Luke was stepping out of a guard post; he had apparently collected all of the weapons and armor that had been in storage. A soft blue light was radiating off of his body, yet somehow not reflecting off of all of the metal that he was carrying. Of course, he was not simply holding everything; he had wrapped it all in a blanket salvaged from a bed, which he had then tied to a long mop handle.

"Hobo, indeed," Taylor sighed with resignation as she moved grumpily toward the post.

The guards of the town were rapidly closing on the area. "Scum, how dare you attempt to steal from Baron Woodswright! Prepare to lose your hands!

For some reason, Luke didn't react positively toward the threat. In an instant, he was in front of the Guard who had just threatened him, his hand raised to crush the man's skull. A vine wrapped around his arm, pulling him backward just before he turned his potential energy into a truly dangerous attack.

Taylor addressed the guards to calm the situation, "Hold! I am Taylor Woodswright, heir of the Baron. I will explain this issue to my father, and you will not be held accountable for the actions of a newly-minted Ascender."

The guards had already been turning pale from the speed at which Luke could move, and every single one of them had felt the brush of death when he had raised his fist. Hearing that he was an Ascender, coupled with the fact that Taylor was going to take the blame, allowed them to retreat quickly. Andre stood next to Luke, staring at him as if he were a dangerous animal; to be fair, Luke had *earned* that glare.

"What in the world is wrong with you? Why would you attack a guard; no, before that, why would you rob an outpost in the first place?"

"I knew they had decent quality weapons and armor. I wanted them." Luke looked at the vine that was still wrapped around his arm, and with a simple pull, it exploded into plant fibers.

"Celestial above, what is your Fitness characteristic at?" Andre gulped as he took in the rippling muscles and shredded plant. Luke ignored him and walked away, heading back toward the forest. "Are you really going to leave without seeing your family?"

For the first time, Andre saw hesitation appear on Luke's face. It cleared up a moment later, and the Murderhobo continued his straightforward march out of town. "I gave up on seeing them long ago, and this quest is mandatory. Can't even remember their names, so why bother going through that all

over again? I need to get back to my world, I need to save...
forget it. I'm not going to slow myself down right now. I can
already feel this brand trying to make me walk. I've decided that
I might as well get some decent gear before I'm forced into
someone else's war."

"Your family probably still thinks you're *dead*!" Andre helplessly called after him.

"*Probably*..." Luke didn't slow down. "...for the best."

CHAPTER THIRTY-SEVEN

The four members of the newly-formed battle team were walking at a leisurely pace - or a frantic jog, for Zed - along a road that had clearly been beaten into the ground by thousands of feet. There was no true rush, only the fact that Luke couldn't handle facing his family after all this time was making them go *now*. Sure, they had orders to go, yet they did not have a specified arrival time. In fact, the majority of them were pleased with what was essentially a break for the first time in decades.

Taylor was not as happy with the situation; she had been looking forward to seeing her family again. Andre had wanted to see his old mentor and teacher, and Zed was looking forward to a pint of ale without a retainer that hated him breathing down his neck. However, knowing that Luke was going to go with or without them meant that they had to put aside their own plans. In all fairness, Andre did not have any living relatives in the village, and Zed was still looked at with suspicion by the people that had known him for what was less than three years ago for them.

"The fact of the matter is that only about a third of the people that went into the Initiate trials came out." Taylor was explaining to Zed as they walked at a human pace. "I was told that part of the issue was the age of the people going into the trials. Normally, they don't start until later, sometime around the twenties. We got 'lucky' because of the need for people to fight in this war. Anyway, starting that late allows people to get into the right headspace; to have a firmer foundation for who they are. Then, when the Sigil is applied, there isn't too much fluctuation. Apparently, many of the people failed simply because the Sigil forced them to maintain an immature mindset. They died for it."

"Seems like *something* the Kingdom should be held *accountable* for." Zed shook his head sadly. "Look at it this way; the Kingdom forced a certain mindset. Most of the people that died during the Initiate training period were those sent to low Mana-density worlds, which means a low time dilation. Correct?"

"I think that is correct?" Taylor raised an eyebrow, not sure where he was going with this.

"Well, clearly, with a higher Mana density, the Sigil has less effect. As an extreme example, Luke over there has clearly gained a totally different mindset than what he used to have." Zed watched as Luke walked over to a tree, sniffed it, and took a bite out of it like it was an apple. The Murderhobo chewed on the wood thoughtfully, then spit it out when he realized that there was no flavor. "There is an argument to be made that the people that were going to come back were the most powerful of the people that went in. In other words, the Hollow Kingdom intentionally sacrificed dozens of people so they could scrape some benefits from those that lived."

"Yes, that's exactly what happened." Taylor nodded at Zed, and his face lit up. However, Taylor's next words crushed his satisfaction. "In fact, I definitely have confirmation from the Archmage that this was *precisely* their plan. Now, pretend I am a normal person, or a Noble; anything except what I *am*. I'm not someone who is bound to the will of the Kingdom until I Ascend, I'm a commoner. You there in your head? Great. Now, tell me what you want to tell me."

"The Kingdom is sacrificing its young-" Zed's eyes rolled up into his head, and he leaned forward while puking violently.

"Oh, look, your Sigil is judging you as breaking one of the Oaths made to the Kingdom: not serving the best interest of the Royal Family." Taylor allowed a crooked smile to appear over her normally frosty expression. "We all do things we don't want to do, but this is one of the requirements for our Kingdom's continued survival. They are making us do things to save *everyone*. Sacrifices *must* be made. What is losing one life when you save a village?"

"A trade that I am not willing to make." Zed wiped his mouth and stood upright. "I would never-"

"How about *taking* a life?" Taylor caught Zed as he started to make a grand proclamation. "We are on our way to the warfront. Are you willing to kill to keep this Kingdom safe? To keep yourself *alive*?"

"I...! That's different." Zed deflated slightly.

"Only your perception of the subject is different." Taylor shifted her eyes forward and walked past the Bard, ignoring his sputtering attempts to respond. "This is why Bards have a bad reputation. All the pretty words; no action behind them."

"Careful with what you say; there are people hiding in those trees," Andre called to his group. Everyone followed his wave toward the trees he was indicating, and people started filtering out of the underbrush.

"Well, well, well. *Someone* has sharp eyes." A roguish man stepped onto the dirt path and crossed his arms menacingly. "This is the King's road, and we are tasked with putting together the funds to improve and maintain it! I'm sure that you will not mind donating to such a worthy cause?"

There was a long pause, where the only sound was the wind whistling through the trees around them. Luke looked over at Andre, then Taylor. "They are making an attempt at robbing us, correct?"

"Yes," Taylor stated flatly.

"No, 'rob' is such a harsh word for this." The man gestured

at the linen sack slung over Luke's shoulder. "We could use some of that gear. Some proper armor and weapons would make our jobs much easier."

"He is specifically... attempting to steal... *my* stuff?" Luke's words were a raging snarl.

Zed rolled his eyes and spoke sarcastically, "Technically *you* stole that first, so... *your* stuff? *Is* it?"

"Here you go." Luke swung the bag over his shoulder, slamming the accumulated weapons and armor into the man. The standard humans in the road had not even seen him move, and Andre only facepalmed in response. The leader of what was clearly a group of roaming marauders was crushed by the huge sack of metal, leaving a broken corpse on the road.

"Dibs on his sword." Luke picked up the sack once more, then looked down at the pancaked man while some of the others ran, screaming about 'Ascended monsters'.

"You are literally carrying a giant sack of swords!" One of the remaining bandits shouted at the Murderhobo. "What could you *possibly* gain from having another one?"

Luke appeared in front of that one as well, and a similar scene repeated itself. He looked over at his party once more, then pointed at the corpse. "Sword. Dibs."

That was enough to make even the bravest remaining among the bandits flee in terror. They didn't get too far, as they were running directly into the forest. Within five minutes, all of them had been collected by the trees they were running past and delivered to the four Ascenders. Each had been tied up carefully with vines, and the giant ball of people and plants began rolling along next to the road as Luke's group continued toward the warfront.

There was an outcry from the captured bandits, especially when they began to get motion sick. However, Andre was having none of that. "I'm bringing you to the warfront as conscripts. No, *hey*! Listen, you can all do it my way... or you can try your luck with him."

Complaints stopped after that, though it was clear that no

one was really happy with the situation. Conversation among the Ascenders lapsed when the group realized that they couldn't discuss their personal experiences anymore, for fear of their Sigils reacting. An entire day passed as the group talked over trivial topics and tried to get closer. Taylor started wavering between letting the conversation remain lacking or just tossing the bandits into a pit. However, before she had made her final choice, Andre resolved the issue by causing sticky plants to grow over the captives' eyes and ears.

"Thank the celestials that *citizens* of the Hollow Kingdom don't count as 'servants' of the Kingdom." Zed gulped as he contemplated how close he had come to dying from Luke's actions. With their involuntary companions secured, the group used the rest of their walk to talk about the trials they had gone through. Taylor and Andre dominated the conversation, with Zed mostly chiming in to get details, and Luke grunting. On the third day of travel, a group of *actual* sentries made their presence known.

"Halt! This is the King's road and leads to the warfront. Turn back, unless you are on official business." The leader of the sentries called. In an instant, Luke was in front of the man. His hand was wrapped around the sentry's skull, but a harsh *chime* made him pause.

"Oh." Luke looked at Zed. "This one not bandit?"

"No, that one *soldier*. Many protect Kingdom. Very Official. Wow." Zed shakily informed Luke, who let go of the soldier... after stealing his sword. It wasn't sneaky in the slightest; he tore the entire scabbard and belt off the man and tossed it into his oddly half-empty sack. "By chance, did you have a stroke, or are your speech capabilities just naturally declining?"

Andre spoke up before anyone could get too angry. "Greetings, loyal heroes of the Hollow Kingdom! We are a part of the new Ascender's Corps, and have been tasked with helping this front until we have either won the war or been given new orders! Where can we go to announce our presence?"

The sentries calmed down nearly instantly, smiling at the

figure that had suddenly turned into a golden Adonis in their eyes. The leader took one last look at the sword that had been stolen, but reluctantly gave up on getting it back. "Welcome, Ascenders. I'll show you to your commanding officer, and you can explain to him that I will need a new weapon, if that's fine by you."

"Of course," Taylor replied graciously, getting a thankful smile in return.

"There's more swords?" Luke butted into the conversation, getting a glare in return from the man.

"...Yes. This is a warzone. If we aren't making them, you can always take them off the people you kill at the front." The sentry started walking, as did the group. The ball of bandits and vines got a confused look as it rolled along, but it was not even close to the strangest thing that they had ever seen.

"You're saying that I can keep all the weapons of anyone I kill out there? What about armor?" Luke was questioning the sentry intently, and the man was getting annoyed.

"Yes, that is how it works. Spoils of war. You can keep it, or turn it in to the logistic group for the coin value of the gear." They were passing through the camp at this point, and only Luke and Taylor didn't flinch at the sounds and smells that were washing over them. Blood, sweat, latrines, death, screams, the clash of distant weapons... Taylor didn't react because her spells were keeping the scent away, and Luke didn't react because he was so used to the stench.

They only paused once, to unload all of the bandits into a forced conscription area. Without the giant rolling ball of plant matter, they were able to move much faster. They got closer and closer to the front, finally reaching a command center. The sentry walked up to the door, knocked briskly, and stood back. A ragged aide-de-camp threw the door open almost instantly, looking over them but letting his eyes linger on the sentry. "Report."

"Sir, Ascenders fresh from the training of the Kingdom. The four of them are here to report in and take on an assignment." The sentry waited there until he received a salute in reply.

"Understood." The officer glanced at the group tiredly, "Listen, there will not be a terribly huge amount for you to do here. Most of our Ascender assets are held back; people like you only go in if an Ascender shows up in *their* battle group. Go find a place to hunker down: there's your orders. If we just let Mages and such do whatever they want, this war will get out of hand far too quickly. This is a defensive war; all we need to do is discourage them enough, and they tend not to press the attack."

The group was generally okay with that, even though it meant they would be here for a long, long time. "I'll get you set up with the nice tents, in the officers' quarters. We will get you situated and introduced to the men tomorrow, so just get some rest tonight. One question for you all…?"

"Sir?" Andre tried to speak respectfully, though his stomach was threatening to rebel as another scream reached his ears.

"Didn't you say something about… *four* of you?"

Andre, Taylor, and Zed looked at each other and around with paling faces. At that precise moment, bellowed words trickled into their ears from a distance.

"*Bum Rush!*"

CHAPTER THIRTY-EIGHT

Luke had gotten bored simply *walking* when there was a fight that was clearly in progress. His sack of swords and armor had mostly been absorbed by Walking Arsenal by the time they had reached the encampment, though he needed another one hundred and fifty steel swords before he would be able to generate his own with his Mana. Sure, he was in the process of absorbing one right now, thanks to that sentry guy, but *one* sword was not going to cut it.

"Ha! Cut it! I'm still funny." Luke laughed uproariously as he jogged at a fast pace toward the front. He could see trenches in the distance, places where men could hide from artillery spells or duck into during a cavalry charge. As he moved, the last of the equipment he had... salvaged from the guard post finished vanishing into motes of mana. Luke decided to throw away his ragged, damaged blanket. He grabbed an entire tent as he went through the area, a small one, and didn't even bother to fold it up.

He got closer to the battle, and the ground under his feet became muddy and bloody - in a word: disgusting. Luke didn't mind. He moved faster, *faster*, and finally was in range. Words tore from his lips, and in his excitement, he bellowed. *"Bum Rush!"*

Luke crossed the last one hundred meters in a flash, his legs pumping as fast as they could. He swung his fist, hitting a surprised soldier that had been planning on skewering one of his countrymen with a sword. *His* new sword.

Damage: 119 (Blunt)

The soldier that he hit collapsed; dead in an instant. Luke waited for the Potentia updates, but nothing appeared. He spat on the ground and furiously growled, "They aren't even worth Potentia? How weak *are* they?"

Grabbing the sword that the soldier had been planning to use as it fell, Luke pinned the tent that he had brought with him to the ground. Three more basic attacks, three more soldiers defeated, and three swords added to the pile. Now that the tent had been pinned down in each of the four corners, Luke went on a rampage. There was simply nothing the standard soldiers could do to stop him. Their attacks hit him, arrows slammed into his body - most landing on his mana-made armor and falling off - but Luke continued moving. "Time to get geared up!"

The arrows stopped after barely penetrating his skin, and the swords created sparks as they skittered off of his glowing armor. Five, ten, thirty men dead on the ground in under two minutes. It would have been more, faster, but Luke was taking the time to carefully remove their armor and pile everything onto his pinned-down tent.

Even so, he was moving faster than any standard human could hope to match. There was one last push to try to defeat him; clearly, they were not thinking straight because of the rush of adrenaline in their minds. All the charge of the full battalion of soldiers did... was make Luke grin.

"Bum Rush!" He didn't bother to control himself. Luke simply barreled directly into the group as it ran at him. Anyone in his way was crushed, and when he stopped, he was surrounded on all sides. His fists began to lash out; for most of the people Luke attacked, the last thing that they saw was a glowing afterimage of goat horns closing in on their face.

"Soldier! What in *tarnation* are you doing? Ascenders are not allowed to take the field!" The shout was coming from Luke's side of the encampments, but he ignored it in favor of stripping the weapons and armor from the fallen battalion of men. "You are going to force them to send out their Mages!"

That didn't even give Luke pause; instead, he turned to look at the man running toward him across no-man's-land in excitement. "Mages…! Will they have magic weapons or armor?"

"Does it *matter* if they have them? Can you survive getting hit by a meteor?" The Officer was shouting in his face at this point, and only Luke's Sigil kept him from reducing this man to a meat paste as well. "I am ordering you to get your rear behind our front lines! I'll be taking you to the General immediately!"

"Who are you?" Something about this Officer was ringing a bell in Luke's mind. He looked down, "Nice boots."

"I am Captain Baker, and you are in direct violation of the Ascender accords!" Captain Baker grabbed at Luke, but the Murderhobo simply continued doing what he was doing, and the Captain showed surprise as he was easily dragged along. "Are you trying to bring the full might of the Dynasty of Dogs down on us?"

"You can't order me to do anything. We're the same rank. One hundred ten… one twenty?" Luke shook his head and stopped counting. "I need ten more, be right back."

With that, Luke left a flabbergasted Captain standing over the newly-acquired gear, and charged into enemy lines once more. Ten bodies and swords were rapidly thrown toward the Captain, and he dived out of the way to allow them to land on the spread-eagle tent. Luke returned to the Captain, pulled the swords that were holding the tent out of the ground, and finally rolled everything up into a makeshift sack. He tossed the blood-dripping sack over his back and coolly regarded the man in front of him. "All right, where are we going now?"

"Abyssal crazy Ascenders!" Captain Baker started running back toward the encampment, with Luke easily keeping pace with him despite carrying over a hundred swords and a bulging sack full of armor. "There's something *wrong* with you, isn't there, boy?"

"Not anymore! Got the swords I need." Luke replied directly as he hopped over a trench. "Armor too. Needed something for my head and legs; been trying to make goat hide work, and it just never did."

"Goat hide? What?" Captain Baker looked at Luke askance, then turned to face him fully. "Hold a moment, I know you… you are the son of that leatherworker we got our boots from. What's it been, two years? Three? What happened to you, lad?"

Luke didn't reply, though his eyes did wander to the tracks that Captain Baker was leaving in the mud. There was a symbol there, the same symbol that now appeared on his Sigil. Captain Baker seemed to have calmed down, and the realization that he knew the man he was running with had put him in a different frame of mind. "You don't even know it, but you made a huge mess of things here. I'll do what I can to put in a good word for you. I suppose no one has explained the rules, if you have just arrived?"

"That sounds correct." Luke didn't actually care about the rules, but if it would keep him from having to do annoying things, he would agree every time.

"On the plus side, you wiped out a swath of our enemies, which should be enough to give our men a day off. Unless you royally pissed off the enemy commander, of course. I guess we'll see by tomorrow," Captain Baker sighed, and they slowed down as they made their way through the Officer's area and arrived at the tent that Luke had seen his group approaching earlier. "General, Captain Baker reporting in! I have a SitRep for you, a critical incident."

The aide-de-camp came out, took a single look at Luke, and

went back indoors. A few moments later, a man who was clearly a General and in charge of the area stepped out. There was something about him, an aura of power and authority, which made Luke realize that he was in the presence of another Ascender. That made sense to him; if the person with the most authority in the area was a standard human, the Ascenders would have run roughshod over him. In fact... oh. Luke realized that he had already seen Generals back when he returned to this world, and they were all Ascenders as well.

"Report, Captain."

"Sir! An Ascender fresh out of the Initiate ranks arrived today, this man here, and joined at the battlefield immediately. He killed nearly two hundred opponents before I was able to stop him, took only about... four and a half minutes." Captain Baker explained as succinctly as possible, swallowing deeply as he realized how short that timeframe had actually been. "He had not been taught the rules, simply rushed in as soon as he got here. I don't think he was trying to destroy our battle rhythm; he was just over-enthusiastic."

"I'll be the judge of that." The General locked eyes with Luke, giving him a stare down that would have made a normal person cringe. "I got a report from the Archmage about a troublesome individual that would be joining us shortly. I can only assume that you are the... Murderhobo, is it?"

"That's what I'm told." Luke was clearly uninterested, his entire focus on the weapons and armor that were contained in the rolled tent he was holding.

"I suppose you have not been informed as to exactly *what* that title means." Power was gathering around the General. He was clearly displeased with the dismissive attitude Luke was displaying. "I was told that the Enchanter who applied that name didn't even understand exactly how apt a title it was. A Murderhobo is a derogatory term for a criminal Ascender, a person who wanders the world, unattached to any community, indiscriminately killing and looting."

Luke simply shrugged. It sounded like the name was fitting.

The General narrowed his eyes further, practically squinting at Luke. "By the Enchanter's report, he named you that because you said that your portal leads you to a place called 'Murder World', your gear was all over the place, and you smelled terrible. In fact, he wanted your class name just to be ' hobo', but you were too powerful to offend so directly. That clearly did not work out well for him, as our healers are still working to stabilize his condition."

"However, that was proof that your Sigil does not work as it should. You should not be able to attack members of our Ascender Corps, nor should you be able to be so disrespectful to the Military Officers around you." At this point, the aide-de-camp stepped out of the tent and handed a file over to the General. The General opened it, read over a few lines and nodded, then handed it to Luke. "There is only one thing that we can do. You need to be stationed further away from our area, where your tendencies will not impact people like they will here. Here are your new orders."

An awkward silence stretched, with the General holding out the folder, and Luke ignoring him. Finally, the General barked, "Take the folder, and get out of my sight!"

Luke's Sigil lit up, and his hand stretched out to take the folder. As soon as he did, information poured into his mind.

Quest failed: Assist the warfront! You lose two months' worth of pay. A new Quest has been assigned.

Quest gained: Sending monsters after monsters (Repeatable). You have been deemed too dangerous to remain in the same area as other humans. You and your team will now be employed as Kingdom-sanctioned bounty hunters, gaining pay and resources only by completing dangerous and deadly tasks that others are deemed too valuable to be sent to complete.

Your first task is to reclaim a mountain pass in the Northeast section of the Kingdom; a map has been provided. The pass has fallen to the Dynasty of Dogs, but the method they used to capture the pass is unknown. There are reports that monsters are involved. Succeed, or die trying.

Reward: Pay and Merit commensurate with the danger and difficulty of the mission. This will be evaluated by your Sigil once the mission has been completed. All rewards must be received in person by your Commanding Officer. Failure: death.

"Any questions?" The General was hoping to see doubt, fear, uncertainty. All he got in reply from Luke was a smile.

"I'm not seeing a time limit."

CHAPTER THIRTY-NINE

The four team members were marching through the woods again, but this time, everyone except Luke was in a very bad mood. Zed glared at the Murderhobo and had to hold back his scream of frustration. "Seriously, when you notice a flaw like a lack of a time limit? You keep that to yourself. You could have just... *left*! Gone to do anything you wanted to do for the next several decades, or until one of the members of the nobility caught up to you! Instead, you taunt the General right to his face!"

"I admit, was not my smartest move." Luke's eyes were always roving, scanning the environment for threats or resources that he would be able to use. "I didn't realize that it was possible to modify quests."

"If they can *make* them, why couldn't they *change* them?" Taylor questioned him. "The logic is very simple; you need to use your head."

Luke was quiet for a while, but then he turned and locked eyes with Andre. "I have been alone for the vast majority of my life, and for most of that time, I was desperately hoping to get back in contact with my friends and family. However. I have forgotten you. Tell me what I have missed."

"Are you trying to become friends with me all over again?" Andre bellowed, slamming his Livingwood staff on to the ground and causing plants in the area to wave around wildly. Luke tensed up, preparing himself for the inevitable combat. "*Excellent*! I'm glad you are reaching out; let's talk!"

Everyone except for Andre was dizzy at that instant change in demeanor; the Druid simply started speaking. "We touched on our situations lightly, so let's dig in deeper. I was tossed into the Druidic Grove world, and found that my master had an extremely sadistic streak. He used me as a test subject for his plans to advance his career, and the worst part... is that everything was *successful*. It worked amazingly well, and I gained power *fast*."

"Later on, it turned out that he was actually a very nice guy, and we became good friends. Let me see... I can tell you this, but you can't tell others, agreed? Good. I reached level eight, and am focused in Capacity. The thing that set me apart in the first place was my massive mana pool, and my goal has always been extraordinary changes in territory. This means that I need huge reserves of mana, else my goals are not achievable."

A short period of silence followed, then Zed stepped in. "That's it? What your *focus* is when talking about a sub-characteristic? What about your powers? Things that you can do? ... Nifty anecdotes, perhaps?"

"All of these are things that I refuse to share." Andre shook his head gravely, "I can tell you that I use *abilities*, not powers, yet I cannot tell you what they are. I found that if I give away this information lightly, others will know my weaknesses. I am much safer in our Kingdom than I was in The Grove, but there are still limits to what I'm willing to share."

"Because it has been decades for all of us? Because we don't know each other anymore?" Taylor spoke in an even tone, assessing what he was telling her and looking for flaws in the story.

"Admittedly, that thought has crossed my mind," Andre told the others, and Luke nodded at the words.

"I am glad. Trust is never *given*. Good to know that I am not abnormal." Luke didn't see that the others winced when he made that comment.

"At least you'll be useful in reclaiming the pass," Zed told Andre after considering for a few moments. "Make a few trees slam things to death; abyss, make them walk and control them like golems! Them we can ride in style and-"

"Oh, right. I also can't intentionally kill any sentient creature," Andre rattled off the restriction, and Zed almost exploded.

"You can't *kill?*" He waved an angry hand at Luke, "He has a gear fetish, and you can't *kill?* What's wrong with you, Taylor? Are you a bed-wetter?"

Surprisingly, that made Taylor's previously *always* ridgid face turn beet-red. A blast of force took Zed off his feet and tossed him into the underbrush. "Mind your tongue! Even if we are party members for a short time, remember that I am the next Archmage-apparent! Keep your filthy words to yourself!"

"That was... out of character. Touch a nerve, did I?" Zed slowly got to his feet, blood dripping from a cut across his forehead... and tears slowly seeping from his eyes. He then silently rejoined the group and walked along without speaking or tending to his wound.

Taylor took the opportunity to offer the information that she was willing to part with, "I am a subclass of Mage called a 'Namer'. I have reached level seven, and have reached the highest levels with my Senses. My Physical Reactions and Mental Energy are nearly equivalent in power. I use spells to take down my enemies from a distance, and I have no such restrictions on killing. I simply cannot use disease-style spells."

"Is that a restriction of your class?" Andre hesitantly asked; he was uncertain what had made her attack Zed, and he did not want to come in contact with her wrath.

"A small one, based only on the specific components that I

use," Taylor explained matter-of-factly, turning her eyes to the horizon.

"I have reached level nine." Luke instantly had the attention of everyone around him, and their expressions were full of shock and doubt.

"Did you not devote any of your gathered Potentia into your... powers?" Andre put forward the question they were all wondering about.

"I did." Luke's face twisted, and he snarled at his resurfacing memories. "I was trapped in a small area for *decades*, and got to the point where I had killed so many of the same thing, so many times, that I simply got no Potentia for years at a time. Though, I did train in such a mana-rich environment that my sub-characteristics have all increased fairly massively. I believe that I terrified the Enchanter who tested me. That was before I kicked him through the wall for trying to fry my brain. In terms of what I specialized in? I suppose my Fitness? It just reached over forty points."

"Celestial *Feces*." Zed whispered so softly that it was only heard because he was surrounded by Ascenders.

"My power? I suppose you mean my skills. I don't have many, but my most powerful one is based on having access to armor and weapons." Luke unfurled the tents that he had been carrying everything in for a full day, giving it a shake to show that it was now empty. He simply dropped the tent on the ground and continued walking after that. "I am able to absorb them, then use them with my mana instead of having to wear them. However, the more I have, the more damage I can deal and receive."

"Let me be clear; if we get anything that I can use, I *will* be taking it." Luke's words were a threat, not a simple assertion. "I have my own goal, and I will not let anyone or anything stand in the way of it. The only reason I am not back in Murder World right now is that *Don* cut me off!"

They continued walking through the forest quietly after Luke's outburst, and Zed finally allowed his boredom to overcome his grumpiness. "Hello everyone, I am a True Bard, and I was able to reach level four in the last two and a half years. Not all of us were able to go to some luxurious alternate dimension to train, and my training has consisted of moving between populated areas to tell stories, as well as spreading inane propaganda on behalf of the Hollow Kingdom."

There was no comment, so Zed kept speaking. "I use what are called 'Masteries', and they are based on controlling, subverting, and bending others to my will. What I mean is, bending others to the will of the Kingdom. Guess what? I can't use masteries on other Ascenders that are part of the Kingdom! I *also* can't use them on regular civilians, unless ordered by the Kingdom! Do you have any idea how difficult it was to gain the number of levels that I did?"

"My master nailed me to a tree to teach me how to give it nutrients so that I could eat one apple a day for about three months," Andre blithely stated.

Taylor joined in on the gripe session, "Archmage Don threw me off a cliff and made me survive in an area populated by tier five and higher spellforms for the last few years."

"I spent forty years alone, with a majority of that devoted to killing goats, eating hallucinogenic berries, and losing the love of my life." Luke's words made the others look at him questioningly. "She isn't dead, I simply have to progress further in Murder World to get her back."

"I thought you were alone there?" Zed's question got him a glare in return. "Right, a subject not to bring up. Two of those in a single conversation, lovely. Well, I clearly specialize in the sub-characteristic 'Charisma'. I'm hoping that our time together will get us great stories, so that I can start gaining Potentia and levels again in the near future."

"How about you, Zed?" Andre thumped the thin Bard on the back. "Any restrictions on killing?"

Zed shrugged at the question. "Just can't kill people that are citizens of the Kingdom. Not without orders at least."

"Same as the rest of us," Taylor chimed in with a grin.

"I could." Luke's words stopped the conversation cold. "Wouldn't even make me blink."

"Bandits don't count." Andre tried to move the conversation along, letting out a nervous laugh.

"Bandits?" Luke thought for a moment, shrugged, and kept walking.

CHAPTER FORTY

Their journey was not a short one, since they were walking at a fairly normal pace to allow Zed to stay with them. Most of them were used to solitude and silence, and only Zed was used to having regular conversations. Yet, roughly a week had passed since their awkward attempt at reintroducing themselves, and *Luke* was becoming more and more twitchy. Eventually, it got to the point that Zed, who had been dying for conversation and kept getting shut down, couldn't handle it anymore. He turned on Luke, and exploded, "*What?* For Celestial's sake, *what?*"

"Do you not see that the forest around us has been reaching out toward us the whole time we've been walking? Now that the trees are getting closer together, I'm not sure how much further we will be able to go before we get attacked. I am debating whether I should destroy them before they can ambush us." Luke's words were calm, but he radiated a killing intent that almost made his teammates step away from him. "One moment; I need to make sure my weapons and armor are ready."

"Weapons and armor? You're barely clothed with the canvas pants and shirt we forced you to wear. *What* weapons and armor? You keep *eating* them." Zed looked scornfully at the ragged garments that Luke was wearing only because they insisted that he not walk around naked.

"Skill check, Fully Geared. No. Walking Arsenal. Gotta get used to that. Old habits." Luke ignored Zed and scanned the status screen that popped up.

Gear

Head: Simple Metal Helm (Crafted). Effect: +7% of overall health is added as armor. Head is considered armored when attacked. Strength: Slashing/piercing attack reduction (40%). Weakness: Blunt force, lightning elemental damage reduction (-1%).

Shoulders: Simple Metal Pauldron (Crafted). Effect: +3% of overall health is added as armor. Shoulders are considered armored when attacked. Strength: Blunt force attack reduction (10%). Weakness: Lightning elemental damage reduction (-8%).

Gauntlet: Metal Gauntlet (Stone Ape). Effect: +10% of overall health is added as armor. Hands are considered armored when attacked. Strength: Slashing/piercing attack reduction (80%). Weakness: Blunt force, magical, elemental damage reduction (2%).

Torso: Simple Metal Cuirass (Crafted). Effect: +5% of overall health is added as armor. Torso is considered armored when attacked. Strength: Slashing/blunt attack reduction (60%). Weakness: Lightning elemental damage reduction (-10%).

Legs: Simple Metal Greaves (Crafted). Effect: +4% of overall health is added as armor. Legs are considered armored when attacked. Strength: Slashing/piercing attack reduction (30%). Weakness: Lightning elemental damage reduction (-9%).

Feet: Ornate Leather Boots (Crafted). Effect: +1% of overall health is added as armor. Feet are considered armored when attacked. Strength: Slashing/piercing attack reduction (10%). Weakness: Blunt force attack reduction (-9%).

Right Hand: Battering Ram Knuckles. Effect: +5% physical damage (Blunt). Right hand treated as a weapon when attacking.

Left Hand: Simple Steel Sword. Effect: +3% physical damage (Slashing/Piercing). Attack range increased by 1 meter. Left hand treated as a weapon when attacking.

"I doubt that those trees are going to be able to throw around lightning bolts… I can take them." Luke muttered to himself, a bad habit that he had gotten into after being alone for so long. *"Death to trees!"*

"Please don't attack the trees," Andres' serene voice sounded out, the first time that he had spoken in several days. Still, his plea was too late. Luke had attacked with his left hand, shattering the trunk of a tree and leaving a deep hole that radiated cracks in a large boulder that was right behind it.

"They're attacking us!" Luke insisted as the tree fell over with a crashing groan. He inspected his left hand and the boulder, pleased with his increased attack range from the absorbed sword. "On the plus side, there is no rush. We can get to them; they can't get to us unless we get close! I can attack at a distance now!"

"Is an extra arm length considered 'at range'?" Zed idly mused.

Andre watched the tree fall over helplessly, feeling a twinge of pain as it did so. "Luke, I am binding the trees as we walk. They're not reaching out to attack us, they are accepting the bond that I am offering. I'm using the opportunity of walking along our border to start taking control of the flora of the kingdom. Eventually I will make everything in the Kingdom work together in harmony, and the accumulated Potentia and mana generated by this harmonious air will work to improve the lives of our citizens. This will extend to everything from becoming Ascenders, to simple improved fertility, and healthier children. So again, *please* stop attacking the trees."

"Does that have something to do with the reason why you are bleeding?" Luke stepped closer to Andre; whose eyes widened in surprise and filled with caution.

"How did you know that?"

"You smell like blood, and no matter how much time has been passing, it always smells fresh. Does that have something to do with your abilities?" Luke sniffed at the air again, then his eyes wandered to the palm of Andre's left hand.

"It does; that is as much information as I would like to share." Andre hid his bleeding hand from view, pulling his hands into the extra-wide sleeves of his green robes.

"I had wondered what Druids did. Makes more sense now when I hear it laid out like that." Zed offered easily. "They bleed on things and make them grow."

"That is *not* what Druids do. Luke, leave the trees alone." Andre's voice was firm, and this time, more demanding than polite.

Luke looked at the trees one more time, then glared at the Druid. "This wouldn't be the *first* time I've been attacked by trees. If you are wrong about them, don't come crying to me!"

"Trees attacked you? *Trees?*" Andre stopped walking, an idea starting to form in his head.

"Fine. It was bushes. They were poisonous."

"That's different, and you know it. Look." Andre pulled a hand from his sleeve and started moving it side-to-side. As he did so, all of the plant life as far as the eye can see followed along with the motion of his hand perfectly. Luke started glowing blue as he devoted mana to his armor. "That's pretty. I am waiting for it to all go out of your control and need to be destroyed. My expectation is clear."

"Literally can't happen. Not only are they bound to me, they are bound to me *willingly*." Andre sighed as Luke shook his head.

"If they are bound to you willingly, they could *leave* your control willingly. Don't worry. I'll keep an eye on them." Luke lapsed into silence, and the group continued walking. Over the next day, the forest around them began to thin, shifting into grasslands and prairie.

"We are getting close to the pass. If you have high enough senses, you can see the mountains in the distance. The area that we need to reclaim is in there." Taylor pointed out, directing her comrades. "Prepare yourselves; the rest of the trip should take a day at most."

Zed didn't see anything, so he simply shrugged and

continued walking. "If you say so, then all right. Another question: if this pass is so important, why has the Kingdom not worked to get it back? Why are *we* going there?"

"Did you all notice that the grass is moving?" Luke looked around in concern.

"That's me," Andre told him with a long-suffering sigh. "I have my work cut out for me; grass takes a lot of time. Don't worry. *Again*, it is going to be under my control."

"Good to know. I'll keep an eye on it."

Taylor spoke up before another argument could break out, "The pass is so far away from population centers that it doesn't make sense to go and spend a huge amount of resources capturing it. Normally it would be a trade route, or a military asset if we were in an all-out war, but the current border skirmish has not gotten to that point. Since only merchants are heavily affected by the loss, it has never made sense to send an army. I think that the only reason they sent us is that all of the scouts that have been going there in recent months have not been returning."

"Question for you! Why do you know all of this, and we do not? If anything, my Bardic Knowledge should be what is telling us what we need to know," Zed challenged her. "I read the same report that you did, so I should have the same information that you do. *But*, you seem to keep pulling facts out of nowhere."

Taylor was sick of being questioned over and over by Zed, so she finally gave him a complete answer. "My training was not merely upon how to gain my power. It was over *all* aspects of the Kingdom; its management, its logistics, everything that I needed to know in order to make decisions as the Archmage. With the time dilation, I was allowed to study as much as I wanted, and nothing ever went out of date due to waiting too long to read the reports. I will just know *more* than you. It is to be expected. Also, Zed, I don't know if I like you very much."

"The feeling is mutual. You are a willing pet of the Kingdom, and I know that you saw what happened when my abilities were revealed." Zed's reply was instant; it seemed that he had been bottling the rant up for a while. "I am *bound* to do what I am told, and there is no end in sight for me. You simply need to get strong enough - quickly enough – for the end to be in sight. For me? The only way for me to do that is to be among people, lots of people, for a *long* period of time. My handlers seem to hate Bards, and thus refused to give me what I need to advance. Now I'm with all of you, in the wilderness, once more away from people."

"*You* wanted to come with us," Andre pointed out evenly.

"It was go with you, or continue being forced to keep my mouth closed as I wandered in the Kingdom. Do you know that is the only way to keep me from gaining Potentia? Not allowing me to speak or catch attention from other people?"

Luke looked over at him, "Do you gain extra Potentia from complaining? If so, you should be level five already."

Taylor and Andre let out soft chuckles, and wry grins appeared on their faces. Even Zed had to hang his head for a moment to compose himself. "All right, fair enough. I'll try to chill a little; I know that my situation isn't your fault. In fact, without you, I would be in a much worse situation… however, I do have some demands."

"*Bo~o~o.*" Andre called out. "Why are you in a position to make demands?"

"Because I have trained my voice; I can literally complain for a week straight. I have enough Fitness that I don't need sleep for that amount of time. Your call!" Zed waited for a long moment, then smiled. "I *thought* so. Here it is: all I need is time in every city that we pass to tell the people in the area about our adventures. That is the only way I will be able to benefit from working with you in terms of empowering myself. If we do that, I promise I will be the best companion you have ever had in your travels."

"Deal," Taylor told them.

"Done," affirmed Andre.

"Don't care." Luke leveled a lingering look, "You don't get Potentia from fighting?"

"You only get it when you participate in combat, and the things you'll fight would kill me in an instant. Not like you can keep a beast off me long enough for me to hit it and get out of the way." Zed perked up happily after Luke nodded in understanding. Knowing that he had finally gotten a win - after several years of training under people who clearly hated him - brought his mood up instantly. "Now that we are actually a party working together, let me show you some of my Masteries!"

CHAPTER FORTY-ONE

"That was a stricture called 'Pass the Time'," Zed explained as the group looked around in a slight daze. "It is a Mastery of mine, a way for me to tell an engaging story in a way that makes the mind fold in upon itself. Obviously, there are side effects, so I cannot use it when we are in dangerous situations, but it makes long distance travel much more palatable."

They were standing at the foothills of the mountain range, and after he started talking, none of them except for Zed felt the passage of time as they walked. Andre mindlessly continued binding plants, Luke seemed to doze off, and Taylor went distant-eyed.

Finally, Zed took a deep breath and smiled, ready to announce that they were at their destination. Before he could get the words out, Zed suddenly choked as Luke's hand wrapped around his neck and he was lifted in the air. The Murderhobo bellowed in his face like a lion, "You told us that your abilities would *not* work on us! What else have you been lying about? Should I kill you right here so that I know that my mind is my own? Can you make hallucinations? Zed! *Can you take them away?*"

Luke's eyes were wild, and veins were sticking out on his forehead and neck. Zed was struggling in his grasp, but there was nothing that he could do against the raw power contained in Luke's body. He glanced at the others for help, but both Taylor and Andre were staring at him with cold eyes, ready to let this play out however it would. Zed struggled to speak, and Luke almost decided to finish the job, but his Sigil chimed and his hands released Zed of their own accord.

Zed lay on the ground coughing, the spittle coming out of his mouth flecked with drops of red blood. Finally, he was able to hoarsely shout, "What is *wrong* with you? I didn't lie, I *can't* use abilities on anyone! I don't *have* abilities!"

"So, you simply twisted your words to change their *meaning*," Luke growled at the fallen Bard. "You were trying to lull us into a false sense of security, so that you could trap us within our own minds when we were not expecting it."

"Hello, I'm… a Bard." Zed started to stand, but a line of liquid fire zipped past his face, courtesy of Taylor. Zed swallowed his words and some blood. Settling back, his voice rasped out, "Well, then. The ground is just as comfortable of a place to explain. First off, let me start with a way to calm you down. I hereby swear on my Sigil that I will not use my Masteries, or any *other* type of power I may gain, to harm any of you three unless it is to help or save you. All *set?*"

His Sigil chimed and a new line slashed across on it, signifying that the oath was binding him. Taylor and Andre calmed down immediately, and Luke did as well after they explained to him what had just happened. After this, Zed continued, "All I was doing was trying to make sure that I was going to be safe. The three of you are clearly much more powerful than I am, and have much more combat utility. I didn't know if you were just taking me into the distance to execute me. It has been a serious concern in the past."

"And the *reason* you messed with our minds?" Taylor demanded as soon as his words stopped flowing.

"I swear to you, it was only an attempt to help us arrive

where we were going in a timely manner! We were all caught up, and people were getting grumpy with each other because of the distance that we had to travel yet. Now, we are within a few hour's walk of our destination, and everyone should have been very pleased and happy with the outcome. Instead…" Zed motioned at the blood on the ground as well as his manhandled flesh.

"Next time, you should make sure to *ask*." Taylor nodded meaningfully toward Luke, "It seems that it takes a while for his Sigil to come into effect, long enough to kill. Perhaps you should think on that before you just do *something*."

"Zed, listen." Andre knelt next to his friend and looked over the blossoming bruise on his neck. "For us, we have all been away from each other for *decades*. What do you think that does to a person? Especially *us*, who seem to have been dropped in the abyss or constantly needing to watch our backs? Beyond that, Zed, remember that we only *actually* knew you for… um."

"Under half a year. He came to our town about six months before the testing." Taylor supplied helpfully.

"There. The rest of us knew each other our entire lives, and look at how we act toward each other." Andre allowed his sadness about that fact to seep into his tone and expression. "Now, we are thirty to fifty-year-old people in the bodies of eighteen year olds, and we were all *just* starting to trust everyone in the group… then one of us *instantly* uses that trust to mess with our minds. I feel that Luke's reaction is… *justified*, if overdone."

"Right, well, got it. Fast travel is *out* in the future." Zed shook his head, rubbed his neck, and stood all the way up. "I got us here; time for *you* three to do some work."

The Bard crossed his arms and refused to look at them anymore, so the others simply started to ignore him; except Luke, who kept throwing dangerous glares at the man every once in a while. Taylor stepped up, working to clear the air as well as progress their mission. " I will scout the situation. Until then, we need a few other things to happen. Luke, guard the area. Andre, how long will it take for you to set defenses across the entirety of the exit of this pass? We need a plan for retreat, there needs to be a reason *why* our scouts have not returned in the past."

"I'll need a solid few hours." Andre got to work right away, reaching into a pocket and pulling out a handful of seeds.

"And me?" Zed stood in a profound position, his arms behind him as he exuded the air of an expert.

"Set up camp, no fire. We can't let whatever is in here know that *we* are here." Taylor's words made Zed wilt like a flower in the summer heat. While the other three were looking at her, she simply vanished from all of their senses. "I'm off to figure out what's going on; be ready for when I return."

"Where are you?" Zed called out as the others started moving. "Did you see where she went? Guys? Sheesh... I'm supposed to set up camp? What is *Andre* going to do to create defenses? And what is Luke guarding *against*?"

Zed looked at the others for support, but found Andre surrounded by a wall of thorns that were already starting to crawl across the ground. The Druid was holding a giant bow, and would reach a hand down to the thorns to pull up an arrow made of the wood. Using the newly grown arrows, he attached and fired what looked like small wineskins. As these small packets hit the stone above them, the sacks burst into scatterings of seeds, which turned into plants that grew far too fast to be natural.

Zed watched the process in amazement for a few long minutes, then looked over at Luke to share his enthusiasm for the magical display. The Murderhobo wasn't paying attention, instead standing next to a huge boulder that had clearly fallen from higher on the mountain.

"This looks suspicious."

Luke started scratching at the stone with a finger, creating a shower of powder with each touch, while Zed simply let his head sink into his hands. "What the *abyss* have I gotten myself into?"

"If what you've gotten into *isn't* the supplies to set up camp, you don't need to worry about it," Andre called from his new perch atop a nearby stone. The bow was gone, and his planted seeds were growing into a thorny maze even as he spoke. Every once in a while, he would point at something to direct the growth of the defensive wall he was making.

"A rock this size doesn't just stop after only rolling a little bit." Luke dug his hands deeper into the stone, creating gravel with every motion.

"It landed over a hole, so just leave it alone," Andre called over. He had already sent roots through the area; he would obviously know where there were holes and where there were other things in the ground. "By the way, if we recapture this area, we need to let the Kingdom know that there's a huge amount of natural coal, iron, and other resources in these foothills. This could turn into one of the largest ore mines in the country, if we play it right."

"You think that was why they took the pass?" Zed quizzed as he got to work, expertly setting up their tents and getting dinner ready. He was mixing ingredients and stirring powders at a speed that would make professional chefs glare in envy. "Hey, how hungry are you guys?"

"Are those shadows moving?" Luke was on all fours, watching shadows slowly creep across the ground. "I haven't seen this before."

"That happens when the sun starts to go down. You've seen night before, Luke," Andre explained with a smile at the man's actions. "Zed, why were you so against us having you set up camp? You're amazing at it."

"Just because I'm *good* at something doesn't mean I want to be forced to do it," Zed replied just as easily. "Looks like it's going to rain soon. I hope Taylor gets back before then."

"I'm here." Taylor's cold voice cut through the area, drawing their attention to the shivering Mage. "Guys. It's worse. It's so *much* worse than we thought it was."

"Please feel free to expand upon your explanation." Andre

climbed down from his rock, pulling a thick blanket out of his backpack and offering it to her. She ignored him; her own cloak was more than sufficient.

"The pass… it wasn't taken by the Dynasty of Dogs." Taylor locked eyes with the Druid. "This place was taken by the Anarcanists; there is a massive scar in the center of the pass. There are *thousands* of monsters surrounding it, and the worst part…"

Taylor paused, just a *second* too long for Zed to handle. "What? *What?* Finish the story!"

"They have a leader." Lightning cracked into the mountains far above them, and the *boom* of thunder echoed for long seconds. "An intelligent monster."

"*The sky is attacking!*" Luke shouted at them as his fists began furiously pounding the air above him.

Zed slapped his forehead and groaned in defeat before turning and shouting at the Murderhobo. "That's *rain*, you moron!"

CHAPTER FORTY-TWO

"I heard you clearly when you stated that a huge amount of enemies were waiting in there," Zed smiled weakly as they huddled all together in the cramped tent that he had managed to set up before the rain began falling, "but what does that mean for us? Do we flee and bring back an army? *Two* armies?"

"There is simply not enough information." Taylor replied after a moment of thinking. "We don't know where they are coming from, and we don't know where they are going. We need to, at a *minimum*, keep an eye on them."

"We can take them! Look at how powerful we are as a group!" Andre waved at the vast forest of thorny death that was even now creeping toward the center of the pass. "I think that together, we can do anything we set our minds to!"

"I wouldn't mind seeing if I can get some Potentia from them," Luke shrugged as he went back to watching the rain fall, fascinated by the sight. He hadn't seen anything like it for decades, and it brought forth a strange nostalgia. "The waterfall! That was kind of like this!"

By now, no one flinched at his random outbursts. Zed reached out and patted Luke on the arm. "Yes, waterfalls and rain are *very* similar. The big difference is how *concentrated* the water is in any given area."

"Stop being condescending, Zed." Taylor turned her head and took in the whole group. "Look, I don't think that you are all taking me seriously when I tell you that there are tens of *thousands* of monsters in there right now. Luke, you can be swarmed to death just like anyone else. Andre, you can't kill the leader, he's *got* to be sapient."

"And Zed shouldn't be forced into the fighting." Andre blinked in shock as a voice which sounded exactly like his spoke out.

"What the...? I didn't say that! Wait, is that really what I sound like?" Andre looked suspiciously at Zed. "Did you just mimic my voice?"

"*May~be.*" Zed winked at the huge Druid. "It wasn't an incorrect statement, though; my fighting skills are basically nil. I can charm people for a while, then lull them into false security, but then I need to rely on killing them while they don't see me as a threat."

"You should focus more on stealth, if that's what is keeping you alive," Taylor ordered him sternly. Zed waved her off with a non-committal grumble. "I have serious doubts about our ability to fight this horde, and yet I can't imagine that the Kingdom is *oblivious* to what is waiting in here. I think they have *some* data, and assume it is a minimal risk, but not that it is this bad."

"What do we do?" Andre sat upright and gazed at the person who had become the unofficial official leader of the team.

"First, we set up defenses and a fallback point. You've already started by getting the thorns going, but we need a secure area as well that can keep us safe if we need to hunker down. As fast as we are, monsters tend to be more powerful overall if they match your level. Remember, they've spent their entire *lives* in high mana concentrations; we only visit." Taylor rose and walked to the edge of the tent, right where the fabric met stone.

"I can make the last-resort fallback point, but I'll need to concentrate on this really hard. If anything happens, you all need to handle it, or I might accidentally drop the mountain on us. Just so you know, this will likely alert them that we are here. I think it is necessary, though."

"Sure, but what are you-" Zed was cut off as Taylor whispered a single word.

"*Fissure.*"

Purple mana tinged with black streaks erupted from her hands, flowing into the stone and causing the ground to grumble. The sound was soft at first, but as she maintained the spell, it became loud and insistent. Zed was knocked to the ground as a line of broken stone opened in the mountain wall and a stone room slowly formed.

Very slowly formed. The shaking continued, and the noise was maintained, but after ten minutes, the process was very boring to watch. So, Zed and Andre's head instantly snapped to attention when Luke spoke up. "There. That stone I was looking at earlier."

"Yes, Luke?" Andre prodded when Luke went quiet.

"It moved."

Zed blew an exasperated blast out of his nose. "*Lots* of rocks moving in the area, Luke. Taylor is making an earthquake. I wouldn't be surprised if a landslide killed us all."

Even so, all three of the men watched the boulder with varying levels of intensity. So, when tiny legs popped out of the sides, all of them saw at the same time. There was no delay between the legs appearing and Luke getting on his feet and rushing at it.

"I *knew* it!"

The fist of the Murderhobo met the side of the rock with a ringing *boom*, and a pile of stone fragments and dust exploded out from the point of impact. There was a *clack*, and Luke came flying out of the cloud. A hasty vine whipped from Andre and slowed Luke enough that he was able to get his balance, though the plant was pulped by the force.

What had been a 'boulder' was now fully revealed as some kind of humanoid hermit crab monster. If a centaur was a cross between human and horse, this was a cross of crab and man. Instead of human hands, there were oversized pincers. Little legs allowed it to scuttle around at surprising speed, and it had eye stalks coming from the top of its otherwise human head.

Zed felt his hair whip around as Luke zipped past him, and a second shower of stone - and this time ichor - blasted from the impact point. "Where is your weak point, crab man?"

An arrow followed closely behind the hobo, bending around him to slam into the monster and detonate into spores that defied natural distribution; instead coating the creature and bonding to its carapace as if they had been applied with glue.

Interaction between a Binding ability and a concentrated mana source has created a temporary overlap.

Luke damages Stone Scuttler: 222 (Blunt damage).

"You can do it! Take that bad beasty down!" Zed called encouragement as he tucked and rolled to avoid the high-speed stone that was flying everywhere. His next words were tinged with surprise. "Also, not sure if this is normal, but I can see the damage that you're doing!"

"I can't see what he's doing? Or are you talking to me?" Andre's voice was calm as he focused on controlling the root system of the ferns that were sprouting all over the creature. There was a sharp *crack* as they managed to tear off a section of stone armor.

Andre damages Stone Scuttler: 36 (armor break).

"Oh, I can see yours too!" Zed was ecstatic. "You can't see each other's notifications? Yes! I can be our group tactician! I'm useful! Luke, that section that just fell removed all the armor from that spot, hit there!"

Luke was in the air in an instant, pouncing like a starving tiger. His left hand came down on the small opening, and a ghostly sword sank a full meter into the fleshy area that had been exposed. Spine severed, the beast stiffened, then went limp.

Luke damages Stone Scuttler: 149 (Piercing damage). Coup de grace! Overkill! Exp gained: 14 (42 split by three party members. T1 Stone Scuttler destroyed.)

Recently gained Potentia has been absorbed to induce the formation of a Mastery based on previous interaction!

"Celestial Saints and golden lyres! I got a Mastery! Oh, I think that it was nearly dead already, but that attack was extra effective, Luke." Zed was cheerfully looking over the notifications. "How many times did you hit it?"

"Three." Luke rumbled at him, examining his own status. "I got Potentia for that. But we are on the base world... nothing here has given me Potentia. How did?"

"Well, to be fair, all you have killed so far are some random soldiers and a tree, so it should be hard to make a judgement call on Potentia. Also, please use full sentences." Zed judgmentally looked at the mess that was coating Luke and frowned. "Didn't you say you had armor? Where did it go? Why aren't you wearing any?"

"I am."

"Right, but see... you *aren't*. You have a blood-covered canvas shirt and pants." Zed lightly shrugged and held his hands in front of himself. "There's a really easy way to see if someone is wearing armor, and you are clearly not. Visual sensory organs are *usually* pretty accurate about this."

"Throw a handful of sand at me." Luke ordered after a small snort of annoyance left his nose.

"No."

"Zed. C'mon." Luke motioned at himself, so Zed grabbed some sand and stone shards and tossed them at the Murderhobo.

"Happy, you-?" Zed's retort stopped as Luke's silhouette lit up to reveal mismatched blue armor, which faded away in less than a second. "It appears you have armor. However, I wasn't *wrong;* you aren't *wearing* any."

"A speechless Bard is something I'd pay to see, normally." Taylor turned from her pet project and studied the twisted remains of the Scuttler. "Fallback point is set; it has water, air supply, and is designed to hold off anything up to tier five for at least an hour. We can rest there tonight. Tomorrow, we need to make our final call on what we are going to do about this situation. Zed, can you share any information on your Mastery?"

"Taylor, I can see everyone's notifications in combat! I lost all the Potentia I somehow gained, but it turned into a permanent feature!" Zed proudly announced. "It's... oh. Oh, my goodness. It's tier *four*! Multitarget! I can talk to all members in my party at up to five kilometers away, see their health and mana values, and the damage they take and deal! Damage *types*, as well!"

She met his eyes and nodded approvingly. "Good to know. Group-style support powers are a rare thing, according to the records of the Hollow Kingdom. You just became useful. If I don't need to handle coordination, I'm freed up to be more active in combat. How far away can you be?"

"No idea! I can *talk* up to five kilometers, but can I hear you? Ambiguous!"

"Just to be clear, you have figured out a way to handle long-range communication?" Taylor's words held a deeper meaning that Zed didn't catch.

Zed's voice seemed to speak directly into her ear. "Oh, yes. I can cast my voice, and I'll work on improving this Mastery even higher when I can."

"Well... congratulations. You now have a combat role, and now I can't justify leaving you in a safe location when we go off to fight, like we had all planned to do." Taylor walked into the stone safe room, followed by Luke and Andre.

Zed simply stood outside, his face frozen in shock, with a single finger in the air as if he had wanted to point *something* out... but couldn't.

CHAPTER FORTY-THREE

The night passed quickly, with the four of them taking turns on watch. Though it was past sunrise, their encampment was still dark thanks to the towering mountains. The four began their information-gathering mission, pausing every once in a while for Luke to check on 'suspicious' boulders.

"These are all fine." He stopped testing after about fifteen minutes, and they began to pick up the pace. The thorns and other hardy plant life in the area bent away from them as they passed, allowing passage without the group having to tear through them. "That Scuttler must have been a scout of some kind."

"It is fully possible, as we discussed, that the enemy knows we are here." Andre nodded as the others looked at him for clarification. "Whether it was pheromones, telepathy, or perhaps it might just be the fact that making a stone room is *loud*; we need to assume they will be on guard for us. Constant vigilance! *Whoa*! Look at that flower! I've never seen that before!"

Everyone else was fairly nonplussed as they watched the normally cheerfully competent Druid leap at the flower like a toddler and start inspecting it closely. There was a flash of mana, which drew Luke's eye, but in that same moment it appeared; Andre finished his investigation. He walked away from the flower, smiling, and the flower itself seemed to stand a little straighter. "It's a Mountain Willow Wind! It has stamina-restoring abilities, and I bet it would be useful to you, Zed!"

"Oh?" Zed appeared intrigued. "I do get tired...?"

"Right, well, not exactly for the medical properties. When the wind flows over the flower, it produces a crisp sound. Depending on the age of the flower, the tone will change. If you had a bouquet of them at different ages, you could literally hand a lady a singing bouquet that makes her feel invigorated as she smells them!" Andre had barely finished speaking when Zed had scurried over to Andre's previous post by the flower, now also inspecting it just as gleefully.

"There aren't any seeds! Andre, can you grow these things at will?" Zed's hopeful voice and desperate stare made Andre start laughing hard enough that he doubled over. "Stop *laughing*, man; I need *answers*!"

"I have everything we will ever need to make as many as we want," Andre reassured the Bard. "I think that you and I will have a *very* good time when we get to a city."

The two of them high-fived, the slap sounding like an arrow landing on stone. No... wait. Luke pushed the two of them to the side and redirected an additional twenty percent of his mana to his cuirass. The boost to his chest armor granted sixty-two and a half points of damage absorption. With so much defensive power, the next half-dozen arrows that slammed into him caused no damage; though his armor was getting danger-ously close to breaking.

Impact! Simple crossbow bolt, piercing damage: 9!
8!
16!
14!
5!
1!

Simple Metal Cuirass. Armor: 9.5/62.5. Mana devoted to upkeep: 30% (14.79/97.35 mana. Time until armor repairs and mana is unlocked for use: 15.2 seconds!)

"Turn off robust messaging during combat," Luke growled at his Sigil, swiping the words out of his vision. "That Enchanter must have reset the combat settings to default, abyss him."

His glowing phantasmal armor showed the damage as cracks all over his cuirass, though Luke knew from long practice that they were just visual aids for him, and didn't actually impact the protection of his armor. He currently had greater concerns; his eyes were locked on the creatures that had managed to attack them. "Taylor. Tell me how they snuck up on us."

"A moment." Taylor stared at the creatures, and her massive Senses allowed her to understand them with a single glance. "Ah. Just like the Scuttler, they were a part of the stone in the pass until just before they attacked. These are 'Scuttler Sentries', looks like they can use simple tools and such. Their crossbows are nearly reloaded, so prepare yourselves."

Zed dove behind a stone outcropping as more bolts flashed through the air at them. The others, prepared for the attack now, used their own methods of defending against the attack. Luke slapped the bolts out of the air, Taylor slightly shifted and let the bolts fly past, and Andre allowed the bolts to pierce and therefore get collected by a swinging vine. The Druid looked at the withering vine and sniffed disdainfully. "Poisoned bolts, and a contact poison. I'll start working up an antidote right now. Also, they use tools, meaning they must be smart-ish. Luke, since you touched, you must be poisoned. Sit down and wait for the antidote, or you might die."

"I'm fine." Luke scoffed at the thought of sitting out a fight. "I love poison. Makes me tingle."

"They're smart enough that you're out of the fight, Andre?" Taylor directed her question at him while keeping her eyes on the attackers that were clinging a few dozen feet up the rock wall on either side of them.

"Hmm? Oh, not at all. They just need to die from natural causes if I attack them. Or I can hold them down and *you* can kill them." Andre demonstrated by linking his mind to a small shrub that was providing cover and using it to swat at a sentry. It screamed, jumped to the side, and fell off the ledge. "There, that one died from falling. Not my fault the ground killed it; all I did was scare it. Before you ask, no, I can't grab people and *throw* them to their death; that wouldn't work. Tried it. I get a warning if I'm getting too close to breaking the rules."

"*What* rules?" Taylor wasn't waiting for an answer; at least she wasn't waiting on an answer before attacking. She sprinted toward the stone wall, not slowing in the slightest as she reached it. Then she was running straight up the pass wall as if it were still flat ground, utilizing one of the effects of Fissure to ignore the fact that she was defying gravity. The others watched as she drew level with the attackers, and a huge wave of ice settled over a dozen of the creatures before shattering and killing them easily.

"Mm. Nice boots," Luke stated approvingly as he watched the Mage move. Realizing that there was an entire wall of enemies still remaining, he took action. Though he wasn't as directly mobile as Taylor, his huge Body stats allowed him to grab outcroppings and hanging root systems and swing up the wall as if he were a gorilla moving through dense forest. In moments, Luke was at the top and slamming his fist into the first of the sentries.

Zed started throwing his voice, keeping the others updated as his Sigil gave him information. "Taylor managed to destroy a ton of those things with a spell called… Shatter Shot? Luke just killed his first… third… fifth… right, he's getting them pretty good. *Oh*! *Andre*! Luke just took a bolt to the head! No, wait. He's okay, somehow; keep fighting. Luke, what *was* that? How did something like that hit you?"

"Stay calm and give us updates that matter!" Taylor tried to force Zed to focus, knowing that he was unused to battle.

"Not used to ranged fighting," Luke grunted angrily as he caught a metal crossbow and squished it with a quick squeeze. "Everything so far on Murder World was either melee or a mind-bending magic type. I can block things, but I'm used to fighting things that are *there*, not so much things that have been coming at me for a while."

"Treat the arrows like they are *snakes*, then!" Taylor's command passed through Zed, and Zed saw Luke actually pause for a moment before continuing with his rampage. Then, oddly, the Murderhobo was somehow *better* at slapping the bolts as they came toward him.

"How? How did that help him...?" Zed quizzed Andre, even as the Druid pulled back a huge vine and released an arrow at the opposite end of the long ledge that Taylor was fighting on. The arrow hit the wall far above the stone-covered ambushers, and exploded into fine particles from the force. "Also, how can you miss so *badly*?"

Andre laughed at the question, kicking Zed playfully as he crouched behind the stone. "Tell Taylor to send fire into them real quick, would ya?"

Zed did so, and a blast of flames instantly flared out, turning into a concussive wave as all the spores and particles caught and exploded. In an instant, Taylor's side of the pass was free of monsters. She took a running leap, stayed in the air *far* too long, and landed a dozen feet behind Luke. Andre winked at Zed, "She helped Luke by making him think of arrows like... hmm, ambush creatures. Taylor said 'snakes', right? They pop out, and you need to kill them or get bit. She was just putting the fight in a frame of reference that he under-stood, and that seemed to have been enough for him to catch on to the new type of fighting."

Though he wanted to understand the topic more fully, Zed held off. The main reason was that combat had ended, and he had gained Potentia. *Lots* of Potentia.

48 Stone Sentries defeated! Potentia distributed based on participation! Andre: 400. Taylor: 1,600. Luke: 1,200. Zed: 900.

"I got Potentia from *combat*? Bards can't get Potentia from *fighting*! How... why did I get so much?" Zed's hands were trembling as he opened up his status sheet and read through what the top line was telling him.

CAL Scan
Level: 4
Current Etheric Xenograft Potentia: 1,311/800 to level 5!
You are able to increase in level! Do so now? Yes / No.
Level up initiated! Integrating Etheric Xenograft Potentia into host! You have one level to use, where would you like to add the bonus? Body / Mind / Presence / Senses.

"Presence, Sub-Characteristic Charisma." Zed felt the Potentia drain from his Sigil and into his body, and he fell to the ground in ecstasy. When his eyes reluctantly fluttered open, he looked at his abridged status.

Current Etheric Xenograft Potentia: 511/1,300 to level 6!
Body: 4.5
Mind: 7.5
Presence: 24.5
Senses: 4.5
Health: 100
Mana: 158
Mana regen: 2.3 per second

"I knew traveling with all of you would be worth doing." Zed stared up at the three faces glaring down at him. "What?"

"Zed. We had no idea if there were more enemies around." Taylor reached down and pulled Zed to his feet, then backed away strangely quickly. "Did no one ever tell you that you should only level up in a safe place?"

"Ah... no. I guess I've never been in an overly dangerous place...?" Zed's excuse fell flat.

Taylor shook her head and walked on, keeping her lips sealed tight. There was no need for her to rant or rave about his thoughtlessness. Luke went with her. Andre closed in on Zed, "You know that there is a physiological reaction to each sub-characteristic increasing, yes? You increase your Mind, you pass out as your brain resets itself. Senses? Prepare for pain and such. Body? Get ready to feel like snakes are coiling around you."

"Thanks for the tip and the imagery; what's on your mind?" Zed quizzed as they joined the others in the hike.

"You just increased Charisma, with your clothes on. Know how I know?" Andre pointed down. "Charisma going up makes you feel *real* nice. Might wanna calm down before you chafe."

Zed flushed a bright red and hoped that Taylor had been too focused on his poor timing in leveling to... examine the area.

CHAPTER FORTY-FOUR

Luke paused as he felt *something* in the air. Something familiar. "I am uncertain what that is. Someone explain this to me."

"You mean the increased mana density?" Andre stretched into a comfortable pose. "Yeah, that's pretty high. Feels like going home."

"Feels like there's danger," Luke rebutted with a grimace. "There's a bug... it's watching us."

"Not a bug; it's a Scar," Taylor explained to the group. "There's a portal to another world there, one that has more ambient mana. No one in our Kingdom knows how they are made, but they aren't like normal portals. These ones are... torn. They are also actively hostile to people. The portal *itself* is hostile. There is a way to close them, but it's a suicide mission. They are stabilized on the other side, and closing them means getting trapped as soon as you destroy the stabilizer. Then, there is no guarantee that they won't get opened again in the future."

"Why open them, then?" Zed spat at the thought of the people that would make these things, specifically designed to kill people over time.

"There has only been a single coherent statement from the

Anarcanists." Taylor made 'spooky' hand gestures with her hands as she quoted, "To save the world from devastation, devastation we will wreak! To prevent the powerful, the powerful we will create and destroy. Struggle, *struggle*! You deserve to exist!"

"That's the *coherent* statement?" Zed pulled out a small instrument and started tuning it. "I'd hate to hear the others if that's the best one."

"The other one that was mostly understandable was, 'Fear the caverns, for they too have teeth. The stars are gone when you look away, but they... can still see *you*'." Taylor chuckled at the odd looks she got in return.

"What'cha got there, friend?" Andre got closer to Zed, examining the small... thing.

"New thing I thought up. I call it a 'Ukulele'. Really helps to keep my hands busy when I'm nervous. Also, makes telling stories into a kind of singing!" Zed was about to dive into the specifics of his instrument when Taylor turned to face him.

"I *do* hope that you aren't planning on letting everyone know our precise location by playing that. I know we made a lot of noise, but this pass widens out to become about a mile wide soon. Letting them know *exactly* where we are is a bad idea."

"You worry too much." Even though he argued, Zed still put the instrument away. "I bet you like violins better anyway, don't you? You do; I can see it in your eyes. Ugh. Nobility. Also, how did you not see all these creatures the first time you came through here?"

"I like violins, but if *you* really came up with this... thing, then I have no basis for comparison. I might like this new instrument better. As to the creatures," Taylor vanished from his view, reappearing next to Zed's side. A glowing spark traced a line of heat across his neck. "You *know* that I specialize in Senses. If you weren't all lumbering around, those Sentries would still be waiting safely and quietly. I didn't see them because they were *rocks*. There was literally nothing special about them."

"That's not totally accurate." Andre spoke up to counter her, getting a glare for his trouble. "*Luke* knew that there was something wrong with the rock back at the fallback point."

"Oh... yeah, but *did* he?" Zed tilted his face down and arched an eyebrow to fully express his skepticism. "This is also the man that killed a tree, was suspicious of grass, and punched rain. Could it be that he's just nuttier than a men's latrine?"

"The regular rocks in the area are five-a-four-d-four-one. The Scuttler was four-eight-three-e-three-four." Luke's voice floated over gently, and a glance told the group that he was crouching and moving softly through the sparse cover that the rocky pass allowed. "How are you all so unconcerned about the fact that all these stone creatures are letting us pass them without attacking? I feel like it's an ambush. Is it just that you're all used to seeing your enemies coming? Or you just don't care about the ambush?"

"You saw more of them?" Andre looked around, "Where?"

"This area is stuffed *full* of rocks."

"What were those numbers?" Taylor cinched her robe carefully so that it wouldn't get in her way. Thanks to Luke, she was now expecting a fight at any second.

"Color codes." Luke blinked twice when Taylor didn't react. "Really? *You're* the Senses specialist. Tell your Sigil to assign everything a color code, then use your Senses to read all the numbers in real time. How do you not know how to do this? *I* didn't have a trainer."

Taylor didn't answer, she was trying to deal with the influx of data suddenly streaming from her Sigil. Her eyes were watering in seconds, and it felt like she was about to overload her brain. She shut that function off, and looked at Luke while blinking away tears. "How do you... *function* like this?"

Luke continued scanning the area, his eyes resting on certain spots regularly. "It turned on about six years before I was forced to return here, and it took me *five* years to figure out how to shut it off. By then, I was pretty used to it. Works pretty well in the dark when there is no light. Follow the moving numbers to find what is coming at you. Different colors of dark. Dark doesn't move by itself. Great for fighting ambush predators."

Taylor looked at Zed with a grimace. "Yup. He's even more insane than we thought he was. In a useful way, though."

"I'm fully sane." Luke had finally had enough of the talking down. "*I* don't need to conform to your weak social norms. *You* need to get stronger. I've tasted insanity before… it needed a little bit of tartar sauce."

"Everyone stop." Taylor knelt and started drawing on the ground. "Once we crest this ridge, we are going to run into the first wave of defenders. I'm sure you could all feel the hostility increasing as we got closer; well… we are just about to the point of no return. Whatever intelligence that Scar has or doesn't have, it most certainly has self-preservation. This is not a battle to destroy it, or even fight at *all*. This is us attempting to determine the likelihood of an attack on the Hollow Kingdom. We make an assessment, we run. Understood?"

The others nodded, and they took extra care from then on to go unnoticed. Upon arriving at the crest of the pass, they peeked over and felt their hearts tremble. It was clear that this pass had once contained a forest, but it had been stripped to the bedrock to provide fires and… defenses? Andre tried not to get too mad about the loss of yet another old-growth forested area in his Kingdom; at least he hadn't bonded to this area yet.

There was an utterly *massive* monster hoard in the area. Thousands upon thousands of Scuttlers filled the pass, but most concerning were all the humanoids that were patrolling the area on foot or horseback. 'Humanoid' typically meant sentient, and if the monsters weren't attacking them… then it must be because they were being controlled by the humanoids. The term of 'Humanoid' didn't mean *human*, only that they could pass as human from a casual glance. In fact, all of the ones walking around wore thick cloaks, shielding their faces and leaving their true identities a mystery.

All of this paled into nigh-insignificance at the sight of the

Scar. The pulsing reddish-purple opening between dimensions drew the eye and the mind, inflicting an instinctive fear. Taylor lightly paled, then spoke softly to the others, "It's *bigger* than it was yesterday."

"That's what she said," Zed whispered back. Luke nodded, though he wasn't sure why Zed had said that. It was clear that Taylor had just spoken, there was no need to explain this to him.

"I can close that by punching it." Luke informed the others, certain that his skill would be able to manage that.

Taylor ignored their commentary and continued, "It has to be at least one hundred and thirty feet tall, and forty wide. Yesterday it was one fifteen, and thirty-four."

"What does that mean?" Andre was the only one to engage properly.

"There's only two reasons that a Scar would keep growing: allowing a more powerful creature through, or to begin terraforming the surrounding area. This is either going to become an incredibly potent enemy, or a country-scale invasion at the minimum." Taylor took a deep breath. "At the rate it's growing, there's no way an army could get here soon enough to make a difference. We need to shut this thing down."

"Didn't you just tell us about how closing a Scar is a suicide mission? That there's no guarantee that it will *stay* closed?" Andre spoke up indignantly.

"It is. But I'll gladly do the right thing so that I can save countless people that are counting on us to protect them. This thing..." Taylor waved at the Scar, "is death. Not just for us. Not even just for the Hollow Kingdom. It might release enough forces to swallow the whole continent. Listen, I'd never sacrifice someone else, or make you sacrifice yourselves, but I'll happily be the one to close it. I just need you all to keep me safe while I figure out how to do it."

"I can punch it closed," Luke again told them, only to be ignored once more.

"We also need to get close enough to get *into* that thing," Zed pointed out bleakly.

"All I hear is that there's killing to be done." Luke stood up and cracked his knuckles. His team gaped at him with white faces as he stood silhouetted against the skyline for their enemy to see. "I could go for some killing. Plus... the quest says that the reward will be proportional to the risk. I feel like stopping a world-scale invasion is pretty *risky*."

The others could only scramble to their feet and run after him as Luke activated Bum Rush and turned a Scuttler into paste a hundred feet away.

Potentia gained!

"Paste? Aw... I miss Cookie."

CHAPTER FORTY-FIVE

"Abyssal *Murderhobo!*" Taylor shouted in a fury, then forced herself to a calm state. "Andre, we need a wall at our backs. We need thorns for the fleshy foes, and thickets to force the armored enemies to come at us how *we* want them to come at us. Zed, sit."

"*Sit?*"

"Sit." Zed reluctantly sat, and a column of stone lifted him into the air. He shouted once, then went quiet as the stone surrounded him and left him with small viewing holes. Now Zed could get a bird's-eye view of the area, without *too* much fear of the fairly inaccurate bolts that they had been attacked with earlier. "Keep us up to date."

"Please make sure to let me down if you think you are going to die," Zed's voice sounded in her ear. "How high up am I?"

"About forty feet; stop whining." Taylor glanced over to see Luke already engaged in combat with dozens of enemies. She took a deep breath and stomped her foot, vanishing from her position and appearing next to Luke just in time to slash out with an unreleased Scatter Shot. Using the spell like a sword, she began hacking through the tough shells of the Scuttlers. She alternated between releasing the power as a full spell and containing it, making her an excellent mid-range fighter that could support her teammate.

Luke - unlike Taylor - was having an *excellent* time. This constant swarm of enemies felt nostalgic, and brought him back to the fun parts of killing the goats in Murder World. "I wonder if I can turn this area into a blood slide...? The pass *does* slant downward here."

"Head in the fight, Luke!" Taylor demanded as she released a Flame Lance into a tight cluster of Scuttlers. The spell detonated, tossing charred monsters into the air and filling the area with the scent of baked lobster. "Ugh... I'm never going to enjoy seafood again."

"Never had it before." Luke slammed his right fist into a Scuttler. He had cancelled his shoulder and leg armor, freeing a total of fifty percent mana that he had been able to devote to his attacks. That resulted in a total of a forty-five percent damage increase when it was diverted to his Battering Ram Knuckles, which meant he could *potentially* hit for five hundred and ninety-two blunt damage if he landed a perfect attack.

It wasn't going to happen. Not with the wild flailing and dodging that he needed to also focus on. Maximum power meant that you needed to focus and bring your entire body into alignment for an attack, and that usually only happened under controlled circumstances. Still, a glancing blow could deal over a hundred and fifteen points of blunt damage, plenty for these basic creatures. Luke punched one in the face, and the stone covering turned into shrapnel that drove deep into its head.

Potentia gained!

"Celestial abyss, *shut up*." Luke snarled at his constantly chiming Sigil. "Devote all Potentia into Walking Arsenal until I say otherwise. Turn off Potentia gain notifications!"

Ding!

Please confirm-

"Yes!"

Ding!

This is your confirmation that all Potentia-

"Ahh!" Luke screamed and ignored the Sigil, shifting his mana to empower both hands evenly and slamming them into the next target over and over. The nice thing about his ability was that he could fight like a brawler. Luke had been worried that equipping a sword would mean that he would need to *hold* it like a sword, and he had been glad to find out that he wouldn't need to do so. A punch, and a meter-long blade appeared over his fist and stabbed things. Perfect for what he needed.

Over the next twenty minutes, Luke and Taylor had been able to move forward a net total of five feet. They had constantly needed to abandon their positions in order to maintain firm footing, even though both of them had powers that granted balance and sure-footedness. All of the blood and carcasses made footwork treacherous.

Walking Arsenal has reached level three! 0/500 to level 4!

"We aren't making any progress!" Taylor stated coldly as yet another blast of ice shattered Scuttlers in a line. "We should fall back and regroup-"

"What are you *talking* about?" Luke laughed at her stricken expression. "We've only been fighting for twenty minutes! We already moved forward! At this pace we will only need another… thirty hours! We'll be to the Scar in no time!"

"Thirty *hours* of constant fighting?" Taylor spun up a Flame Lance, letting it blow away a squad of reinforcements.

"Way less than I thought we would need!" Luke's bright smile brought Taylor right back to her childhood, but she got ahold of herself and shook off the strangeness of seeing her one time friend still in the body of a mid-seventeen-year-old. This was the first time Luke had seemed actually happy since coming out of the portal - the first time he had seemed like *himself* - but she was already practically out of mana.

"We need to fall back so I can recover my mana, Luke!" She hated to interrupt his happiness, but she wouldn't die so that he could get a few chuckles.

"Go ahead; I'll keep at it! Come back when you have a full arsenal ready again!" Luke activated Bum Rush and slammed into the line of attackers, creating an opening that Taylor used to zip back to the... forest?

"Welcome back, Taylor!" Andre called out as she entered the oddly silent copse. "I set up a meditation area *there*. Should boost mana regen, especially with the mana density in the area!"

"Meditation area...? Andre, this place needs to be *defensible!*" Taylor forced herself to sit and focus on calming her mind. She felt her mana regen kick into high gear, pleased with the result even though she was still lightly fuming over the seeming lack of protections.

"Don't worry." Andre's voice turned hard. "Nothing under tier six could walk into this core area without having to destroy every plant in the way."

"I don't... how can you be sure?"

"I can't move from this spot, but everything in thirty meters that grows is actually considered the *same* plant. This whole place shares the same health, which means they would need to be able to destroy this area in a single hit if they want to get in." Andre let his eyes flutter closed as he returned to making a cycle. Mana and Potentia flowed into him, out to the plants, and back to him, since they were a *part* of him.

With every second that passed, more plants sprang out of the ground. Andre had also been spreading grass seed along the path as they had traveled, and he was hoping that there would soon be a verdant path that connected him to the rest of the area in the Kingdom which he had bound to himself. Then this small area would be *really* hard to crack. "Abyssal *Murderhobo*. If he had just given me a few days to get all of this ready...!"

"Speaking of ol' Lukey," Zed's voice spoke to the two on the ground, "any idea why he is doing *more* damage over time than he was doing before? It isn't a lot, but while you were out there, his damage average increased a few times, and really suddenly."

"He's devoting all the Potentia he's getting directly to his abilities." Taylor stood and prepared to return to the fight. "It'll peter off; there are so many of the same type that he's gonna stop getting much Potentia soon."

"Shoot! Andre, Taylor! There's a calvary charge coming!" Zed's words made Taylor speed off, and Andre closed his eyes. "People on horseback, holding lances!"

"I'm sure of it now. These Scuttlers are nothing more than beasts. I'll take care of them, you focus on the cavalry!" A wave of mana exploded out from Andre, forcing the growth of thorny vines all around his defensive copse. Andre began to pant as his mana slowly refilled, but his mind was focused on binding the vines with a singular purpose: anything that came into the area needed to be beat to death or torn open. Scuttlers started dying in droves along the thicket's boundary as the plant life pulled them apart or suffocated them. The Potentia they released was sucked up by the plants, making them stronger, hardier, and finally... more numerous.

As more appeared, Zed began to notice a strange message appearing over and over. He traced it to Andre, and blanched.

Damage taken - health regained - damage taken - health regained...

A glance at Andre revealed that there were small vines that had latched onto his arms and legs. They were thorny, and Andre was clearly bleeding heavily. Zed swallowed as he watched the fighting, only now truly realizing exactly how invested his team was in growing more powerful.

"One sacrificed his mind. Two offers her life to protect others. Three is eaten by his creations to bring life and death. What is four... what am *I* willing to do for the power to change the world?"

CHAPTER FORTY-SIX

Luke was yanked to the ground as two people on horses ran past him while dragging a net. He started skidding as they dragged him, but he was released in an instant as the horses slammed into a razor-sharp stone spike each. They collapsed forward, and Luke was sent flying as if he had been in a sling-shot instead of a net. He flipped in the air, Innate Balance coming to the rescue and allowing him to prepare for the new threat.

The people didn't get off the horses after they were impaled, and that was when Luke realized that they were *not* separate creatures. "What in the-"

"*Down!*" The order came, but Luke didn't duck. That wasn't in his nature. Instead, he struck out at the threat, using his left hand to cleave another of the horse-creatures in half. The body split around his mana-made sword, the momentum of the beast soaking Luke in viscera.

"Luke, these are called 'Centaurs'." Zed's cheerful voice appeared in Luke's ear as he tackled another man-horse to the ground and punched it wildly. "It appears we found the theme of the invading world. They are all chimeras!"

"No idea what that means, Zed. Tell me." Luke threw the horse half of his opponent at another charging group. The loss of morale was visible, but he could see them steel themselves for their attack.

"Sure thing, sugar-booger!" Zed stopped playing around when he heard the dark threats Luke began muttering in reply to his gentle teasing. "Chimeras are creatures that are essentially hybrids. They have pieces of at *least* two things grafted together. Centaurs are pretty well-known, obviously horse and man. The Scuttlers make sense as well now, I'm thinking crab and man at the *minimum*."

"How does this help us?" Luke demanded as he took a blow across the head.

Simple Metal Helmet. Armor: 4/17.5

"Well, it lets us know that they will have both the strengths *and* the weaknesses of the types of creature they are made of. Horse and man? Likely afraid of snakes? Got any snakes with you?" Zed trailed off as he tried to think of anything actually helpful. "Well... the less 'creature' there is, typically the more intelligence there is. Centaurs are smart enough to work in groups and use tools, but they are too much horse to be able to create a real civilization as we know it."

"The *point*, Bard!" Luke Bum Rushed at another small herd, taking two to the ground upon impact. The Centaurs whinnied at a frequency that would have caused damage in a weaker person, so Luke punched them in the face to cut off their noise. Noses and facial bones shattered; the remaining sounds were garbled and wet.

"The *point* is that their commanders, the intelligent threats, will be *mostly* Humanoid. The more person-like they are, the more effort you should put into killing them as fast as possible."

Luke liked that explanation. "Good. That was actually useful. Tell me more things like that."

Zed's next words were also informative, though in a different way. "There are two herds closing in on you from either side! They have lances, you need to move away from there!"

"I'm not afraid of a horse with a silly *stick*." Luke coldly cut off the incoming warnings. "Tell me more about things I should be on the lookout for."

"*The lances*, look out for *those!*" Zed's fear caused Luke to slap a Scuttler out of the way so he could judge with his own eyes how dangerous this opponent was. He *felt* more than heard the thundering hooves, and his eyes widened fractionally when he saw that the lances glowed enough to indicate enchantment. While the Centaurs were still a long way away from him, dozens of lances discharged a figurative *river* of lightning at him.

"Abyss."

Armor break! Simple Metal Helm, Simple Metal Pauldron, Metal Gauntlet (Stone Ape), Simple Metal Cuirass, Simple Metal Greaves, and Ornate Leather Boots have reached armor: 0.

Mana pool expended! 80% mana must be regained in order to reactivate the broken armor!

Health: 92/250 (Paralyzed, 4 seconds remaining.)

Luke read all of the messages as he stared at the sky. He slowly fell flat on his back. He couldn't move, and his clothes were on fire. He had a high enough resistance that the weak flames didn't really damage his skin, but it was still uncomfortable to feel his clothing carbonize. The thundering hooves drew closer, but another sound drowned them out as Taylor tore open a Fissure in front of the leading herd. Their screams cut off as they fell, but only because the ground slammed together again with a ringing **shriek** of tortured stone.

Though he was feeling something pulling him, Luke only managed to wriggle. Taylor's voice stopped even that, "Knock that off; I can barely manage to haul you and fight as it is!"

"No… the lances." Luke weakly pushed the words from his charred throat.

"Yeah, you should have listened. There is a *reason* we need to have team cohesion. *Listen* when someone tells you to watch out!" Taylor's voice fell on deaf ears as Luke's paralysis wore off. "Learn to duck-"

"No, the *lances*. I want them." Luke forced himself up and took a step toward the fallen centaurs.

"They are buried right now; you'd need to attack that other herd in order to get even a *few* lances." Taylor grabbed him as Luke took a shaky step toward the regrouping centaurs. "That wasn't an invitation. *Enough.* You're injured and naked; fall back for now. We need a new plan."

"What?" Zed's faux-shocked voice echoed in their ears. "You *aren't* going to just keep attacking them directly? Your face is still intact; why not hit them with *that*? Abyss, go *bite* them to death!"

"You're not helpful." Taylor calmly yet firmly pushed Luke back, knowing that if he didn't want to go, there was no physical way to make him do it. Luckily, in his current addled state, he was more receptive to listening to what she was saying. "Luke, we need to regroup."

"Can you just... throw me? Get me right in the center of that Scar. I take out the leaders, you mop up the scattering army by dropping the mountain on them." Luke's voice was firm, though slightly slurred. The blood running down his forehead made Taylor think that he might have a concussion.

"How does your head feel?" They were moving steadily toward the fallback point that Andre had made, though Taylor needed to blast their way through a few times.

"Is fine." He punched a Scuttler, and luckily his weapons were still available; otherwise, he would have broken his hand. "Only took... twenty hits on the head so far? I was fine until the lightning."

Sparks started to flash across Luke's entire head, increasing in intensity until they became sparkles, then planes of mana began to form. After a long moment, the same thing started happening all over his body, and Taylor realized that it was his armor reforming. "Are you doing that?"

"Huh? Oh. No." Luke looked at his arms as the sparkles

faded and the shifting mana once more became invisible. "When the armor breaks, it needs to reform. Whatever mana was in it was locked until the full amount invested is regenerated. Then it just stays that way unless I shift it again."

"It's a passive ability?" Taylor let the fact that she was impressed seep through her voice, working to keep Luke distracted and amiable. There was far too high of a chance that he would charge back into the fight if she didn't.

"Mostly. There are active components to it as well. Oh." Luke stared into the distance, a clear indication that he was looking at a notification. "It hit level four."

Taylor tried to control her eye twitch. Luke had gained well over a thousand Potentia in under thirty minutes? She checked her own notifications, finding that her portion had been closer to seven hundred, and most of that was due to the sheer differences in monster types that she had killed before. New always meant more Potentia. "That's great! Big changes between levels?"

"Literally nothing that I can clearly see. Just a way to pass time until the next tier." Luke took a deep breath, feeling his mana reserves top off at the same time. "Welp, time to go do some killin'."

"Abyss, hold *on*, will you?" Taylor grabbed him, then went cold at the look he gave her hand. She knew in that instant that she had nearly died, and only the fact that Luke had already been straining against his instincts so they could talk mid-battle saved her life. "I'm… sorry, that was a bad idea."

"Yes."

"I'm not going to launch you at the Scar. We're at the fringes of the horde, and we still can't easily kill everything. I mean, because of the swarm tactics. Obviously, you can punch things to death. However, your idea of dropping the mountain on them was a good idea. Let's go talk to Andre and figure out how and where we could cause a landslide." Her idea was sound, so Luke nodded and entered the strange, still oasis that had no place in this bloody battlefield.

"Welcome back! Can you please let me down now? I need to pee." Zed called from his tree-tall perch.

"I'll make you an arrow slit." Taylor's calm reply made Zed groan. "Just keep watch. If something too strong comes, we need to be prepared. How are you doing, Andre?"

"Good." Andre opened his brilliant green eyes and stood, shaking off the vines that were clinging to him. "It is a fine balance, teaching plants to kill without directing them to do so at my will. It's an interesting experiment, though!"

"Convincing other things to do the work for you. That's an impressive way to get around the requirement of not killing directly." Luke plopped to the ground with a sigh, basking in the calm atmosphere. "Are you sure you aren't a Bard?"

"Was…" Andre looked at Luke with clear excitement, "was that a *joke*?"

"He has a concussion." It pained Taylor to see Andre slump at the explanation. They had once been best friends, and now none of them really knew each other. Though the change was the clearest with the Murderhobo, all of them had spent a life-time apart. "Luke had a good idea; I want to create a landslide and use the distraction to get to the Scar. Can you help me find the best place to create a Fissure, and shear the wall? The higher the better."

Andre became introspective, hesitating before responding. "How much time do we have?"

Thunder filled the area as a herd of lightning lances discharged into the trees around them. Taylor watched as vines whipped out and put out the fires that had been started as a result.

"Work fast?"

CHAPTER FORTY-SEVEN

"Here we go." Zed was watching the walls of the pass intently. A thin layer of moss had coated it as far as his eye could see, and over time, most had fallen off aside from a few areas where large green 'X's showed what Andre had hoped were stress points. Taylor was heading to the largest of them even now, using her stealthy ways to cross the distance.

Since she needed fairly close proximity, and the mana she devoted to the process would light her up like a beacon, Luke had happily offered himself as a distraction. The Murderhobo had somehow convinced Andre to use his vines to catapult him at the centaur herd that was waiting for them, and they had timed the release of the hobo with the next burst of electricity. While the monsters were distracted by the light and sound of their thunder lances discharging, Luke had activated Bum Rush, sprinting forward.

Just before he broke through the brush, the vines had wrapped around his waist and arms, lifting and sending him in a single enormous leap over the heads of the centaurs and into their midst. A wild-eyed Murderhobo had fallen from the sky and wrapped himself around the torso of a centaur before headbutting it. His mana armor flared, preventing him from hurting himself, and Zed had gotten a far-off thumbs up. "Thanks for the reminder that I can use every part of my body in combat!"

Though he hadn't been serious when he told Luke to attack with his face, and in fact had been insulting the concussed man, Zed felt flattered that the idea was working out. Still, Zed hadn't been able to keep his eyes on the rest of the battle. Luke was brutal, and his attacks left twisted and terrible remains. Among the unarmored foes, there were very few that could survive more than a single hit, and there were only so many times Zed could watch a centaur get split into both a horse corpse and a man corpse before he got ill.

So, Zed turned his eyes once more to the bright green 'X' on the side of the mountain pass. His grip on a vine, which Andre had supplied, was tight; and he was near to panicking. As soon as Taylor reached out to him, he needed to tell the others to start running. He also needed to leave the safety of both the stone column he was on and the oasis that Andre had created. Zed, a Bard that had *barely* higher characteristics than a standard human, was going to need to run through monster-infested territory and hope that the plane-walking, super-powered, incredibly *violent* members of his team remembered to wait for him and keep him alive.

"Well... at least I'll get a good story out of it." Zed checked his Potentia gains, and noted happily that he had already gained over two hundred since Luke had started fighting again. Through trial and error, Zed had found that the key to getting large chunks of exp was to point out things that combatants would otherwise miss, or needed to hear. Otherwise, he got nothing. Chatter didn't do anything, and inane conversation had actually *slowed* the flow of Potentia. He was glad he had tested the mechanics of the exp splitting his new Mastery allowed, but he *really* wished it was spelled out better.

Zed was so lost in his thoughts that he almost missed Taylor whispering to him across the distance. "Zed, I hope you can still hear me. I'm starting. You need to go now."

He sent a hasty affirmative, then told the others and *jumped*. Zed whimpered as the ground started approaching *far* too fast... then the vine went taut. He swung out like a jungle man, at a lower speed than Luke had managed; though it didn't feel like it. Zed was flying directly at a large thicket of thorns, but the vine twitched and he was sent sailing toward... "What in the *abyss*!"

A massive green *bear* was staring at him! He was getting closer; it opened its mouth as he neared. Zed squeezed his eyes closed, then felt a soft **thump**. Andre's chuckle made Zed's eyes crack open, and he froze as he realized that he was sitting *on the bear*. Andre spoke out, "Zed, meet Arthur. He has reluctantly allowed you to ride upon his majestic back. Please make sure to properly thank him later."

"Andre there is a bear." Zed squeaked out in a high-pitched jumble of words. Then his mind caught up to the conversation, and he looked at the bear below him. "He's green... and I can see through him."

"He's my bound Cave Bear." Andre explained simply as the bear started to lumber out of the area. "He is not actually physically present; this is a mana-clone of him. If he came here personally, he would be stronger, but could also be killed permanently. He was already hesitant to leave The Grove, and the low mana density on our world gave him the final push to decide against staying on this world when I returned."

"Why is this the first I've seen him?" Zed managed to say the words in a normal register.

"He came through the portal for a few seconds when Archmage Don brought me back, but you must have been traveling at that point still. Short answer: he takes a lot of mana to summon. Now, there is no maintenance cost, but his *mind* is here, even if his body is back home. Since there is a time difference, that means if he is here for an hour, his body is asleep for six. The limit is clearly shown here; what if he is attacked while

I need him here? He just... dies; fully unable to protect himself."

"Ah." Zed nodded, pressing himself close to the bear as they broke through the brush and his terrifying mount shot forward. "I can... see why this is a rare occurrence."

"Yup; hold on, Arthur wants to move faster than just walking." Andre was having no issue keeping up with the bear-relling beast, yet they were moving far too fast for Zed's comfort. "Luke, we're going!"

Luke joined them in a flash, a stack of lances held under each arm and a satisfied expression on his face. "Got what I needed. Where's the-"

Rumble.

"Oh, there it is." A flash of purple in the distance caught their attention, a ring that morphed into a pillar of light. It looked like a star had touched down on the pass, and the effect was similar. Thousands of tons of rock tipped and fell, almost in slow motion. The ground began shaking, and the subsequent earthquake simply became exponentially more powerful over the next few minutes.

The three of them were sprinting toward the still-tumbling scree, very pleased that they were at the highest point of the pass. The rock followed the slope, and a vast multitude of chimeras were caught under the stony torrent of death. Zed's head jolted up, and his eyes followed a particular rock that seemed to be falling at a different angle. "Luke! Andre! Taylor is there; she just went unconscious!"

Luke looked up, then down at his lances, then up at the falling stone that had a smidge of Taylor's white robe dangling over it. "Well, we had a good run together."

"*Save* her, you cheese wheel!" Zed felt ashamed that his honed mind had only been able to come up with that very lacking insult.

"Throw me!" Andre demanded instantly as he charged at Luke. The Murderhobo prepared himself, dropping the lances. "At *Taylor*, Luke!"

Realization dawned, and Luke shifted positions quickly; then caught Andre and hurled him even as the Druid jumped. The fur-robed Druid shot like an arrow at the falling rock, vines exploding away from him and into a massive spider web as he got close. Taylor was scooped off the rock almost gently, and the 'web' closed around them, rolling into a ball that cushioned their fall as they hit the ground.

Arthur, Zed, Luke, and Luke's re-collected lances were sprinting toward the ball before it had reached the ground. Taylor came flying out of the vines, though a few of them anchored to Arthur and tied her to his back like a bedroll. The remaining vines settled around Andre's body and he once more appeared to be dressed only in a simple fur-and-flower robe. His Livingwood Staff flipped off the bear, and Andre caught it just in time to swing it up and around into a centaur's knee.

As the staff swung, a multitude of spores were released from small sachets connected to it. The seeds burst into bloom, and everything they landed on started to scream as roots twisted into them and began releasing capsaicin directly into the impacted areas. "Go, run, *run!*"

Luke was starting to lag behind slightly, the unwieldy lances forcing longer turns and increasing the difficulty of leapfrogging over the unstable and still-settling rocks. Andre glared at him as he joined the others on Arthur. "Drop those! I'll make the wood in them walk the weapons to a safe spot!"

There was a long moment of hesitation, but then the lances were tossed. They started inching like worms toward a space between some rocks, and Luke felt satisfied that this teammate hadn't yet betrayed him. The Scar was looming closer and closer, but the monsters were regrouping around it. Some were departing through the portal, and Luke knew that there would be no such thing as the 'element of surprise' when they got close to it.

What he wasn't counting on was the time differential. Creatures began *pouring* out of the scar, far more than should have been possible. They were coming so fast that some were getting crushed by the sheer numbers that followed, unable to get away. With a quarter mile to go, and thousands of monsters between them and their goal, Luke started to get uneasy.

"Something is wrong." His voice demanded attention from the others. "They aren't attacking. They... they aren't defending either. Something has changed. I don't understand this, but the mana is swelling around the Scar. We need to wake Taylor up."

The portal *pulsed*, and even as far away as they were... the creeping certainty of death washed over them.

CHAPTER FORTY-EIGHT

A hooded figure stepped out of the portal, and in an instant…
the Scar was reduced in size by at least a third. The sheer
amount of power this one being represented must be utterly
huge if the stabilized portal weakened that much just to let it
through.

"Wake her up, wake her up, wake her *up*." Luke muttered in
manic repetition, a strange desperation flowing through him.
The hood worn by the creature made it impossible to understand what he was looking at, but a single glance made Luke
feel like he was swimming through a pool of blood. The sheer
killing intent bearing down on them screamed 'massive
Charisma and Capacity'.

This was a Mage of a high order, and the only being that
Luke had encountered with even *close* to the same feeling was
Archmage Don. "Andre, do something."

"How am I supposed to be able-?" Andre was cut off as Zed
reached over and caressed Taylor's face.

In his most lecherous tone, Zed whispered, "Wake up,
sleepyhead. You fell asleep in my arms and were here all *night!*"

"*Noo!*" Taylor awoke with a scream as one of her worst

nightmares played out in reality. The shift between unconsciousness and fight mode was instant, and only Taylor's exhaustion saved Zed from an instant Flame Lance to the heart. "What...! Did it work?"

"Yup! You nearly died, though!" Andre cheerfully informed her. "Great to know your real feelings toward me, by the way. Also, it looks like the whole dying thing may still happen. Any idea what we should do about... that?"

Taylor directed her weary gaze to the Scar, and her focus sharpened instantly. "It shrunk... what came through? Oh... oh no."

"I was really hoping to hear 'that isn't so bad, we can handle this,'" Zed fumed from his position on the still-charging bear.

"That's... it's so strong. I've never felt a power fluctuation from a monster like that, except once: a sentient thunderstorm. The storm was a tier *ten* existence." Taylor swallowed; her mouth too dry to say much more.

"Stop. It's doing something." Luke pulled them back to the moment, just in time to feel a mental shockwave pass over them. For an instant, Luke wanted to destroy his group, then himself... but he tensed his body and shook off the insidious demand. Still, in the next moment he was rolling his eyes as he held a rabid Andre off. The Druid was gnawing on the skin between Luke's thumb and index finger, but couldn't manage a single point of damage to the mana-armor of his gauntlets.

Taylor seemed to move... inward? Like a wineskin that was squeezed suddenly, she convulsed once, and then she was fine. Zed didn't even blink at the mental order that had tried to control him, but the bear that he was riding on started bucking wildly. Were they not tied on, Taylor and Zed would have been tossed off and swarmed by the chimeras that were sprinting at them in orderly, neat rows. Luke noticed the difference, and let the others know. "That thing has control powers; it took direct control of *everything*."

"Not possible. It must be directly controlling relays of some kind. Find the most humanoid being in any group and kill it.

That'll add a ton of strain to the boss over there, and it might collapse the entire structure," Zed explained succinctly, just as Taylor fell forward on the bear, her eyes rolling back into her head as her overuse of mana came back into play.

Andre came back to himself a moment after Luke slapped him 'gently'. Arthur calmed down in the same moment. "What...?"

"You two find me monsters to kill. Get close to that Scar!" Luke ordered as he devoted most of his mana to his left fist and made a slashing attack at a group of Scuttlers. The extended - overcharged - mana blade cut through their stone carapaces like butter, but a standard attack from one cut Luke's bicep open enough that blood began pouring down his arm. "Best defense is *defense*, blast it! I keep forgetting that!"

He evened out his mana flows, blocking the next few attacks that would have bit in deeply. His punches and slashes needed to remain single-target to make a kill with one blow, and in the following minutes, Luke fought a desperate battle as the chimeras attacked from every direction with repeated, machine-like precision. Arthur roared as spears were used to puncture his energetic flank, and Zed screamed as he saw death approaching.

"*There!*" the words were practically forced into Luke's ear as Zed managed to notice a black-robed humanoid a dozen feet away. Luke had moved as soon as his attention was called to the beast, and with a *crunch* the monster was decimated; the top one-tenth of its body just *gone*.

The orderly attacks fell away, and the monsters were just angry beasts once more. There was a moment where they appeared to have lost attention, and were confused by their surroundings. Luke went through them like a hurricane, and his Sigil let him know that Walking Arsenal had reached level five. "Quantity over quality is fine... just be worth *something!*"

A slash to his side pulled Luke's attention to another robed humanoid. The strange part was that the attack had gone into a joint between Luke's armor, bypassing the protections they afforded him. He looked at the wound, then at the assassin. He could clearly see that the being had a human face, and on that face was a smug smile.

I Have Concerns has detected a new and potent poison! Assessing, assimilating… I Have Concerns has reached Tier 3, Level 1! Assimilating!

"Thank you." Luke's heartfelt gratitude made the monster glare and realize that something was wrong. "Without you, I would have had no idea how to level that skill up."

In the next instant, the humanoid was bisected by Luke's mana blade, and the Murderhobo had returned to his team's side. Shrubberies had appeared around the combat Zone, their roots drinking down the blood that was spilling in the central area and keeping the ground firm and solid. Fungus and mold coated the fallen bodies, and Andre was allowing Bloodthistle to empower them to be even faster without needing to provide the mana cost. The residual mana in the creatures' flesh and blood allowed the plants to chew through the dead corpses at high speed. Andre welcomed Luke back with a nod, then refocused on creating an oasis in this spot before they were overwhelmed.

"On your left, Andre! Luke, behind you, left hand upward slash!" Zed called instructions, getting the others to focus on their attacks. Andre was protected by Arthur, and Luke slammed two charging centaurs together, dropping their broken bodies to put a barrier between him and the rest of their herd.

Over the next thirty minutes, they held their ground against an unceasing tide. A full hedgerow had grown around them, shielding them on all sides and gaining additional defense by incorporating a good amount of the stone that coated the Scutlers. With the 'wall' in place, Luke allowed himself a small breather and checked the notifications that were waiting for him.

Walking Arsenal has reached Tier 8, Level 6!

I Have Concerns has reached Tier 3, Level 4! Assimilating!

"What was *in* that poison?" Luke grumped at the fact that it hadn't even bothered to provide a basic hallucination. There was no answer forthcoming, so he continued on his rampage. A group of Scuttlers in front of him detonated into frozen shards, the first signal that Taylor had awoken.

"Welcome back!" Zed cheerfully stated as Taylor sat up. The Bard was evidently loopy from the constant twisting and turning that Arthur had subjected him to. "What brings a pretty place like you to a girl like this?"

"Mana shift." Taylor was clearly exhausted still, making Luke wonder exactly what had happened to put her in such a state. "All the mana that the Scar has been pouring into the world is getting drawn back to it. Something is about to happen. Something terrible."

Luke looked to where the 'boss' was standing. The robe it was wearing, black with a series of red and gold trims, was whipping around wildly. It appeared that the creature was at the center of a whirlwind, as well as being obscured by a heat haze. It became harder to see the creature over time as the mana became denser... and *denser*.

"Why are they leaving?" Zed's question was the first thing that drew attention to the fact that the attacking waves of creatures were stepping back and away. "I wasn't *happy* that they were attacking us, but I at least *understood* that... Taylor... why are they backing away?"

As much as she wanted to be able to answer that question, Taylor could only bite her lip and stay silent. Her eyes were searching for the *slightest* nuance that would explain the situation. This vigilance allowed her to see the exact instant that something *did* change near the Boss. "It's creating a magic circle?"

"What does that do?" Luke shot the question at her sharply.

"Like what I do?" Andre was startled, and squinted in an attempt to see the far-away figure better. "That thing is a Druid?"

"No, it's... a magic circle, for Mages, is how high-tier spells are cast when you want to use them at full power. Anything above Tier Five requires too much concentration, too many components, to simply *cast* it. Unless you are just... so powerful.

A magic circle appearing means that the spell was cast correctly up to a certain point, then sealed so that the next portion could be cast." Taylor launched a Flame Lance at a larger group of monsters, though they ignored their dying comrades for the most part. "Each circle that appears around the inner one means another layer of the spell being cast correctly. I only spot two, so… we have a chance to stop it?"

Zed eyed the distance and the army that separated them. "I have a doubt to throw into this optimism."

"We could try to take shelter and hope that it won't be able to hit us?" Andre chimed in hopefully.

"I agree with Taylor. Kill our way there before it can cast." Luke started moving forward, catching the ire of a pod of Scuttlers. Almost casually, he slapped them to death in passing. After he had fought them a few times, he had learned the best way to massacre them. "Is it just me, or are they giving up less Potentia? Zed, you check that, I don't want to let the Sigil into my head until I need it."

Zed, happy to have *something* that he could do, looked into the distance. "Yup… looks like you are getting only about a third of what you were at the start of combat."

"So, I need to kill three times as many for the same effect." Luke's Bum Rush directly at the Boss forced the others to scramble, coming out of the safer area and into the attackers once more. However, the response from the armies was… pitiful.

"Third, no *fourth* circle is up!" Taylor gasped, working to free herself from the clinging vines. "Andre, make these things let me go!"

"Done." Andre fired arrow after arrow into the air, and spores and seeds rained down on their foes before exploding into either thorns, Stink-sacs, or simple rooting vines. However, the response was still muted, the creatures barely even attempting to fight their way free. "Something is wrong."

"*Fifth* circle!" Taylor recoiled in horror as a massive tsunami of blood erupted out of every chimera they could clearly see, the epicenter being the Boss. Red washed out their vision as far as they could see, slowly settling to the ground. The beasts slowly fell to the ground, tens of thousands of bodies falling to the ground at once creating a strange, unique sound.

Zed looked at himself, then at the dripping blood around them. "Was that the attack? It didn't do anything."

"No…" Taylor gulped loudly as the blood started streaming toward the Boss. As it moved, the settling of the sea of red revealed thousands of desiccated corpses left behind. "It just killed its own army. That wasn't the spell… it just used everything it was linked to as a *component*."

CHAPTER FORTY-NINE

"Tier seven!" Taylor screamed as they all charged toward the Scar at full speed. A quarter mile was nothing to this group normally; however, they were continually ambushed by straggling chimeras that hadn't been consumed by the spell. The Scuttlers especially would erupt from the blood and corpse piles, trying to pull Zed down from Arthur's back.

"Why are they all after *me*?" Zed screamed as yet another Scuttler jumped at him only to be sliced apart by Luke. Its head bounced off Arthur, and there was enough life left in it to snap at Zed's leg. He jerked himself out of the way just in time, "Celestial, are these things part *eel* or something?"

"Snakes do the same thing! They want you because of your Charisma! They 'feel' that you are the most powerful, so they want to take you down first! Great job being bait!" Andre called as his vines pulled a charging centaur down and into a seated position. With a shout, mana exploded from him and a hedgerow formed just in time to block a series of lightning strikes coming from lancers. "I'm... y'all, I'm outta mana!"

Luke took a pouch from his waist and tossed it to him. "Take a *sniff*. Do *not* drink that."

As the words left his mouth, a group of Stone Sentries slammed into Luke, creating fracture patterns over the entirety of his armor. Taylor blew them away, and Luke rolled forward onto his feet easily. Andre popped the top of the waterskin and took a hesitant sniff. Angry red blisters appeared all over his face wherever the vapor touched, and his veins started to bulge like he was having a wild heart attack after running a hundred miles.

"Ahh!" Andre *dumped* mana into the area around him as blood ran from his nose and eyes. An almost electrical storm of mana surrounded the group, causing their enemies to hesitate long enough for either Luke or Taylor to force their way through.

Luke grabbed the waterskin from the mana-charged Druid and snorted. He tossed back the drink like a shot, his armor fixing and the cracks vanishing in an instant. Luke smacked his lips and shook his head at the Druid, "Didn't take you for a lightweight. Aren't you supposed to have a massive Capacity?"

"Was that *liquid mana?*" Taylor took her eyes off the eighth circle that had just appeared in front of the Boss, her eyes almost hungrily staring at the waterskin. "I'd like some."

"You know what it is." Luke handed the near-empty waterskin over even as he shook his head. "Not a chance that you can open it. With a low Capacity, that would count as seeking your own death. I bet your mana channels would burn out in an instant."

Taylor grabbed the top of the skin, but her Sigil chimed and forced her numbed fingers to let it go. "Abyss. *Abyss!* That attack is about to go off."

"What is it?" Zed, even at the cost of his life, wanted to be involved. "If we make it out of here, we're going to have the most *amazing* story!"

"All I know is that the spell is approaching tier nine. It used the death of *thousands as a* power source, so the spell has to have something to do with either death, or blood, or maybe reshaping? As a nine, it's a... country killer. That spell has enough power to wipe out a city, at the *minimum*. It is only *kinda* being used against us; the remaining power will destroy… I don't even know how much. The entire mountain range?"

"The spell hasn't been cast yet." Something about Andre had changed. He dropped to the side, sliding off of Arthur, and let his bare feet slam onto the ground. Mana whipped around him, and in an instant, a dust devil had formed around him. The particle-filled whirlwind exploded outward, making the surviving chimeras stumble. The ground between the team and the boss of the Scar *shifted*. Without a better way to understand it, Luke only saw that a direct road had been suddenly built into the pass. Their speed increased, and chimeras that had been waiting - partially buried in the ground - were trapped in the hardened stone.

"Did I just witness a Druid reaching the *Third Circle*? He bound himself to the earth itself! Ha! Yes!" Zed's voice was filled with awe, and the others could practically hear the sound of his thoughts: coins falling and clinking into a large sack. "*We* can do this! Go *team*! I believe in *us*! Andre, the path is great and all, but make the earth stab them or something!"

Taylor ignored them all, her focus on the rapidly approaching Boss. "We've got at least a few minutes before it gets that spell to tier nine! We can do it! Kill him!"

The ground shattered as Andre created a jumping-off platform for Luke. The Murderhobo in question didn't bother to ask. "*Bum Rush!*"

He crossed the remaining distance in a flash, the entirety of his remaining mana redirected to his right hand. The weakness of Mages was their need to cast uninterrupted. It was a well-known weakness, which made the next moment all the more confusing for Luke.

The hooded figure didn't move… didn't move… yet was *gone* in the next moment, just as Luke's fist *whiffed* through the spot where it had been standing.

"An illusion?" Zed screamed the question at Luke. "Were we hallucinating?"

"Pff. I *wish*."

No one heard Luke's words, since Taylor had directed a warning at them. "He's over *there*!"

Luke sprinted at the huge magical circle that hung in the air in front of the boss monster. He could barely make out the hooded figure, but could clearly see that strange mystical markings crawled along the outer edge of the magical circles. A little over one-third of the final circle had been completed, making it easy to see exactly how much time remained as more and more was filled in. Something screamed a warning to him just before he dived into the circles, and his eyes took in the free-floating physical components within their boundaries.

Though he wasn't concerned that the mana itself could hurt him, thanks to the pure mana-ignoring effect of 'I have Concerns', there was something about this structured power that told him that touching it was death. The circles and boss *blinked*, and Luke's eyes focused on Taylor, who had just tried to jump into the rings. "Taylor, that's death!"

"I'll discharge my entire mana pool into that to interrupt it if I need to!" Taylor replied, sprinting at the new location of the Boss.

"Will a huge influx of mana destroy it?" Luke's question caught her off guard, but she knew what he was getting at.

"Do *not* put pure mana into that!" She ordered firmly. "It's a draining spell right now, and the only reason it isn't ready to cast is that there isn't enough ambient mana to fuel it. It is pulling in everything from miles around. *Structured* mana introduced to the system would rewrite a section enough to make the spell self-destruct!"

"Are you sure?" Andre had caught up, and Zed held onto Arthur as he lumbered at the Boss and missed a swipe.

"No, but it would make something *other* than the intended effect happen!" Taylor's exasperation was shining through her normally cold demeanor. "It *should* just explode."

"But we are *right next* to it!" Zed snarled at her, his face flushed with fury. "Just because *you* are so willing to die for the Hollow Kingdom doesn't mean *we* are! Stop trying to kill us!"

"But that's the *only*-" Taylor was cut off as Zed hopped off of Arthur and stalked close enough that their noses almost touched.

"Celestials above and Abyss below, if you finish that statement, I am going to blow up harder than that spell would!" Zed's teeth were clenched so hard, he would likely need healing. "If the only way forward is to die for something, find *another way*! If it is impossible, *make* it happen!"

A grating laugh caused them all to freeze. They turned as one to face the new location of the boss monster. "I do *love* watching lower life forms quibble."

The circle was approaching the halfway complete point, but this was the first sign of true intelligence any chimera had displayed. It knew their language? Zed was the first to react, unsurprising since it had suddenly turned into a verbal battle. "I'm just going to go over to your home plane and wait this out. Unless you plan to send… whatever *that* is into your own house? To be fair, I wouldn't blame you. If everyone around me was as ugly as the rest of your people, I might be tempted to chuck a few killing spells at them, too."

"Insulting our appearance? It's just so… *cute*." The Mage's face was clearly visible, though painted by the shifting red and gold colors of the spell circle it was building. "Tell you what. *You* go through that portal; I'll keep you as a pet until I get bored of you. You get to live at least a *little* longer!"

"Why are you attacking us?" Taylor demanded from the man. "What do you even get out of this? You come from a mana-dense world, we can't be worth almost *any* Potentia for you! If you are trying to become a Paragon, this place will do nothing for you!"

"Why, I'm here for *resources*, of course!" The boss flickered and appeared in a new spot as a dozen vines whipped through the space where he had just stood. "Tut, tut, that won't do. As I was saying, there is so *much* here! And on such a *backward* world that is barely protected! Almost no beings, hardly any *under-standing* of magic, and so *many* food sources!"

"Too many people? You have a population issue?" Taylor's mind was whirling with data and ways to mitigate the situation. "I can offer you land, and the resources you want. All you need to do-"

"Hush now, shush now, settle down," The being told her, almost gently. "I am not *given* things. I *take* what I want. From how much you struggled against my cast-offs, my *components*, I know that your people will have no defense against my actual military force! We will sweep across this world and take it for The Twisted. It's a small offering, but a welcome one. I'll tell your Anarcanists that I thank them for providing a doorway, before I feast on their hearts to gain a few additional *scraps* of power."

"You aren't working with them?" Andre pressed for information as Luke threw a rock at the Boss. The attack was caught in one hand, though there was a brief flare of surprise on its face. A glow had appeared over its hand just before the rock stopped, a clear indication that there were magical protections in place.

"Pah." The humanoid creature rolled its oddly square-pupiled eyes. "You were clearly not listening. We *take* what we want. We don't 'work with'. We dominate. We flood the world. We eat every scrap, and only when a world is an empty *husk* do we move on to the next."

Attacks came from every side. The bear attacked, the Druid scattered seeds, the Mage blasted, and Luke ran forward screaming wildly.

It didn't matter. The hooded creature *blinked* again and again, reappearing with the circles nearly ninety percent complete. Deceptively slowly, the spell circle completed and began to glow brightly. Zed screamed in fear, as they were directly in front of the spell. "*Do something!*"

"He keeps moving! I can't get close enough to kill him!"

Luke's anger was pure frustration; he wanted to *punch* that smug, goateed face!

"I can't hold him!" Andre admitted sadly as he watched the end coming. "Somehow, I can't even get the smallest spore on him!"

"What *is* this thing?" Taylor threw spell after spell at the circles, which shifted out of the way each time they got too close.

"You wish to look upon the face of your death?" The boss laughed at them, treating their attacks like children throwing tantrums. "Certainly! I'd be *more* than happy to let you know who defeated you so easily."

His robe tore away, revealing thick, hairy legs with cloven hooves. Above the waist, he was pure human until the top of his head, where a pair of thick horns curled back and around. "Gaze upon me and despair! Gethedrel the Red Dread shall personally take your lives!"

"Yup. Whole world full of ugly." Zed catcalled one final insult.

Gethedrel raised his hands and snarled. "Enough of this. Blood of the willing, wash over the world and bring its resources to me. All shall be collected. All shall be used in the service of the powerful. Until nothing remains! Spell of the ninth tier, activate!"

The ninth circle flared, and completed.

"*Reduce, reuse, recycle!*"

CHAPTER FIFTY

"Not like this!" Zed screeched, his organs and skeleton able to be seen due to the approach of the intense red light shining toward them. An ocean of bloody illumination was expanding in a sphere; upward, side-to-side, and even digging through the ground as it moved. Only a second into activation, the spell was already moving as fast as a normal man could run... and *gaining* speed.

"Everyone get behind me!" Andre stood tall, power flowing out of him and into the ground. With everything he could put into his abilities, he bound himself to the earth and threw a hill-sized rock directly into the light. It was broken to the smallest bits in an instant as the light touched it, but strangely enough his connection remained. He realized that the hill had been separated out, and everything that it had been composed of was separated into neat piles of ores, mulches, and stones. "This spell... all it does is tear apart, neatly stack, and store what it touches?"

"We are mostly made of water, but that doesn't mean I want to get turned into a pool!" Zed fell to the ground, all the fight having left him. A second, maybe less, until everything was gone.

"*Cleanse!*" Taylor's voice sounded, and the three males were pulled into a heap and tied together by their clothes. "Unsummon Arthur right now! This is already going to be too close!"

"What?" Andre got out before he found Taylor laying across all of them, as spread-eagle as she could manage. The remainder of his words couldn't be heard over the roar of the red flood and... something else.

A klaxon call drowned out all other noise; the scream of strange butterflies that had appeared the instant before the red light touched them. The all-encompassing red light reached for them, then simply vanished as the butterflies spread further and seemed to eat a tunnel through the assault.

"Three, four, five..." Taylor was counting, the panic in her voice rising with each passing second. Just after she said 'eight', the light was gone, flowing over them and into the distance as an unstoppable tsunami. The four began to fall, dropping a dozen feet as the ground beneath them vanished.

"How?" The voice shook the air as they rose to their feet. Luke looked up, seeing an unending river of resources flowing out of the red light and forming into neatly stacked piles. Hills - more properly - at this point. Gethedrel was walking toward them, but he seemed exhausted and drained. "You should be dead. Your constituent parts should be impossible to determine at this point. How. *How* are you still here?"

"A benefit of being so beautiful." Zed's voice was muffled, seeing as he was still under Andre. "You wouldn't understand."

Flames boiled out of Gethedrel, only to be countered by an explosion of ice and water vapor, courtesy of Taylor. "Mongrels! I'll eat your *hearts!*"

Luke was tossed at the creature by a vine, and his left fist caused a brilliant light to shine around Gethedrel before it vanished. Luke was *furious*. "Stand still so I can kill you!"

"No! For it is *I* who shall be doing the killing!" The wind began whipping, in this case, literally. Thin streams of solidified air began lashing out at Luke, causing his armor to light up with every attack. Not even bothering to continue paying attention to the Murderhobo, Gethedrel released more air. This sent all the spores that Andre had released flying back at him. Obviously, it wasn't a danger, but it did still disappoint the Druid.

The scene repeated over and over, only interspersed with the spells that Taylor was throwing at him. Something had to give eventually, and it turned out to be Luke's armor first. With a sound of shattering glass, Luke's cuirass shattered into motes of light. Angry red lines began appearing on his skin, and blood began to flow.

"Ah, *finally,*" Gethedrel chuckled as the small tears of blood dripped from the whip-cuts. "I was wondering how much punishment you could take. Well... no need to hold back! Thank you for the meal!"

Blood shot out of Luke in a fountain, and Gethedrel opened his mouth to taste the coppery blood. After a deep gulp, the chimera started laughing. "Such *power* in you! This taste...! How much Potentia have you gained in your short life? There must be the hopes of a million invested within you! It... it's..."

Gethedrel stumbled and Luke sank to his knees, the loss of blood taking a serious toll on him.

Health: 110/250. Weakened: Blood loss. Damage output reduced by 30%! Bleeding (minor): -2 health per 5 seconds.

I Have Concerns has taken effect! Someone was foolish enough to try a taste, huh? Initiating the unicorn-goring!

"What is happening?" Gethedrel tried to vomit out the blood, but it stayed in him, as if it had a mind of its own. "So... so *disgusting!* Do you *all* taste like this? What is in your blood? You're *venomous?*"

"I'm *poisonous.* Venomous would be if I bit you."

"Pathetic creatures! How *dare* you!" A Shatter Shot took Gethedrel off his cloven hooves, but he *blinked* to another position mid-fall. Mana built up around him again, and his eyes were leaking bloody tears. "This is a potent venom-"

"Poison!"

"-but I've survived worse! I am done playing with you; it is time to start the invasion!"

"Abyssal demon! Stand and fight!" Andre shouted as he attacked over and over again. It was useless; his attacks couldn't land on the otherworldly beast. Arthur may have been fast enough, but the bear had been unsummoned just before it was hit by the red light. Andre had taken Taylor's advice, not wanting to see what would happen if the summoned version of Arthur was pulled apart.

"I can't land another hit either," Taylor admitted after her initial excitement about blasting the invader once had faded.

"I could kill it if I could land just *one* clean hit," Luke snarled, yanking open his waterskin and downing the last of his liquid mana. His wounds healed quickly, and his armor *snapped* back into place. "Tell me how to force a demon to hold still."

"What?" Zed did a double-take at Luke's words. "That isn't a demon."

"I don't play guessing games, Zed. Andre called it a demon. Spit out the answer or shut it." Luke's growl emanated from deep in his chest.

"That's a *Satyr*." Seeing Luke's lack of understanding, Zed explained, "These creatures are all chimeras, yes? That one is well-known, a magic-focused cross between a human and a goat. A Satyr can-"

Zed almost fell over as Luke Bum Rushed Gethedrel. The Satyr gathered a wash of mana into its hands, "This again? *Enough!* Die for your impertinence, you-"

"*Baaa!*"

Gethedrel froze in place, then took a slow step toward Luke before coming to his senses. "What was th-"

Goat Call was super effective!

Luke damages Gethedrel: 89 blunt damage!

The mana shield around Gethedrel flared and shrieked.

The Satyr himself *blinked* away, staring at Luke with a shaken expression. "How are you able-"

Once more Luke was in front of him, but as Gethedrel tried to blink away, Luke activated *Goat Call* again. The Satyr froze for a split second, and another punch landed.

Luke damages Gethedrel: 125 blunt damage!

The mana shield shattered, and Gethedrel screamed as Luke's mana-created horn dug deeply into his left eye. "No! *No!* I will not be defeated on this backwards plane!"

His next blink brought him next to the Scar, and he dove through before anyone could react. Taylor watched as Luke followed closely on the Satyr's hoofsteps, diving through only a moment after Gethedrel had made it in. "Everyone in! The time difference!"

By the time the other three had joined Luke in this new plane of existence, both he and Gethedrel were bloodied and heaving for air. Gethedrel took another hit, landing heavily on the ground. A thin mana shield wavered into existence, shattering as Luke hit it, but taking all the damage. "You think you've *won*? Y-you're right! I... I admit defeat. I'll make any concession-"

Critical hit! Luke damages Gethedrel: 433.21 blunt damage!

Gethedrel's head exploded, and the rest of his body flopped to the floor, a light bleating noise escaping his exposed trachea. Luke stood over the corpse for a long moment, his breath starting to slow after only thirty seconds. "I..."

Potentia distributed based on participation! Andre: 1,500 Taylor: 2,600 Luke: 3,200 Zed: 700.

Quest completed: Sending Monsters After Monsters (Repeatable). Return to the quest assigner for your rewards!

"You did it!" Zed squealed at the Murderhobo. "Now we just need to find a way to close this Scar, and the reward will be *massive!*"

"I don't think we need to worry about that." Taylor stated sadly, waving her hand behind her. The Scar had already snapped closed. Only the faintest distortion in the air remained to indicate the massive energy structure that had once stood there.

"How? How did that-" Zed's complaint was cut off when Andre kicked Gethedrel's clenched right hand and revealed a shattered stone disk.

"It was a trap - a failsafe - or a getaway attempt." Andre sighed knowingly, knowing that they were abyssed. "Either we were lured here in the unlikely event that he died, so that his armies would eventually eat us, or... he never thought that we would be so quick to join in, and he was trying to escape by slamming the door behind him."

"I *hate* goats. They always have something planned." Luke finished his thought. "What's going on, now? Where are we?"

"Before we fall into despair," Taylor spoke pointedly at Zed, who had already dropped to the floor in a despairing fetal position, "we need to remember that we can hold out. We can work together and figure out a new way home. If the door exists-"

Feet pounding on the earth began to shake the ground, and bestial roars suffused the area as uncountable millions of creatures realized that their master, their protection against the rest of this world, had been slain. There was sorrow in the howls, fear... and *rage*. They were coming. They would destroy the ones that had done this before they lost their lives to the hordes of the other pillars of this plane.

"A-as I was saying," Taylor's pale face allowed her true emotions to seep through, but she powered on, "we may have saved not only the Hollow Kingdom, but our entire world! Even if no one knows our names, or remembers our stories, we can rest in peace knowing that... we.... Luke, what are you doing?"

Power was gathering around Luke and accumulating on his fists. He lashed out, and the world reverberated.

Wub.

"Weak point right here. Can't go to Murder World, but I can go back to ours. As much as I appreciate what you are saying, I'd like to live." Luke was beating on the distortion in the air at an even pace over the course of the next few minutes, and with every blow, more and more mana came from *somewhere* to assist in opening the door between dimensions. "Just gotta tenderize it a little."

"You can't just *punch* a hole back into our world!" Taylor tried to help Luke save face. "I don't know what you are doing, but-"

"Tier Eight: *Open Up!*" Luke shouted as he lashed forward one last time. A portal appeared, and they could see their world beyond it. Luke dove through right away, seeming to move in slow motion on the other side as soon as he crossed.

"You!" Taylor froze in shock as Zed dove through as well, having gotten to his feet in record time. "You can't use a Tier *Eight* spell in under three minutes! This is impossi - *yipe!*"

"To be fair, he *did tell us* that he could punch it closed a few times. If he can do something that ridiculous, why couldn't he punch it open?" A vine grabbed Taylor and tossed her through the portal, and a chuckling Andre followed after her, moments before the portal snapped closed and the area was overrun with monsters.

EPILOGUE

"That's all for tonight, folks!" Zed called to the enraptured tavern audience. "Come back tomorrow if you-"

"*Boo!*" someone called out, making Zed's eye twitch. "That's not what happened!"

"Please explain where I was *wrong.*" Zed's overly calm voice and dangerous tone was missed by the too-drunk barfly.

"Everyone knows the Fields of Blood was the first real triumph of the Terraformer!" The words of the barfly caused a roar of agreement to sweep the area. "He became the youngest Druid of the Third Circle in *history,* and leveled the entire mountain range in the battle against the Dynasty of Dogs! The resources he carted back to the Hollow Kingdom are *still* the lifeblood of the country!"

"All of that is true, except the claim that *he* was the one that transformed the mountains into plains." Zed shook his head knowingly. "Next you are going to say that it was Taylor the Archmage who-"

"Healed the Scars of the land?" Another person was influenced by the first. "Of course it was! Your story suggests that it was the *Murderhobo* that closed the Scars? Everyone knows that it was the structured magic of the Archmage that made closing Scars possible!"

Zed stood slowly, and the rumbling crowd quieted, unknowingly swallowing back fear. "It doesn't matter if you *believe* my tale. Know that I tell you the truth, and not the propaganda that these false 'Zed' characters have been giving you. I'll tell you now, creamy lies certainly spread easier upon the toast of life than the cold and chunky truth does. The true story is here if you want it. Otherwise, feel free to listen to a new take on an old tale... somewhere else."

"That's another thing!" Someone snapped their fingers and pointed at Zed. "You're too *young* to be Zed the Mindbender! If you were him, we'd believe you if we wanted to or not! That's the truth, and we all know it!"

"A *True* Bard is exactly the age you need him to be... to hear his story." Zed snapped back, starting to get sick of this rabble. "I will be back for two more nights, but then I will pass on. Feel free to join in, or not."

Zed stepped outside of the tavern, and looked at the sky. "Looks like the rain finally let up. Should be clear for... just long enough."

He closed his eyes with a deep sigh, and rubbed the long beard that had not been on his face only moments ago. When he reopened them, crow's feet and wrinkles showed for a bare moment; and the wisdom of ages appeared in deep-set eyes. All the changes were gone in an instant as he turned to face the young man that had followed him outside.

"Mr. Mindbender, why did they laugh at you? I could... I could *see* the story." The youngster swallowed deeply as Zed smiled at him. "Can you tell me why you are the 'Mindbender'? You called your old team different names the whole night... I don't understand."

"Ah, lad." Zed shook his head. "That was a lifetime ago, and on the other side of the defeat of the Dynasty of Dogs. When there is no war, the people in charge of old monsters want them to go in a cage. There is no place for war heroes in a time of peace. Nowhere except old stories that can be used... the *next* time a war comes around."

"In fact, two nights should be just enough." Zed got a faraway look in his eyes, and the young man next to him could have sworn he was hearing hasty warnings, snapped orders, and the marching of boots.

"What happens in two nights?" the young man asked, almost afraid to hear the answer.

"Why, Rupert... I already told you. All the way back when I started my tale. This world, this entire *civilization*... is ending." The smile on Zed's face was dark. "The truth is, in two days, I'll be the one that ends it."

"How did you know my...?" Rupert gasped as he saw behind the illusion that Zed was using. "You really *are* him! Your Sigil! *Oh, Celestials above it's*... it's..."

A few minutes later, a middle-aged man stepped out of the tavern. "Rupert? Son, what are you doing out here? Are you... Rupert! Are you alright?"

"Dad! I saw...!"

"*What*, Rupert?"

"There was... something. Something *terrible!*"

The father looked around, swallowing nervously. "I think this might have been a long night. Let's get you to bed."

There was no movement, and the father began to grow cautious. "What is it, boy? Are you ill?"

"No, I just needed to tell you..." Rupert looked at his dad and shook his head sadly. He couldn't remember the thing he had seen; only that it was incredibly important.

"*Something.*"

ABOUT DAKOTA KROUT

Author of the best-selling Divine Dungeon and Completionist Chronicles series, Dakota has been a top 5 bestseller on Amazon, a top 6 bestseller on Audible, and his first book, Dungeon Born, was chosen as one of Audible's top 5 fantasy picks in 2017.

He draws on his experience in the military to create vast terrains and intricate systems, and his history in programming and information technology helps him bring a logical aspect to both his writing and his company while giving him a unique perspective for future challenges.

"Publishing my stories has been an incredible blessing thus far, and I hope to keep you entertained for years to come!" -Dakota

Connect with Dakota:
MountaindalePress.com
Patreon.com/DakotaKrout
Facebook.com/TheDivineDungeon
Twitter.com/DakotaKrout
Discord.gg/mdp

ABOUT MOUNTAINDALE PRESS

Dakota and Danielle Krout, a husband and wife team, strive to create as well as publish excellent fantasy and science fiction novels. Self-publishing *The Divine Dungeon: Dungeon Born* in 2016 transformed their careers from Dakota's military and programming background and Danielle's Ph.D. in pharmacology to President and CEO, respectively, of a small press. Their goal is to share their success with other authors and provide captivating fiction to readers with the purpose of solidifying Mountaindale Press as the place 'Where Fantasy Transforms Reality.'

Connect with Mountaindale Press:
MountaindalePress.com
Facebook.com/MountaindalePress
Twitter.com/_Mountaindale
Instagram.com/MountaindalePress

MOUNTAINDALE PRESS TITLES
GameLit and LitRPG

The Completionist Chronicles,
The Divine Dungeon,
Full Murderhobo, and
Year of the Sword by Dakota Krout

Arcana Unlocked by Gregory Blackburn

A Touch of Power by Jay Boyce

Red Mage and
Farming Livia by Xander Boyce

Space Seasons by Dawn Chapman

Ether Collapse and
Ether Flows by Ryan DeBruyn

Dr. Druid by Maxwell Farmer

Bloodgames by Christian J. Gilliland

Threads of Fate by Michael Head

Lion's Lineage by Rohan Hublikar and Dakota Krout

Wolfman Warlock by James Hunter and Dakota Krout

Axe Druid,
Mephisto's Magic Online, and
High Table Hijinks by Christopher Johns

Skeleton in Space by Andries Louws

Chronicles of Ethan by John L. Monk

Pixel Dust and
Necrotic Apocalypse by David Petrie

Viceroy's Pride by Cale Plamann

Henchman by Carl Stubblefield

Artorian's Archives by Dennis Vanderkerken and Dakota Krout

89477068R00210